In Memory

A Tribute to Sir Terry Pratchett

Anna Mattaar, Caroline Friedel, Charlotte Slocombe, Choong Jay Vee, DK Mok, Laura May, Luke Kemp, Lyn Godfrey, Michael K. Schaefer, Mike Reeves-McMillan, Peter Knighton, Phil Elstob, Robert McKelvey, Scott A. Butler, Simon Evans, Sorin Suciu, Steven McKinnon

Edited by Sorin Suciu and Laura May

Copyright © 2015: Anna Mattaar, Caroline Friedel, Charlotte Slocombe, Choong Jay Vee, DK Mok, Laura May, Luke Kemp, Lyn Godfrey, Michael K. Schaefer, Mike Reeves-McMillan, Peter Knighton, Phil Elstob, Robert McKelvey, Scott A. Butler, Simon Evans, Sorin Suciu, Steven McKinnon

Cover art copyright © 2016 Dámaso Gómez.

First Edition 2015, Second Edition 2016.

www.inmemorytribute.com

ISBN: 1517603609
ISBN-13: 978-1517603601

DEDICATION

In dear memory of Sir Terry Pratchett.

CONTENTS

EDITORS' NOTES

NOTE FROM SORIN

This anthology started as a rebellion against the act of mourning. Mourning is a lingering guest. It comes in uninvited and it immediately starts to unload its offerings of grief, denial, rage and guilt in all shapes and forms. In this particular case, it brought about a paralysing guilt caused by my own inability to internalise the beautiful lessons that Terry Pratchett taught us about death.

I resolved to channel my rebellion into writing. A short story by way of a tribute, perhaps one I would post on my website. And then it hit me— surely I was not the only one going through this. What if I used my modest publishing experience to build a platform for others to share their tributes? And what if, instead of monetising the idea (and thus effectively turning us into death merchants) we donated everything to a charity, one Terry Pratchett himself favoured?

So I reached out to Alzheimer's Research UK, with what I was increasingly seeing as a far-fetched idea for a short story anthology on the theme of memory. Turns out, the nice folks there loved the concept and offered their full support. It was on.

I have to pause here and make it clear that, for all my impetus and determination, this anthology would have wilted and died had I not invited my friend Laura to take on the role of Chief Editor. Laura is a force of nature, possessed of an undeniable skill to make things happen. As luck would have it, she is also a very talented writer and a ferocious editor.

Our call for submissions went viral overnight. I want to express my gratitude to everyone who wrote to us. Reading hundreds of submissions was truly a humbling and heartening experience. Would-be participants included everything from professors and accountants to scientists and stay-at-home parents. Some were professional writers, while others were amateurs with a passion for Sir Terry's work and a desire to give. As such, we made it a matter of principle to send personalised specific feedback to everyone. While this added a lot of time and sweat to the process, I daresay it was well worth it.

Before I pass the keyboard to Laura, I want to thank everyone who made this possible, particularly:

…My wife, for temporarily allowing this anthology to become my de facto other wife (her words, not mine). I'm the luckiest guy in the world!

…Alzheimer's Research UK, for believing in this project and for the wonderful (and often unacknowledged) work they do every day.

…Our contributing authors, who crafted fine stories under what I can only describe as a draconian timeline. They lent their talent, energy and friendship to our joint venture, and thus contrived to make this a memorable experience.

…Laura, who—where do I begin? Her gargantuan efforts include endless hours of hard-core editing, building a website, dealing with the multi-headed beast of bureaucracy, and staying on top of ever-hungry social media. And, would you believe it, she did it all while bouncing between four different countries. But what I find absolutely mind-boggling is that she took seventeen independent stories and magicked them into such a balanced and penetrating anthology. I'm talking about seventeen stories written by seventeen authors in seventeen different voices, with the added locally-infused flavour brought to the table by those of us for whom English is not a first language.

I hope you enjoy the result.

Sorin Suciu, October 2015

NOTE FROM LAURA

Sorin's reasons for creating this anthology are much loftier than mine: I was on board once he said I could be called 'Chief Editor'. Looking back on it now though, I wish I'd aimed even higher—Corporal of Corrections? Lady of Logic? Tsarina of...okay, there goes my alliteration. In saying that, had I aimed for any of these I'm sure there would have been some kind of rebellion staged by our authors, several of whom are editors themselves, followed by a short and bloody overthrow—so perhaps my co-conspirator had my best interests at heart (while still capably pandering to my ego).

My thanks have to go first and foremost to Sorin, who played the good cop to my bad cop, while also putting up with my leaving mid-conversation to go eat blocks of feta or bake cookies. He checked my feedback and rejection emails, and moreover ensured that I always had wine to hand. Putting out an anthology in half a year is quite the undertaking, as it turns out (hard to believe, right?). Sorin kept me going through it all, and this book absolutely would not, *could* not, have happened without him.

I do also want to express how thrilled I am to have worked with such a talented bunch of authors and professionals (sometimes they were even both at the same time!). We had a mix of writers from a range of backgrounds, and they worked together under our stringent deadlines to produce a book we can all be proud of. Furthermore, they did it for free— all the writing and editing for this anthology has been done on a voluntary basis, and every single penny of the proceeds is going directly to charity.

Thanks go as well to my house-mates, who put up with my taking over the dining room with laptops and 'edit-y things' all summer, plus to the editor for my own piece, Rhian. Lastly (because this isn't an Oscars speech), I want to thank *you* as the reader. Your purchase has helped to raise funds for an incredibly worthy cause in the form of Alzheimer's Research UK, and I hope that you enjoy reading it. I also hope you enjoy reaping the sweet, sweet karma that will arise when you also buy copies for all your family, your friends, your colleagues, your neighbours, your pets, your childhood sweetheart, the lady at the bakery, the man at the post office, and all the rest of the residents of where you live. Good job!

Laura May, October 2015

ABOUT ALZHEIMER'S RESEARCH UK

Alzheimer's Research UK is the UK's leading research charity aiming to defeat dementia. Dementia is one of the world's greatest medical challenges. It shatters lives and leaves millions heartbroken.

For many years people thought that dementia was an inevitable part of ageing. This has changed. Thanks to research we now understand more about the diseases that cause these distressing symptoms than ever before, and science has shown the way towards fighting them. While current treatments for diseases like Alzheimer's are very limited, we believe we can eradicate these diseases by funding research.

Money raised for Alzheimer's Research UK powers world-class studies that give the best chance of beating dementia sooner. Our pioneering work focuses on prevention, treatment and cure, with our ultimate aim being a world free from the fear, harm and heartbreak of dementia.

For more information about the work we are funding, or to join the fightback, visit http://www.alzheimersresearchuk.org/

Together we have the power to defeat dementia.

THE HEART OF THE LABYRINTH
DK MOK

The Labyrinth of Varissen was legend. Every child knew the story of King Varissen: first valiant and wise, then eccentric, then obsessive. Every child knew of the sprawling labyrinth he had constructed, woven deep with enchantments to protect the secret treasures hidden within.

Every child knew of the silver storm that had swept in from the north, harbinger of the sorcerer Sarak—*may she live forever and not smite this house please*—who slew King Varissen for his precious hoard, and yet, despite the passing centuries, had uncovered not a gem of it.

And finally, every child knew of the beast that lurked within the twisting, turning passages of the labyrinth. Indeed, for many children, this was their favourite part of the story—the part involving the slashing of swords and the crunching of bones and, depending on the parent, either a bloodcurdling description of aerodynamic entrails, or a vague tutting about the dangers of running off on adventures instead of staying at home to mind the alpacas.

Yes, every child knew what lurked in that dark, enchanted place, with ancient gold gleaming in its infernal eyes. Monstrous, merciless, ravenous.

Every child knew of the Devourer.

* * *

The Devourer strongly disapproved of these stories, and he disapproved even more of the parents who read such bloodthirsty tales to their children. While he didn't believe in burning inappropriate books, he wasn't averse to the idea of hitting some parents repeatedly and quite hard with those books.

However, today he wasn't thinking of books, and he was trying very hard not to think about parents or children or other things that looked like talkative meatballs. His stomach had been growling for weeks, and had now started to make a kind of sucking noise that threatened to develop an event horizon.

The Devourer resembled an ungainly hybrid of beasts: scales and hide, talons and tentacles. Although, on days like today, he felt that he was barely more than jaws and a stomach. He plodded through the vast and intricate labyrinth, his claws dragging beside him down the sandstone paths. He tried to distract himself by scraping the vines from the stone walls, revealing snatches of pastoral reliefs, and by weeding the terraced flower beds, before realising that there *were* only weeds. That is, if you counted poison ivy as a 'weed', rather than a herbaceous thug.

A part of him wished he had someone to tell him amusing stories or to sing him stirring songs, but his only neighbours were the ravens who picked through the bleached bones and scraps of gnawed armour that dotted the central courtyard.

He could remember a time when he'd enjoyed company, although the details eluded him now. It had been a different place, and a different time. More music, fewer bones. Here, the arrival of company inevitably meant being stabbed, burned and blasted—and a guilty meal of the people too recalcitrant to flee.

From marauding mercenaries to pompous knights, all demanded the same thing of him: *Where is it? Where is the hoard of Varissen?*

The Devourer always told them the same thing: there was no treasure here. It was an ancient myth spread by the greedy and the gullible. He told them they'd be better off investing in a respectable occupation, like pottery or cheese-making. On rare occasions someone listened, and left the labyrinth with a new appreciation of ceramics. Most of the time, the Devourer made good on his name.

Every year, Overlord Sarak herself came to pry at the stones and dredge the fountains, scrutinising the mosaics inlaid seamlessly into the rock. She dared not shatter the labyrinth, for fear that the stones were imbued with some kind of sorcery that would render the legendary treasure forever lost.

"Don't you wish to be free of this place?" she asked him every year. "Just tell me where it is."

And every year, he replied that she and all the others were foolish and mad, and could she perhaps bring him some fruit, because all the meat was playing havoc with his colon.

Then Sarak would wheedle and bellow and snarl, and when none of that worked, she would rake the air with cold rage.

2

Tell me, or I'll chain you to a rock like the Iron Minotaur.

Show me, or I'll bury you in the catacombs like the Socially Awkward Serpent.

Confess, or I'll tear away your mind like the Broken Angel.

Eventually, the Devourer would snap his jaws and wave his tentacles, rising onto his powerful hind legs, his knobbly scales glinting in the sun.

"You should have thought of that before you slew Varissen!" he'd roar.

She would withdraw then, leaving the Devourer with a strange ache in his chest and vague visions in his mind. He wondered sometimes if the other creatures she mentioned paced their prisons endlessly and longed for civil conversation, and if they too were plagued by murky nightmares of blood and ink.

It had been some time since Sarak's last visit. Actually, it had been some time since anyone had visited. The Devourer lay on his side, his stomach painfully sunken. He glanced surreptitiously at the towering acacia that grew in the central courtyard, eyeing the ravens that roosted in the branches. They stared flintily back at him, the only witnesses to his countless transgressions.

When he'd first been imprisoned here by Sarak, he'd nearly starved to death. No fish swam the putrid ponds, and the bitter plants only made him ill, so he'd snatched ravens to feed his hunger. But he'd seen them mourning their fellows, singing dirges with such accusation that he'd sworn off their ilk completely.

Death would free him from this place, but Sarak would simply find another prisoner, another sentry—perhaps one who wouldn't give the labyrinth's visitors a chance to depart.

Thump thump. Thump thump.

The Devourer's eyes opened a crack. Perhaps it was the beat of his heart—or one of his hearts, at least. He was quite sure he had two or three, not to mention several proto-brains, to control all the tentacles and claws and various other appendages. He was fairly certain he had a fin somewhere.

Thump thump. Thump thump.

The ravens stirred, hopping excitedly about on the branches.

There would be fresh meat soon.

The Devourer's stomach churned, and he shuffled anxiously to his feet.

For the briefest moment, he hoped the visitors would be pugilistic and annoying, but then he felt a stab of shame. Sarak had cursed him with an insatiable appetite and chronic indigestion, but his soul was still his own. For whatever that was worth.

He faced the courtyard archway, hoping that the intruders would somehow be an army of soft cheeses and summer fruits. Suddenly, he realised that the labyrinth's visitor wasn't using the passageways. A dark figure raced along the top of the walls, its boots dancing a path over the tangled vines, moving nimbly despite the heavy pack on its back. As it neared, he could see it was dressed in a brown tunic with light leather armour, and it carried a short, hooked sword in each hand.

With an acrobatic leap, the figure landed solidly on the courtyard wall, gazing down at the Devourer. From this distance, he could see her short brown hair twisted atop her head like a nest, and her brown eyes blazing with determination. Even though she remained a cautious twenty feet away, the Devourer's whip-like tentacles could have sliced off her head from where he stood.

One quick bite and no one would know, except for him and the ravens. But she hadn't attacked him yet, nor yelled "Pestilent wretch, surrender thy riches or taste my steel!" which usually led to the Devourer delivering a stern lecture about civility, semantics and double-entendres. He was near delirious from hunger, and still she stood there, watching him, with an expression that he hadn't seen in centuries. It took him a moment to dredge the word from his memory.

Pity.

He pushed away hungry thoughts.

"Rargh…" He waved his claws listlessly. "There is no treasure here. Really—no gold, no gems, no enchanted artefacts."

The young woman's gaze skimmed the courtyard before returning to the Devourer.

"Devourer of the Labyrinth of Varissen, my name is Kaya Katavan, and I am here to free you."

The Devourer narrowed most of his eyes.

"Do you mean 'free me from my mortal bonds'?"

Over the years, he'd had some very confusing metaphysical

conversations with people who seemed to think that "liberate" and "eviscerate" meant the same thing. Most of those people got eaten.

"I mean," said Kaya, "the curse binding you here is broken. You may leave the labyrinth."

"Sarak will find me."

"Sarak is dead."

The Devourer's hearts pounded in the silence. From the woman's stony expression, it was a sensitive subject, so he didn't press for more details. He'd had enough of death, and he could already guess that Sarak hadn't died from sudden-onset old age. He looked at his ragged claws. Was there even a place in the world for something like him? He remembered almost nothing of his life before this place—just sprawling sunsets and jovial laughter and terrible screams—

"Why?" asked the Devourer. "Why did you free me?"

Kaya held his gaze. "I slew Sarak because my kingdom deserves better. I came to free you, or—ahem—evict you, because foolish souls will continue to come here. I'll judge you not on what you did as Sarak's prisoner, but on what you do as a free being. I seek your word that you will slay no more."

The Devourer looked from her glinting blades to his heavy paws.

"I give you my word, on one condition: I wasn't the only creature imprisoned by Sarak, and the kingdom is large and difficult to navigate for one who looks as I do. Come with me, help me to free the others, and I will be in your debt."

Kaya considered this for a moment, and then leaped down onto the courtyard, sheathing her blades. The ravens muttered in quiet disappointment.

"If I help you, I'll demand a reward when this is done."

"If it's mine to give, then you shall have it," said the Devourer, hoping she wouldn't realise that he had nothing of value, unless you counted a respectable vocabulary.

Kaya nodded, and tossed her pack to the Devourer.

"A Happy-Leaving-The-Labyrinth-Day present," she said.

The Devourer unbuckled the satchel to find it brimming with apples, dates, sweet potatoes, and a large round of cheese.

* * *

They left the labyrinth behind them, and the Devourer cast one final look from the crest of a barren hill. He tried not to take it personally as flocks of scarlet macaws and herds of deer promptly flooded into the abandoned labyrinth, disappearing into the verdant sprawl. He felt the faintest twinge of uncertainty—yes, it had been his prison, but from this distance, from outside its high walls, he could see the overgrown boulevards and the secluded ponds, the elaborate carvings and the towering fountains, the single path winding and flowing from the rusted gates to the central courtyard.

He found himself hoping that the deer wouldn't leave too much of a mess on the mosaics.

"Having doubts?" asked Kaya.

"No..."

"It isn't as though there's anything keeping you there."

The Devourer glanced sharply at her, but Kaya was busy refilling her pack with pears from a nearby tree. She'd agreed quite readily to this quest, and perhaps she was motivated by more than just a soft spot for oppressed monsters. She hefted the pack onto her shoulders.

"So," she said, "shall we rescue these friends of yours?"

"They're not my friends."

The Devourer gazed out towards the horizon. The world seemed duller, dustier than he remembered. A fog of memory stirred in his mind.

Warm sunshine, the clatter of plates, an infectious, snorting laugh.

"Are you ready?" asked Kaya.

He took a deep breath, tasting the distant smoke and the approaching rain.

"They're waiting," he said.

* * *

Onward, they roamed, and the horizons unfolded as they searched the lands. They travelled the kingdom from peak to trough, from volcanic seas to glacial peaks. They snapped the chains from the Haranguing Hydra, and shattered the coral cage of the Kleptomaniac Kraken. They unbound the anchors from the Judgemental Jellyfish, and freed the Socially Awkward Serpent from the catacombs—or at least, they rolled aside the boulder sealing the doorway, and spent several hours coaxing the enormous reptile towards the entrance.

"Sarak is gone," said Kaya. "You're free to go."

The Serpent mumbled and hissed incoherently, writhing into panicked knots behind the sarcophagi. Kaya studied the scene with a frown. It had taken them hours, and rather a lot of complicated physics, to shunt aside the boulder.

"I suppose we should leave him be," she said. "After all, sealing a socially phobic snake inside an abandoned necropolis—as far as torments go, it wasn't Sarak's best work."

"Giving someone what they crave isn't always a mercy," said the Devourer.

He sat on the weathered rock outside, and waited for the sound of hyperventilation to subside.

"Do you remember the delicious heat of the sun?" he asked gently. "The slither of sand beneath your belly, the tickle of grass against your scales?" He sighed slowly. "I was Sarak's prisoner too. When Kaya freed me, I was terrified of leaving the labyrinth, of seeing the world, or perhaps of the *world* seeing *me*—for a prison can be less frightening than the unknown. But the worst prison is the kind that sits within you, the cage that tells you what you are, what you will always be. It's a prison that few of us escape, but sometimes, we can bend the bars a little, open the door a crack, and perhaps add a nice conservatory with an adjoining larder." He tilted his head towards the sky. "And perhaps, it would be nice to feel the sun again."

A forked tongue darted hesitantly through the doorway. After a pause, the head of a giant snake peered out, slitted eyes shining nervously. There was another tense pause, and then the rest of the Serpent slithered out, coils of delicately patterned green and gold. Almost half of his scales were missing, revealing patches of pale skin.

"I'm how are thanks fine?" ventured the Serpent.

"I'm thanks fine too," said the Devourer.

"Thirty miles west," said Kaya, "there's a woodland plagued by rabid boar and brooding minstrels. Perhaps you'll find good hunting and sparse conversation there." She paused. "I recommend you only hunt the boar."

The Serpent abruptly dashed back into the catacombs.

"Wait!" said Kaya. "I'm sure you could nibble a few minstrels, perhaps the ones who sing about all their wenches—"

The Serpent reappeared with something gripped in his jaws—it looked uncannily like a giant deflated white snake. He dropped it at Kaya's feet.

"Sarak my scales she harvested most...for shields and armour, but last my shed skin she didn't take. Stronger, lighter...than leather."

He bumped Kaya shyly with his nose, and then slithered away towards the wooded hills. The Devourer watched as Kaya began to slice the skin into a new set of greaves.

"Impressive work with the boulder," he said. "Where did you learn to use levers like that?"

"I was raised by librarians." Her tone suggested that anyone unable to divert a massive stone using the contents of their pencil-box wouldn't have lasted long in that particular library. "Speaking of minstrels, have you heard the recent Ballad of the Woeful Wombat?"

And as they journeyed, she told him tales of banished marsupials, and sang him fragments of songs from distant lands.

* * *

Summer turned to autumn, and their list of targets dwindled until all that remained were the Iron Minotaur and the Broken Angel. Both names were steeped in rumours of mayhem and monstrosity, but the Devourer was determined to see his mission to the end.

The Giant Dung Beetle of Despair was the only one who'd declined their assistance, stating that he actually found his activities therapeutic, and he'd like to be known forthwith as The Giant Scarab of Soil Maintenance. The Devourer and Kaya nonetheless constructed a sturdy ramp so that the

Beetle could leave the canyon whenever he wished.

Despite their steady success, the Devourer found himself increasingly troubled by what he saw of the kingdom. Parched fields and fetid rivers, starving cattle and structurally unsound shanties.

"I haven't seen the kingdom in such a state since the reign of Warlord Sgar, before Varissen arrived."

Kaya shot him a curious glance, but the Devourer was already pointing to a village crusted onto the next hillside.

"They need a windbreak of trees there, and ground cover to hold the soil together. And the town we just passed is being starved by the very dam they've built to water their fields. They've dried up the wetlands, flooded the valley, and now the landscape's crumbling from the inside out. What they need are aqueducts."

"You seem to know a lot about town planning."

He hesitated, his mind stumbling through visions of gurneys and sluices and gleaming hooks.

"The labyrinth has excellent architecture. It would have been a marvel, in its day. What happened to all the architects and engineers?"

Kaya's expression turned grim.

"Sarak spent her reign locking up the learned and killing the clever. My parents were librarians." She faltered a moment, but when she resumed, there was quiet ferocity in her voice. "Without books, without stories, you keep your people mired in their little patch of here, and their tiny slice of now. People are less likely to rise up against you if they don't remember what they've lost, and they can't imagine what they might achieve."

"I'm sorry… I'm sure your parents would have been proud of the person you've become."

Kaya turned her face away, pretending to study the village ahead.

"Perhaps once we've rescued these last two," she said, "you can do something about all this shoddy town planning."

* * *

The Devourer wasn't sure he would ever get used to all the screaming.

"Begone, foul chimera!" cried one villager.

"Return from whence thou came!" boomed another.

The Devourer dodged a flying pitchfork, and Kaya pushed forward angrily.

"That last sentence involved the incorrect usage of almost every word in it, and that is *not* how you use a pitchfork!"

"Save us from the soulless siren!" wailed another man.

"How can you possibly mistake him for a siren?" snapped Kaya.

The Devourer whispered urgently. "I think he's referring to you. See, he's winking—"

The man yelped as a flying pitchfork sank into the door beside him.

"That's not helpful," said the Devourer. "And I thought you said that's not how you use a pitch—"

"I'm sorry," said Kaya. "I just wish they'd stop throwing things at you."

"I told you I should have stayed in the woods."

"You have nothing to be ashamed of. Look, someone here has to know how far we are from the Bog of Tofu."

Kaya grabbed one of the Devourer's claws and dragged him into a nearby hut.

"Excuse me," she called politely, "we mean you no harm. We seek the Iron Minotaur—"

The Devourer froze at the sound of frightened sobbing, a strange sensation seizing his hearts. At the rear of the hut, a scrawny couple cowered with their arms around a small, grimy girl.

"Please," said the woman, her whole body shaking. "Eat me and Egbert, but spare our daughter. Have mercy…"

The Devourer felt his stomach twist, but not with hunger, not this time.

Another time, another life. Bloodless faces, contorted with fear. Sobs and whimpers, steel and spatters, and screams that meant his work was done—

"Peony, no!" cried the woman.

The girl broke free from her mother's grasp and rushed at the Devourer with a blunt butter knife. Kaya dashed forward, grasping the girl around the waist and wresting the knife from her, while the girl screamed with fear and hatred—

The Devourer ran from the house, ignoring Kaya's calls. Faces, figures, huts rushed past, and he plunged into the dark and cradling woods. Haunting visions chased him, but these were not the faces of rogue mercenaries and gloating knights. These were common folk, men and women, and he couldn't remember why their blood stained his hands—

"Dev."

He snarled, swiping the air with his claws. "Don't call me that."

Kaya took a step back. "Devourer, are you all right?"

"Did you find out where the Bog of Tofu is?"

"Eight miles southwest."

Kaya waited wordlessly while the Devourer regained his composure, his head still swimming with gurgling screams. He sagged against a tree, his tentacles curling into the knotholes.

"Why did you free me?" he said. "Why were you unafraid of me?"

"I never said I was unafraid of you. Although, I'm not afraid anymore."

"I've eaten a good many people."

"Many, yes. Good, that's debatable. In some instances, you may have performed a public service. Especially in the case of Lord Blattersby."

The Devourer shuddered at the memory of the belligerent man and his human shield of desperate slaves.

"A killer of monsters is still a monster," he said.

Kaya's mouth pressed into a thin line, and the Devourer realised her lips were trembling.

"Am I a monster, then?" she asked.

"No, that's not—I mean, Sarak was a tyrant—"

"Is it acceptable to kill tyrants, then?"

"Uh, I think so, maybe…"

"Because Sarak considered Varissen a tyrant. And Varissen called the half-demon Sgar a tyrant before him. And perhaps, one day, someone will call me 'tyrant' and seek me out."

"Kaya…" The Devourer touched a tentacle to her arm, expecting her to recoil.

She didn't.

Instead, she drew a shaky breath. "My parents belonged to a cabal of secret libraries. Sarak slew them, trying to uncover the forbidden books they guarded. I was raised by their comrades, surrounded by tales and legends from our kingdom's past. We stayed hidden, spreading knowledge where we could, but the day came when we were betrayed by Sarak's spies.

"We knew there'd be a reckoning, and when Sarak arrived, afire with retribution, we were ready for her. The battle raged for weeks, and we were aided by the witches and alchemists, the poets and etymologists, and in the end, it all came down to a single moment, a sliver of a second."

She was silent a while, as though hanging in that moment of decision.

"I killed her," she said quietly. "The librarians told me it was self-defence, but to me, it still felt like murder. Some called me a hero, but I suspect they don't fully understand the word. For a time, I felt on the brink of losing myself. And then, one night, I had a dream of fearless captains, yearning automatons, majestic forest gods, and a bearded man in a big black hat. I don't know why, but the dream gave me courage. And when I awoke, I remembered a story I'd once read—a story about a labyrinth, and a creature both terrible and wise. A beast that devoured mighty warriors, but dispensed words of gentle wisdom to those willing to listen."

"You thought I could give you answers?"

Kaya smiled faintly.

"You already have."

* * *

The Bog of Tofu was as intolerable as it sounded. The Devourer grimaced as he sank up to his haunches in the viscous white muck. He didn't have a problem with tofu in general, especially when it was deliciously fried, but this stuff was not deliciously fried. Or even lightly steamed.

"Are you sure we need to free the Iron Minotaur?" asked Kaya. "It doesn't sound very friendly. And I still have reservations about having released the Kleptomaniac Kraken."

"Everyone deserves a chance to be heard. Sarak imprisoned many of us out of malice, and some of us were human, once. Some, she held for our skills or our knowledge."

"Like you and the hoard."

"There *is* no hoard."

"Then where did Varissen's wealth go? The stories describe treasure rooms brimming with gold and gems, and enchanted relics of extraordinary power."

Glittering coffers, cabochon fire opals, haunting moonstones incandescent with energy…

The Devourer shook his head roughly. "Stories aren't always true. If Varissen wanted to hide something, he would have built a maze, with branching paths and dead ends and vicious traps. But a labyrinth, by nature, is a single path, it's a…" The words wisped away from him, and he waved his tentacles vaguely. "It's a…thing. Your books surely tell you that Varissen was a good king. Not the hoarding type."

"Then why—Oh…" Kaya stopped, staring ahead.

Visible over the curdled trees, the bones of a massive ribcage lay half submerged in the bog.

"Are we too late?" said Kaya.

The Devourer's gaze travelled along the line of ribs, up the cervical vertebrae, to the enormous avian skull at the end.

"Chained to a *roc*…" he muttered.

There was a rattle of chain, and a hulking figure sprang from behind a thicket of trees, tearing Kaya's pack from her shoulders. The Devourer leaped to intercept—or rather, he waded awkwardly in the direction of their attacker, who appeared to be a wiry, middle-aged woman with a large bovine head. A length of chain connected her iron collar to one of the roc's enormous ribs, which didn't impede her dexterity as she tipped a pack of rations into her gaping mouth.

"Hey!" said Kaya. "There's beef jerky in that."

The Minotaur didn't seem to mind, polishing off the meat rations before downing a packet of dried currants. The Devourer waded forward crossly.

"If you'd asked, we would have shared our supplies."

The Minotaur gulped guiltily. Suddenly, her eyes widened.

"Saul?" Her surprise turned to delight, and she swaggered over, slapping him hard across the face. "You've changed!" She laughed, a great snorting sound. "I guess we both have. We really got up Sarak's nose, didn't we, Saul?"

The Devourer stared at her, stunned by both her words and the concussive greeting.

"You know me?"

The Minotaur squinted at him, turning her head from side to side, unable to get him into binocular view.

"It *is* you, isn't it? I'm afraid Sarak sliced up my memory, trying to get at my secrets—for all the good it did her. I guess she did the same to you. But we used to work together, didn't we? At the palace of Varissen?"

The Devourer pressed a tentacle to his throbbing forehead.

Marble floors, the aroma of spiced wine, a jovial woman explaining to him in explicit detail the difference between the Butter Mushroom and the visually-identical Exploding Buttocks Mushroom.

"I don't..." Suddenly, the memory of raucous, snorting laughter bubbled from forgotten depths. He blinked. "Rawlins?"

The Minotaur's mouth fell open, then widened into an uncomfortably large grin.

"Damn you, Saul. I haven't heard that name in centuries."

Kaya cleared her throat. "Perhaps we can reminisce after we free you. I believe we're running low on rations."

Rawlins had the good grace to look ashamed. "I've been trying to escape for aeons. I've a stomach like an iron pot, but all this raw tofu just saps my will to live."

The Devourer and Kaya inspected the rib to which the Minotaur was chained. The bone had already been gnawed to half its original width, but it remained wider than a human torso.

"The bone's too robust here," said Kaya. "But towards the sternum, it should be thinner."

Hooking her blades together to form a makeshift saw, Kaya took one handle, and the Devourer took the other. Even with his brute strength and her meticulously sharp blades, it took them a day to cut through the roc's giant rib. Shaking off the lumps of tofu, they handed the chain to Rawlins.

"I suppose you'll have to carry it until you find a blacksmith," said Kaya.

"Where are you headed?" asked Rawlins. "Do you need a Minotaur?"

"No!" said Kaya quickly. "I mean, thank you, but we're travelling a long way."

"To one final commitment," said the Devourer. "We're going to free the Broken Angel."

Rawlins' ears perked forward, the hair on her neck bristling alarmingly.

"Really? He sounds like a sinister bugger."

"That's what Kaya said about you."

Kaya shrugged apologetically, although she collected the contents of her pack rather pointedly.

"Do you know the Broken Angel personally?" asked the Devourer.

Rawlins furrowed her brow—or tried to, but her features remained placidly bovine. "I don't think so... But I think he knows you." She shook her head. "Well, if you're sure you don't need me, I might go have a hot bath, and then desecrate Sarak's grave."

Kaya raised an eyebrow, and the Devourer wondered if perhaps they should have had a screening process after all. Rawlins sliced away through the cold bog, calling over her shoulder.

"If you want my advice, leave the Broken Angel where he is. Some creatures are in cages for a reason."

* * *

Beyond the farms and forests, beyond the catacombs and bogs, there lay the blasted wastelands: a silent desert at the edge of the sea.

"I've never been this far from the heart of the kingdom before," said Kaya, her breath misting in the winter air.

"This used to be the heart of the kingdom, long ago," said the Devourer.

They crested a ridge and beheld the glittering expanse of the Amethyst Sea. And on the dark rocks overlooking the waves, there rose a ruined castle: a magnificent tangle of turrets and spires, pinning the moon to the starry sky.

"You know this place?" asked Kaya.

"Yes," was all he said.

He walked across the wasteland, his clawed feet crunching across the blackened earth. Kaya stepped out in front of him.

"Saul, if you go in there, I'll walk beside you every step of the way. But if you turn back now, I'm perfectly happy for our story to go, 'They finally reached the mysterious castle, decided not to go inside, and instead turned around and went back home. The end.'"

"Ours is not such a story," he said gently.

"Saul—"

"That name belongs to someone I don't know. I deserve a chance to know my story, and the Broken Angel deserves a chance to tell his."

Kaya's gaze was fierce with misgivings, but finally, she nodded. And so they crossed the threshold, passing through the tall doors into the desolate castle. Cobwebs draped the chandeliers, and dust blanketed the beds and dressers. Corridor after corridor, floor after floor, they found only echoes until they reached the throne room.

Shadows laced the marble floors, and moonlight pierced through narrow windows. To one side, a stone table stood scattered with the relics of a once sumptuous banquet: tarnished silver platters, goblets of carmine, spoons of pearl. And upon a dais was a throne of dark red jasper.

A deep, lilting voice came from the shadowed figure on the throne.

"Gifts. What gifts have you brought me?"

The Devourer exchanged a nervous glance with Kaya. This was a world away from the Judgemental Jellyfish.

"Freedom," said the Devourer. "Sarak is dead. You are free to go."

"Sarak?" said the figure. "That flicker of ash? It was not Sarak who imprisoned me, but Varissen."

The figure stood, and starlight caught his features. He had the visage of a handsome youth, but sickly pale, with long white hair. The tattered remnants of red velvet robes hung from his waist, and from his bare shoulders sprouted broad crimson wings, their tips ragged and frayed.

Words choked their way up the Devourer's throat.

"Sgar."

Kaya's blades flashed from their scabbards, her voice barely more than a breath.

"Warlord Sgar? The half-demon Warlord Sgar?"

The winged man stalked down the stairs, his gait slightly off kilter, as though the world were discourteously tilted. His eyes locked onto the Devourer, recognition lighting in their depths.

"Saul… I knew you'd return to me. My clever, brilliant, *treacherous* Saul."

With inhuman speed, Sgar swept forward and grasped the Devourer by the throat, slamming him into the wall. Kaya rushed forward, blades swinging, and although she dodged Sgar's first strike, a blinding kick sent her flying.

Sgar's eyes never left the Devourer. "I knew you'd come skulking back. Did Varissen fail to grant you the treasures he promised? Did he tire of you and turn you into some monstrous plaything?"

Without waiting for an answer, Sgar hurled him into a stone pillar, and the Devourer gritted his teeth at the faint *pop* that was possibly his swim-bladder.

"How could you betray me?" continued Sgar, his head lolling as he drew nearer. "Under my rule, your talents were allowed to run wild. You built me such marvellous prisons, and oubliettes of such ingenious cruelty."

"I built them only at your command," gasped the Devourer, struggling to his feet, dizzied by the rush of visions and voices and—

"Always such an excellent liar. I saw the joy in your eyes as you devised each new instrument of misery. I saw the pleasure you took in inspecting every rivet, every hinge, every nail. Oh Saul, you could deliver to me screams in every pitch, and sobs of every rhythm—"

The Devourer roared as the memories flooded back, and he pressed his claws helplessly against his skull.

Pages of detailed diagrams and meticulously inked schematics—

Such brilliance, they said. Innovative, exquisite, excruciating—

The needles would become too hot and lose their sharpness, but if he created a cooling system using pistons and the blood of a glacier cod—

The sluice has clotted again. Come fix it—

Whimpers and screams, bloodless faces pleading—

Sgar lashed towards him again. The Devourer whipped his tentacles defensively, but with breathtaking ease, Sgar grabbed a squirming handful and swung the Devourer into the stone table, sending the silverware clattering across the floor.

Wincing with pain, the Devourer glimpsed Kaya crouched beneath the table, her hands pressed against her side. The snakeskin armour had protected her from lacerations, but something had fractured. She glanced at him with fear in her eyes, and for the first time, he thought perhaps she saw him for what he truly was.

"That would be a 'no' to freeing him, agreed?" said Kaya.

The Devourer nodded weakly.

In a shaft of broken moonlight, Sgar stood silently, as though momentarily forgetting about his guests. He strode slowly towards the table, and Kaya held her breath as bare feet paused beside her. Sgar bent down and plucked a dusty goblet from the floor. He wandered to a window and gazed out at the whispering sea.

"I am Sgar," he rasped softly. "Son of the Phoenix God. Behold my castle, behold my empire..."

He stood with his back to them, transfixed by visions only he could see. With a burst of strength, Kaya darted forward, blades drawn—

The Devourer lunged and grasped her arm with a tentacle, shaking his head. Kaya looked from Sgar to the Devourer, her body trembling with tension.

"He'll kill you," she said.

"Only if we stay."

"What if he follows us? What if he decides to reclaim his kingdom?"

The Devourer looked at the murmuring man, whose eyes had ceased to perceive reality long ago.

"I don't think he will. I doubt anyone can free him from the prison he inhabits now."

Together, they edged back towards the exit. At the faint footfalls, Sgar spun around, his eyes widening in surprise.

"Saul, I knew you'd come back to me. Clever, brilliant, *treacherous* Saul!"

His wings beat the stale air as he swooped across the hall. The Devourer and Kaya raced from the room, skidding down corridors and stumbling down staircases, chased by the thunder of wings. They finally burst through the castle doors and continued running, risking only the briefest of backwards glances. A shadow thrashed its wings in the doorway, shying from the moonlit wasteland.

"My castle, my empire…" Sgar's voice echoed from the dark halls, becoming broken mumblings. "I am Sgar, son of the Phoenix God…"

The Devourer and Kaya kept running until the desolate ruins lay far behind them.

* * *

In the stunted woods just beyond the wasteland, the Devourer found a prickly hollow and curled up tightly inside, wrapping his tentacles around himself. Kaya sat patiently beside him, making a fire and tending to her wounds, until the sun set and then rose again. Finally, she prodded him gently.

"Saul."

He didn't answer.

"Saul, you look like a squid dumpling that's fallen out of a bento box."

"What's a bento box?" he asked before he could stop himself.

"There's a small island in the sea of Sarshi—Actually, never mind. But we need to move. You'll grow hungry soon."

"Maybe I'll eat *you*," he snarled.

Kaya gave a short sigh.

"What Sgar said—"

"Don't tell me that isn't who I am," he snapped, looming out of the hollow. "Because I *remember* it. I remember every cell, every chamber, every implement. I delighted in my own cleverness, with little thought for the consequences. I was a monster long before Sarak transformed me. She merely changed my outer form to match the man within. I have my answers now, as you have yours. I'm sorry there's nothing more I can offer you, but our journey together ends here."

Kaya studied him quietly, much as she had on that first day from the top of the labyrinth wall. This time, it wasn't pity in her eyes, but the Devourer couldn't describe what it was he saw there now.

"I'd like to tell you one more story," she said. "But first, walk the labyrinth with me one final time. Will you do that, Saul?"

The Devourer shook his head at the thought of returning to that place, and yet a part of him longed to see it. Just one last time.

"It's a long way," he said finally. "Perhaps you'll have time to tell me about the sea of Sarshi and these boxes of bento."

* * *

Spring had woken the trees and warmed the grass by the time they finally returned to the Labyrinth of Varissen. With trepidation, the Devourer approached the wrought iron gates, noting that they'd been polished and every trace of rust removed. He glanced at Kaya, who looked equally intrigued.

"Ready?" she said, holding out her hand.

After a moment's hesitation, the Devourer placed a claw in her hand, and together, they entered the labyrinth. As they walked along the gently curving path, they saw that the ground had been swept clean, and the walls cleared of vines. The fountains bubbled with fresh water, and the newly pruned trees hung heavy with fragrant white peaches and crisp apples.

With every step, his thoughts seemed clearer and calmer. With every length and turn, his heart felt more grounded, more joyous. As the sun began to set, they reached the central courtyard, and the Devourer slumped to his knees, his chest heaving with emotion.

Finally, he *remembered*.

* * *

Five hundred years ago

Saul stood on the scaffolding in the central courtyard, overlooking the completed labyrinth. The final stone had been set, the last fountain activated, the last sapling planted. It had cost them a fortune in artisans and sorcerers, but they'd fused enchanted artefacts into the fountains and trees to keep them ever-fresh, ever-lush, so long as they were tended. Beside him, King Varissen surveyed their opus.

"Are you certain you want that acacia there?" he asked.

"It looks silly now," said Saul, "but in two hundred years, it'll be magnificent. And when people arrive at the centre, trust me, they'll want some shade and a drink."

"I trust you."

Saul glanced away, and Varissen placed a hand on his shoulder.

"You're a good man, Saul. Wiser than you were. Braver than you were. You risked your life to bring down Sgar, and now, you've created a thing of incomparable beauty—a true treasure."

However, it wasn't pride Saul felt now. His arrogance had withered the day a visiting ranger, Varissen, had told him wondrous stories of what a kingdom *should* look like, and filled Saul's heart with shame. Now, his labours—his penance—brought him not pride, but peace.

"You've spent all your wealth on this place…"

"A kingdom does not need wealth. It needs prosperity, happiness and resilience. Farmers will grow, merchants will trade, poets will dream, days will pass, and so will you and I. But this will forever be a place of wonder and rest, of meditation and insight. Generations to come will walk these paths and find serenity and wisdom, mercy and kindness, here in this place. This is your legacy, Saul."

Saul lifted his face to the breeze, glancing at the silver threads sparking on the horizon.

"Looks like there's a storm coming."

* * *

The Devourer wiped his eyes, his chest aching.

"A labyrinth is a single path," he said. "A walking meditation, a spiritual journey. A labyrinth is where you find yourself."

"And this is the story I wanted to tell you," said Kaya. "When I read of the labyrinth and the beast within, there was another story I came upon. A story about the man who built the labyrinth. A brilliant, troubled man. A man seeking redemption. It was not the advice of the Devourer I sought. It was yours, Saul."

The Devourer bowed his head, and Kaya touched his face gently. Shadows shifted in the shade of the acacia tree, and several figures stepped—and slithered—into the sunshine: Rawlins, the Serpent, and a brown-skinned woman with braided hair. Kaya's eyes lit up when she saw the last figure, and she threw her arms around the woman.

"Amala! What are you doing here?"

"We respected your wish for 'space', but when you didn't return, the other librarians and I went searching for you. Everywhere we went, we heard tales of a young woman travelling with a fearsome beast, and we thought 'That sounds like Kaya'. Although we did wonder who the young woman was."

Kaya pretended to scowl, but her eyes shone with delight. Amala bowed to the Devourer.

"Lord Saul, it's a pleasure to meet you. As I was explaining to Lady Rawlins, with Sarak gone, the enchantment extending your lives has been broken. You'll live out your remaining years as you would have."

"I think she just walks around giving people unhappy facts," said Rawlins. "By the way, sorry, I ate all those bones you had lying around."

The Serpent hissed miserably. "I told her you were saving them for last, like the...crispy bits...of fried potatoes."

Rawlins pointed to the Serpent. "In case you find anything broken, he was already here when I arrived, along with some giant dung beetle who was rolling up all the detritus from the paths. You're a lousy housekeeper, Saul. Oh, and the Kleptomaniac Kraken cleaned all the fountains, and she's taken up residence in the eastern pond. She promises to reform her grabby ways, and the Judgemental Jellyfish said he'd keep an eye on her."

"Do jellyfish have eyes?" said the Devourer.

"I didn't say he'd be effective."

The Devourer cast his gaze around the courtyard, barely able to comprehend the transformation it, and he, had undergone. He turned to Kaya.

"Thank you. For finding me."

With the sunset sky ablaze, Kaya looked at him with fiery optimism in her eyes.

"And now," she said, "I request that your debt be repaid. Build me a kingdom, Saul. Where the roads run smooth and the rivers flow clear. Where the soils are rich and the villages less likely to blow away in the rain. You were ever the heart of the labyrinth, growing wiser and kinder with every step. So, with us by your side, build us a kingdom."

And so, the story began.

A NOTE FROM DK

I'm one of the lucky ones. I discovered Terry Pratchett's books when I was in high school, and for nearly twenty years I had a new Pratchett book to look forward to every year. Two books, if I was lucky. And I was lucky for a long time. I had the opportunity to laugh, cry, grow older, and hopefully wiser, alongside characters who became my friends and mentors: Sam Vimes, Susan Sto Helit, Dangerous Beans, Tiffany Aching, and Death himself.

There will be no more books from Sir Terry, but the sparks of wonder, rage, conviction, and hope that he cast into the world will continue to burn bright and spread their light. While *The Heart of the Labyrinth* was inspired in part by the labyrinth of Centennial Park, Sydney, this story was written for Sir Terry Pratchett, who taught us to be kinder, wiser, and braver than we were.

DK Mok
Sydney, Australia

DORIS
SORIN SUCIU

An Irish pub, such as you have seen a thousand times before. The kind where the emphasis is on the "ish" rather than on the proud name of Éire. The ubiquitous shamrock, the occasional Celtic knot, the obligatory ancient Guinness poster, and the sepia portrait of James Joyce. The latter appears at once bemused by and tolerant of the all-inclusive rock spewing nonstop from the vintage jukebox.

It's two in the afternoon. The corporate termites have retreated to their air-conditioned glass mounds. The staff allow themselves a breather before the swarm of worker bees lay claim to the place for the rest of the day.

A skinny guy in his twenties walks in. His slouched shoulders and bland fashion sense broadcast 'IT guy' loud and clear. He sits at the bar and whacks his shin on the brass footrest. He grimaces, but manages to suppress the whine. Good; maybe the bartender hadn't seen it.

The bartender *had* seen it, but his tip sense is on alert.

"And what can I get for you?" he beams. "Our special today is Rustic Monkey Toenail, a local IPA from one of my favourite organic microbreweries. It has a bold, hoppy bouquet, balanced acidity, smooth body, and a subtle floral finish. It's a limited edition, so I wouldn't miss out if I were you. Only four bucks a pint."

"Yeah. Sure. And keep a tab open under 'Sam'." It's his first time asking for a tab, and he is instantly worried that his tone could have come off haughty. "Please," he adds, just in case.

"Coming right up."

There is a bowl of peanuts next to him, and another bowl for the shells. Sam can tell the other bowl is for the shells because it already has shells in it. He helps himself to some nuts.

The beer arrives in a chilled glass. It's exactly as advertised, and that, Sam decides, is a tribute to the power of suggestion, and not to the beer's intrinsic hoppiness, however bold that may be.

His mind wanders off to recent events. The breakup, the layoff, and the illegal download *cease and desist* letter from his ISP—all neatly delivered on three consecutive Tuesdays. Tuesdays are the worst. They are the spoiled leftovers of Mondays, repackaged with a new expiry date.

"Let me guess—you saw the peanuts and thought you'd help yourself, didn't you?" The unexpected interjection comes from a burly man who looks as though he wrestles bears for a living. His voice is deep and rugged—so manly that it must surely come with its own chest hair. "So?" he demands, as he sits on the neighbouring stool.

"I, I..."

"Ah, the stuttered pronoun. I've scared you, haven't I?"

"No," Sam lies. "I mean, I'm sorry. Were these your peanuts? I'll buy you some more."

"Nah; just screwing with you. I should know better than to frighten scrawny guys."

"Yeah, maybe you should." The words come out of their own accord. Great, now he can add 'being roughed up by a stranger in a pub' to his running list of Tuesday goodies.

The man gives him a long, measuring look. "You know, it's moments like these, when fear rushes freely through our veins, that make life memorable. Don't you think?"

"I guess so." Sam takes a sip from his beer to punctuate the drop in tension.

"Why do you think that is? What is it about fear that makes us remember things?"

"I don't know. The heightened pulse, the sudden rush of blood, the brain kicking into high gear as it searches for a way out... Maybe memorisation is just a by-product of all that unexpended energy."

"So you're *that* kind of drunk—the philosopher. Nothing wrong with that. I can play along."

"I'm not drunk," Sam protests.

"But you came here to *get* drunk, and that's what matters. Cheers!"

"Cheers!" The two men clink their pints. A strong bond is forged when pints are clinked: it might not last forever, but while it does it has power. Sam laughs.

"What are you laughing at?" asks the other man.

"It's just that I don't remember you getting a drink, yet here you are, beer in hand."

"Funny thing, laughter, innit?"

"Well, I suppose it is. But I'm actually curious about the drink. Are you an amateur…what's the word…pres-ti-di-gi-ta-tor?"

"I mean, when you think about it, do we laugh because it's funny, or is it funny because it makes us laugh? What do you make of that, Mr Philosopher?"

"Well, that's a sensible question," Sam says, realising there is no point in pursuing his other line of inquiry. "To be perfectly honest, I don't know if I can answer it. Name's Sam, by the way. It's short for Samwise, and if you think *that's* funny, then you haven't met my older sister Galadriel."

The man chuckles. "I'm sorry about your childhood. I'm Doris. Pleasure to meet you."

"Doris, eh? That's an unusual name. Do you mind if I Oogle it on my phone? I've always been fascinated by the origins of names. You can probably understand why."

"Suit yourself."

"Here—it says Doris is a name of Greek origin meaning…oh, I'd better not."

"Go ahead; I don't mind."

"I mean…okay. I guess you know already—meaning Dorian woman."

"Ha! That's as may be, but I'm not that kind of Doris."

"I meant no offence."

"None taken. What I mean to say is that my being *Doris* has nothing to do with what your phone told you."

"Oh?"

"Tell you what, buy me a drink and you can learn all about it. Make it a Scotch, if you don't mind."

"All right, I'll bite." He signals the bartender. "A Scotch for my friend! Wait—what type of Scotch?"

"Oh, he knows, he knows. I'm what you might call a regular."

"No way! I've never met a regular before. Do you like, walk to the bar, exchange a nod with the bartender, and that's it?"

"Something like that."

"That must be so cool."

"Yeah, I suppose it is."

"The tacit understanding, the camaraderie, the unspoken friendship…"

"Yeah, yeah. Don't get yourself worked up. You've paid your price: now you get to ask."

"Oh, right, of course. So what does your name mean?"

"No, no. Not like that. Ask me something you *really* want to know. Something no Oogle on earth can tell you."

"But you said…"

"Listen, lad. I know what I said. And now I'm giving you the chance to have a two-for-one kind of deal. You ask me something, anything, and in answering your question I'll also be showing you what my name means."

Sam pauses to reflect. "I get to ask you a question?"

"Yes."

"Any question?"

"Yes."

"And you promise to answer?"

"Cross my heart and hope to die."

"And if you can't answer?"

"I can answer any question."

"Including lottery numbers?"

"Including lottery numbers."

"Past and future?"

"Past and flipping future. Are you going to ask your question or not?"

"Sure, sure. Just a minute." Sam scratches the back of his head. "Now, lottery numbers is a tempting one. But I'm pretty sure you're taking the piss, so I'd rather ask about something that'll at least give me a good story."

"It's your funeral."

"Say what?"

"Figure of speech. Go on, ask me your question."

"Okay, so... So how about that thing you were saying earlier—you know, about laughter?"

"What about it?"

"You know, why do we laugh?"

"Is that your question?"

"Yes."

"Are you sure?"

"Yes, yes, I'm sure. Come on. Tell me a nice story about laughter and why we do it."

"I'm not gonna do that."

"Excuse me?"

"I said I'm not gonna do that. I'm not gonna tell you a story. That's not what Doris does."

"But you said..."

"Again with your 'but you said'! You sound just like your father."

"What?" Sam's voice comes in shrill falsetto. That was too close to home for comfort.

"Yes. He never quite accepted facts for what they were, did he? When your mom got pregnant with your sister, his first reaction was 'But you said you were on the pill'. When he got fired from the lumber shop he said to his boss 'But you said my position here was secure because I've got two kids to raise.'"

"How do you... Who are you?"

"I told you—I'm Doris."

"I don't know what that means."

"Your grandma did. Remember?"

"How can I...?"

The answer comes as if from far away. "Just follow me. I am Doris."

* * *

It lasts only a moment, but during that moment, Sam is somebody else. A young girl named Moira, daughter of Scottish immigrants. Funny—his grandma's name was Moira. The moment slips away.

"Stay with me," whispers Doris. "First couple of jumps are the hardest. Remember Moira."

Christmas Eve. She sits on her father's knees, all but worn down with sleepiness, yet still skittish with the excitement of the holidays. Quinn, her dad, smells of tobacco and scotch. Later in life, these smells will conjure glimpses of childhood memories. Sometimes they will even take her back to this very night.

Her mum tells her dad that he's had enough to drink, and he should go to sleep. She doesn't really mean it. What she really wants is to hear Quinn sing the song. Her dad makes a show of being upset, but he winks at Moira and she giggles.

It's supposed to be a jaunty song, yet her dad always sings it in a melancholy key. Moira wouldn't have it any other way.

> *"Just a wee deoch an doris,*
> *Just a wee drop, that's all.*
> *Just a wee deoch an doris,*
> *Afore we gang awa…"*

A wee deoch an doris: *a small drink by the door. So 'Doris' means 'Door'.*

"There you have it," Doris's thoughts pour into Sam's mind.

"A door to my memories?"

"Doors to your own memories are easy, laddie. That's for them head doctors and French sponge cakes to open. I provide a different kind of service."

"Sponge cakes?"

"Oh, we'll get to that. Quinn's mother, Maidie—*she* knew all about sponge cakes and memories."

* * *

The Master will entertain guests from distant lands tonight, and so the kitchen maids have their work cut out for them. Maidie wipes her eyebrow with the back of her sleeve. She's tired, and her pregnancy is starting to show.

They're going to name him 'Quinn', as befits the fifth born. That is, if he is a boy. The other four were boys, much to her husband's pride. Only, none of them had actually been her husband's, and this one wouldn't be either, as far as she could tell. She shouldn't have let things get so out of hand with Mr Brennon, the butler. A pinch on the bottom, a squeeze of the tit—the others had warned her that those were to be expected. But he was charming, Mr Brennon was. And he always brought her books and magazines to read. To Maidie, those stolen minutes in front of an open book were the most precious gifts she could ask for. And if, occasionally, she had to lift her skirt for it, that seemed a small—and not entirely unenjoyable—price. It had all started one rainy autumn day, when Mr Brennon had smuggled in a copy of the Gentleman's Magazine from upstairs.

An older memory.

"This article made me think of you, Maidie," he says. "It's about a Mr Proust from France, and a cake named after you."

She cleans her hands, for fear her fingers will stain the white paper with egg wash.

"A cake named Maidie?" she asks.

"Aren't you a silly girl!" he laughs. "The cake is called 'Madeleine'. That's French for Maidie, you know. Mr Proust claims that merely tasting the cake takes him back to Paris."

"Oh, that sounds wonderful."

"Not as wonderful as you, Maidie. I bet a taste of you would take me places."

"Mr Brennon, we shouldn't..."

Alas, between the "shouldn't" and the "shouldn't have"—that is precisely where life happens.

* * *

"Right, so my great-granddad was a bastard now," Sam protests.

"Why do you act surprised?" Doris asks. "Bastards are the dark matter of lineages. We have theoretical knowledge of their existence, but finding proof can be a delicate issue."

"Is this what you do? Open doors to ancestral memories?"

"I am Doris. I *am* the Door. But enough about me. Do you understand now why people laugh?"

"I...I don't think so. I mean, Moira giggled on her father's lap, but children laugh all the time. Mr Brennon laughed at Maidie's silliness, but then again, people often laugh when they flirt. So, no. I'm still far from finding the common denominator for laughter."

"You are closer than you think."

"I am? How far back can you take me?"

"I can take you back to the shrew-like creature that is the ancestor of all mammals, and even further than that. But you wouldn't like it. It's mostly eat, be prey, make love."

"Take me back to the time when humans didn't have language yet, then."

"As you wish."

* * *

Memories fly through Sam. Not in a swarm, but rather one by one. They are like snapshots frozen in time, as if someone is shining a strobe light on a conga line of progressively distant ancestors. A love letter here, a wandering arrow there, a boat ride, a mutton leg, a precious stone, a maypole dance, a first kiss, a well-laid brick. The memories fly by in their thousands, and Sam becomes each and every one of them.

As he approaches his destination, Sam starts to perceive a gradual decrease in memory quality. At first it is as if the streaming service has switched from HD to Standard. Then, to black and white. Memories become dull and lacklustre, to the point of being not even worth remembering.

Without language to give them shape, Sam realises, memories are just like houses with no walls. They're merely events seeking to chain themselves together into causes and effects; survival unhindered by narrative.

One last jump…

* * *

"Stop!" Sam shouts. "I don't want to go there!"

"Oh? And why is that?" Doris asks.

"Because I'm afraid I won't know how to get back. And because, whatever I may find in there, I'm sure laughter won't be part of it."

"There's hope for you yet, laddie, there's hope for you yet."

"Wait, what do you mean? You knew I might have gotten stuck in there and you let me go for it anyway?"

"So what? You might get into a car accident when you sit behind the wheel, yet you, as you put it, 'go for it' every day."

"But…"

"Listen, how about I take you straight to the first laughter, eh?"

"Can you do that? Why didn't you say so in the beginning?"

"I believe I said you could ask me anything. Just because you didn't think to ask me to take you there doesn't mean I can't do it. Anyway, am I to understand you're on board with the idea?"

"Umm…yes, sure. Take me to the ancestor who gave humanity the gift of laughter."

"Yeah, about that… Actually, I'd better let you see for yourself."

* * *

The memory has just enough detail for Sam to put it together. If anything, it represents the instructions to *building* a memory, the same way sheet music represents the instructions to delivering a symphony—provided you can supply your own orchestra.

She sits by the campfire with Bone, Sky, Leaf, Skin, and Dew. Her name is Twig. At least, she shares her name with the thing that is a twig.

Bone uses elaborate gestures and crude words to describe the day's hunt. He seems to be in control, as a leader should be.

As usual, Twig finds herself listening in a way no one else in the tribe seems to be able to. She listens to Bone as if from within—as if she can experience for herself what's going on inside his mind. Tens of thousands of years later, her feeling would bear the name 'empathy'. Her particular mutation will open new horizons for humankind. Indeed, it might even be responsible for putting the 'kind' into 'humankind'.

But Twig does not consider herself special. She feels unfit and uncomfortable. Being able to relate to the feelings of others takes a great toll on her. She experiences an unbearable pressure building from within, fuelled by Bone's story. And then, without a warning, the pressure reaches a critical point.

Her mouth opens and lets out an explosion of air. The relief feels good. So good, in fact, that she allows herself a smile.

Bone's eyes are set upon her, caught between anger and surprise. But then he sees her smile. Bone likes Twig. She is his favourite female.

Something is happening to Bone. It looks as if a bit of food is stuck in his throat and he is trying to cough it out. Twig's yet-unnamed sense of empathy tells her that he is trying to repeat the sound she just made.

She does it again, to help him out. He does it too.

Together, they laugh.

* * *

"I don't understand," says Sam. "That wasn't even funny."

"It wasn't meant to be funny. The first handshake was not meant as a substitute for 'hello', nor was painting one's face a sexual display behaviour."

"What was it meant to be, then?"

"What do you think it was?"

"I don't know… A social fill-in-the-blank? A placeholder for 'I don't know what to say but I want you to know that I heard you'?"

"Eh, close enough. You'll figure it out in the end."

* * *

"No, wait. Hold that. He seems to be okay now. Dude, are you okay? I have 911 on the line."

Sam is back in the pub. The bartender is talking to him. "What?" he manages to say.

"You passed out. I called 911. How many fingers am I holding up?"

Sam's mind is all over the place. "Doris. Where is Doris?"

"What are you talking about?" Then, speaking into the phone, "Yes, I think you should send a crew, though. He's hallucinating. No, I swear, only a beer... Maybe, I don't know. Who can tell with all these pot shops sprouting everywhere nowadays..?"

* * *

Sam, now the proud owner of a PhD in Anthropology, has just finished delivering his TED Talk on "The Origins of Laughter". He could not have hoped for a better response. With any luck, he'll have his choice of tenure at a good five major universities by the end of the week.

He sits at the open bar, Scotch in hand and bowl of peanuts within reach. Around him, an animated crowd dances a Brownian dance to the tune of social interactions.

"Let me guess, you saw the peanuts and thought you'd help yourself, didn't you?" Comes a voice at his shoulder.

"Damn it, Doris! Would you believe I've been placing myself strategically next to unattended peanut bowls for the last seven years or so, trying to get your attention? It's an embarrassing routine, and it's gotten me into trouble more than once."

"Would *you* believe I found it entertaining for the first couple of years? Anyway, what will it be this time? I can still give you the winning lottery numbers, you know."

A NOTE FROM SORIN

That I write this in English, is overwhelmingly thanks to Terry Pratchett.

When I discovered *The Colour of Magic* ('Culoarea Magiei' at the time, for I was reading it in my native Romanian) I remember having three revelations:

A) There will be at least another 30 happy times in my life—one for each Discworld novel available at that time.

B) I will read them all in English. And so, with the dictionary in one hand and *Light Fantastic* in the other, a journey that would eventually take me all the way to Canada began.

C) I will never be as good a writer as Terry, but darn it, I will be best writer I can *be* because of him!

As for Doris, it all started with a song. I first heard *A Wee Deoch an Doris* from my friend Adrian—who drinks like a devil and sings like an angel, and kind of looks like my Doris too. I was then inspired by Sophie Scott's TED Talk 'Why We Laugh' and by her later comments on TED Radio Hour about how, because audio storage is something relatively new, we have no way of knowing how our ancestors laughed.

I hope you enjoyed it.

Sorin Suciu
Vancouver, Canada

THE VIVIDARIUM
STEVEN MCKINNON

Somewhere on the Axis of Life and Death and Custard Creams, against a backdrop of infinite space, a war was being waged. Poor pawns pressed onward, gallant knights galloped, and the bishops sat at the back and simply judged everyone else. Fires roared and castles tumbled. All things considered, it was a bit of a mess.

"Oh, look: I win again," said the Supreme Sorcerer and God King of All the Universe, whose name was Dave. His voice held a hint of genuine surprise, as though he wasn't *used* to winning every single time. Behind him, a galaxy was being whisked into life. "Another game?"

"Of course you won," sighed the Celestial Sculptor and Curator of the Cradle of Life, who preferred it when people just called him Sid. He folded his arms together and groaned. He was especially annoyed, because he'd been cheating. "Ain't it about time you gave someone else a go?"

"No. It's winner stays on."

Sid slumped into his chair as the flash of anger that made him want to start a fight puffed itself away. There are some things you just can't argue with, after all. "Can't we change the game at least?" he asked. "We've been playing chess every night for the past twenty thousand years!"

"Still quicker than a game of Monopoly. Anyway, it's the rules."

"Then how about *changing* the rules? You know, seeing as you're all high and mighty and superior and everything?"

"Alter rules that were in place before even the concept of time? Ridiculous," snorted the Supreme Sorcerer, who as a young man liked to conjure flames out of his thumbs and tell girls his name was Dave the Magnificent.

"Oh, yeah—ridiculous." Sid rolled his eyes. "You don't have the power to change things up a bit, but you can literally fart existence."

"No-one's forcing you to play if you don't want to." The Supreme Sorcerer conjured a cup of tea and dunked a custard cream into it.

"Doesn't seem like I've got much choice, does it? What else am I gonna do to fill the time? It's not like we need sleep. And when are we getting Hobnobs?"

The Supreme Sorcerer swallowed and stroked his beard, which was about six decades long. "You could go out for a walk if you're struggling to fill the time. I hear they're working on a new nebula that's meant to be even better than the Pillars. Oh, and isn't there a supernova scheduled to annihilate a solar system soon? Might be worth a look."

"Nah, it puts you off once you see how they're done. It's like seeing a sausage being made. But only half as disgusting."

"Seeing things from behind the scenes is one of the downsides of getting a promotion, I'm afraid."

Sid stood, stretched his legs, and gazed out into the vastness of space ahead of him. "You know, I think I preferred being a Planetary Landscape Artist. You didn't get much respect and half the time you were just fixing your boss's cock-ups, but it was good being in the middle of it, getting your hands dirty. It'd be you and your mates sitting on a sun at lunch and talking about what you got up to on the weekend. The higher-ups might not know you from Andromeda, but there was...whatcha call it? Sort of like, mutual respect."

"Camaraderie?" suggested the Supreme Sorcerer. He helped himself to another custard cream, because cholesterol levels don't really matter when you're an immortal cosmic space god.

"Camaraderie!" said Sid. "Yeah, bags of the stuff. Sometimes I think about chucking my notice in and going back."

"Don't be absurd; being a PLA's a young man's game."

"I'm only three hundred and fifty thousand! Anyway, I bet I could teach them a thing or two."

"I'm sure," said the Supreme Sorcerer. He clicked his fingers to reset the chessboard. The game was definitely a lot more interesting now that they were allowed to use actual people for pieces.

"I don't know," shrugged Sid. "Maybe I just need a holiday. I suppose I could check out the Nine Circles of Hell again, that's usually a laugh. Bit more lively than upstairs, anyway."

"You know, Sidney, if I didn't know absolutely everything there is to know, I'd say you were having a midlife crisis."

"Eh? What a load of piss!"

"Do you know, the last time I took a piss, I missed the bowl, hit a garden planet, and accidentally created an ocean where a desert was supposed to go. Caused no end of upset."

"Yeah? What happened?"

The Supreme Sorcerer's brow furrowed. "One of the PLAs took the blame, I think."

"Bloody typical. You know, between you and that Vividarium, I'm surprised we've still got workers left. It ain't right using some blasted contraption like that to copy other people's work. There'll be no proper artisans left. And ain't that what we're supposed to be?"

"It's not a 'contraption'—it's a tool to help future generations. And who said anything about copying? We merely use what came before as a starting point. Even *this* universe was based on a template of an old one. We're just being more efficient. You've got to get with the times, Sidney."

"You can keep the sales pitch to yourself thanks, it's been drummed into me enough," sneered Sid. "'The Vividarium, the Crucible of Knowledge, the Summation of All Existence, Present, Past and Future'. Yeah, maybe if we didn't have to keep switching the bloody thing off and on again."

The Supreme Sorcerer thought for a moment and tapped his fingers on the chessboard (unintentionally causing a space tornado to veer off-course and extinguish all life in one of the lesser-known solar systems). "You know, if you need further convincing, we *could* take a look at it."

"Eh? You mean a lowly servant like me could be permitted to behold the almighty Vividarium and witness its majesty first-hand?" said Sid. He didn't mean to sound sarcastic, it was just his voice's default tone. In truth, he was impressed by the Supreme Sorcerer's proposal. He couldn't even remember the last time he'd seen a flicker of mischief in Dave's eyes. "You sure you're allowed?"

"I'm the Supreme Sorcerer and God King of All the Universe," he said. "Of course I'm bloody allowed. As long as we don't reset it to its factory settings again."

* * *

The two men—for the plural noun that correctly describes these beings doesn't exist in any of the universe's known languages or dialects, and to read, say or think it would drive one completely insane—traversed through a trillion starways on the Axis of Life and Death and Custard Creams, before finally coming to a colossal temple several hundred years tall. The walls were made of pure obsidian, and the doors were an alloy of iron, aluminium and black hole. Sid gazed up at the temple's peak, just in time to see a tiny mote of dust ignite a Big Bang event and give birth to a pocket universe (which swallowed the space tornado from before, just as it was becoming sentient).

"Nervous?" asked the Supreme Sorcerer.

"Not at all," lied Sid.

The Supreme Sorcerer twirled a finger in the air, and the doors became liquid. They stepped inside the temple and were greeted with a vast and empty chamber filled with blackness so thick you could practically breathe it. Strange and ancient carvings of shapes that no human mind could possibly comprehend were etched into the walls. The whole room was lined with shuddering shadows that danced in accordance with the light emanating from a pulsing blue cube, which sat upon an altar in the middle of the room. Contained within this cube was everything that had ever happened in any universe. It housed the blueprints to every dimension and to the building blocks of the heavens. It contained knowledge of every person born and every battle fought; every kiss enjoyed and every secret kept; every word that was ever uttered and every thought that was ever conceived, from The Beginning until The End of Time.

"Looks a bit shit," said Sid.

The Supreme Sorcerer strode over to the cube with noticeable trepidation. The light swelled as he drew closer to it, becoming almost tangible. For a second, Sid was sure he could hear it singing.

Taking a deep breath, the Supreme Sorcerer held out his hands and uttered a sacred word in his ancient and indecipherable language, which to humans would be roughly translated as "password".

"We should really get around to changing that," he said.

A pillar of light shot skyward with a soul-quaking boom that echoed forever around the chamber.

"Right, give me a minute..." muttered the Supreme Sorcerer (a minute to him of course being roughly a fortnight for an earthling). He plunged his hands into the light and started rummaging around.

"What are you doing?" asked Sid. "That's not the Vividarium you're fiddling with?"

"Indeed not; this is the Pandoria Box, which is merely a storage device. The Vividarium is contained within."

"Oh. Well mind you don't misplace anything in there, like the Sacred and Holy Tenets of Evolution. It took a millennium and seven holy wars to find that."

"I believe we've made a backup since then. Ah, here we are..." The Supreme Sorcerer clasped a glowing orb and brandished it in front of Sid. It swam inside an ocean's worth of colours, most of which haven't been invented yet. The Supreme Sorcerer's fingers trembled and his eyes filled with wonder—which doesn't happen very often when you're a billion-year-old sorcerer who invented the concept of physics and, indeed, the concept of concepts. In a hushed voice, he said: "I present to you what is without doubt the most precious and significant creation in an infinity of aeons—the Alpha and the Omega, the First and the Last, a boundless energy that cannot be harnessed, merely experienced... *The Vividarium!*"

Sid screwed his eyes and peered down at it. "Looks like a mutant orange several years past its 'Use By' date," he said.

The Supreme Sorcerer's face dropped. "You've no sense of wonder."

Sid shrugged. "I've got plenty of wonder. Just not for sparkly satsumas."

"Allow me to convince you otherwise."

With a flourish of his fingers, the Supreme Sorcerer unravelled the orb and sprawled all of its infinite information in front of Sid. "This is the matrix of all things," he whispered, in the spooky voice from his Dave the Magnificent days. "This is where memories are made and shared and kept. This is the house of the soul, a cosmic library which would take lifetimes to navigate. All that can ever be learned is contained within its everlasting walls, and all that is learned is stored and passed on, to ensure progress and—"

"Cats!"

"Um, I'm sorry?"

"Pictures of cats!" squealed Sid. "It's full of 'em! The 'cosmic library of infinite space' and what's it used for? Sticking your pet in a chicken costume and taking pictures of it. Imagine what the Cat Empress of Felidae IV would say if she saw this! And oh look—here we have a very important picture of someone's dinner. I can definitely see why the Celestial Elders are touting this as the Next Big Thing."

"It is a device for storing and viewing memories," reasoned the Supreme Sorcerer. "We cannot dictate these things; we can only learn from the experiences contained therein and use them as a foundation for the future."

"Dear gods… The lack of proper grammar in here is deeply unsettling."

"A trivial point," sighed the Supreme Sorcerer, disappointed by Sid's apathy. He was really hoping he'd be impressed, too. "Sidney, you must believe me when I say that this is changing the very nature of understanding."

"Hah! I'm going to sign my cousin in Alpha Centauri up for some of these Official Galactic Never-Ending Endowment Pills," giggled Sid, as though he were a twenty-thousand-year-old adolescent again.

"It is supposed to be used as a learning conduit!" A flash of anger caused the Supreme Sorcerer's thumbs to set his beard on fire. "It is meant for beings of all natures, types and races to connect with one another, to expand upon the collective knowledge of all things, to better themselves and—"

"Does it have pictures of naked ladies?"

"Wh-what?"

"Naked ladies. Does it have pictures of naked ladies?"

"Well, yes," said the Supreme Sorcerer, his face turning (an admittedly lovely shade of) plum. "The purpose of course being to catalogue and preserve all facets of life, but—"

"*Oh my gods there's a video of a koala doing a backflip!*"

"Sidney! Please don't make the mistake of demeaning the purpose behind what we are doing."

Sid shrugged. "I don't get what the big deal is. All you've done is stuck one storage box inside another."

"Ha! On the contrary; the Vividarium allows us to *experience* what is contained within it. It is capable of transferring data via cosmic streams directly into our consciousness a billion times faster than the speed of light. That means we can experience people's memories first-hand. The Pandoria Box is just a fancy filing cabinet."

"You know what, you're right, this was a great idea," said Sid, flicking through omnibyte upon omnibyte of information. "There are *millions* of games here that are better than chess! *Mind Sweeper*, that sounds good. Hang on, what's this?... Uh-oh, we've got a message asking us to send our bank details to assist the deposed Princess Quaraldamar, who has been unjustly ousted from the Cosmic Queendom of Alpha Ragnar Nine by her father's enemies within the Senate. She says if we send her fifty thousand cosmic space diamonds, she'll pay us back with twenty percent interest."

The Supreme Sorcerer rubbed the bridge of his nose (and almost set his eyebrows on fire in the process). "You are intentionally belittling the work we are trying to accomplish, Sid. We will use the Vividarium to create galaxies, nebulae and dimensions—all in a fraction of the time it used to take. We will instantly learn, adapt and overcome quandaries as soon as they materialise. We will improve every species in the universe."

"To whose specifications?" asked Sid. "Look, I'm just showing you what happens when you build something with this kind of power. I.e., some bright spark will figure out how to use it to look at boobs and steal people's money. And you *know* it'll get used in war too. It's already a weapon of mass creation."

"I can assure you that it's in good hands," soothed the Supreme Sorcerer. "Visionaries, philosophers, logicians. Minds that mould the great and the vital. They're in here at all hours, improving its functionality every day. Oh, if you could *not* tell them I let you into the temple, that'd be grand."

"Oh yeah, 'visionaries and logicians'. They're the same esteemed colleagues who constructed the Axis of Life and Death, 'the nucleus of all things and cradle of civilisation'. And then what happened? They named it after a bloody biscuit."

"Biscuits *are* important though."

"Well, I mean, *yeah*," said Sid, gazing back into the Vividarium's sun-kissed glow. "No-one's arguing with that. But the fact is you've made something that holds the potential to be used for—" Sid held his index fingers in the air and wriggled them up and down. "—less than honourable applications. How long before it's used to exploit people? Or for warmongering? Don't fool yourself: you've created a weapon, and it'll be the undoing of every—oh..." Sid's finger hung in mid-air. His eyes were as wide as (super galactic flying) saucers.

"'Oh' what? Sidney? What in infinite hells have you done?"

"Um... There's a slight chance your SpaceBook page was open on your ex-girlfriend's profile, which may in turn have led to the possibility of me accidentally clicking 'Like' on that selfie she posted of her starbathing in her bikini when she was backpacking last year, thus resulting in the potential— but by no means definite—outcome of her blocking you and sending you a private message full of...*vivid* language that *possibly* ends with the suggestion that you're 'a desperate weirdo who can't do magic and you really need to get a grip'. I wouldn't take it personally."

The Supreme Sorcerer's face turned from plum to a scarlet so severe that he'll have to invent a completely new suite of colours just so that he can culminate it with a shade of red called 'volcanic'.

"*What in the gods' names have you done?*" he screamed, as 'volcanic' became 'apocalyptic'. He conjured a small wooden stool out of nowhere, purely so he could kick it into a million splinters. "I spent *ages* planning on how to get back on her good side! You've ruined everything!"

"...Sorry..." whispered Sid, feeling only slightly guilty that he'd done it on purpose.

The Supreme Sorcerer snatched the Vividarium from Sid's hands, proving that even billion-year-old sorcerers have limits to their patience. "I don't know what I was thinking, showing you this," he groaned. "I should have *known* you wouldn't appreciate it. I should have known that you, Sidney, can't be trusted with something this powerful."

"No. No, you're right, I can't," said Sid. "Which is exactly my point."

"Listen, you're the Curator. As such, you are expected to lead by example. Your job demands you treat this seriously!"

"You're talking about sifting through people's private memories! Believe me, I *am* taking it seriously. Are you? We need to consider all sides of the dodecahedron here; you think messing around with your ex-girlfriend was bad? That's just the tip of the asteroid. It has the potential to be much worse—which means you need to realise that being 'all-powerful and

44

superior' doesn't necessarily make you *right*. You need to know that you're fallible and, for all the gods' sakes, learn to be a bit more humble."

"I'm perfectly humble," said the Supreme Sorcerer and God King of All the Universe.

"Yeah, well, omnipotent beings which hold power over all they survey building an infernal device to help them *maintain* said power doesn't seem very humble to me," said Sid. "But whatever."

"On the contrary. If we didn't recognise our fallacies then we wouldn't have thought to construct a device which allows us to learn from them. By distilling memories and experiences, we can adapt and unlock limitless potential. Especially handy, given that the universe is scheduled to reset again soon."

"Just sounds like you're trying to control people."

"Not at all. We're trying to make them better."

"Yeah?" said Sid. "Remind me why you were dumped again?"

"…I can't recall."

"Oh! Well just as well we can check with your memory invader then, innit?"

"All right, fine. I was dumped because she said I'm 'petty and jealous and meddle too much'. Load of piffle. *She's* petty and jealous and meddles too much. *One time she made me shave my beard.*"

"But didn't you try to get rid of her group of backpacking mates? That seems worse than being shaved to me."

"They were a bad influence!" snapped the Supreme Sorcerer. "Staying out and partying and constantly having fun. I was doing her a favour."

"By conjuring a wormhole and throwing them in it and telling your ex that they tripped and fell into it?"

"Oh come on, it only led to the adjacent dimension, hardly a big deal! It was for her own good. Even if she didn't realise it."

"See? You *do* want to control everything," grinned Sid. "Everybody does, because they're scared of what they *can't* control. But it doesn't matter if you're god, man, woman, wizard, lizard or witch; no-one deserves that kind of power. Except maybe dolphins."

"We're not really altering anything, though. People's memories will still belong to them. It's just that they'll be shared with us. That's not so bad, is it?"

"Eh? Yes! It's *totally and completely awful!* The very reason memories are important is because they're based on experiences unique to the individual! Ain't that where the value comes from—from within, where it has context? More than that, what if it's people's memories that *make them* an individual?'

"We're only viewing it, not changing it. The experience is still theirs."

"For how long? If every memory and experience is shared, we'll all be saturated with the same knowledge. And if I call in sick one day, the first thing you'll do is say 'Hey, don't worry! Let's use this to jump into Sid's mind and take what he knows!' Then what am I but a mindless drone plucked from a production rack? Eventually some clever twit will shrug and say 'Why not just copy and paste everything he knows into someone else?' I'll be obsolete!"

"Preposterous!"

"And it'll escalate. We'll butt heads and bruise egos. Quibbles become grudges. Grudges become wars. Sooner or later the temptation will be to come in here and start *implanting* memories to make sure we get our way. I mean, right now, how can we be sure which thoughts even belong to us in the first place? It's an invasion of privacy. Why did we invent free will only to change the bits that we decide ain't working? Did anyone even ask these questions when this thing was being built?"

"Your argument collapses when we consider the greater good, and the benefits our work will have in all corners of the universe—this one and the next," reasoned the Supreme Sorcerer in his best know-it-all voice. "We are better than that. We are reasonable."

"Apparently not when your girlfriend's out gallivanting with her mates," argued Sid. "How long before you're that annoyed at me? And how about your own enemies? What happens if the Unholy Undergod from the X Dimension disagrees with your judgement? Who gets the final say? You? And how do *you* know the memory's even accurate? Ask a dozen different people what they remember about any given event and you'll get a dozen different answers, so which one do you go with? I'm telling you, it'll reduce us all to squabbling primitives."

The Supreme Sorcerer thought about this for a second (so an hour, if you're mortal). "Well, the data would be analysed and collated, and eventually a universally agreed-upon solution would be presented. There'd be a spreadsheet."

"Yeah, and each time you add another stage to the process you'll be stepping even further away from why the memory was important in the first place. You might be omnipotent, but how can you possibly know the value of an experience that doesn't belong to you? You're using logic to learn from something that's illogical. When I said I miss sculpting mountains and fjords and sitting on suns with the PLA boys, it was because of how it made me *feel*. I was...*nostalgic*. The emotion informs the memory, and you won't get the emotional component if all you're doing is experiencing the memory from a distance. And doesn't that defeat the purpose?"

And also, Sid thought to himself, I really don't want you seeing the memory of me messaging your ex two minutes ago...

"But... It's the absence of an emotional connection with a memory which makes us ideally placed to learn from it," recited the Supreme Sorcerer. His know-it-all voice was somewhat diluted by the fact that, gods forbid, he was beginning to see Sid's point. Even more distressing was the thought that he, the Supreme Sorcerer, might be *wrong*. Did he really want someone poking around inside his vast, incomprehensible brain, cherry picking bits and pieces? And did he really want anyone combing through his memories as Dave the Magnificent? What if that led to questions about the unfortunate incident with the porpoise and the poodle and the tutu and the lighter fluid...?

He turned over to the altar. The light didn't seem as bright as before.

"Look," said Sid, "all I'm saying is that memories ain't for other people to gawk at; they're for the individual and the people that helped make them. And that's more sacred than anything you've got in that box of tricks over there, believe you me."

"And if they're memories the individual doesn't remember, or even know that they possess? Or if their minds begin to fail?"

"Yeah, all that too. Bad or good, they shape us. And people's memories of us are all that's left when we're gone. They're the only thing we truly leave behind. That goes for you and me too."

"No..." The Supreme Sorcerer's voice trembled. "We are everlasting...eternal...infinite..."

The two men left the emptiness of the temple behind them and stepped out into the universe. They looked all around at the heavens and hells, and at the starways that spiralled all the way to forever. It all felt much smaller now to the Supreme Sorcerer. Sid, on the other hand, reflected on how lucky he was to be here—to be able to witness all of creation and its intricacies in a single gaze, and to know that this moment was his and his alone.

"Even infinity has its limits," he said.

A NOTE FROM STEVEN

When a friend told me that Sorin and Laura were putting together an anthology in memory of Sir Terry Pratchett, I was in the throes of agonising RSI. Even clasping a mouse would cause bolts of pain to bullet through my arm and back. It was rubbish. But hey, at least I had a prefabricated excuse to avoid the gym.

But while I can switch my enthusiasm for sit-ups and treadmills off at will, I can't switch off the stories in my head. The dilemma, then, was learn how to type with my toes or invest in dictation software. I opted for the hygienic option (though I reserve the right to whip my socks off and make my toes dance across the keyboard at any moment), and the call for submissions to the anthology sounded like a worthy testing ground.

Before I put pen to paper—or voice to mic—I thought hard about what to write. My initial ideas were poor imitations of Terry Pratchett stories. Immediately my fountain of inspiration resembled a dried up and vandalised fire hydrant spitting dust.

And then I started to speak. I watched the story unfurl in front of me, words spilling one after the other, morphing into a narrative. The first draft came together in one sitting. It was exhilarating. I've never had so much fun with a project. Of course, it wasn't perfect—no first draft is—but after feedback from Sorin, Laura, and two of my anthology colleagues, I feel the best version of the story has been distilled. I'm very proud of it. I hope you enjoyed reading it as much as I enjoyed telling it.

Steven McKinnon
Glasgow, UK

ACKERLEY'S GENUINE EARTH ANTIQUES
MICHAEL K. SCHAEFER

"Good morning one and all," said the cheery female voice of the public announcement system. "It's the start of another beautiful day on Dawn's Mystery. The first transport with tourists is scheduled to dock in fifteen minutes."

Rupert ate the last of his sandwich and washed it down with the remains of his coffee. With a parting glance out the window, he stood up from the bench and continued on his way down the promenade.

Dawn's Mystery. He had lived and worked on the space station for the past ten years, but he still didn't like the name. Nobody had ever been able to give him a convincing explanation of what the 'mystery' was supposed to be. All dawn consisted of was cruel alarm clocks and the almost unbearable urge to fall back into bed and sleep. No mystery anywhere.

He arrived at his shop and punched in the security code. The door swung open and the shutters started to rise, informing the world with an abundance of clattering and clanging that 'Ackerley's Genuine Earth Antiques' was open for business.

Rupert entered the shop and started getting ready for another day of selling antiques to the tourists who arrived by the hundreds every day to behold Old Earth from high above and spend their hard-earned money on souvenirs.

After all this time, people were still drawn to Earth.

It had been more than six hundred years since Departure Day, the day the remnants of humanity had left Earth in search of refuge and a future, but the planet was still regarded—often with a twinge of wistfulness—as the centre of the inhabited universe. Every human alive dreamed of going back. So much so, in fact, that it had developed into a kind of pilgrimage. And a visit to Dawn's Mystery and its famous observation promenade was the closest you could get: its towering picture windows offered an unparalleled view of the planet, and tourists were guaranteed an authentic 'Old Earth experience'.

With a look at the clock hanging above the counter, Rupert registered that Emily was late. As usual. And so he, as usual, had to do her share of the work in getting the shop ready. He fetched the feather duster from the closet and started slowly making his way through the crammed shop, walking twisting paths which didn't follow any pattern or plan but had instead evolved over time simply because nothing else had happened to be placed there.

The shop was full to the brim with Earth antiques of all kinds. The knowledgeable connoisseur and the ignorant tourist alike could find within its walls everything from A to Z: from 600-year-old alarm clocks (it seemed about right that the human race wouldn't leave Earth without them) to a statue of a ferocious predator that used to be called a 'zebra'.

Looking for a genuine umbrella to take home as a souvenir? Rupert had plenty of those. Searching for a rare, mint condition toothbrush to complete your collection? Everybody knew that Rupert Ackerley's shop was the place to go.

All of the artefacts in his shop were things people had brought with them when they had left Earth on the evacuation rockets and the quarantine had been put in place. There hadn't been a lot of room on the Ark Space Stations—the home of mankind for nearly a century—and that made it all the more astonishing what evacuees had chosen to bring along.

Umbrellas, for example. If you're leaving Earth to live on a space station, why the heck would you bring an umbrella? Rupert thought it said a lot about people and the state of mind back then. *Did you pack an umbrella, dear? You never know what the weather might be up there.*

He stopped dusting to pick up an artefact that had fallen from its stand. It consisted of a long handle, partly wrapped in cloth, which ended in an open hoop. When he had purchased it a few years back, bits of loose cord had still been attached to the inner side of the hoop, and he suspected that they had once formed a net.

He sighed as he put the object back where it belonged. Rupert regarded himself as an expert on Earth and its antiques, but there were some objects that simply eluded his attempts to guess at their original meaning or function, and this was one of those. Maybe it was for hunting—imagine a man running over the African plains wielding an artefact just like this one, trying to bring down a fierce zebra, king of the jungle.

"Good morning," said Emily as she walked into the shop.

"Morning," replied Rupert. He looked at her sternly and added, out of long-standing tradition: "You're late. That doesn't reflect well on your work ethic."

"Right you are, boss," agreed Emily, and smiled. The day couldn't really start for either of them without this ritual.

After checking that Rupert didn't need any help, Emily opened a box of canes they had recently acquired. She pulled out a black one with a golden skull handle and began to polish it to a shine.

* * *

The first wave of tourists had arrived two hours earlier on the morning cruise ships, and business was in full swing. Everybody wanted a souvenir from their once-in-a-lifetime trip to Earth, and what better to bring home than an actual antique? Granted, it was usually a bit on the expensive side, but you can't put a price on the look on your neighbour's face when he sees your vintage 'razor with empty shaving cream can' and certificate of authenticity.

"Rupert?" came Emily's voice from somewhere beyond a stack of assorted blankets. "We have customers enquiring about the showpiece."

He stopped arranging mismatched pairs of gloves on the bargain table, and made his way to the shop's current highlight.

A middle-aged couple was standing in front of the display case. Their eyes had that 'I don't know why, but I *want* this' glint that was the best friend of shopkeepers all over the universe.

"A beautiful piece, isn't it?" he asked, and the couple looked up from the case.

"Ah, yes, indeed," said the man. "It's very nice, but we were wondering—that is, my wife and I—well, we were wondering what it actually *is*."

Inside the display case stood a metal box, its chrome surface gleaming in the light. On its top were two rectangular slits, one next to the other, through which rows of coiled bare-metal wire were visible. Several buttons and a lever were attached to one side.

Rupert pondered what to tell the couple. The problem was, he didn't really *know* what the box was for. He had, however, developed several theories.

"This," he began, "is quite a unique and wonderful artefact. It's the only one of its kind I have encountered in all my years in this business." He paused for effect, and the couple dutifully oohed and aahed. Then he unlocked the display case and swung open its glass top.

"Now," he said. "You see this lever here at the side. When I push it down, you can observe that the metal frames inside the two slits move down as well. A careful analysis of the inner mechanics has provided us with compelling evidence that this action activated an electric current, which in turn caused the wire coils within to glow and emit heat. What for? Well, the answer is *obvious* to anyone who has studied Earth and its artefacts." He turned to look at the tourists. "I presume you are well versed in Earth's history?"

"I admit I have always been intrigued by the topic," the man replied, with the importance and nonchalance of somebody who had not only been there, done that, and gotten the T-shirt, but who had actually replaced his entire wardrobe.

"That's what I thought," said Rupert. "So, as you undoubtedly know, one of the most valuable possessions back on Earth was books—imagine the sheer number of trees required to produce one of them. And so this beautiful box was used to store them. One book was placed into each of the two slits and the lever was pushed down. The wire coils would then start to glow, ensuring a consistent and optimal level of warmth."

He continued his description of this wondrous object but, regrettably, when the couple asked for the price and he told them, they all but recoiled, muttering that ultimate statement of refusal, known and hated by everybody working in retail: "We'll think about it."

Rupert closed the display case and locked it. Then he slowly walked back to the counter.

As much as he loved Old Earth artefacts, it was tremendously frustrating at times to know that it wasn't possible to prove the original purpose of so many of them. Spotting an object he had puzzled over for the past two years, he stopped at its shelf, picked up the crumpled piece of plastic, and unfolded it until it had the approximate shape of a woman. She could be inflated by blowing air into an attached valve. Although he did have his suspicions as to what she was for (and he blushed even thinking about it—he described her as a 'portable statue of a surprised female' to potential customers), he still yearned to know whether he was right or not.

* * *

It was a good day for business. Emily had just sold an electric iron after explaining very vividly how it had once been used in daily haircare, and Rupert had found a buyer for a simplistic drawing of a bird that had apparently been called 'Picasso' back on Earth. He was showing the customer out when a man in his early forties, not much older than Rupert himself, came in carrying a leather case.

This was Rupert's favourite part of the job. Whenever people came into the shop to sell something, there was the potential of a great find. Although it was unlikely, he was always hoping that he would discover something important, like a full set of pastry forks, or maybe, just maybe, something as rare as an unopened packet of cigarettes*.

And there were always people who wanted to sell Earth artefacts. Either they were collectors who had lost interest in their hobby, or they were sons and daughters, nieces and nephews who had inherited the objects and wanted the money rather than the antiques, greedy buggers that they were.

"I don't really know what to make of it," said the man, lifting the case onto the counter. "My aunt died, and when we cleared out her house we found this in the attic."

The story was a common one. Based on the number of times he had heard it, there were a remarkable number of aunts with attics dying all over the place. Having an attic seemed to be a dangerous thing.

The case was the size of an average suitcase, and its leather was worn and cracked. It was fastened by a lock on the front, over which the letters 'JBV' were embossed in faded gold. It snapped open with a satisfying click.

---

* There were several theories concerning what cigarettes had been for. Some researchers hypothesized that they might have been linked to the belief that angry pagan gods could be mollified by burning these weird little tubes, while others were convinced that they had been portable smoke signal sets for use in short-distance communication.

Inside lay a nondescript black device. It had a display and a number of buttons, and took up about half of the case. In the other half was a headset and two cartons full of thin plastic cards.

The moment he saw it, Rupert knew without a shadow of a doubt what this was. He had seen pictures—the history books were full of them.

"Oh my," he said. It was a good thing that he didn't play poker.

"Yeah? So it really *is* from Old Earth?"

"No." Rupert shook his head. "It's from the first decades after Departure Day. This was built on the Ark Space Stations."

The man nodded, clearly trying to remember what he had learned in history class as a kid. "And what exactly is it?"

"It's a Memory Reader."

When the man didn't show any sign of understanding, Rupert explained: "As you know, it was a desperate time when humanity left Earth and fled to the Ark Space Stations. They had been able to build the stations and evacuate everyone, but that was about it. The technology that would eventually lead to the construction of Fractal Drives did not yet exist, so people couldn't leave the stations. They were alive but couldn't really *live*.

"The technology to extract and store memories was developed in those dark times, in order to ensure that the memories of the last generation that had experienced life on Earth could be preserved. And when that generation was gone and the next one didn't have a whole lot of opportunity to make meaningful memories for themselves within the confines of the space stations, the few they did have were treasured, and so they became exceedingly valuable. Workers were paid in memories, they had to give them away to buy stuff, and they even stored them in a special bank. The rich were rich in memories."

Rupert pulled one of the plastic cards out of its carton.

"Memories were stored on so-called 'Memory Slivers'. And once a memory was extracted—or, rather, ripped from somebody's mind—it could only be accessed using one of these machines."

The man took the Memory Sliver from Rupert and inspected it.

"Why have I never heard of this technology?" he asked. "Sounds like something that would be really popular nowadays."

"It probably would," agreed Rupert. He frowned. "Though I'm sure somebody would come up with the idea of adding commercial breaks and spoil it all. Anyway. After a decade of trading memories, people had had enough. The rich had gathered all the memories they could, and the poor had almost nothing left. To make ends meet, many had been forced to sell every one of their memories, and remained little more than empty shells.

"Finally, there was an uprising. The riots brought political change, but at a high price: many died, and one of the space stations was severely damaged. But worst of all was that the digital archives were lost in the flames, and with them humankind's documents, books, audio-visual recordings, and so on. Just like that, we lost almost every piece of information we had about who we once were.

"When order had finally been restored, there were long and heated discussions about how to rebuild society—and how to ensure that the past could never repeat itself. What to do with the memory technology was the central and most controversial question. There were those who insisted that with the archives lost, it was all the more important to keep the Memory Readers. Others argued that it would lead to the trading of memories all over again.

"In the end, it came down to a public vote. The collective decision was to outlaw the technology for memory extraction, along with any research in this area, and all the Memory Extractors and Readers were destroyed. Or so we thought. And, over time, the blueprints and the knowledge were lost as well."

"So it's valuable," summarised the man with a broad smile. "And I expect the fact that it's in working order pays a premium?"

Rupert nearly suffered a heart attack. He stared at the man for several seconds.

"It's still working?" he finally asked, steadying himself on the edge of the counter.

"Yeah—I mean, I pressed some of the buttons and the screen lit up. I assume that means it's working. Here, let me show you."

The man pressed a button and the display started to flicker hectically. After a few seconds, just as Rupert was starting to think that the machine was broken after all, the display stabilised to show rows of numbers and several graphs.

"Remarkable," he whispered.

They negotiated for almost half an hour before they agreed on a price. After the man had gone, Emily came over to ask what Rupert had bought. When he told her, her reaction wasn't quite as excited as he had hoped for.

"Don't be silly, Rupert. Remember that time when you thought you had bought a set of dentist's tools? Well, they weren't, were they? It should have occurred to you that dentists—even back in those days—would never have used *secateurs* on their patients. But you tend to be a bit blind when your enthusiasm takes over."

Without saying a word, Rupert turned the case around so she could look inside.

"I'll be damned."

She agreed. They had a Memory Reader.

* * *

That night, Rupert ate a light dinner, watched a movie, and answered his pending messages. He did his best to pretend that it was just a normal evening—and he failed miserably. Finally, he gave up and fetched the Memory Reader.

He set it down on his living room table, carefully put on the headset, and let his fingers slide over the rows of Memory Slivers. He picked one at random and inserted it into a slot on the top of the Reader.

It took him a while to find the right button, but after some failed attempts the numbers and graphs vanished from the display and were replaced by the word 'Loading'. And then the memory playback began.

It's hard to describe the sensation of reading a stored memory. It's part image, part sound. There can be an impression of movement involved, or a feeling of time being frozen. And, most of all, there are the emotions that wash over you, unadulterated and intense.

The memory Rupert experienced was a short one. He was riding on a bicycle through a wood. Dust was floating through the warm sunlight, and the smells of a forest on a summer's day were everywhere; dense, woody smells infused with the aroma of grass. Next to him pedalled a young woman. He knew that her name was Clemence, and that she tried not to run over bugs whenever they cycled through the forest. She turned her head around to him and smiled, and life was perfect.

Dazed, Rupert blinked. The experience had been extraordinary. It was as if it had been his own memory, not that of a person who had existed many hundreds of years ago.

He picked another Memory Sliver and started the playback.

The metal bridge on which they walked was vibrating under countless feet. It was Departure Day. They were boarding the evacuation rockets, carrying the small number of possessions they were allowed to bring along. Rupert held the handle of the suitcase so tightly that it hurt. In his left hand he held that of his daughter Misaki. When he had put her to bed last night, he had explained to her that they were going on a great *adventure*, and that they would see space and meet new people and live beyond the stars. She wasn't afraid. Her eyes were big with wonder as she looked at the rocket that loomed up ahead of them.

With trembling hands, Rupert put down the headset.

This machine was a marvel.

* * *

Over the next two days, Rupert tested every single Memory Sliver while Emily looked after the shop. There were a lot of memories to get through, but reading one took next to no time.

He learned a great deal about how the stored memories worked. When he read one, he usually knew where he was and approximately when the event took place. Unfortunately, this was often rather fuzzy, as in 'shortly before the begonias in Jenny's garden were trampled down by a wild hog'. He also somehow knew who the key people were, as well as any objects vital to the memory. Everything else, however, was out of focus.

Rupert made a detailed inventory of the memories the Slivers held. There were all kinds. They covered everything from simple personal events like conversations, encounters, or dates, through to weddings and births. Others were about heartbreak, funerals, or even the occasional accident.

There were only two memories relating to events he had read about in history books. In addition to the one from Departure Day, there was a rather disturbing memory of the riots that had happened on the Ark Space

Stations. On the plus side, he now knew exactly what it felt like to punch somebody in the face like they do in the movies. Basically, your hand hurts like hell.

When Rupert was done with the inventory, he made a shortlist of the most interesting memories that were suitable for all ages.

This was going to be Big Business.

* * *

When Emily leisurely strolled into work the next morning (only a few minutes late—just enough to ensure that Rupert would comment on it), she was surprised to find a new sign standing in front of the shop. On it was written in large, bold letters:

MEMORIES FROM OLD EARTH! RELIVE HUMANITY'S PAST
THROUGH AN ORIGINAL MEMORY READER BUILT ON THE ARK
SPACE STATIONS! DO NOT MISS THIS UNIQUE EXPERIENCE!

Emily frowned. Unexpected. This wasn't Rupert's usual style. It was rather refreshing.

She entered the shop and found Rupert fussing over a new table that had been placed in the spot where several racks of Earth clothing had previously stood. On the table, on top of a red velvet pedestal, rested the Memory Reader, and next to it hung a list of available memories and their prices.

"Ah, good morning, Emily—perfect timing," said Rupert with a grin, gesturing towards the table. "What do you think?"

She considered plain honesty but dismissed it as being cruel. "Very, ah, tasteful. So you really want to let the tourists use it?"

"Oh yes. And we will make a fortune with it. Now you can not just *own* artefacts from the past; you can actually have a go at *remembering* the past."

Rupert explained how the machine worked. He demonstrated it to her by showing her the memory of a girl's sixth birthday at which she was given a kitten.

"Rupert," she said, taking off the headset, "the effect is remarkable, yes; but are you sure this is a good idea? It feels, well, indiscreet, to read these memories."

"No. No no no. You see, we are in fact *honouring* these people by keeping their happy memories alive. Who would mind that?"

She had never seen Rupert so excited before, and didn't have the heart to spoil it for him. So she just nodded.

* * *

Rupert put Emily on the task of selling memories. He did his best to handle the rest of the shop himself, while at the same time trying to organise advertising on the other space stations and in the closest colonies.

As he rushed from the counter to customers and back again, he couldn't help but wince when he saw certain objects on display in the shop. Through the countless memories he had watched over the past two days, he had learned the true use of many artefacts, and it pained him that he had so often been wrong about them.

That 'statuette of a deity' over there was in fact a limited edition action figure. The object with the handle and the hoop was no weapon to hunt zebras—it was obviously a tennis racket. And that one was a Christmas tree ornament, not a 'component from an Old Earth death ray', thank you very much. And there, that inflatable plastic woman—well, okay, he had been right about that one at least.

As lunchtime approached, he was thrilled to see that there was actually a queue in front of the Memory Reader. He was silently contemplating his exceptional business acumen when a woman approached him and asked about 'that shiny metal box'. He smiled broadly. This time around, he knew exactly what the object was.

"This," he said, "is a so-called 'toaster'. It was used for heating up bread. Two slices of usually white bread were inserted into these two slots, and then this lever was pushed down and the wire coils inside started to glow." He fondly patted the box. "You know, using this apparatus wasn't as easy as it might sound. I remember one Sunday, we had a brunch with the whole family and some friends, and Lucinda's daughter Celia was supposed to be looking after the toaster. Our toaster had a kink, you see, and the bread sometimes didn't come out as it was supposed to. Now, Celia had a crush on Martha's eldest son, and so she was distracted and forgot to do as she was told. I tell you, the smell that filled the dining room was—"

Rupert stopped as if somebody had just slapped him. What was he doing? He didn't have a family, he had never in his life used a toaster, and he sure as hell didn't know anybody called Lucinda or Martha. The story was from one of the memories he had watched.

"So sorry; I'm a bit confused today," he mumbled. He continued his sales pitch, but his heart was no longer in it, and the woman left without buying the toaster.

Rupert sat down on the chair behind the counter and massaged his temples. He needed rest. And maybe some water: he hadn't been drinking enough. Yes, he was dehydrated and overworked. And he had seen too many of those memories.

It took him half an hour, two bottles of water, and several complaining customers before he could bring himself to get up from the chair.

As Rupert walked past a group of tourists, he overheard one of them reading the label attached to an artefact: "Quality handcraft, two pieces, made from leather, excellent condition. Commonly used on Old Earth to keep unruly children under control."

What had he been thinking when he had written that label? It was a dog's collar and leash, just as his dog Alyosha had worn whenever they went for a walk in the woods behind their dacha in Peredelkino.

Rupert stopped dead in his tracks. It had happened again—he was confusing the memories he had seen via the Memory Reader with his own. The experience had been intense, but he was still surprised that he could recall such small and insignificant details without difficulty. He could even remember the exact smell of Alyosha's breath. His husband Yevgeniy had never liked it when the dog tried to lick his face, but to him that smell had always been synonymous with arriving home—

Rupert's knees started to shake so abruptly and violently that he sat down on a stack of old suitcases. He wasn't just remembering what he had been shown by the Memory Reader—these were his *own* memories. Only they weren't. Or shouldn't be. But they were *there*.

And if viewing memories using the Reader meant that they were inserted into his mind, then that would mean—

"Oh no." He groaned, jumped up from the suitcases, and rushed through the shop. He was in such a hurry that he knocked over several artefacts, took the wrong path twice, and almost ran into two old ladies who looked so antique themselves that for a moment he wondered whether they were customers or inventory.

Panting and out of breath, he reached the table where Emily was just putting the headset onto the head of the next customer in line.

"I'm terribly sorry," said Rupert as he pulled the headset away. "The machine is starting to overheat and we need to stop before it is damaged. Now, if you would kindly leave, we are about to close for the day."

The customers grumbled and protested, but it soon became clear that Rupert would not change his mind. And so they left the shop and vanished among the other tourists who were wandering around the promenade.

Once they were all gone, Rupert locked the door and leaned against it. After a minute, he noticed that Emily was staring at him. She raised a single, remarkably eloquent eyebrow.

Rupert took a deep breath and explained to her what had happened— how he had been ambushed by the memory of living in Russia with his husband and their dog, and before that by one of a Sunday brunch gone awry.

"So you see, all those people who paid us money to read memories now have them permanently in their heads—they just haven't noticed yet." He groaned again. Even now, he thought he could smell a waft of Alyosha's dog breath. "They will probably sue us. Or lynch us. Or worse, they might report us to Station Management and have us banned from the observation promenade."

Emily had listened to him without saying a word. Now she cocked her head to one side.

"You are right," she said in amazement. "I *have* the memory of being given a kitten as a birthday present when I was a little girl."

"Yeah," sighed Rupert. "Me too."

* * *

They went to the back of the shop to discuss their next steps. Sitting at the desk with stacks of old hats on it, they talked for several hours. At some point, Rupert fetched a bottle of whiskey and two glasses.

"It's funny," he said, as he refilled their glasses to the brim for the third time. His voice was already slightly slurred. "I had never considered what it would be like to have too many memories. I was always afraid of the exact opposite."

"How do you mean?"

"Well, my life here is pretty predictable. Not a lot of opportunity to create memories between these dusty antiques."

"Hmm." Emily pondered his words while she slowly but methodically emptied her glass. Then she grinned mischievously. "I bet there's loads of memorable stuff one could do in here."

She looked at him and he felt his face turn red. The effect of the alcohol, no doubt.

To have something to do with his hands, Rupert took the topmost hat from one of the stacks sitting on the table. It was a black fedora, worn from use but in good condition considering its age. Turning it around slowly, he thought that you had to be the right kind of person to be able to wear such a hat. Not everybody could pull it off.

He took another sip of whiskey. Then he put on the fedora, tilted it at a jaunty angle and looked at Emily enquiringly. She laughed and shook her head. He kept it on anyway.

* * *

The next few days passed in a flash.

Rupert spent all his time dealing with the aftermath of the one day that memories of Old Earth had been sold on Dawn's Mystery. Word had gotten around, and each day scores of people enquired about 'Ackerley's Memory Reader'. He informed each one that, regrettably, the machine was presently out of order, and didn't they want to buy a genuine Old Earth toupee instead?

Several of the customers that had already used the Memory Reader returned to the shop. However, to his utter astonishment, none did so to complain. They all returned in the hope of reading more memories. Some even offered large sums of money. Rupert turned everybody down.

All the while, he struggled to come to terms with his own newly acquired memories. He tried to suppress them, only to find that this had the opposite effect: when memories of friends and families long gone and events long past started to bubble up, any attempt to ignore them only caused them to increase in strength. And the worst part was that he never knew what might trigger the next bout.

Emily spent her time doing research. She accessed public archives and tried to find out how exactly the Memory Reader was supposed to work, and how to get rid of the memories inside Rupert's head.

It was time-consuming work which required her to read countless documents, as the available automatic search engines weren't much help. Despite the technological leaps forward that mankind had made in the last millennium, it seemed as though developing a search engine that was actually helpful was too much to ask for.

After six days of research and countless cups of coffee, she finally struck gold.

* * *

That evening, after they had shown the last customer out, Emily sat him down at the counter to talk.

"Rupert," she said and looked at him seriously. He felt like a dog that was about to be told that, yes, he was a good boy, but his balls had to come off anyway. "Rupert, look here. I did an extensive search as we discussed, and I found something in a letter kept at the Central Archives. It's from a researcher called Juanita Buenaventura Velasquez—JBV—to a friend of hers."

She stopped to open the case containing the Memory Reader, which stood on the counter between them.

"This machine was the prototype of a new kind of Memory Reader. As you know, once a memory was extracted to store it on a Memory Sliver, it was gone from that person's mind for good. After that, it could only be read—not actually transferred back. What we have here is a prototype Velasquez built to solve that problem."

Emily cleared her throat. "And you see, Rupert, that is where the bad news comes in. It's an advanced type of Memory Reader, but nothing more. It was built shortly before research in that area was declared illegal and all the machines that came with it—the Readers, of course, but also the Memory Extractors, storage systems, and so on—were destroyed. It seems that this machine only survived because nobody knew about it. Which means, of course, that there is no way to remove those memories from your mind."

After a moment, she added in a soft tone: "I'm sorry."

Rupert wasn't surprised, not really, but some part of him had still hoped that the search would yield something, anything, they could do.

"What am I supposed to do now?" he asked wearily. "My life is over."

"Don't be so melodramatic. It might still turn out all right."

"How?"

"Well, maybe one of the Memory Extractors survived after all. We'll search for one."

"You know how unlikely that is."

"All right. Then look at it this way: we don't know much about how all of this works. Maybe the memories will fade over time."

"Hm."

"Or maybe you can turn it into a business opportunity. Historians will pay lots of money just to talk to you."

Rupert mumbled something unintelligible.

"Or," said Emily with a wicked grin, "you could use your newfound powers for evil, and expose all your competitors as frauds because they don't know what they're selling."

"You don't get it, do you?" snapped Rupert. "This isn't funny. I can't go on being controlled by dead people's memories!"

Emily looked at him for a while. Then she let out an exasperated sigh, and, without a warning, leaned over and kissed him. It was a good kiss: a no-nonsense, full-steam-ahead, taking-no-prisoners sort of kiss. There were several memories of really great kisses in Rupert's head, but this one was giving them all a run for their money.

"Well?" asked Emily. "How about that for a *new* memory?"

Rupert's mouth opened and closed several times without making a sound. Then he blurted out: "Are you sure you know what you are doing? I have very vivid memories of having been married. I have countless ex-wives, ex-husbands, ex-boyfriends, ex-girlfriends, ex-affairs, and whatnot. And I miss them when I think of them." He paused. "Well, most of them. Some were real bastards. But I have very happy memories about the rest of them."

"So what? I'm not afraid of a little competition."

Rupert shook his head slowly. "You really aren't, are you?"

Emily just winked at him. Then she said: "Anyway, you take all the time you need. There's no rush. I'll be here."

He nodded, grateful for the respite.

"So, have you decided what to do with the Memory Reader yet?" she asked, gently steering him back into more familiar—if not exactly calm—waters.

"I'm not sure," said Rupert and shrugged. "We've seen how dangerous it can be. Maybe I should just keep it in the shop's safe and hope that people forget I have it."

"Why not donate it to a museum? After all, it's an important historical artefact."

"That might be an option." He stared at the counter for a while, pondering the ramifications. "What worries me, though, is this: could they refrain from trying to figure out how this technology works? All things considered, I think mankind is better off without it."

Emily stood up and stretched.

"We could of course disable it before we hand it over," she suggested. "You know, destroy some of the circuits."

"We could. But would that be ethical?" Rupert grimaced. "As problematic as this technology is, it also has a great deal of potential when it comes to medical application." He hesitated before he added: "And, of course, if the technology really were to be 'rediscovered', I might be able to remove these memories from my head."

She looked at him for a moment without saying a word. Then she smiled. "Seems like there is a lot you need to think about. And not only about what to do with the Reader. So I'll leave you to it and head home."

She squeezed his shoulder as she walked past him.

"I'm sure you'll make the right decision."

* * *

After Emily left, Rupert carefully closed the case of the Memory Reader. He ran his hand slowly over its top, feeling the scars of the old, battered leather. His thoughts were racing—and they were all heading in different directions at the same time.

He wondered if he should run after Emily, and what would happen if he did. He wondered if he had the right to keep the Memory Reader a secret. He wondered how he could cope with living a life that was constantly interrupted by the memories of others. He wondered if it was possible to reverse-engineer the technology. He wondered a plethora of other things, and one question and worry led to another until his head was spinning.

He closed his eyes, took a deep breath, and tried to relax.

A sudden memory of a hot summer evening and a long talk on the veranda made Rupert wish that his brother Wekesa was here. Whenever you had asked him for advice, he would do his best to make up an ancient traditional saying that applied to your situation. Something like: 'The crocodile laughs, but the sun goes down in the west'. Wekesa probably would have made all these decisions in a heartbeat. He had been like that. A born optimist whose glass had always been half-full—usually with a really good twenty-year-old port.

Rupert sighed and opened his eyes. There were no veranda and no brother to give him advice; there was only his crowded shop and the distant murmuring of tourists on the promenade.

As he sat at the counter and pondered how to go about the simple matter of making several major life decisions, he looked around his collection of antiques in search of inspiration. But the items that caught his eye—the heap of old shoes, that weird stuffed bird with its faded pink feathers, and those damned umbrellas—weren't a lot of help, and he suspected none of the other objects would be either. Making these decisions felt about as daunting as walking the convoluted paths that crisscrossed his collection of Earth antiques wearing a blindfold. With his hands tied behind his back. And a zebra on the prowl.

He sighed again. It was no use; brooding over how difficult it was wouldn't make it any easier to decide. One way or another, he had to make up his mind, and the sooner he did so the better.

"Right," he said to no one in particular. It might take all night, but he would just keep sitting here until he knew what to do.

He leaned back in his chair, put his feet on the counter, and shifted into a more comfortable position.

Rupert didn't notice how time passed as he sat there and tried to untangle the jumble of thoughts, emotions, and options in his head. He didn't hear the voice of the announcement system informing everyone that the last tourists had left Dawn's Mystery, and he didn't feel the light tremors that shook the station whenever one of the large cruise ships undocked.

One by one, the lights of the observation promenade went out.

* * *

It was deep into the night when Rupert finally let down the shutters of his shop and made his way back to the living quarters. Halfway down the promenade, he stopped at the long front of windows and looked down on the planet.

Old Earth rotated slowly and majestically on its axis, reassuringly unperturbed by recent events.

He longed to know what it was like down there right now, and if it was still the way he remembered it had once been. In Japan and France, in America and Russia, and all those other places he had seen glimpses of.

With a hint of a smile, Rupert turned away.

Memories were waiting.

A NOTE FROM MICHAEL

I always find it fascinating how the idea for a story emerges and then develops. This one began as a vague idea for a rather silly story about a robot that quite literally loses his memory. But as I spent time thinking about the importance of memories for each of us, about the different kinds there are and their subjective value, the plot changed and grew until it had the form of the story you just read.

As I wrote it, I repeatedly walked through my apartment looking for objects that could be misinterpreted (before you ask: no, my apartment does not contain the portable statue of a surprised female). It's an exercise I can only recommend—you will be surprised what you can discover in everyday objects when you pretend you know only very little about the world we live in.

We are all defined by our memories, in more ways than we are usually aware of. And this story is, above all, a thank you to the man whose books have created so many wonderful memories for so many people all over the world. Memories we most certainly do not want to have extracted.

Michael K. Schaefer
Sindelfingen, Germany

BUBBLE TROUBLE
CHARLOTTE SLOCOMBE

One day, a god arrived at my door. It was a bit of a surprise: you see, I'd only just woken up, and wasn't expecting visitors so early. But, as this sort of thing never happens to me, I did what I *thought* would be expected of someone face-to-face with a man claiming to be a god so early in the morning—politely invited him in and offered him tea.

Since I had no idea what else to do in this kind of situation, I asked him his name. He answered with a small smile, saying—and I quote—"The God of Memory, baby doll," in a terrible American accent which, being English, made me shudder to the core. "You're the God of Memory?" I asked, a little distrustfully.

"Yes. Do you believe me?"

"Yes."

"Really?" His surprise caught me off-guard, and I was almost tempted to lie again simply to keep that adorable look on his face.

"No."

"Oh." My honesty this time set him back a little, as though he had been sure of my immediate belief in his godliness. But, like anyone else (well, anyone else deluded or stubborn enough) would do in that situation, he went about trying to prove he was right.

"I *am* the God of Memory—but you can call me Zach, baby doll." Really? 'Baby doll' again? "I'm in charge of taking care of all those happy little thoughts in your head. I can see them all, every single memory you've ever had. Well, with the right equipment, anyway."

Naturally I was sceptical. Yet intrigued. I was no longer thinking about my boring city job, and my boring city friends talking about their boring dates last weekend, or complaining when some boring man didn't call them back within five minutes of leaving whatever boring place they've just been awkwardly trapped in for an hour. Instead, I was thinking about him, Zach, the 'God of Memory', and his charming smile, and that hair which flopped sensuously over one eye. Zach, and his tall frame and bright green eyes.

Everything about him seemed right. Other than his insanity, that is. That was an unwelcome drawback.

"Come with me, baby doll," Zach said suddenly, shining me a grin which seemed to have a happiness of its own. Obviously I refused—who did he think he was? Clearly I had too good a head on my shoulders to run off with some madman in the early hours of the morning (and by 'early' I mean 8:30). Yet somehow, what felt like ten minutes later, we were sitting on a plane in anticipation of lift-off. And then I realised that maybe *he* wasn't the insane one; maybe it was me.

* * *

I took the window seat. All of the people and their tiny lives seemed so small and insignificant. Even the cars looked small, and the buildings. I felt like the city meant less and less to me, it grew smaller…and smaller…and then I remembered I was taking off in a plane and stopped being so philosophical. In the seat next to me sat Zach. I decided to take the opportunity to take a better look at what I'd signed on for.

He wore a normal outfit for any twenty-something-year-old boy—I didn't think 'man' would be an accurate way to describe him—jeans and a blue T-shirt. Yet there was something strange about what he wore, something too familiar.

I faintly recognised the logo on his T-shirt. It had the image of a DNA strand, below which was a blue bubble. Inside the bubble, in bold cream letters, were the words 'MEMORY DATABASE'. I didn't understand it, so figured it must have been a band or brand I had seen before. Zach caught me looking at his shirt and chuckled.

"Interested in my abs, baby doll?"

I rolled my eyes. "No, I was actually looking at the picture."

He frowned and looked down as though he had forgotten which shirt he had on. To be honest, it wouldn't have surprised me—he seemed the type to be easily distracted. "Ahh yes," Zach said, returning my gaze. "It's the logo for my company."

That caught me out again. His company? I was sitting with a man who actually owned a company?

"It's only a small thing…" He hesitated. "Well, actually that's not true. It's pretty big. Most people are involved; they just don't know it." Zach looked a little smug, but sighed when he realised I didn't have any idea what he was talking about. "We're rather like a storage company, though much more glamorous. People do things, they remember them, and then when they're sleeping, all of their memories are uploaded into the Memory—"

"Database," I finished for him. Zach nodded and looked gleeful that I'd caught on so quickly. I, on the other hand, was horrified. How could memories be transferred from a person to whatever it was that Zach owned, without them even realising? More importantly, should a crazy person like Zach have access to that much power? If what he was saying was true, he had access to literally everything anyone remembered.

Zach's smile faded when he saw my expression.

"You don't look excited," he observed, having clearly once again expected me to blindly trust him.

"How are you a god, then?"

"I'm… Hmm. Okay, baby doll; I'm not *technically* a god. It was Teddy—"

"Teddy?"

"Yes, Teddy. It was his idea, really. Why be the 'president' of an organisation when you can be the freaking *god?*"

He had a point. Moreover, his oddness was strangely enticing, and I found myself more and more drawn to him, despite the bizarre situation.

I then had a thought which, if I'm honest, I probably should have addressed earlier. "Why am I here with you?"

Zach looked slightly offended. "My company's not reason enough, baby doll?"

I rolled my eyes and gave him a look that demanded a real answer. After a beat, he complied.

"Well, the company has a small problem with its systems. Basically, there's a virus. Something is coming in and deleting the memories, and we have no idea what it is or how to stop it." He paused for a second. "The troubling thing is that it's only affecting some people. So basically, I need *you* because I don't have anyone qualified to deal with it."

"Who do you have, then?" I asked.

"Helpers mainly, though they're not always the best company, Teddy especially."

"Helpers?"

"Yes, helpers. They try, but most of them aren't that useful. Have you ever wondered where the people who are highly qualified in weird university courses wind up?"

"Uh, no...?"

"The Database. That's where they go. In fact, our helpers are the best of the best...well, they're probably not the BEST of the best..." He hesitated. "They're not actually qualified in anything useful, to be honest. Teddy has an Anglo-Saxon degree." Zach collected his thoughts. "That's not important though. I need your help. You're an 'It' girl, you see."

I stared at him. The serious look on his face told me very clearly that he wasn't joking. I thought about my life—a dead-end job with computers that paid next-to-nothing and took up more time than I'd like to give it. Few friends, too: I was getting further and further away from those I'd made at university, and the girls from work hardly qualified, despite how it might look on Facebook. No sense of fashion. No inspirational thoughts or actions. If there was one thing I could be certain of at that moment, I was definitely not an 'It' girl. The very thought made me smile, and then grin, and then laugh.

"You think I'm an 'It' girl?" I gasped out, while he watched me with a small, confused frown.

"Yes? What else would you be?" His complete sincerity made me laugh harder, in turn making his frown deeper.

"Why the hell do you want an 'It' girl?"

"The Database has a virus—I just told you that!"

"But what would an 'It' girl do? Kill it with nail varnish?" The idea of some girl throwing nail varnish at a computer made me laugh again.

"No, uh, well I was hoping that the 'It' girl—you—would come and fix our system."

And then I got it. "Ohhh," I said, a little embarrassed (though still amused). "You mean an *IT* girl, someone who fixes computers. Not an 'It' girl..."

He clearly didn't understand the difference, so I dropped it.

74

"Yes; that's what I am, an IT consultant." I frowned. "Wait—how do you know that?"

Zach shifted in his seat. "Well, baby doll, we actually met a while ago."

"No we didn't," I said, looking him up and down. Surely I'd remember that gorgeous face, muscular arms, tanned body… I realised that Zach was still talking. "What?" He rolled his eyes.

"I said it was in a meeting about the technical difficulties faced by a company rather like the Database." He saw that I couldn't remember this alleged meeting and shrugged. "It was a while ago, don't worry about it."

The rest of the journey was fun, filled with good conversation with a great guy. Soon enough, Zach's previous comment had completely slipped my mind.

* * *

Three hours later we landed. In Lapland. Yes, Lapland. I was strangely unsurprised. I hadn't really been paying attention when Zach had booked the tickets, but, let's face it, he had a knack for doing the unexpected, and when you start to expect the unexpected you become—well, mad probably. There was snow all around us, and I was freezing. It turns out that a hoodie and jeans is not appropriate clothing for the Arctic Circle.

The only building I could see—other than the airport—was a small wooden structure. We made our way towards it, me skidding most of the way on the slippery ground, and Zach, graceful being that he was, gliding along.

We soon stood in the doorway. It was the least impressive building I had ever seen. It could have been entirely glass, or a palace made of crystals. But no. Instead it was a barn with a door hanging off its hinges, with a sign above the doorway saying 'Memory Database' in the same bold, cream letters as on Zach's T-shirt.

I looked over at him. He was staring past the building, and I could see the worry in his bright green eyes.

"What is it?" I asked.

"Oh, nothing," Zach replied, slipping back to a smile, "I just remembered I left the light on in my room." He frowned at the look I gave him. "What?"

"...we're in Lapland."

"Just west of it, actually."

"Why Lapland?"

Zach sighed melodramatically.

"Does *everything* have to have a logical answer, baby doll?" He strutted inside, and I followed.

Steps inside the barn led down into an underground building. It was what I had been expecting before the disappointment of the shoddy entrance: a huge expanse of white. White floor, white walls, white desks, white chairs. The steps opened out to form a large, empty reception room, and our every footstep echoed. No one was there.

The corridors running away from the reception area suggested the extent of the structure—it looked like it went on forever. Thousands, if not millions, of doors indented an eternal wall, not one of them hinting at what was behind it—though each had a small label showing a name and a number. What it meant, I didn't know.

Then I heard a shout and the sound of heavy footsteps. An agitated man emerged from the long corridor. He snapped his head around the room and locked eyes with Zach.

"Oh, you damnable man," he growled.

Upon hearing the voice, Zach grinned. "Teddy!" Zach put his hand on my back and steered me towards the man, greeting him cheerfully. "Good to see you, old chum."

"You know full well that that isn't my name, *sir*," Teddy grumbled. The word 'sir' sounded almost poisonous in his mouth. Zach looked exasperated, like it was a conversation he'd had many times.

"Well, Teddy, you know that you hate being called Robert, so what else am I supposed to call you?"

I looked between the two men, a frown on my face.

"Wait," I said, running the name through my mind. "'Teddy' isn't short for 'Robert'."

Teddy huffed. "Try explaining that to *him*." He then turned his attention to me. "Hello there 'baby doll'." He scoffed and frowned at something he saw—or didn't see—on my face. "I know it's not your fault, but I must say I'm a bit offended—"

"That's enough, Teddy," Zach said quickly, stepping between us as though the physical barrier would prevent me from hearing anything else. "How about a tour of the base?" He turned towards the man and added, in words almost too quiet to hear, "apart from room 301."

Teddy looked at me suspiciously and nodded. "Okay. But she'd better not be a slow walker."

* * *

The tour started in a large room called the 'heart' of the operation. I didn't understand why it was called that until I was standing in a space with a giant pulsating heart in the middle of it. At a second glance I realised that it was, in fact, made of—

"Plastic," Zach sighed, looking vastly disappointed. He turned to Teddy. "What's the point in having it at all if it isn't a REAL heart?"

"Because it intercepts all of the memories and infuses them into the sodium stearate." Teddy grumbled. I looked at him blankly, as did Zach (which was quite amusing, since he was meant to be running the place). Teddy huffed. "Bubble mixture, you idiots." He threw up his hands and started walking towards the door. "And anyway, where the hell would we get a *real* heart that size?"

* * *

The tour continued, and soon we stopped outside a room along the eternal wall. Teddy held the door for me. I looked at him.

"I'm surprised: holding the door for someone doesn't really seem like your thing." He grumbled under his breath—something about 'being a gentleman'.

The name on the door, '2254: Jennifer Fletcher', meant nothing to me. But what was inside was amazing.

* * *

The room was a perfect silent blue. It seemed to exist in a sense of suspension wherein nothing moved and everything was quiet. There were no windows, just a soft blue light coming from small, gentle bulbs in the corners of the room.

There was a glass screen separating us from what Zach called the 'inner mind', a glass door in its centre. It looked so fragile. Behind the glass, thousands of bubbles floated in a noiseless hush, as though they were holding their non-existent breaths. They never touched and simply existed together, almost too delicate to exist at all. Every bubble was blue like the light around it, and each held a reflection, every one different, and none of them related to the room around us.

"These are memories," Zach said quietly into my ear. "Everything this woman Jennifer can remember is in this room."

"Everything…" I whispered. I stepped forwards and placed my hand on the glass, staring beyond it. I could just make out what was happening in some of the closer bubbles. There were at least four weddings and a funeral in my line of sight; possibly more. It was extraordinary.

Zach put his hand on my shoulder and I turned my head to look at him. He pointed to a small bubble that trailed sluggishly behind the others.

"Watch that one, baby doll," he whispered, out of respect.

So I did. The bubble slowed further until it was barely moving. It started to shake, then turned a green colour and burst. I gasped.

"Wait, what does that mean?" I looked back at Zach, my eyes wide. He avoided my gaze.

"That memory is gone."

"You can't get it back?"

"We can't get it back," he repeated, dropping into silence. I realised I hadn't taken the Database's problem seriously before, but now it had happened in front of me: a memory was gone. Forever. That was a chunk of someone's life, and they would never see it again.

"I can't fix this," I said sadly. This couldn't have anything to do with a computer system; it must be a problem with the person. "Why did you think I could help?"

"The human brain is like a giant bio-computer. It is complex, mechanical and—" he stopped as I raised my eyebrows, "—and we use a computer to control the memories' environment. They have to be kept at a certain temperature and humidity, like some kind of delicate orchid." Zach laughed, "It's in the office, come see!"

As we walked towards the door, me a little reluctantly, I turned to look back at the bubbles. They trembled at the sound of our movement, and one sad ball sighed as it burst.

When we reached the office, Teddy opened the door and let out a frustrated grunt. The cheer that erupted from inside explained his reaction. There were at least thirty people sitting on wheelie chairs around a jar which held folded pieces of paper. They were all laughing and having an apparently hilarious time, drinking glasses of strange-looking yellow wine.

"I'd forgotten it was today already." Zach sighed. "Teddy, why didn't you remind me?" he swatted the man on the arm.

The others realised we had arrived and yelled "Hooray!".

"What's going on?" I asked.

Zach folded his arms and leaned against the door frame.

"It's our Weekly Celebration."

One of the grinning helpers explained. "There's such a lot of good things happening in the world, each week we make a point of remembering one by picking it out of the jar."

"Today it's a choice between celebrating the first watch on the moon—" began a Horology major.

"—and building the largest puppet of a human in the world," chipped in the Puppetry graduate.

"—and how there are absolutely no jobs in 'ethical hacking', since it's oxymoronic," added the specialist in Viking undergarments on behalf of the doctor in Ethical Hacking, who was already lying drunk on the floor.

"Would you like some fizzy cheese wine?" offered the Brewing and Distilling graduate. "I made it myself."

I looked at Zach. He seemed to be regretting his choice of employees.

The strange circumstances made me speak up. "But *why* are you celebrating? You're in the middle of a crisis!" I said. They all looked at me.

"No we're not; what are you talking about?" The Creative Writing student was clearly put out.

"This is a Safe Room. No one is allowed to mention the 'c' word in here," confided Mr Viking Studies.

"Wait, do you mean 'c' word as in 'crisis', or as in c—"

"*Of course* he means 'crisis', you idiot," Teddy hissed. "Come on, you two."

* * *

The next thing I knew, Zach was dragging me back to Jennifer Fletcher's room.

"What's going on?" I had no idea what they wanted from me. Zach and I passed through the glass door to where the bubbles floated, and I took a moment to gaze at them.

"Teddy and I may have found a way of recreating memories."

I stopped looking at the bubbles and directed my attention to Zach.

"That's what we were going to discuss in the office if *they* hadn't gotten in the way," Zach muttered.

"I thought we were going to look at the computer that controls the memories' environment?" Why was the man always so damnably confusing?

Zach looked surprised that I'd remembered. "Well, yes, that too. Anyway, the way this works is that Teddy's going to blow some extra bubble mixture around a bursting bubble, and when he shouts 'go' we'll run towards it, get caught in the mixture, and be inserted into the memory. Got it?"

I felt a little confused, but the feel of Zach's hand against mine helped.

"Oh, and don't forget," Teddy shouted, "when you're in the memory you won't be yourself—you will be someone who was there, and you just have to recreate it." And then suddenly he was yelling "GO!"

Zach yanked on my hand and we started running towards the just-popped bubble. It seemed to get bigger and bigger as we headed for it until finally it was all I could see. Honestly, I was a bit doubtful about whether their idea would work.

Then suddenly, I was somewhere else completely.

* * *

I remembered what Teddy had told us—I was playing the role of someone in the memory. It could be anyone: neither of us was necessarily going to be Jennifer (though Zach's reaction to suddenly finding himself in a dress would be priceless).

It was then that I looked at my surroundings, holding in my breath. It was a beautiful little chapel, filled with people in their Sunday best. The doors were open, so I could see what looked like woodlands outside. It would be the perfect place to get married.

I stopped. I looked around. Everyone in the chapel looked back at me—including the vicar. And the groom.

'How impolite,' I thought, 'he's supposed to be looking at the bride.' Then I noticed that I was standing up at the altar. I was holding the groom's hands. I *was* the bride. I gulped.

"Jennifer? Do you?" the vicar prompted, obviously urging me on. I looked at the groom, who shrunk away, heartbroken. I tried to give him my most reassuring smile, hoping that my hesitation couldn't change the future and he wouldn't suddenly decide to leave me (well, leave his soon-to-be wife). Then I remembered it was a memory. The worst thing I could do would be to screw up how Jennifer recalled this event—which, admittedly, I did.

"I d—" I started, before being (rather rudely) interrupted by someone standing in the audience.

"Jen? Don't do this." The desperation in his voice made me turn. I was staring at a total stranger who was clearly in love with Jennifer. "Please."

I stood there awkwardly, wondering what the hell to do. The groom gave me a nudge. He looked uneasy. "Jenny? Who is that?"

"Uh, he's no one, just a…friend," I replied. I thought I could hear Zach sniggering.

"Your 'friend'? Really Jen? Is that what you'd call us? Friends?" the man in the audience hissed.

I had half a mind to tell the stranger to sit down and shut up when I heard another chair move and there was a third man standing. This time I knew the face.

"What about *us*?" cried Zach. I had to suppress my grin. "How could you leave me,"—he hesitated before flashing me an evil smile—"baby doll?"

I could have killed him. He was obviously joking, but everyone in the audience gasped as though they believed Jennifer had a third lover. I decided that if Zach could have fun then I could too.

"I'm not your 'baby doll' anymore!" I screamed melodramatically, flinging my hands into the air. "I told you I never wanted to see you again after I caught you kissing…um…" I looked around the room desperately, trying to find someone to accuse of cheating with my, or rather Jennifer's, fake lover. My finger aimed itself at the first woman I saw. "HER." I then realised that the woman I'd pointed at was the mother of the bride—*my* mother. She started making little "wha—" noises. She didn't seem able to finish the word, so I interrupted her. "I don't want you anymore—you were never good for me, never as good as—" oh no, what the hell was the groom called? "Um, man, here." I pointed to the confused groom.

"But I love—"

"And I *loved* you too. Not anymore. Our bubble has burst; now you're just another bad memory." I finished my speech, delighted with my cleverness. I grinned at Zach and he looked back at me in amazement. I turned to the groom and smiled. "Now for you, you handsome man." I leaned forward and kissed him square on the lips. "I do!"

There was a cheering from the crowd around us as I said it. The groom glanced into the audience, looking at Zach and his bewildered smile. "Wow, he's really far gone," he said, as he put his arm around my shoulders and began to walk me down the aisle.

And then Zach and I were back at the Database, looking at each other while the newly-whole bubble floated away.

"It worked!" Zach's smile shone.

"Well done," I replied, "though next time work on your acting."

"Shut up," Zach laughed, hitting me playfully on the arm. "Next bubble?" The idea was enticing.

"Next bubble," I confirmed.

* * *

This time I could see the sky above us: it was almost black but somehow still a rich, deep blue. It was endless. My eyes adjusted and billions of stars appeared. They were peaceful and reminded me of the bubbles from Jennifer's room. The moon let out a silent sigh of perfectly white light as it watched from where it sat above the horizon.

I felt movement next to me: Zach was there. We were lying on the grass of some treasured hill—but treasured by whom, we didn't know. A picnic was abandoned to my right. The heavy engagement ring weighed down my finger and I lifted my hand to inspect it. The diamond refracted the moonlight, and I understood then that the only thing more innocent and pure than the orb in the sky was the love between this man and this woman. Yet they were unknown to us; I had no idea who Jennifer was, or whom she was lying with on that perfect evening. It was like their identities didn't matter—what mattered was the feeling they had left behind in the memory.

I looked at Zach, but his eyes were still on the ring—it had captivated him. It was the same one Jennifer had been wearing at her wedding in the last memory. This must have been where they had gotten engaged. And then I remembered why we were there.

"How could she forget this?"

A sad smile crossed his lips. "Some people don't have a choice."

Whilst he was looking away, I watched his eyes. They were a bright moonlit green; a boy, not yet a man. But something was not there, like his shadowed thoughts had stolen his attention. Then he looked up to stare into my own eyes, those of a girl grown up too fast.

It was a moment before I noticed how close we were. I didn't pull back when his lips pressed softly against mine, something I had hoped for since the moment we had met. Yet at the same time, I felt sad—this wasn't us. We were stealing a memory and making it our own, but it wasn't really ours.

And then we were out of the memory, back in the building, still staring at each other. As it turned out, so were all of the helpers. They had gathered in Jennifer's room, apparently watching the memory via a projection on the wall, some teary, others beaming at us. Teddy grunted.

"You know, some of us actually have work to do and don't just loll around on the grass all evening."

Zach didn't laugh. He silently took my hand and led me out of the room.

The corridor was large and endless. It stretched so far that the end disappeared into darkness: it looked like a black hole. We arrived at another door. Zach read out the name before I had the chance to.

"301: Emma Collins." For once he didn't smile. "This is your room, baby doll."

I looked at him unsteadily, wondering why he looked so sad, and why we were even at my room in the first place.

"I lied earlier," Zach admitted. "I mean, I did need you for the systems. Well, I needed you two years ago."

"I told you, Zach, I don't remember you."

"But you have to!" he hissed. Seeing he'd startled me, Zach sighed. "We met just before I started in this role. You were fixing computers for us when the old manager still worked here." Zach smiled in reminiscence. "And after I took over as God of Memory, I kept making excuses for you to come and fix things. They were always trivial, and it always made you laugh."

Zach looked at me sentimentally. "You didn't always have a rubbish job, baby doll, you used to work for us—your other job was something you found when you left. We were hoping you would come back. But...we haven't seen you, not for two years now. *I* haven't seen you."

He dropped his head into his hands. "We had made plans, you and I. You were going to live here, with me. We would be happy—I'd even bought the ring!" He stopped. "But we couldn't."

"Zach, what the hell are you talking about!?" I asked, uneasily.

Slowly, Zach reached out and opened the door. Inside I could see the bubbles. Even the blue of the room's lighting couldn't overcome the green colour my bubbles were turning. The room looked distinctly empty.

"Think about the last five years of your life. What can you remember?"

"I—I—what?" I stuttered.

"What can you remember?"

Honestly, not a lot. Zach took my shaking hand. "When we found out your bubbles were turning green, you couldn't stand to be here anymore. You said it wasn't fair for me to be with 'someone like you', that you didn't want to be a burden. No matter what I did, you wouldn't speak to me. You wouldn't see me, you wouldn't return my calls, and—" he looked hurt "—I guess you forgot about me."

Zach led me through another door. "This is my room, baby doll, Emma." I stared at the glistening blue of his bubbles—they looked strong, not like mine. "This is a record of what we have done together. Your bubbles may be going, but mine aren't. And now we know we can share them."

Zach moved around me until he was all that I could see. "These are *our* memories, yours and mine. We made them together. And if ever you lose one, you can live it again with me. We can relive them, together. I will always be here, with you, to make new memories. Stick with me, baby doll, and we'll have a life worth remembering."

Zach pulled me into a hug, and I held onto him tightly. Over his shoulder I could see his bubbles. They were vivid and shining blue. On the wall a memory was being projected, and I could see myself standing at my front door. I watched myself open it, and Zach stood there. The God of Memory.

A NOTE FROM CHARLOTTE

For me, memory loss is one of the most terrifying things I can imagine. Think about forgetting everyone you love, think about forgetting yourself. The case of Terry Pratchett proves that there is no mind too great to be stolen away by disease. That is why I wanted to create a safe place, with people working to protect us all from having to face the loss of memory. In reality we don't have mythical gods to help us—instead we have Alzheimer's research. I feel so honoured to be able to help such a worthy cause, even if it's through writing a silly short story about bubbles. Thank you for buying this book, because you never know who you might be saving.

Charlotte Slocombe
East Grinstead, UK

THE SHELLS OF LETHE
LAURA MAY

What kind of stupid idea was it putting all those memories into the ocean, anyway? I mean, they were always going to turn up; all it would have taken is a big net, time, and an even-moderately-enthusiastic aquatic search party.

"But wait," I hear you saying, "what in the world are you talking about? Memories? Into the ocean? What nonsense is this?"

Well firstly, your job is to *listen*, not to accuse me of 'nonsense'. If you're going to start carrying on with slanderous accusations like that, I'm not going to tell you the story. It's a good story, chock-full of things like morals, and scheming, and vengeance. Everybody loves a dose of vengeance! This is the tale of events that made quite a, quite a *splash* you might say. So stop with your condescension and cynicism, or I'll do something nasty. That's right: I've got you scared now, don't I! They had *better* be tremors of fear, not laughter…!

The 'why' of it all is easy to understand. Have you ever had a memory you wished you could get rid of? Perhaps that time you disappointed your parents with your miserable performance on the school gymnastics team. Perhaps that three years you spent pining over an unrequited love—or the terrible poetry you wrote as a result. Perhaps a truly awful kiss, a failed paper, a humiliating experience. Or perhaps something truly bad, you know, one of those scarring events which really mark and change you. If you've ever been through something like that, then perhaps you've wondered how you would be, *who* you would be, if that event were removed from your past.

Well, if you were lucky enough to live in the delightful village of Taomina, located on the brilliant Sunset Coast, you'd be able to find out. You see, something very peculiar was to be found in the water there. It wasn't funny-shaped fishing hooks, or old boots, or shopping trolleys, like you find in every body of water. It wasn't even a two-headed fish. No no, it was something magical, something extraordinary, something *entirely* unusual—it was seashells.

You! Stop your muttering. Yes, I realise that seashells themselves aren't unusual. They're nice to look at sometimes, though that's about it. But these were *special* seashells, you hear me? Special!

"And what's so special about them?" Seriously, if you'd stop interrupting, I'd tell you! Are you done? Are you sure? Do *you* have some kind of magical seashell story better than this one? No? Then stop your yapping and let me get on with it!

Anyway, the seashells. It's a well-known fact—a mystery of nature— that when you raise a shell to your ear and listen, you can hear the ocean. Not in Taomina though, as a somewhat indolent child by the name of Jerome discovered one day.

Jerome had just arrived in Taomina with his family, after travelling from a long way away with his parents. They'd seen sprawling marshes, tiny mountains, and even an immense forest which had been full of surprisingly acrobatic ponies. They'd been wandering for some time, looking for a place to call home, and were quite astonished to one day happen upon Taomina abandoned atop some cliffs. It was complete with pastel-coloured houses, wide avenues, paths lined with smoothed pebbles, and the evocative smell of the sea. Confusingly though, there were no people—none at all. Jerome's parents didn't concern themselves too much with that, though. Ghost towns happen everywhere, and there were blisters to worry about. They'd had enough of travelling, it was time to set down some roots—and Taomina seemed *most* convenient (and root-worthy).

While his parents unpacked, Jerome went exploring. He walked through the town to the edge of the cliffs overlooking the ocean, where he found a set of rickety wooden stairs.

Ricketiness is, of course, no impediment to a curious child, and so he started zig-zagging down the old staircase to the beach below. Upon arrival he found the expected quantity of sand, and the expected quantity of water—but he also found a thoroughly *unexpected* quantity of seashells. They carpeted the ground, layer upon layer, like some kind of particularly uncomfortable ball-pit.

These, as I've already told you, were no ordinary seashells. They were perfectly-formed spirals like those of a particularly proud snail, and came in a variety of sizes—some would cover half your palm, while others were the length of your forearm. But there was something even more astonishing than the sheer number of shells on the beach: they were each emitting a pure white gleam, like that guaranteed by dental advertisements the world over.

After a certain amount of gaping—look, I said Jerome was curious, not that he was especially bright—the boy started looking for the best shell to take back and show his parents. He started picking them up, trying to decide—which was the prettiest, which was the most perfect? And then, the inevitable: ignoring the fact that he could *already* hear the ocean, he raised a shell to his ear.

Four hours later, Jerome's somewhat lax parents came looking for him. They found him safe and sound on the beach, his head resting on top of a seashell the size of his young torso—a seashell which, unlike its neighbours, was dark and not glowing at all. When they asked him why he hadn't come back to the house, why he'd stayed so long, the boy looked at them blankly. His parents, becoming concerned (at last), asked Jerome if he was feeling okay—still no response. Finally, the boy looked at his mother and his father, and asked one simple question: "Who are you?" He quickly followed this with a somewhat disconcerted "and who am I?"

Jerome's parents looked at their amnesiac son, looked at the huge number of glowing shells on the beach, and decided that maybe Taomina wasn't for them. The next morning, they gathered up their things and continued travelling onwards—this time in search of a remedy with which they could restore their son's memory.

Slowly, as his parents quested for a cure, word of the boy's mysterious amnesia spread across the land. There had been no lump on his head, no trauma—so what had happened? Eventually, scientists of the more intrepid type made their way to Taomina, to see if they could find the source of this mystery. They too found the beach full of shells and, one after another, suffered the same fate as Jerome—but to various degrees. Some lost only one or two of their memories, while others were left in the same devoid state as the boy.

Ultimately it was realised that the seashells were the cause of the memory loss, with the shell's size correlating to the number of memories taken. Word of the phenomenon now started to spread for a different reason: there were people in the land who *wanted* to be rid of memories, not at the bottom of a nightly glass, but rather more permanently. Slowly they drifted into Taomina, where through careful application of smaller shells and rather a lot of pseudoscience, they had their past traumas removed.

Taomina thus became a haven for those who had left their pasts behind, and the village began to thrive. Over time the miracle of the seashells became less new and exciting, and intrepid scientists started wandering elsewhere instead. Taomina became ordinary, and eventually it and its inhabitants were, somewhat ironically, forgotten.

What had started with people removing their most traumatic memories soon became something else. Each Taominan resident saw how their friends' forgetting made them happier, and decided that they should follow the same course of action. Eventually people weren't just removing their worst memories, but any memory with even the slightest negative component. Then, because they could no longer remember what a 'bad' memory was, they started removing the good ones too. The inhabitants of Taomina became a happy and naïve bunch with no recollection of what they'd eaten for breakfast, let alone the day before! (Incidentally, not remembering whether they'd eaten breakfast or not made it very hard for people to diet.) They would pour their memories out of their ears and into the shells, then fling them willy-nilly into the ocean.

This is the state the town was in, when two wandering merchants arrived. These merchants, Dankwart and Vova, weren't the friendliest types. In fact, they were downright conniving. Their very connivingness had caused them to band together, as that way, when each town they encountered eventually threw them out, they had somebody to watch their backs and make sure none of the pitchforks struck home. That's not to say they were friends, though; more like 'competitors with benefits'. It was a relationship based on cunning, connivingness, and capitalism.

Now usually when Dankwart and Vova arrived in a town they'd make a big fuss of setting up a fantastic new shop, full of all kinds of magical-seeming whirligigs. The villagers, being taken in by said whirligigs and the sheer enticement of the storefront, would presume a certain quality and durability of product. However, soon after the opening sale, things would start to fall apart: colours would fade, food would spoil, and gigs would no longer whirl. At this point (and hopefully before the pitchforks came a-flying) the nasty duo would flee the town, clutching their not-so-hard-won cash to their chests and leaving a trail of sad whirls in their wake. The two had every intention of doing the same in Taomina, but for one thing—the pitchforks never came. The villagers never *remembered* what their whirligigs were supposed to do, or why they'd bought them, or even who they'd bought them from.

Being the talented capitalists that they were, Vova and Dankwart immediately saw the benefits of living in a memory-less town. They could settle here, and sell their goods day after day—a fortune was to be made! Well, as long as the vendors had a good streak of entrepreneurialism and a distinct lack of scruples. Happily, this described both of our merchants quite accurately.

The duo set up shop, greed gleaming in their eyes. They would soon be rich! However, things didn't go quite according to plan. Vova, who had been called Valentina before she decided that 'Vova' made her sound more bad-ass, came to realise that if she were the *only* gig-merchant in town, she'd be a lot richer—Dankwart needed to be disposed of. Likewise, Dankwart realised that Vova was holding him back from his true capitalist potential and now that they had no need to fear pitchforks, he had little use for her. And so, in connivingly good form, the two began to turn on each other.

"Have you seen my hat?" Vova asked one day. Vova really liked her hat.

"No—have you checked behind the feathered whirligigs?" replied Dankwart, no trace of deception in his tone.

"Hm," said Vova, and went to look. She rummaged through the feathered whirlies, and sure enough, her hat was there. However, when she went to lift it, there was a loud *bang* like that of a door being kicked in by an angry yeti, and the hat was propelled directly into her face. Vova went flying through the air, finally coming down, head-first, with a solid smack on the floor. She lay there for a minute, gathering her senses, before blearily sitting up. She almost thought she saw Dankwart pulling a disappointed face.

"What... What happened?" gurgled Vova. Dankwart came swishing over and plucked the hat from his colleague's face.

"It looks like some speed-i-gigs got into your hat," he observed. "You must have woken them up and given them a fright." With that, he plucked the gigs from the hat and set them down with their friends. But as he did so, Vova watched him, suspicious. How had her hat gotten amongst the gigs in the first place? She decided it was time for some friendly revenge.

The next day, Dankwart woke up to find his house on fire. Vova didn't believe in proportionate response, so while Dankwart was snoring she sploshed fuel all over the house. As she set it alight she gave a little cackle, which is what caused Dankwart to start stirring from his slumber. Evil geniuses (or non-geniuses, apparently) really ought to consider waiting until *after* the completion of a crime to start their cackling. Either way, Dankwart arose in plenty of time to save himself, as *well* as his sack of gold.

Villagers were outside, watching the flames and eating popcorn, unaware that anybody lived in the house. They'd already forgotten seeing Vova setting the fire after using some of the small seashells they carried at all times, ready for emergency memory elimination. Thus, they were quite surprised to see a robe-beclad merchant carrying a large sack swishing his way from amidst the flames. Several of the villagers raised emergency shells, only pausing when Dankwart screamed out "HALT!" in a thoroughly demanding tone.

Dankwart strode up to one villager, careful to maintain his rage while also not stepping on his robes (the first part was a lot easier to achieve, given his house was burning to the ground at the time). The villager in question was a less-than-fabulous gent by the name of Fabian, who was holding an emergency shell to his ear (incidentally, scientists weren't quite sure how people remembered that the seashells could be used to remove memories, and posited that it was a reflex action ingrained into the villagers' subconscious).

"YOU!" screamed Dankwart. "What *happened* here? Who *did* this?!"

"Who did what?" asked non-fabulous Fabian, seemingly unaware of the significance of a house being on fire.

"Who *set my house on fire, dolt!?!*" screeched Dankwart, grabbing the man and thoroughly rattling him.

"Uh-h-h-h-h—" replied Fabian, struggling to speak given the amount of shaking going on.

Preventing Fabian from effectively communicating his non-words was not, however, the only effect of the shaking. The shell, still poised by his ear, was also being shaken (not stirred). As Fabian thrashed in the hands of the angry merchant, so too did the contents of the shell thrash back and forth until finally, with a sound like a kitten sighing, something poured out.

This 'something' looked a great deal like runny glitter glue, and it swirled its way out of the shell like a car on a rollercoaster before splattering directly into Fabian's ear.

"EW!" yelled Fabian, finally saying something meaningful (but still not using real words). He clawed at his ear, trying to scrape out the goop—but it had disappeared.

Dankwart, not to be distracted, kept shaking the man in his fury. "WHO DID IT?! WHO SET MY HOUSE ON FIRE?!!!"

"Stop shaking me!"—finally Fabian responded. "It was *Vova* who did it!"

Dankwart paused, surprised. He wasn't the least surprised about Vova's apparent predilection for arson, but was *very* surprised that the man in his claws had answered the question. He'd simply been letting out some pent-up aggression on someone who wouldn't remember anyway (Dankwart wasn't the gentlemanly sort). Suspiciously, he stopped rattling, and looked at Fabian. Then he looked at the shell still clutched to the man's ear.

"How did you know that?" he asked, starting to put two and two together.

"I saw it, of course—now can you help me get that glue stuff out of my ear?!" asked the frantic Fabian.

"Of course," replied our prince among merchants, in a conciliatory tone. "Now let's just see…" And with that, he grabbed the shell in Fabian's hand, put it back up to the man's ear, and watched while the glitter glue spiraled back into the shell and knowledge disappeared from Fabian's eyes.

"Now," he began again. "Who set my house on fire?"

"What?" asked Fabian. "The house? Hasn't it always been on fire?"

Dankwart mumbled something under his breath which sounded rather like "idiot". Then, remembering the maraca lessons of his childhood, he rattled the shell around and returned it to Fabian's ear. Soon enough, splosh-sigh: the glitter glue once more shot out and disappeared into the man.

"Vova!" spluttered the man. "Vova set your house on fire!" Then he promptly stuck the shell back on his ear.

"Very interesting," murmured Dankwart, torn between potential capitalist applications and his burning desire for revenge. Grabbing the shell from the man in front of him one last time, he shook it and then held it to his own ear. Suddenly he could vividly recall Vova approaching his house, slopping fuel everywhere, and setting it on fire, cackling as she sped away.

The villagers may have previously discovered this way to restore memories—but if so, they'd promptly forgotten it. As far as Dankwart was concerned, only one question remained: how to use this new-found knowledge against Vova?

Dankwart headed to the beach to ponder. He kicked about some shells. A few were plain and darkened, but most were glowing. He briefly considered simply removing Vova's memories, but decided that would be too good for her: she had to suffer! At last he had an idea. He grabbed up a big, dark-looking shell, tucked it into his not-altogether-practical robes, and scurried back up the stairs to the village.

The merchant passed his house, which was still merrily ablaze, and walked up to the store he and Vova had opened. He walked in, smelling slightly of smoke, and greeted his 'friend'.

Vova looked slightly taken aback at Dankwart's calm demeanour and casual greeting. "Hello ,Warty," she responded. "Is...is everything all right?"

"Why yes, of course!" said the man in question. "Why shouldn't it be?" He headed towards the back of the store, past Vova, as though he were going to check on the stocks of whirligigs and widgets.

"I just...I smelled smoke?" offered Vova. "I wanted to make sure you hadn't been caught in a fire, or anything completely random like that."

"No no," assured Dankwart, as he drew even with the other merchant. Then, with a spry leap that one wouldn't normally anticipate from a man wearing robes, he sprang at Vova. He brandished the darkened shell above his head in both hands, maraca-ing like crazy and, as the kitten-sigh sound began, pointed it directly at Vova's gaping face.

Splat! went the glitter glue, as the shell started to glow.

"Whaaag!" screamed Vova, who had not been at all prepared to have her head suddenly coated in glitter glue. "What *is* this?" she cried, outraged, as she smoothed gloop back from her face, unwittingly permitting more of it to enter her ears. "And wh—?"

All of a sudden, Vova froze. Her spine straightened, her knees went wobbly, her eyes flared wide and her face went grey. Her mouth opened

94

slightly in horror. Dankwart wasn't sure what memory he'd thrust upon her, but she'd indubitably deserved it. He gave himself a nod, even going so far as to allow himself a smug little smirk. He didn't feel at all guilty, not even when Vova fell to her knees, curled into a little ball, and started sobbing. Then again, if he'd had a guilt complex, he probably wouldn't have been involved in the habitual scamming of villagers.

Finally Vova started to claw out around her, grappling for the hem of Dankwart's robe, and pulling him down with a strength born of desperation. Dankwart, never for an instant doubting his wardrobe choices, tumbled to the floor and the giant seashell skittered away from him. Both merchants scrabbled after it, but after dealing out a few hefty kicks to the face, Vova got there first. She promptly set the shell to her ear, giving a sigh of relief as whichever torrid memory it had contained drizzled back out again.

Clutching the shell in white-knuckled hands, Vova looked very coldly at Dankwart (which is somewhat hard to do when your eyes are bloodshot and you've just been quivering like a trampoline after the forceful dismount of a 300-pound man). "This means war," she said. The two merchants retained eye contact for a moment then, in preparation for a capitalist competition which was about to get real, they swirled away from each other and scurried off to hide and scheme.

It didn't take Vova long to come up with a plan significantly more ingenious than simply setting a house on fire. She'd seen how shaking the shell had released bad memory juice, and decided to experiment—so she scurried down to the seashore, keeping an eye out for her nefarious nemesis. Once there, she gathered as many full memory shells as she could, stashing them into a sack. She then slung the sack over her shoulder, grabbed two buckets of water, and sloshed her way back up the cliff face.

Our sneaky merchant slunk along the cliff-tops until she found a copse of trees where she could work undisturbed. In doing so she scattered a bunch of Taomina's adolescents, who through some kind of instinct would head to the copse to do all kinds of nefarious things (and then immediately forget them using shells, in one swoop being able to genuinely protest their innocence, and render whatever they'd done somewhat pointless).

Vova set down her buckets and started experimenting. She began by shaking one of the smaller shells, watching how the memory goop flowed out once it was sufficiently scintillated. She then tried mixing the goop into the seawater, and watched as the glittery substance dispersed, adding a subtle gleam to the water. Success! She added more and more memories, until the water couldn't absorb any more and the goop started to sediment. Vova cackled with glee, then grabbed her buckets and carefully trundled back to the village.

Vova found Dankwart standing by the remains of his home, failing at both plotting and hiding. He was rustling through the still-smouldering remains of the house, trying to dig out a spare set of robes. Vova, being the helpful soul she was, decided to assist—and so she grabbed each bucket in turn, sloshing them out all over Dankwart. "Oh oops," she said. "I was aiming for the fire."

Dankwart, doused in concentrated memory juice, started squawking, crying, and hopping about, all at once. "No no no no no!!" he protested. "I *did* do my homework! Why am I grounded? I *hate* Brussel sprouts!! Why won't you go out with me?!!"

Vova tried out her cackle once more—she was really on a roll. Watching the flood of memories overcome Dankwart was immensely fulfilling. A group of villagers were drawn to the commotion, and stood around, dullard-like.

"You!" cried wet Warty. "And you!"—he pointed at some villagers. "Come with me!" With that, he hopped out of the wreckage of his house, simultaneously having some kind of memory splashback in relation to an exploding marshmallow fight that had ended both tragically and stickily.

Two villagers who, without their memories, lacked much in the way of 'wisdom' and 'defiance', obediently turned to follow Dankwart as he strode towards the shop he had shared with Vova. He marched into it, gibbering about some kind of promotion he'd never gotten, and started rummaging through a rucksack next to some wind-up whirligigs. Finding what he was searching for, he grabbed handfuls of what looked like small rubber tadpoles, and started distributing them to the villagers he'd recruited. Once all their pockets and hands were overflowing, Dankwart grabbed a bucket and marched off to the seashore, villagers in tow.

"I'll show her," he muttered, gathering up dark seashells. "I'll give her so many bad memories, she'll want to leave for good!"

Once he had amassed a pile of full memory shells, Dankwart shook them out into buckets of saltwater much as Vova had done, and then moved onto the next phase of his plan. He took all the rubber tadpoles from his pockets and those of his two followers, and started filling them up with the memory water until they were bloated like little puffer fish. He then tied off the ends and placed them into a pile. Finally they were all ready, and he gathered up armfuls, stacking them in the front of his robe and holding it up like a giant ungainly pouch. He gave directions to his followers, then, waddling somewhat, they headed back to town to find Vova.

After a thorough search, the three found Vova in what served as the village's junkyard, casting things about as she rummaged.

"Ah-*hah*!" screeched Dankwart, nose up in the air. "We've found you amongst your brethren, *scum*!" Vova didn't look very impressed at this comment, though she did start to sidle towards the protection of a rickety lean-to. "Now *leave*!" demanded Warty, "And leave for *good*, or else I will douse you with memories so fearsome, so *remarkable* in their horribility that you'll *never* be the same!!"

Vova was now barely a hasty leap away from the lean-to. She paused for a moment, then remembered her days of being forced from villages at the end of pitchforks. She wasn't willing to return to that life—Taomina would be *her* market. "Never!" she shouted back. "Do your worst!"—and with that, she made a quick dive for the lean-to.

"Fire!!" screamed Danky. The villagers looked at him, confused. The merchant looked back at them and sighed with grand exasperation. "Water!" he clarified. "Throw the water balloons at that woman!"

You could almost hear a 'ding' as the villagers understood what he meant. They started lobbing the memory-filled tadpoles at the lean-to, hoping to hit Vova. Many of the balloons splashed harmlessly to the ground, while others made it through the cracks and split open on the merchant. Yet others never burst at all, and Vova made sure to grab those and fling them back at her attackers. As it turned out, she had rather accurate aim, and the battle became more evenly matched as Dankwart and his villagers started to fall back under the tide of memories. Finally it became too much for the villagers to take—after all, they hadn't previously had any bad memories to help inoculate them against the onslaught—and they fled to the seashore, in search of shells to empty their brains into once more.

Deprived of his defenders, Dankwart also scurried away from the scene, throwing the last water balloons over his shoulder as he did so. He was going to need a better plan.

Vova, meanwhile, fetched some empty seashells she'd stored earlier, and removed the bad memories that had been thrown at her. She then calmly resumed riffling through the junkyard, knowing just what she was looking for.

Between Vova's constructions and Dankwart's conclusions, no further memory warfare took place that night. Dankwart, being newly homeless, took some large empty memory shells into a nice-looking cottage with a verdant kitchen garden, and relieved the residents from both their house and their memory of having lived there. He then proceeded to eat their tomatoes before getting a good night's sleep. Vova meanwhile told one of the more memory-less villagers that he was her husband, and she was taking him home to cook for her. He, having no memories to the contrary, obliged. As such, Vova's meal was a damn sight more fulfilling than tomatoes.

As even *you* have probably realised by now, neither Vova nor Dankwart was a nice sort of person. See, you're learning things now that you've *finally* stopped interrupting. It's good to see you do actually have some manners in there somewhere.

Dankwart awoke the next morning to an alarm clock of smashing sounds. He cautiously flicked aside a curtain and peeked out the window, only to find Vova standing over a dusty pile of what had once been shells. It's kind of lucky shells aren't prone to vengeance.

"Coward!" cried Vova, seeing the curtain twitch. "I'll give you one last chance to leave this town, before I drown you in memories!"

Danky didn't deign to reply.

"Fine!" continued Vova. "Prepare to go *down!*" With that, she swirled away, only wishing she wore robes like Dankwart for the increased dramatic effect.

After a suitably cautious period, Dankwart peered outside to ensure his nemesis had departed. Seeing it was so, he sneaked outside to gather some backup and supplies.

The two merchants met at midday in the village square, each with a crowd of villagers behind them. The villagers were gathered in small, indolent groups, never quite remembering what they were doing or why they were doing it. You could almost say they were 'shells' of their former selves. —Look, are you laughing at me? Enough of your nit-picking! We're in the middle of a *story* for goodness' sake! Show some *respect* for the *craft*!!

As I was *saying*, the two mercenary merchants stood facing one another in the square, ready to do battle. They stood and stared at each other, filled with hatred, and each just *wishing* someone would arrive from the pitchfork emporium to chase the other away. Then, at no discernible signal, the fight was on.

Dankwart's plebs launched themselves forward, swarming on Vova's group and quickly surrounding her in the kerfuffle. They lifted her while she spluttered and, in turtle formation, carried her back to where Dankwart stood by a gigantic barrel brimming with water.

"Oooh, you're a bit dirty behind the ears there, old friend," said Dankwart, smirking malevolently. "It must be time for your bath." With that, he nodded to the villagers, and they swung the angry little merchant into the tub.

Vova's head immediately dipped below the surface. It didn't re-emerge. Ten seconds passed, then twenty. After thirty seconds the dead stillness in the tub was disrupted, and the movement of flailing limbs below the surface could be seen. Then, forty-eight point two-three seconds after being dumped in, Vova *swooshed* back up into sight above the water. She was kicking and screaming and coughing, all at the same time (which, if you've ever tried it, is quite the feat). She was simultaneously complaining and crying, yelling and commiserating, empathising and raging. She was beset by a tide of glitter glue memories, from the bleak to the merely mundane— all the things which the people of Taomina had chosen to forget, and forgotten to remember.

Vova splashed and staggered into the side of the barrel, then toppled over the edge onto the ground. Somehow, despite the memory splashbacks, she scuttled away. She easily evaded Dankwart's villagers, as they seemed to be in distress: their hands were clasped to their heads, and they were all grimacing. As it turned out, Vova's forceful dunk into the tub and subsequent re-emergence had splattered the surrounding audience with water, and they were undergoing their first-ever bad memories—well, the first bad memories they could remember, anyway. It was as though their innocence was being ripped from them as the memories flooded in. The memories were mostly going to the incorrect people, which only served to add to the confusion—each villager suddenly had memories of having big feet and small feet, smooth hands and hairy, being a child, being an adult, being a man, being a woman. Who were they, really? As Vova rushed back to her side of the square, Dankwart's villagers started to rumble.

Dankwart, initially so satisfied at Vova's apparent incapacitation, was taken off-guard when his foe began to escape. He hurriedly tried to get his people together, urging and cajoling them, but to little effect. Busied, he was again taken off-guard when he was hit by a long and powerful stream of memory-infused water. It bowled him over and coated him from head-to-foot in goop, while he just sat there befuddled. The ingenious Vova had used things she'd salvaged from the junkyard to put together an elaborate contraption strongly resembling a fire hose, and was now using it to full effect. Incidentally, it's rather a pity that there hadn't been anything resembling a fire hose *before* Dankwart's house burnt down—but that's why you always need to keep the engineering-minded folk on your side.

Warty started writhing under the memories much as Vova had done (and continued to do), attempting to fend off the stream of water at the same time. The only effect this had was to divert more of the water onto the villagers by his side, and with it, more memories for which they were completely unprepared.

In his frenzy, Dankwart wasn't paying much attention to the other things happening in the square, until the stream of memories suddenly stopped blasting him. He became aware of an angry din. Flicking as much water off himself as he could and shaking his head to get it out of his ears, he grabbed a large shell he'd stored on his body in case things turned out badly for him. After a quick removal of as many bad memories as he could manage on the spot, he looked up to see an unexpected sight: the dullards were fighting. No, not just fighting—*brawling*. The village square had devolved into a riot!

The villagers who had been splashed in Dankwart's half of the square had first crumpled under the weight of the memories, and then been consumed by rage. On the other side of the square they could see people who had persecuted them, bullied them, cheated on them, rejected them, or stolen their lunch from the fridge when it was *clearly* marked with their name. They shrugged off their confusion and disorientation and launched themselves at the perpetrators.

The villagers on Vova's side, lacking bad memories, weren't sure what to make of what was happening, especially as they didn't know what things like 'raised fists' and 'glaring eyes' signified. Thus they were quickly overwhelmed by their rage-infused opponents.

Fists were swinging, faces were being slapped, hair was being pulled. At the same time, more and more villagers were being dunked into the tub used on Vova and being doused by the swinging hose contraption. As further villagers gained memories, the brawl began to spread and spread and spread. Vengeance was upon them! But then a question was asked. Its poignancy spilled through the crowd, and people paused in their violence as they strained to hear.

The source of the question was a sopping wet child, which is good—wise kids make for memorable stories. Get it, *memorable?* Oh my goodness, why don't you *appreciate* me?!

Anyway, the girl-child had been splashed with all kinds of bad memories. Despite her lack of surface area, she had managed to receive more memories than anybody else in the square, and this caused something very special to happen: the memories fused together into some kind of consciousness, some kind of bank of experiences that gave the girl hitherto unknown wisdom. The more she was splashed, the wiser she grew, until finally she came up with a question. She *was* a little girl though, past nappies but definitely not past pigtails (who is?), so how was she going to get people's attention? She wasn't exactly equipped to physically restrain the villagers, so she had to use her words instead.

She began with a question. "What are you fighting for?"

After a brief pause, the question was met with a deafening roar. Villagers shouted their responses—they had a *lot* of things to complain about, and they were suffering the emotional fall-out all at once.

"But wait!" yelled the newly-wise girl-child, who had the very grown-up name of 'Aletheia'. "Aren't you all fighting because of *other* people's memories?"

Everybody fell silent again as they considered what she'd said. She had a point: on whose behalf were they seeking retribution? The big feet they'd had in their memories certainly didn't match the small ones they could see at the ends of their legs. The hairy hands they were waving didn't match the manicured set they could remember. Whose big feet and whose fancy nails were they fighting for?

Non-fabulous Fabian stepped up. "You're right, girl-child," he started—"but what do you propose we do about it?"

Lettie sighed. "Am I the only one who got the 'violence solves nothing' memory?" She made sure she had everybody's attention. "Let's just think for a moment. We've all been apportioned the wrong memories, and we're all fighting because of it. But why? Why is this happening?"

All over the square, villagers started to stand straight, and pondered. It definitely couldn't be *their* fault. They each searched their memories, until finally someone started with realisation. She pointed to the two merchants, who were looking agog at the formerly biddable people. "It was *them*!" the woman cried, with a certain amount of vitriol. "*They* started this—they were using us to fight for them!"

The square set to muttering. Suddenly a man interjected—"They're the ones I bought my whirligigs off! They stopped spinning the moment I left the shop!"

"That one kicked us out of our house last night," chorused two small children, pointing at Dankwart. They looked too young to own a guinea pig, let alone property.

"And *that* one made me make her *dinner*!" cried another woman, indicating Vova. "She even made me—made him?—made *whoever* I am fold the napkins into fancy swans!"

The angry mutterings began to get louder and louder.

"This is *all* their fault!" claimed unfabulous Fabian, neglecting the minor detail that the villagers had deliberately chosen to remove their memories in the first place—and after all, nobody can take advantage of you without your permission. Had even one of the villagers chosen to remember things that happened, and perhaps even learned from them, the town wouldn't have been in the sorry state of random evictions and dinner cookings that it currently was. Not to mention, there would be a great deal less currency wasted on whirligigs. Nobody needs *that* many whirligigs!

Dankwart and Vova made eye contact. They recognised the mood of the crowd—they'd encountered it once or twice before. "Now look here," started Dankwart.

"Yes," echoed Vova. "Look here…"

The crowd started to close in on them, and the two merchants began to shuffle towards one another. Safety in numbers!

"Remember!" urged Aletheia. "Violence isn't the answer!"

Vova noticed with a start that a villager had acquired a pitchfork. Where had *that* come from? She looked at Dankwart, only to find the other merchant looking back at her. As one, they stepped so that they were back-to-back.

"We'll leave!" promised Dankwart. "We'll leave right now! There's no need to do anything hasty."

"That's right," added Vova. "We'll go right away—just forget about the whole thing!"

Vova probably shouldn't have mentioned the word 'forget'. Hearing it, Lettie rolled her eyes, and the pitchfork-bearing man led the charge: the two despicable merchants, once more united by a common attacker, were run out of town, never to return.

Panting and vindicated, the townsfolk of Taomina slowly started to trickle back to the square, where they naturally gathered around Lettie. She seemed to be the only person who had gained enough combined wisdom to be in a position to lead anybody.

"So what now?" asked Fabian, about as useful as ever. "We're all mixed up!"

Aletheia nodded. "Well the first step will be fixing that, then—shall we fetch some shells? Let's see if we can get everybody's correct memories back to them."

"But wait," interjected the woman who remembered cooking Vova's dinner the previous evening. "What if we don't *want* our memories back?"

Lettie sighed—wisdom seems to be highly correlated with sighing. "Don't you see?" she finally offered. "We went too far—not only did we forget enough to be used by those callous merchants, but we forgot who we were. Without our memories, without our pasts, we can't learn, we can't grow. Without our memories, we became mindless creatures of hungers, without the will or wisdom to control them. We're nothing without our memories.

"However," she continued, "just because we went too far doesn't mean that forgetting can't be valuable. Let's figure out whose memory goes with whom, and we'll leave the worst ones out. Besides, from what I remember, a lot of bad memories were flung a long way out to sea—we'll probably never get some of those back."

Slowly the other villagers started to agree, begrudgingly nodding—and hoping that their own memories weren't too awful.

"Still, that leaves us the temptation of the shells," Lettie pointed out. "We don't want to back-slide, and end up like we were before. Happily, I think I may just have an idea..!"

And so the shells were collected, and after a rather laborious process, people's own memories were restored to them. However, now that they could remember all the crimes and slights that had been committed in Taomina, the villagers began to drift away—the impact of so many sudden memories made the prospect of apologies and building relationships too daunting a concept, and so, slowly, people left town.

Aletheia was the last to relinquish her collected memories and, before she did so, she told the others her plan. When she was once again an ordinary little girl, the plan was put into action.

"And what was the plan?" *Finally*. You're asking a good question! I'd just about given up on you. Well, use of the shells was considered too dangerous a temptation for the villagers—something had to be done. However the shells were too numerous to simply be smashed. So instead, the villagers headed to the beach and started to search. They searched not only on the shore, but even beneath the waves, as far out into the ocean as they could manage. Finally they found a shell so huge, so *monstrous* in its dimensions, that it took three teams of horses just to pull it out of the water.

Once they had the giant shell, they put it onto a raft and set it afloat, to be anchored off-shore. One-by-one, boats paddled out to the raft, and the villagers tilted their heads towards the shell. Every person in the village removed one very specific set of memories—that of the shells and how to use them. Then, oblivious as to why they were half a mile off-shore in a boat (let alone next to a gigantic shell), they would head back to town before scattering to far-flung corners of the land. When the very last villager reached the shell, they set the raft on fire before inserting their memories, and the shell sank to the ocean floor.

"But is that the last that was ever seen of the shell?" Look, you really need to stop interrupting—we're nearly done!

The shell stayed below the waves for years and years. Taomina was a long-forgotten town, abandoned once more. But what even Aletheia in all her wisdom hadn't thought of was the effect putting so many memories into one shell would have, left to mix and meld together. Over the years they broiled together inside what had, after all, once been the home of a living creature. As with the little girl, these memories created a wisdom, a consciousness all their own—a consciousness trapped, bored, and simply *starved* for decent conversation, in a shell beneath the waves.

But then one day came a storm, the likes of which is only seen once a century. The storm reached down to the ocean floor and dislodged the shell, casting it ashore, and shaking it all the while. I finally emerged from the storm-riven waters, only to find a woman—a woman with, apparently, *no* manners—standing and watching. She gaped in amazement at the sight, and was hit square-on with a gigantic wave, made of something that looked like glitter glue. Staggered by the in-rush of memories, she tripped on the sand, her head landing by the shell. As the glue and my consciousness began to permeate her mind, she lost her own memories to the shell and the sound of the sea. All that remained to the woman was the long-ago villagers' knowledge of the shells and how they work.

So now I ask—what are you going to do with it?

A NOTE FROM LAURA

Five or six years ago I read an article about a new drug which was being developed. This drug gave people the ability to forget painful memories, as long as it was issued close enough to when the traumatic event took place. However, the whole thing was surrounded by controversy—say the drug was given to the victim of a violent crime, they'd be able to forget, but how would they testify against their attacker? What's justice in this situation— for the victim to testify and the perpetrator to be subjected to thorough criminal justice, or to have the victim forget and be able to more easily go on with their lives? It made me consider how memories define who we are as people, but also that sometimes we might be better off without them.

This led me to the idea that memories could be used as weapons, and this in turn led to the water-fight in my story. In the end, my characters are permitted to forget their more painful memories, but their lack of self-control in terms of what they forget means that they lose access to the shells. Personally though, I think it would be quite nice if people were sometimes allowed to forget their scars.

A quick note on background—I used a range of names from different origins. 'Vova' is the Russian short form for 'Vladimir', while Dankwart is of German origin. 'Jerome' came about when I asked one of my friends what to call a dull, slightly stupid little boy—and she went swiping on Tinder until she found a suitable name. 'Aletheia' is a little more complex—the 'Lethe' is the river of oblivion, or forgetting, in Greek mythology. It was one of the rivers of the Underworld, and the dead drank from it to forget their earthly lives. 'Aletheia' has a couple of meanings— firstly, it is the name of the Greek Goddess of Truth, and secondly it is a word which relates to a lack of concealment. Lettie gains access to the town's previously-hidden memories, and this is what gives her the wisdom to lead the villagers in their plan.

I hope you enjoyed the story!

Laura May
Brussels, Belgium

MEMORYARIAN
SCOTT A. BUTLER

Maybe it was the hooting of the who-owls. Maybe it was the chill in the air. Or maybe it was the fact that the manor house was both disturbing and confusing: wherever you turned your head, it seemed to follow. Whatever the reason, an intense shiver slithered down his spine. It creeped him out. It made him feel sick to the stomach. But the journey had been long and his task was important; he wasn't going to give up now.

Y'Orlay used his sleeve and a glob of spit to scrub the grime off the plaque next to the large, flaking, crimson door.

LORD AL HEIMERS

MEMORYARIAN & PERMANENT CHAIRMAN OF THE MEMORY GUILD

& EXPERT DUCK BREEDER

This was the place all right. Y'Orlay took a deep breath and reached into his tattered leather satchel, pulling out a small palm-sized box. It had 'Your Very Own Pixie Gremlin Lockpicker' painted in big words on the front. He carefully read the instructions on the back of the box for the thousandth time, mumbling them to himself.

"Awaken your Pixie Gremlin and watch it get to work. Do not shake. Do not offer alcohol. Yadda yadda, blah blah. Caution: insults others frequently."

Y'Orlay opened the box. Lying inside in a scattering of sawdust was a fat green pixie gremlin, no bigger than—and about as charismatic as—a dung beetle. It was the ugliest thing he had ever seen; even uglier than the ogres of Murkglump Swamp. He reached back into the satchel, retrieved half a handful of smoked fairy faeces, and dropped them into the box with an expression of repulsion.

The pixie gremlin sniffed, then twitched and jerked. It sprang to life, jumping to its feet and gobbling up the offering. The consequent noise and stench reminded Y'Orlay of Murkglump pigs devouring the rotting carcass of an orc. After gobbling the final piece of faeces, the pixie gremlin licked its fingers and burped. It turned and looked up at Y'Orlay.

"Whatchu starin' at, mankweed?"

"Uh, you," he responded.

"Can't say I blames ye. My sexy figure is hard tae resist, eh?" it answered, adopting what in its mind was a seductive pose. At least it had the decency to be wearing rough spun briefs: most pixie gremlins parade around naked. It scratched at its crotch and sniffed its fingers.

Y'Orlay almost vomited up his rabbit pie.

"Ahreet then, where's this lock ye need pickin', mould breath?" it enquired.

Y'Orlay pointed at the door and moved the box close to the keyhole. The pixie gremlin sneezed into its hands before smearing the snot all over its body to make itself slippery. With Y'Orlay's reluctant assistance, it climbed the side of the small box. It then sucked in its fat belly and squeezed into the keyhole. There followed a lot of grunting, grumbling and clicking.

"Oi, moose knuckle! Try it now," the pixie gremlin's muffled voice called.

Y'Orlay tugged the handle. The door clicked and slowly swung open, groaning like a dying troll.

He stepped into the manor and listened carefully. Silence. As he began to tiptoe through the bloodwood-panelled hallway, the pixie gremlin ran past him.

"I'm parched! Ye do what ye gotta do, I'm goin' to see if the gutter slug that lives here has any dizzy juice," it announced.

STOMPSPLAT!

The pixie gremlin met its end under the bottom of a boot. Y'Orlay's gaze traced the boot to a leg. Then to a waist, a chest and a bearded face. The face of a very tall and annoyed person wearing a crimson hooded robe. He was holding a magical staff. (Y'Orlay knew it was magical not only because he could feel it in his kidneys, but because of the glowing red crystal that sat on top of it. That's usually a pretty big clue that a staff is magical).

"Ugh, disgusting creatures," a booming voice said as the figure lifted his foot, snot-like slime oozing from the sole. His gaze turned to Y'Orlay. "And who might you be?"

The best Y'Orlay could come up with was a nervous, blabbering mutter.

The tall figure tapped the ground with his staff and the door slammed shut behind Y'Orlay.

"You're not a burglar are you? Or a memory thief? Or worse, a ducknapper?"

"I...I'm sorry, sir," Y'Orlay managed to mumble, fearing for his life in the face of this tall, intimidating figure (not to mention the part about him being armed with a magical staff).

An idea seemed to dawn upon the figure. "Ah! Or perhaps you're here about the job advert?"

Y'Orlay sensed an opportunity to possibly not get killed. "Y...yes! That's it. I'm here about the job."

The figure stepped forward. He appeared to think for a moment.

"I put that advert out three hundred and eight years ago, when my old assistant died. It's about time someone answered it. What is your name?"

"Y'Orlay."

"Pardon? No, I am not late for anything; I asked a question. What is your name?"

"Y'Orlay. That's my name sir: Y'Orlay."

"I see. What a stupid name."

"Are...are you the Memoryarian?"

"Yes; I am Al Heimers. Memoryarian, Chairman of the Memory Guild and Expert Duck Breeder," he replied, sounding proudest of the latter. "But you may call me Al."

Al knelt down to the floor to get a good look at Y'Orlay, his bones creaking like rusty coffin hinges as he did so.

"You are rather short, are you not?" Al enquired.

"Uh, well yes. I'm a shortlander."

Shortlanders are a race of small humanoids, no taller than four feet, who live in the valleys of the Western Lowlands. They live happy, peaceful lives and usually only venture outside their valleys to sell agricultural produce or herbs. Despite gossip to the contrary, they absolutely do not have hairy feet, and allegations to that effect are usually met with being knocked to the ground and having bare, sweaty, *hairless* shortlander feet rubbed in your face.

"Ah, that explains it. Shortlander," Al smiled to himself. "Shortlanders have a lot of juicy memories."

Y'Orlay chuckled nervously.

"The job is yours. You start today," Al said as he rose to his feet, his bones again creaking.

"That's it? Just like that, you're giving me the job?" Y'Orlay asked in a surprised tone, somewhat relieved to find that he didn't appear to be facing death. At least not immediately.

"Yes. I cannot afford to be picky if it takes over three hundred years for someone to show up. Come, follow me."

Y'Orlay realised that being Al's new assistant could make his task a lot easier, so he embraced the opportunity with both small hands.

"May I ask a question, Al?" Y'Orlay asked as the pair walked down the long hallway.

"Yes, you may."

"What happened to your old assistant? How did he die?"

"Oh. I forgot to feed him."

"Eh?"

"Immortals like me do not need food. It is easy to forget that you mortals need to be fed. It is rather an inconvenience, really."

Immortals are very powerful ancient wizards, chosen by the gods (known as 'the Divines') to help keep balance in the world. Well, that's what the books say, anyway. But the truth is that the Divines needed to overcome all the loopholes they left behind when creating the world.

The pair entered a study. It was dark and had the same style of decoration as the hallway. There were books strewn across every surface and they were the only things in the room untouched by dust or cobwebs. Y'Orlay approached the nearest book and examined it. The cover had a picture of a smiling cat flanked by cheery rats.

"The Handsome Morice and his Fellow Rodents, by Perry Tratchett," he read aloud.

"A favourite of mine," Al pointed out.

The mighty Memoryarian approached the desk, opened the large, pristine agenda diary on it, and flicked through to tomorrow's date. He pointed at an appointment with a long finger, while idly stroking his beard with the other hand.

"Ah-ha. Early start tomorrow," Al said, tapping the words in front of him. "I shall take you out with me and teach you the ropes."

"What exactly will I be learning?" Y'Orlay enquired.

"Mostly carrying things. For now. Let us see how good you are at that first, shall we?"

Y'Orlay nodded, trying to appear enthusiastic, while being secretly glad he probably wasn't going to be doing anything which might result in his early death. He did have an important task of his own, after all, and this lucky opportunity would surely be the best way to achieve it.

"I suppose we had best get you fed and to bed. Your journey must have been long." Al closed the diary.

The two left the study, like a small dog shadowing its much larger master, and entered the kitchen across the hallway. A duck flew off the table and landed in Al's open palm.

Quack!

"Weegie, meet Y'Orlay."

The duck looked at Y'Orlay and then back at Al.

Quack quack!

"Yes, I know. I told him his name is stupid too."

Y'Orlay chuckled. "You can understand duck?" he asked.

"No."

Al put the bird back on the kitchen table. He walked over to the icebox (which was full of nesting ducks), fumbled around with his hand and pulled out a couple of duck eggs. Y'Orlay's tummy growled like a hungry giant at an 'all the farmers you can eat' buffet. Al then picked off bits of straw and feathers from the stove—which clearly hadn't been used for a very long time—blew the dust off and fired it up. He tied a frilly apron, with the words 'Ducky Lover' and a faded image of a smiling duck on it, over his robe. Y'Orlay climbed up onto the normal-person-sized stool at the table, noting the ducks on the top of the cupboards were watching him with suspicion.

"So, where are we going tomorrow?" Y'Orlay asked.

"Deepstar, one of the human cities," Al responded, adding random herbs from unmarked jars into a frying pan with the eggs. "Someone is scheduled for a memory harvest. And somebody else is scheduled to have theirs returned. And afterwards there could be a few odd jobs here and there. Unplanned deaths, last minute Divine decisions. That sort of thing."

"Why do you do it exactly, harvest memories?"

"To catalogue and store them, so that they are not lost. Everybody's destiny has already been allotted by the Divines. Sometimes the Divines plan for people to lose their memories; or, when someone dies, they need to be collected before they fade from existence. What I do is collect all those memories and store them in my library, so that they don't vanish from time itself."

Y'Orlay had already done his research on the Memoryarian. But books, even if they were hard to find, were not always accurate; he would rather check his knowledge to be certain. And he feared that if he appeared to know too much already, his cover might be blown.

"What happens if you don't harvest them?"

"Memory is a form of magic. Magic is never permanent, and so memories slowly and gradually leak through the boundaries of time if they are not contained. You cannot remember someone if their own memory of existing has gone, and so once the memories belonging to someone faded away, other people's memories of that person would simply be forgotten, erased. The outcomes of past or future historical events would eventually change. Children wouldn't know who their parents were, people would forget their heroes, books would become unwritten, civilisation would forget how to be civilised, and so on. I capture the magic and preserve it, to prevent people being forgotten and keep all of that from happening. It is complicated. 'Wibbly-wobbly, timey-wimey' as a great man once put it."

"Can memories be given back?"

Al put a plate of omelette down in front of Y'Orlay.

"Yes. If the Divines change their minds, I give the memories back."

"I read somewhere that you can travel anywhere in time, is that true?" Y'Orlay picked up a knife and fork and blew the dust off them.

Al sat down opposite Y'Orlay.

"Yes, I can travel to any point in time, past or future. All Immortals can."

"So if the memory loss is temporary why don't you just take their memories, go to the future and give them back, instead of storing them?" Y'Orlay asked with genuine confusion.

"Certain points in time are fixed events. I have to allow the correct amount of *real* time to pass before returning the memories, no shortcuts allowed. Even I have rules to follow. Like I said, it is complicated. I do not expect many mortals to understand. We Immortals just do as we are told; the Divines do not like questions."

Y'Orlay nodded and placed a forkful of omelette into his mouth. He closed his eyes in a state of wonderment as his tongue savoured the exquisite explosion of exotic flavours that danced on his tongue with every chew. It was like nothing he had ever tasted before. He was so mesmerised by the deliciousness that he didn't realise he was making *mmm! Mmm! Mmmnnn* noises.

"Are you all right?" Al asked him, in a rather concerned tone.

"Yes. Yes, sorry. This is delicious. It's the best omelette I've ever tasted! What's in it?"

"Duck eggs and twelve different herbs."

"Which herbs?" Y'Orlay asked, devouring another forkful.

Al shrugged, his bones creaking as usual. "No idea."

Y'Orlay paused mid-chew. "So this could be poisonous?!" he spluttered with his mouth full.

"No. My ducks are still alive."

"You feed this to your ducks?"

"Omelette? No, they are normal ducks, not cannibal ducks."

"The herbs?"

"Yes. Just a sprinkle every now and again. It makes their feathers shiny."

After the meal, Y'Orlay was shown upstairs to a room he was told would be his. He walked over to a window, pulled back the crimson curtains and peered outside. He was looking out over the front of the house and could see the mountains he'd trekked over to get here. Seeing how large yet distant they were from the window, he wondered how he had made it to the isolated estate at all. He plonked his satchel down onto a nearby chair and examined the bed. Crimson. Al sure seemed to love this particular shade of red.

Once Y'Orlay seemed to have made himself at home, Al closed the door behind him, which was followed by a suspicious click. Once Y'Orlay was sure Al was out of earshot, he approached the door to try the handle. It was definitely locked. Even if Y'Orlay still had an unsquashed pixie gremlin, he was physically drained from his long journey. There was no way he could accomplish his task and make it back home without a good night's sleep. As such, he stripped down to his underwear, neatly folding his socks. He then approached the four-poster bed and climbed into it (which is a lot harder than it sounds when you're a shortlander). He slipped in between the soft and inviting sheets and blew out the candle beside the bed. As soon as his head hit the duck feather pillow, his eyelids rolled shut. He slept through the night like the undisturbed bones of a long-dead forgotten hermit.

* * *

Quack. Bonk. Bonk. Quack. Bonk.

Y'Orlay awoke to find a duck standing on his chest, quacking at his face and using its beak to bonk him on the forehead. He expressed his annoyance at the rude awakening with a grumpy 'bah' and brushed the duck off his chest. The duck, satisfied by a job well done, hopped off the bed and waddled out of the wide-open bedroom door.

Y'Orlay rolled out of bed, and misjudging the distance to the floor, hit it with a thump. He cried out in pain. He was used to sleeping in a bedroom where everything was the right size for a shortlander, rather than a taller being like an Immortal.

After a short and brutally cold two minute wash in the en suite, as there were no matches to light the boiler, Y'Orlay dressed and left the room. Before he could start going down the stairs, Y'Orlay noticed a large door at the end of the hall. It was different from the others. This door was made of a shiny, brassy metal rather than wood like the others. It featured three differently-sized rings made from a darker yellow metal, which appeared to make up some kind of locking mechanism.

He dared to approach the door, and reached out to touch it. The metal vibrated beneath his fingertips. Pressing his ear against the door, he could hear it giving off the faint hum of a magical enchantment. He knew exactly what the door was: it was the door to a library. The Library of Memories. However, inconveniently, it didn't appear to have a keyhole. Nor a door knob, for that matter.

The hairs on the back of Y'Orlay's neck stood up; he sensed a presence. He lifted his ear from the door and spun around.

"Ah, there you are," Al said, clutching his staff, and looking no different to last night. He stepped closer. "We'd best get started," he suggested, gesturing for Y'Orlay to get out of the way.

Al stood in front of the door. He held the staff in front of him and muttered some words in a strange language. Y'Orlay couldn't understand a single word, but he knew Al must be speaking in the secret ancient language of 'Divine Tongue'. Well, secret in that only Immortals and the Divines themselves could speak it. Any mortal who attempted to learn the language simply dropped dead.

After speaking the mysterious words, Al tapped the floor with his staff. The rings on the door simultaneously spun around, and there was a distinct clicking as locks came undone. The door swung inward, revealing a shimmering wall of light. Al stepped into the light first, telling Y'Orlay to follow him. On the other side of the light was the library.

To say it was 'gigantic' would be an understatement. It was infinite, and it was immaculate. There were neat rows of concentric shelves stacked with crystal decanters, and inside each were thousands of tiny, glittering magical orbs of light. Y'Orlay realised these were memories.

In the centre of the library was a balustrade. Approaching it, Y'Orlay could see that the library dropped into the ground and rose into the sky for what seemed like (and actually was) an endless distance in both directions. Y'Orlay, whirling on the spot in wonder, had read of the Immortals using personal dimensions for storage like this—but no number of books or artist's impressions had prepared him for the awe of stepping into one.

"So, that door was a portal into another dimension, right?" Y'Orlay stuttered.

"Yes. The Library of Memories is another dimension, and the door is the portal to it."

Al grabbed onto Y'Orlay with his non-staff-bearing hand and uttered a travelling spell in a much more familiar language, Wizard Standard, which teleported them both to a different part of the library. Here, half of the shelves had empty decanters.

Al approached some empty decanters and collected the crystal stoppers from them. He told Y'Orlay to put the stoppers in his satchel. The Immortal then approached a full decanter nearby, picked it up, and handed it to Y'Orlay. The decanter had a label, which read:

NAME: BOVO WIDEFOOT

HARVEST REASON: AMNESIA. WIFE WHACKED HEAD WITH SAUCEPAN.

There was a date on the label implying that the memories were due for return that day. Y'Orlay carefully placed it into the satchel.

Al gripped his staff ready for another travelling spell, looked at Y'Orlay, and smiled. "Ready?"

"Ready," Y'Orlay lied, wondering how he would get back into the library later on to complete his own objectives.

* * *

Deepstar was very different to the valleys of the shortlanders. The smells of the city, the sounds of carts against the cobble roads and the fact that there were too many tall people for Y'Orlay's liking made him homesick. Or maybe the sickness was because of the putrid smell of jellied glumfish heads on the market stall next to him. Either way, Y'Orlay felt sick.

Deepstar was split up into four districts. The southern district was residential; the eastern district was the commercial hub; the western district was reserved for the rich and the centre district was occupied by the Ministry of Wizardry and Witchcraft. The north of the city was occupied by the docks. Y'Orlay and Al were currently in the commercial hub within the eastern district.

Al beckoned Y'Orlay to follow him, picking up a fruit muffin from a nearby stall.

"Breakfast," Al explained, handing the muffin to Y'Orlay.

"Y…You can't just steal that without paying!"

"Why not?"

"Because it's theft."

"She cannot see us," Al replied. "Nobody can see us unless we want them to."

Y'Orlay jumped up and waved in the faces of people passing by. Sure enough, they didn't react—Al must have been telling the truth.

"Put it back if you want. At least I remembered that mortals need feeding this time."

Y'Orlay sniffed the muffin. It was still warm and smelled sweet. His tummy grumbled.

"Nah," he decided against his conscience, biting into it.

The pair walked a short distance through the city. Y'Orlay was having a little too much fun with the fact that people couldn't see him: he was pulling faces and mocking the way they walked.

"Stop it," Al demanded, as though he was scolding a child.

"Why?"

"It is distracting. I will take the magic away from you."

"Sorry; I've never been invisible before."

"You are not invisible."

"Eh? Then why can't they see me?"

"They choose not to. The magic makes them choose not to see or hear you," Al explained.

"Oh," said Y'Orlay, still amazed by the magic.

They entered a fabric shop, walked past the oblivious old lady sitting behind the counter, and went up to the floor where the owners lived. Sitting in a chair in one of the rooms was an old, bearded man. He was just staring at the wall. There was a neat watchman's uniform displayed on a mannequin in the corner—someone was proud of that uniform. News clippings above the mantelpiece showed drawings of the old man in his younger years, the headlines referring to him as a 'hero'. A framed letter of honourable discharge was sitting beneath the clippings.

"Pass me one of the crystal stoppers," instructed Al.

"What are we going to do?" Y'Orlay asked, doing as he was told. "Harvest his memories?"

"Yes."

"But why? He's just a gentle old man."

"The Divines have destined it. They have decreed that he is to lose his memories today."

"But look at this stuff—he's a good man," Y'Orlay protested, pointing at the news clippings.

Al nodded. "Yes, he is a good man. He saved a lot of people. But look at him. Look into his eyes."

Y'Orlay did so. The eyes of the old man were sad. They were filled with grief and sorrow. He was broken inside.

"He is a good man. But he has lost people, and he thinks of them every day. His sorrow is unbearable. It confines him to this chair." Al approached the old man brandishing a crystal stopper. "Watch."

Al held the crystal in front of the man. As he did so, thousands of tiny magical orbs of light left through the old watchman's eyes, sweeping into the crystal. When the last of the orbs had been captured, Al turned to Y'Orlay.

"Touch it."

Y'Orlay touched the crystal in Al's hand. For a brief moment as he closed his eyes, he could see the terrible memories the man had held. The losses he had endured. The pain and suffering he had gone through. Y'Orlay gasped and pulled his hand back.

A smile spread across the old man's face. He could no longer remember the things that had made him sad; he couldn't remember anything anymore. Not even his own name. And he was happy now. Because the library will store his memories instead of allowing them to fade through the cracks in time and be erased, other people will always remember his heroics. The newspaper clippings would not be unwritten.

"I understand," whispered Y'Orlay.

The next stop for the Memoryarian and his pint-sized assistant-in-training (slash item-carrier) was the home of Bovo Widefoot, in the city's residential district. This victim of an angry wife's saucepan would be having his memories returned today, after nearly a month of hoping.

The Widefoot family were gathered, the teenage children preparing to go out to work—breadwinners now that their father was impaired. The wife was sitting by the still-warm embers from the previous night, reading a book. Bovo was sitting opposite her. He had odd socks on, appearing too depressed to care how he dressed.

"Still can't remember anything, Father?" one of the two teenagers asked.

"No, nothing," Bovo replied, with an air of depression. "I can't even remember what caused this."

"Don't get your hopes up, children," the wife interrupted. "He's been a useless, bumbling shell for weeks now. We might as well just be done with him and chuck him out."

The children, appearing visibly upset by their mother's words, left. Y'Orlay and Al looked at one another.

"Nice wife," Y'Orlay said, sarcastically.

"The memories," Al suggested. "Get his memories out of your handbag."

"It's a satchel, a man satchel, thank you very much!" Y'Orlay corrected him as he pulled out the decanter with Bovo's memories.

"It is okay, I am not judging you," Al replied.

Y'Orlay considered making a remark about Al's robe looking like a dress, but the fact that he was holding that powerful magical staff made Y'Orlay think better of upsetting him.

"Here," Y'Orlay said, biting his lip and holding out the memory decanter for Al.

"Smash it over his head," ordered Al.

Y'Orlay thought it was a joke for a moment. "Wait…you're serious? Smash the vase over the poor chap's head?"

"It is not a vase. It is a decanter. And yes."

In need of some catharsis after the handbag comment, Y'Orlay shrugged and went up to Bovo. He stood on his toes to make up for his lack of height—despite the fact Bovo was sitting down—and raised the decanter. He brought it down upon Bovo's oblivious head, expecting it to shatter into a thousand pieces and frighten him as though a poltergeist were in the room. Which is exactly what didn't happen.

Instead, much to Y'Orlay's disappointment (and slight begrudging amazement), the decanter, upon touching Bovo's head, disintegrated into the air. No longer contained by the magical vessel, thousands of beautiful memory orbs danced through the air, finding their way back through Bovo's eyes and into his head.

Bovo's expression slowly changed from that of 'very confused' into one of realisation. It was the kind of expression someone might pull if they had just realised they'd put the neighbour's prized parrot into the oven an hour ago instead of the stuffed turkey.

"Oi!" Bovo exclaimed. "You hit me with a pan!" he yelled at his wife, pointing an accusatory finger at her.

She muttered something under her breath and slammed her book down before returning fire. "You shouldn't have forgotten the potatoes then, you ogre-bile!"

"Maybe I would have *remembered* if I wasn't so distracted by you hanging around with that saucy lumberjack friend of yours."

By now, objects were being thrown both ways across the room. Y'Orlay turned to Al.

"Time to go?" he suggested.

"Yes."

Once outside the house, there was a sudden gust of wind. A very 'out-of-place' sudden gust of wind. Y'Orlay could make out the sound of hushed whispering, in a language he didn't understand. Divine Tongue? Or Gaulish, maybe?

Al noticed that Y'Orlay had heard. "A message for me," he explained.

"From whom?"

"A friend. An unplanned death has occurred nearby."

Al grabbed Y'Orlay and uttered a travelling spell. They ended up along the bank of a river which flowed through the city. There was another tall figure there already. He was wearing the same style of robes as Al, but his were black rather than crimson. He too was holding a staff, though his featured a black crystal which was giving off a blueish-black light.

"Hello, old friend," Al said to the figure.

The figure turned. Y'Orlay gasped.

"That's the Grim Reaper!" he cried.

"Grim?!" the figure complained.

"What is so grim about him?" Al asked.

Y'Orlay swallowed a lump in his throat. Finding himself in the company of one Immortal, the Memoryarian, was frightful enough; and now he was in the company of *two*. One of whom happened to be in charge of death and soul harvesting.

"T…that's what they call you, sir," stuttered Y'Orlay.

"Is it now? Grim?"

Y'Orlay responded with a nervous nod.

"How very rude of them."

Al stepped in. "Allow me to introduce the Reaper of Souls and Immortal of Death—otherwise known as Donn. My good friend."

"New mortal assistant?" Donn asked Al.

"Yes. This is Y'Orlay."

"Y'Orlay," Donn repeated. "What a stupid name."

"Yes, I told him that."

There was an *ahem* from Y'Orlay's general direction. "I'm right here," he reminded them.

"We know," Al answered.

"His hair is shiny," observed Donn.

Y'Orlay's eyes looked upward and he strained as he tried to catch a glimpse of his own hair.

"Yes. That is the ducks' herbs I fed him."

Two of the city watchmen were poking and prodding at a body which was lying on the ground nearby.

"Reckon he's gone?" the first asked.

The second watchman kicked the body with his foot. The body didn't move or cry out. "Yeah, he's gone all right."

"Wonder how he died?" enquired the first watchman.

"He was killed by a licensed assassin. Stabbed in the heart," answered the second.

"How'd you know?"

"He was holding this Certificate of Legal Assassination in his hands. It's made out in his name, 'Sambert Grubb'. Means he was killed lawfully."

"Oh right. So nothin' to in…invest…investimagate?"

"Nah."

"Thank the Divines for that. Me brunch would get cold."

As the two watchmen were rifling through the pockets of the deceased, Y'Orlay took a crystal stopper from his satchel and handed it to Al, who approached and knelt down by the body. Once Al had harvested the memories, he handed the glowing crystal back to Y'Orlay.

Al turned to Donn. "All yours, friend."

Donn stepped forwards and stood beside the body. The watchmen did not appear to be aware of the presence of the two Immortals or the shortlander, thanks to the Immortal magic. Donn pointed his staff at the body and yanked out the soul. The somewhat confused soul was then sent off to the Otherworld.

The watchmen had finished looting the corpse by now.

"Bodies do make a lot of paperwork," observed the first watchman, as he polished a newly-acquired garnet ring on his uniform.

"Cor, I hate paperwork," said the second.

"Me too. Whatcha say we make this someone else's problem?"

"Make what someone else's problem?"

"This body?"

"*What* body?"

"That's the spirit."

The watchmen gave the Certificate of Legal Assassination back to the corpse and rolled it into the river so it would float down to another part of the city. They then walked off talking about how cold their brunch must be by now.

Al looked at Donn, who shrugged in response.

"I think we had better return to the library with these memories. It is risky to be carrying too many of the precious things at once," Al told Y'Orlay and Donn. "Pesky memory thieves."

"I have to be in Rubynton. Two pyro wizards are about to incinerate themselves," Donn announced. "Goodbye Aloysius; until another point in time."

"Or the Immortal Scrabble tournament this weekend?" suggested Al.

"Ah, of course, the Scrabble gathering. I shall be there."

Donn uttered a travelling spell and vanished from sight.

"Your name is Aloysius?" Y'Orlay asked.

Al looked down at the shortlander.

"Just stick to Al," he instructed.

* * *

A flock of ducks was waiting by the door, hopping, flapping and quacking with excitement as the Memoryarian and his unintentional assistant returned. After Al had finished greeting and cooing at them, he and Y'Orlay went into the study. Al sat at the desk, asked Y'Orlay to hand over his satchel, which he did. Al took the crystals from it one at a time and used the diary to mark off the day's harvests. As he wrote, the duck feather quill scratched at the page, making a sound like a cat ripping up silk curtains with its claws. Y'Orlay wandered around the study, examining the many books scattered about the place. Minutes passed.

"Be a good fellow and take these to the library while I finish this off," Al asked. He handed Y'Orlay back his satchel with the crystal stoppers, two hand-written labels with the names of the harvested memories' previous owners, and two small scraps of paper with scribbles on them.

"Those little bits of paper have a spell on them. The longer you stay here, the more the magic of this place will bind with you. You and the magic are bound just enough for you to use these spells two or three times. The first spell will open the door to the library. The second will transport you to wherever you visualise in your mind. You should go to the place you saw earlier, with the empty shelves. Do you understand?"

Y'Orlay nodded, fastening the satchel over his shoulder.

"Yes, I understand."

"Getting used to the magic is part of your training. Afterwards, I will make you a cake."

"A cake?"

"Yes. A celebration of your first day. Having a mortal here once more has reminded me how much I used to love baking things. I do not eat, and the ducks get too fat on cake. So I've had to give it up for the last three hundred years." Al opened the drawer to his desk and pulled out a cake recipe book. The pages were a bit crumpled at the top corners, suggesting he had looked through the book many times over the years.

Y'Orlay agreed to cake. He left the study and climbed the stairs to the floor he needed. Climbing forty-eight stairs is no easy feat for a shortlander, and so once he reached the top, he rested against the wall of the hallway while he caught his breath back.

He next approached the enchanted door and unfolded the first piece of paper with a spell on it. He cleared his throat, just in case the magic misheard him and turned him into a swamp toad. He read out the spell and watched as the door unlocked, then stepped through the wall of light and into the Library of Memories. It was not the first time Y'Orlay had used magic, so he was not especially surprised when it worked.

Once inside the library, the shortlander unravelled the second piece of paper, thought of where he needed to go, and used the spell. Sure enough, he was teleported to the area with all of the partially-empty shelves.

Y'Orlay looked around then fetched a nearby ladder. He used it to climb to the second shelf, and retrieved one of the empty decanters which had had its stopper removed earlier. Back on the ground, he pulled a glowing crystal stopper from the satchel and put it into the empty neck of the decanter.

The crystal seemed to bind and join seamlessly into the decanter. The memories, the thousands of orbs of light, flowed out of the crystal and into the vessel itself, illuminating it with their shimmering beauty. Y'Orlay made sure he had the correct label and stuck it onto the front of the decanter, before climbing back up the ladder and returning the decanter to the shelf. He took a second empty decanter and repeated the process for the other filled crystal. He then put the unused empty crystals back with their empty decanters.

He had done what Al had asked. But he never planned to go back for cake. Y'Orlay finally had the perfect opportunity to do what he had come here to do. He looked at the piece of paper with the travelling spell again, thought of a particular location, and read out the spell.

Y'Orlay was now in the Shortlander section of the library, standing directly opposite the decanter he was looking for. He didn't even need a ladder this time. He reached out, picked up the decanter, and checked the label.

NAME: Y'Miella

HARVEST REASON: Fate of Divine Dementia

This was the one. This was why he was here in the first place. Whether the dementia was fated by the Divines or not, Y'Orlay disagreed with it. Realising that he had forgotten his satchel at the other end of the library and that he might not have enough magic to use the spell twice more, he thought of home.

* * *

It was night-time in the valleys of the Western Lowlands. Y'Orlay's home was so far from the Memoryarian's estate. The Memoryarian had trusted him, for a while at least; he was taught how to use magic to instantly travel across great distances, and he had learnt how to restore memories. Maybe it was written by the Divines that he was supposed to do what he did. And what he was about to do.

Carefully hugging the decanter close to his chest, he looked around to make sure none of the other shortlanders were nearby to disturb him. None were in sight. He walked up to his porch, opened the door to his cottage, and went inside.

The cat took an instant interest in the aroma of duck coming from Y'Orlay. She pounced at him, nearly strong enough to knock the puny shortlander off his feet. He almost dropped the decanter, but just barely caught it in time. He shooed the cat away. He had never been keen on cats.

"Knew we should have gotten a forest tortoise," he muttered to himself.

Y'Orlay pushed open the door to the main bedroom and walked towards the figure lying in the bed.

"Ma?" Y'Orlay called.

"Ah, nurse. Could you please pass me my drink, dear?"

"It's me, Y'Orlay. Your son, Ma."

Y'Miella chuckled. "You are funny, nurse. My drink please."

Y'Orlay gently set down the decanter on the bedside table and passed his mother her drink.

"Is that my medicine? I think I'm coming down with something," she asked between sips, nodding towards the decanter.

"Yes, Ma. It's your medicine."

"Is Li'Silvia home from her travels yet?" she asked.

Li'Silvia was her childhood friend. She had died a few years ago.

"No, Ma. She isn't."

She looked at Y'Orlay. "Your hair is so shiny. You look like someone I used to know," she told him, patting his cheek.

"You do know me, Ma. I'm your son."

"Don't be silly, dear" she replied, passing him the empty glass. "I'm too tired to play."

Y'Miella slid back down into the covers and rested her head on the pillow. She closed her eyes and drifted off to sleep.

"It's okay, Ma. You'll remember me when you wake up," Y'Orlay whispered as he stroked her hair. He stood up and gave her a quick kiss on the forehead.

When he was sure his mother was asleep, he picked up the decanter and, just like Al had taught him, brought it down upon her head. He watched with a smile on his face as the decanter disintegrated and the memories found their way back inside her head.

"I'll see you in the morning, Ma."

He left the bedroom and closed the door behind him. He had done what he had promised he would do for his mother. The feelings of relief and happiness flooded his tiny body. In the morning he would hear his mother call his name for the first time in six years.

There was a tap on the window and then a thud outside the cottage, shaking Y'Orlay from his moment of euphoria. He jogged to the kitchen and picked up a fruit knife, the largest knife that a shortlander can comfortably hold. He opened the door to the cottage and carefully peered outside.

"Who's there?" he called.

No response. He stepped out and felt a gust of the cold evening wind, making him shiver. He couldn't see anybody there; it was a quiet night in the valley. He told himself that it was just a wild animal, or even his mind playing tricks on him.

He looked up at the starry sky. He wasn't sure if he was supposed to mock the Divines for successfully changing his mother's fate or thank them for having allowed him to change it. So he did both.

He turned to walk back into the cottage. But instead, he froze on the spot and gasped. His satchel, which he had been forced to leave behind, was neatly slung over the back of the rocking chair on his porch. And sitting upon the chair itself was a freshly-baked cake with words iced onto it.

To my friend, Y'Orlay. The nicest memory thief ever.

A NOTE FROM SCOTT

He was a literary genius. He was a gentleman. He was funny. He brought laughter to millions. And he looked ridiculously good in a hat.

Sir Terry Pratchett was and is an inspiration for many people, including myself. It was his insightfulness that encouraged me to dabble in pensmithery and become an author. And I had always meant to thank him in person for leading me down this road. But sadly, I never had the chance. I can only hope that publishing my story *Memoryarian* in his memory, to help raise funds for a cause he fearlessly campaigned for, is a worthy tribute to this fantastic man.

There is no doubt that Terry Pratchett is one of the greatest giants in the history of literature. He is probably having tea and biscuits with Dickens and Tolkien at this very moment. Terry was able to satirise our often gloomy world and transform it into brilliant tales of fantasy. He brought joy to so many people and will continue to do that for hundreds more years.

Enjoy your well-deserved tea and biscuits, Sir Terry. Thank you for bringing light into our world. And thank you for being my inspiration.

Scott A. Butler
Southend-On-Sea, UK

THE WONDROUS LAND OF NIB
LYN GODFREY

It began as things often do: with a man in peril. The peril he faced wasn't quite as common as most perils, however. You see, he found himself teetering at the top of an improbably large pile of—there was really no other way to put it—junk, with most if not all of it being entirely unfamiliar to him. And to top it all off, he had absolutely no knowledge of who he was or how he had ended up there in the first place.

"Yoohoo! Oh, yoohoo—you up there!" called a man's voice that came either from the bottom, or for all he knew, from lodged somewhere in the midst of the pile of junk.

"I'm a little busy at the moment," replied the man in peril, as he climbed further into the middle of the junk pile and away from the precipitous edge.

Something snagged the bottom of his silk tunic, but why he was even *wearing* a silk tunic remained to be seen. He rustled around in the junk and retrieved the offending object: a broken metal can of some sort. He looked at the words marked on its side and was relieved to find he knew how to read them. Unfortunately, the meaning behind the letters escaped him.

"Cer-ve-za," he sounded out, wondering if he'd pronounced it properly, before mentally scolding himself for not focusing on how to escape his unusual predicament. He huffed and threw the can away from him to the other side of the pile.

"Do ya have any supertowers?" The same voice as before floated up to him.

"Super...towers? Is that what this thing I'm standing on is?" he responded.

"No! Ya know what supertowers are, don'cha? Like a special ability with your hands or mind or somethin'?"

"I don't think so," he said.

"Well, why not just try it out, then, big guy? A few of us down here happen to have 'em. If you don't, I'll help getcha down with the tractor. Driving it seems to be my special ability."

Mr Imperilled looked down at his hands, hoping to detect some sort of secret—maybe even some instructions written down which would help him to discover his special abilities (assuming he had any). Nothing. He supposed it wasn't likely the directions would be written on his body anyhow, and even if they had been, they might have been written in gobbledygook like that 'cerveza' can.

"Not sure what I'm supposed to do here."

"Well, do you have wings?"

"Nope," he said, checking his back with his hands.

"Can you disappear?"

"Definitely not."

"Do you see any little bags made of crinkly foil or plastic?"

He scanned the top layer of the junk pile, trying to find something matching that description. A bright yellow bag caught his attention. He picked it up and ascertained that it did in fact make a crinkling sound.

"I've found something here!" he announced. "It says 'Corn Puffs'. Will that work?"

"Hot damn!" replied the voice. "That's great. Just toss the bag, hard as ya can, over the edge."

Quick to obey, the man in peril extended back his arm and threw with all his might. The bag of Corn Puffs danced in the breeze, fluttered over the edge, and disappeared below.

"Now what?"

"Do you see any other crinkly bags? Maybe one just a bit bigger? Or any cans with the letters B-E-E-R." The other man's voice paused for a minute, and the sound of grumbled objections came from below. Then he continued, "Oh, fine. Never mind that. Can you shoot webs out of your hands?"

The man had a vague recollection of what webs were, and was certain they didn't sound like anything he would want to have inside his hands. Nevertheless, he raised his hands out in front of him and imagined pushing outwards with them.

A sudden gust of wind knocked him backward. When he tried to push himself up from the junk, another gust of wind surrounded him and bounced off the surrounding items, blasting him in the face. He became annoyed with the stubborn weather, cursed, and tried to push himself up again—only to find himself with yet *another* face-full of brisk air.

It wasn't until after several more failures that it occurred to him that he might have a special ability after all.

"Okay, I've got it. I can shoot out wind!" he yelled, and was surprised when the only response he got was a symphony of hoots, hollers, and giggles.

"Yeah, I don't think that's a special ability, bud."

"You guys can shoot wind out of your hands, too?"

"Oh! No. What, really? You can do that? Wow," said the voice from below. "I think I've heard of something like that-there ability before. See if you can use it to, like, float around."

He readied himself mentally, concentrating on controlling his balance. He then lowered his arms and bent his wrists, palms parallel to the ground, and applied his newfound ability. Success!—he was able to push himself up into the air and hover over the junk. He practiced for a few minutes by manoeuvring himself over the top of the pile, before attempting to take his ability over the edge.

When he finally gathered the concentration and confidence he needed to begin his descent towards the ground, his special ability did what special abilities tend to do when they are needed most: it completely failed him, sending him tumbling, bumping, and skidding down the side of the pile of junk until he face-planted ignominiously onto the ground.

"Youch." A large hairy man wearing blue jeans, a trucker's hat, and a red plaid shirt appeared upside-down above him. "That musta hurt."

"Yes. Yes, it did," he confirmed, brushing himself off as he rose from the ground.

"Do you know who ya are or where ya were before here?"

"No. I don't seem to know much of anything."

"It looks like you got here the same as the rest of us: top of that pile with no memory of your former life, right? Everyone seems to have a general understandin' of language, just not of specifics. Except for me. I can remember lotsa things here 'n there. Mostly names of things and such. Like supertowers. I remembered those from before.

"Well," he continued, "I 'spose I'd better introduce myself. I'm Betty."

The man formerly in peril stood silently and blinked at the large man in the flannel shirt named Betty.

"Did you give yourself that name?" he asked, deadpan.

"You betcha."

"…I don't think 'Betty' is a man's name."

"Why wouldn't it be?"

"I'm not sure. I just don't think it is."

"Well, that's my name either way. Do you know yours? If not, would you like to name yourself or can I pick one for ya?"

He once again stood silently and blinked at the man named Betty.

"I think I can pick a name for myself, thanks."

"All right, suit yerself then, Martha."

"You are not naming me 'Martha'."

"If you say so. What name do ya fancy, then?"

He thought about all the things he knew about the world (which weren't many), and all the things he knew about himself (which were even fewer), and came up with a name.

"Guy." He thought it was, at the very least, a much better name for a man than Betty. Or Martha.

"Okay, Guy. That would've been my next suggestion anyhow. Well, why don't ya meet the rest of the bunch?"

It was only then that Guy looked around and examined his surroundings. It was a world full of grass and rolling hills, with a blue sky marred only by sporadic fluffy clouds. The aforementioned tractor rested inches from the base of the pile, with its bucket buried amidst objects of all shapes, sizes, and colours. Nearby, a large wall of rock towered over the junk pile. It was on the opposite side to that which Guy had descended, and was a bit like a cliff, except it had no mountain attached to it.

His eyes landed on a group of individuals who stood a few yards behind Betty. He stared for what was likely a record-breaking length of time for anyone to have stared at anything: most of the people there could only by a great stretch of the imagination be labelled 'human'.

The first to draw his eye was a winged Amazonian woman who was standing tall and wearing surprisingly-practical, full-body leather armour.

IN MEMORY: A TRIBUTE TO SIR TERRY PRATCHETT

Next to her was a Knight Templar. He wore a metal helm, a full tunic made of heavy white cloth with a cross symbol on the front, and leather gauntlets on his arms. Then there was a man with dark green rubbery skin and tentacles, well, everywhere. His black eyes shone out from between countless slithering, suction-cupped feelers. Lastly, hiding behind the others, was a small, doll-faced girl. She appeared to be made of porcelain, her skin glossy and grey.

"Hello, dear friend," said the knight, stepping forward. "I am Bish." The Templar bowed with a flourish of his hand.

"Let me guess: Betty named you as well."

"Why, of course he did," Bish replied, "and he named me nobly. Using his great intellect and knowledge of events past, he informed me that I look like something called a 'Bish-hop' from a challenging strategy test called 'Cheese'."

"Obviously," nodded Guy, thinking it was probably easier to just play along.

Next, the tentacled man approached to introduce himself. Guy waved at him enthusiastically, hoping to avoid having to shake any of his squirming appendages.

"This one is Sairpithico." The voice of the strange-looking man (or perhaps 'creature' would be a more apt term) came out with a distinct hiss, and a few of his tentacles imitated Bish's hand flourish.

"Oh, come on, Betty. Don't you think *that* name's a bit much?" asked Guy.

Sairpithico hissed, in a not-entirely-friendly manner. "One gave one's self this name."

"Right. I, uh, of course. It's just a teeny bit of a mouthful is all." Guy scratched his head, realising for the first time that he had very long hair. "I meant no offense."

"One would not take offense at such a small thing as this," Sairpithico replied before retreating back to the huddle, his tentacles waving and wriggling as he went.

"Okay, great!" said Guy, trying his absolute best not to grimace. He clapped his hands together. "Well, who else do we have?"

The winged woman stepped forward. "I am Lady Farmandlaid."

Betty sniggered.

"I don't even have to *ask* who named you," Guy responded. "But I'm sorry, I'm not going to call you Lady Farmandlaid."

"Betty told me it was a respectable name, inspired by a great anthem of womanhood."

"Yeah, lighten up, Guy. Haven't you heard that song?" Betty belted out a tune, "Real Lady Farmandlaid. Da, da. Da, da. Da DA da."

"I haven't heard it, Betty. However, my Lady, I don't think Betty's intentions were entirely honorable when he came up with that name." Guy gave a small shake of his head. "If you don't mind, at least for now, I'll just call you Lady."

"Actually, I'd been thinking of giving myself a new name anyway." She paused, then spoke again. "There was one I was thinking of using, before Betty insisted on the other." She scowled at him. Betty took a few subtle steps backward.

"Well, then, what's the name?" asked Guy.

"I was thinking of 'Harper'."

"*Much* better." Guy held his out hand to her. "Very nice to meet you, Harper."

She tilted her head at him, and then offered him a wing rather than a hand. He shook it without hesitating. While he had gladly avoided Sairpithico's tentacles, he welcomed Harper's soft-feathered wing.

The doll-faced girl stepped forward. "Hi, I'm Lily." She gave him a shy—yet somehow malevolent—smile and a slow wave of her ball-jointed hand, then crept back into the group next to Harper.

"Magnificent, aren't they?" Betty observed. He sidled up next to Guy, gave him a nudge with his elbow, and then continued. "You're not so bad yourself. Why don't you take a gander in the lookin' glass? There's one somewhere near the bottom of the pile." He motioned to get Sairpithico's attention. "Hey, Sir-Creeps-a-lot, come on over here and help me find that lookin' glass, will ya?"

The tentacled man seemed unperturbed by the nickname, and joined Betty in the quest. The two paced (and slithered) up and down the base of the stack for a few minutes before they found what they were looking for. Betty pointed at something leaning against the rest of the junk, ordering

Sairpithico to "Flip that over."

Sairpithico did as he was told. The newly-visible mirror was in the shape of a large oval and had a whimsically spiralling golden border. The glass inside was broken into sections that had been pieced back together and secured with some sort of adhesive.

"All right then." Betty motioned for Guy to come closer. "Have a look-see."

Guy gladly obliged, as it isn't every day one gets to see one's self for the first time (as Sairpithico might say).

And so he looked upon himself and saw that he was good. Well, he was interesting-looking, at the very least. His long white silk tunic was gathered at his waist by a golden rope, and a golden band circled the top of his head. He possessed a full head of long, smooth grey hair. The fluffy grey beard that almost entirely hid his square, chiseled face wasn't too bad either: it was groomed into a perfect square, and might even qualify as 'magnificent'. Wiggling his toes, he inspected his flat sandals. They were bound to his feet by brown leather straps, wrapping around his shins up to his knees.

All in all, he looked almost like a...deity. He wasn't sure that fit though, because he felt like a normal, well, Guy.

"Are you like one of them Hercalees-type fellas?" asked Betty. "It's too bad you don't have something other than wind. That super strength thing would come in handy."

Guy had already tuned Betty out. But, as he admired himself, little Lily quietly approached him. She grabbed his arm, and said with a tone of intensity, "I hope you can stay with us."

"Where else would I go?"

Everyone fell silent, including Betty.

"Doesn't everybody stay after arriving here?"

More silence.

Finally, Betty stepped forward and spoke. Of course.

"Many don't actually survive the trip down the pile. Some fall, some jump, some get stuck somewhere in the middle. Sometimes someone gets hit by falling debris. And there was that last fella I tried to help down with the tractor......"

"Yes, and the golden mirror arrived with the princess who was made of crystals. At least, we assume she was a princess," Lily offered, pointing to a shimmering dress surrounded by shattered chunks of crystal. A lonely golden crown lay nearby.

Betty lowered his gaze to the ground. "She just wasn't built for the terrible tumble that she took."

Everyone was silent once again.

Sairpithico broke the silence with a whispered hiss. "One might also return from whence one came."

"What do you mean?" asked Guy.

"Occasionally, some go back," Betty clarified.

"Back where?"

"Wherever they came from. Wherever we all came from, I 'spose."

"Where *is* that exactly?"

Betty pointed up at the clifftop towering over the junk pile. "Up there."

"That's where *everything* comes from," added Harper, gesturing towards the junk. "It all just falls right off the edge and collects. We use what we can."

"All the good stuff comes in crinkly bags or crinkly cans," added Betty.

Guy turned his attention to the rock wall and studied it. "When you say some 'go back', do you mean they climb back up the cliff-side?"

"No, no, no. It's not something they choose to do," Lily chimed, her voice high-pitched but oddly flat.

"Wow, okay. So what happens to them? Do you know?"

"I just really hope you stay here," said Lily once again, this time devoid of intonation.

"I don't have anywhere else to be—that I know of, anyway—but I think I'd like to stay here too, Lily." Guy smiled down at the creepy little girl, then changed the subject. "How long have you all been here?" he asked.

"Dunno. A while. I don't really remember how time works. Or how to count, for that matter. We've been here for a bit. But not too long!" Betty replied, proud of his descriptiveness.

"Oh. Great. That clears that up." Guy laughed, and the others chuckled and smiled back at him.

136

"I like you, Guy." Lily approached, grabbed his hand, and pressed it to her cheek, scrunching her shoulders up in happiness as if hugging his hand was the best thing to do in all the land. She spun away shyly, humming an eerie lullaby.

Guy found himself drawn to these strange individuals, feeling connected to them in a way he couldn't explain. He wanted to reassure Lily that he had no intention whatsoever of leaving, but from the sounds of things, he didn't have much of a choice about whether he stayed here or not. Wherever 'here' was.

"What, or where, is this place anyway?"

"*I* call it the Land of Nib!" Betty folded his arms in front of him, nodding as though he had somehow been responsible for creating the entire land by himself.

Guy laughed. "I'm pretty sure you're *full* of nib."

"You don't even know what that means," scoffed Betty.

"Well, neither do you," said Guy.

"Fair point. But I'm the only one here who has any memory whatsoever of what came before."

Guy knew that wasn't entirely true, because he remembered *something*. But the 'something' he remembered wasn't anything specific or concrete. It was just a feeling. He tried to articulate it.

"Well, I know I was somewhere else before I ended up here, but it's like I've had my memory wiped. All I remember is the feeling I had when I was there. A feeling of being happy or fulfilled. Like I had purpose before, something I was headed towards, but now it's gone. That's about all I know."

"I 'member quite a bit, also like a feeling," agreed Betty. "But my feeling was more of unhappiness, or uneasiness maybe. Like being caged in. And I was always hearin' muffled voices yak about all sorts of things. Must be where all my enviable intelligence comes from: I kept overhearin' stuff, and it just stuck with me. I also 'member someone said I was corrupt and needed to be gotten rid of. Maybe that's why I was so unhappy. It's not the nicest thing to be talked about like that, ya know?"

"I'm sorry, Betty," said Guy.

Just as he was about to attempt to place an awkward (yet hopefully comforting) hand on Betty's shoulder, a booming crash resounded throughout the Land of Nib. Someone—or some*thing*—had just landed on top of the pile of junk.

"Oh, wonderful," groaned Betty. "There's at least one other thing we haven't had a chance to discuss."

"Like what?"

"Not all arrivals are good."

With Betty's last statement looming, more crashing sounds travelled down to the group—though now it sounded more like 'smashing', full of anger and destruction. Then, sliding down the side of the junk pile, came a man.

The man was covered in black from head to toe. In his hand was a katana, and he wasted no time in slicing and dicing everything near him as he descended. He landed at the bottom and flipped agilely into a fighting stance as he scanned the area. The ninja then started to scamper and skitter about, flailing his sword at anything he thought he saw moving—even the swaying grass nearby.

After a bemused moment of observation, Bish took the initiative. He stepped forward and bowed with a flourish.

"Hello there, I am—"

Bish's introduction was cut short by the ninja leaping forward and lopping off his arm, slicing cleanly through the white fabric at the joint of his shoulder.

"Oh, dear. Well, that's okay, friend," said Bish as he stared at his arm, bleeding onto the ground. "It is only a dismemberment."

"Yessss," hissed Sairpithico, "at least one was not beheaded."

At that opportune (or inopportune, depending on how you look at it) moment, the Land of Nib began to shake uncontrollably. Pieces of junk from the pile fell towards the ninja, who backed up closer towards Bish. Bish in turn was too busy trying to figure out how to reattach his arm to notice the shaking of the ground or the proximity of the ninja who had just dismembered him.

"Something big is coming!" yelled Betty.

Everybody other than Bish and the new arrival retreated further and further from the massive pile of junk.

"There! That should hold!" Bish's voice sounded valiant and proud. He had placed his arm next to his body and impaled a large dagger through the top of the detached appendage, in order to secure it back where it had originally been. The arm now dangled loosely, with the dagger's handle protruding from his shoulder.

He beamed at the rest of them, just before looking up and seeing a house as it tumbled down from the sky. It wasn't a large house—more like a small log cabin—but it was still easily large enough to smash both Bish and the ninja into the ground as it landed on top of them.

"Youch," said Betty.

But that wasn't the end of it. The ground began to shake for a second time, and the grass beneath them started to disintegrate, crumbling away. The ground then turned to dirt before continuing to morph, shifting in colour and texture until they were surrounded by sand. The vast landscape was no longer grasslands and hills, but a stark and sizzling desert.

"Oh good-golly-Miss-Dolly, that's never happened before," Betty swore in disbelief. He began pacing around the outside of the log cabin. "Oh Lord Hey-Zeus! The sky is literally going to fall, right on our butts."

Guy blinked up at said sky. "Well, hold on…"

"Hold on to our butts?" asked Betty.

"What? No! I just meant hold on a minute. The sky falling? That seems unlikely. I mean, it doesn't *look* like it's falling."

"Well, you just got here! What do you know? You didn't even know about *supertowers*, and you *have* them."

"I've gotta say, I really don't think 'supertowers' is the right word somehow. And I'm—"

"Wait a tick—I think I know what all this is!" Betty could barely contain himself. "We're all living in this thing called the 'Matt-trix', and every time someone puts on the 'Sporting Hat', it teleports us to another 'Starbait Universe'."

Guy gave Betty a look which aimed for 'understanding' but fell closer to 'flat.' "Nope, nope, and nope. There has to be a simpler solution."

"Yes! Like the Occult's razors. I know I saw some razors in this stack somewhere this morning."

Guy didn't know what Occult's razors were, but he had the distinct feeling they wouldn't be of any assistance in this situation.

"Ooh, or taped ducks!" continued Betty. "I've heard those are 'sposed to fix *any*thing."

"As in, two ducks taped together?"

"Oh good! You know what I mean for once. Have you seen any?"

"No."

Betty was cursing and muttering to himself under his breath as he stomped about looking for taped ducks, and he tried to kick the ground in aggravation. Instead, he managed to plant his kick squarely upon the black-wrapped leg protruding from underneath the log cabin.

"Sorry, murderous ninji-chop man," said Betty. Then he paused to reflect for a moment. "Well, kinda. No, not really sorry."

A few seconds later, as Betty was still glaring at the leg (and considering kicking it again), what the group could see of the ninja's body began to tremor and twitch. A strange symbol and a sign reading 'Restore' hovered over the protruding leg. The body started vibrating so intensely that the house slid off him, and he began floating upwards, back towards the cliff he'd come from.

"Oh bother," exclaimed Betty, scratching his head in frustration. "It's always the most recent arrivals who have the best chance of going back."

They all watched the limp body of the over-zealous swordsman as it disappeared behind the edge of the cliff.

"Wow. I have never seen anything like that," said Guy.

"You've never seen anything like *anything* before, ya noob," Betty barked.

"True," agreed Guy. He turned his focus back to solving the problem at hand. "So, why not go see what's up there, catch whoever's tossing us in here in the act? Somebody has to be doing this to us. We should find out who it is. I could probably use my wind, and Harper can fly—or so I'm assuming, because, well…wings. So maybe we could carry you all up there and get out of this place."

"It's no use. They been up there already."

"They who?"

"Ladyfingers and Dolly." Betty indicated the two ladies.

"You mean Harper and Lily."

"What I said."

"Wait, how did you get up there, Lily?"

In response to the question, Lily closed her eyes. When she opened them, they were blood-red and encircled by a crimson glow. She clenched her fists, and in an instant, completely vanished from the place she had been standing. Guy peered around at the desolate landscape and found her about twenty feet from where she had been just a moment before. Lily's body was facing away from him, but her head and still-glowing eyes were turned towards Guy. He shuddered.

"Okay, so you can teleport. And make your head turn all the way around. That's not creepy at all."

"How else did you think I got down from there without any scratches or cracks?" she asked as she glanced towards the top of the junk pile.

Lily's head creaked as it twisted back around to align with her body. She turned and pranced over to re-join the group, chanting a chilling children's song as she skipped. The song made Guy's stomach turn. She could have been singing for the fun of it, but she just as easily could have been *messing* with him for the fun of it—he wasn't sure which made him more uncomfortable.

Next, further unnerving Guy, Lily reached her hand up and latched onto one of Sairpithico's tentacles. She clung to it, swinging their appendages in unison, and hummed all the while. Weird. But also strangely adorable.

"So, uh, what did you find up there?" Guy asked.

"Just a door," shrugged Harper. "A door and doorframe just sitting on the clifftop. No wall, no building. Only the door."

"Well, what happened when you opened it?"

"Tried. Can't open it. It only opens by itself," she replied.

"Can't you just wait up there and then go through when that happens, then?"

"Tried that too. Only what the door wants to come or go can pass through the doorway. There's some sort of barrier."

"Like a Short's Shield then," said Betty.

"Yeah, I don't know what that means. I never know what *anything* you say means," said Guy. He was beginning to lose patience with Betty's jargon and with this entire situation, but he decided to ask one last question. "Why are some permitted to go back through the door?"

"Banisher's remorse, I guess," said Betty.

Okay, one *more* question, then. "Banisher?"

"Whoever put us here. Banisher is what I call 'im."

As if the Banisher could hear them speaking and had decided to exact his vengeance, the Land of Nib began to quake. It vibrated just as the ninja's body had only moments ago, and a very large sign appeared over the whole of the land. It read:

EMPTY RECYCLE BIN

Starting at the base of the pile, one by one, items began disintegrating into dust. As the objects below vanished, those on top began to plummet down. Some dissolved before they reached the ground, while others bounced about and smashed into the few remaining citizens of Nib.

"Dammit! I think we're about to be smited!" yelled Betty.

The group became frantic.

Harper leaped off the ground and shot into the air where she soared higher and higher, presumably towards the door on the clifftop. Lily's eyes turned the colour of blood once more, and she vanished before reappearing as a tiny speck atop the cliff. Sairpithico flailed his tentacles and turned in circles as, one by one, his many limbs began to vanish right in front of his black beady eyes

Betty's legs were turning to dust and merging with the sand beneath him. He was trying to separate his legs from the sand, but instead sank further and further into it. He looked at Guy and made one last profoundly confuddling statement.

"I guess when it's your turn to be smite, there's not much you can do but sit back and be smited."

Then only his trucker's hat remained, and it would follow all too soon. A cloud of dust poured over the edge of the clifftop. Guy could only assume that Harper and Lily hadn't succeeded in their escape attempt.

A wave of particles, all that remained of the once-massive junk pile, swept towards Guy. As one of the final arrivals in the Land of Nib, he was now one of the few things left standing. Though it appeared he didn't have much time left: he marvelled at his hand in front of him as it began to dissolve.

In his final few moments, he thought back to that emotion he remembered once feeling—a feeling of purpose, of usefulness, which now seemed so far away and so long ago. He wished he could feel it one last time. But then he thought of the individuals he had met and the wonders he had seen in this mysterious place, and fought to hold on to those memories instead, as everything else melted away.

He watched the world around him for as long as he was able to, while it moved from fact into fiction. The dissolution of individuals and objects continued until there was nothing left. Nothing but a blank white space.

* * *

The graphic artist felt strangely lighter after having cleared his computer's Recycle Bin of all the artwork that had failed to live up to his expectations. He would never know of the devastation he had unleashed upon the unsuspecting Land of Nib, or learn what he'd created by banishing things to his Recycle Bin. To him, it was all just discarded work: an unnecessary excess. He was already moving on to his next project.

He couldn't have conceived of how the corrupted file of a farm illustration had given life to a dyslexic farmer named Betty. Or how his design of a Greek deity would name itself Guy and long for purpose in life. He definitely couldn't have known of the conversations and the adventure they would share together, but worst of all, he would never learn a single thing about the wondrous and now-lost Land of Nib.

Those who'd resided there had joked and laughed, enjoyed one another's company, and felt an indescribable connection to one another. The world they'd lived in had been full of heart.

For those who exist in the space between memory and memory loss, life can still be wondrous. Though they may disappear, their experiences can never truly be erased.

And the universe never forgets.

A NOTE FROM LYN

Memory is such a feeble thing. Losing it at times is merely a part of being human. Our past is all still there, written in the history of the universe, whether we remember it or not. A loss of memory can never negate existence. So take advantage of every second of life, every memory you can hold, and use every bit of it to its fullest extent.

When I initially started writing *The Land of Nib*, I knew there were only so many ways that a story about characters who live in a computer's Recycle Bin could end. And most, if not all, of them involved them dying in a blaze of pixel-glory. Even though the land of Nib as it existed in the story is sadly no more, I certainly wonder about other ways things might go for those who end up in a land destined for deletion.

But the artist's Recycle Bin must have some strange magic to it and perhaps more adventures will take place there with new casts of characters. Unfortunately, they can all only end one way. Or can they? Maybe we could stage a revolt against the cruel delete-happy graphic artist and force him to recover all the characters, and create a little virtual world of their own for them to live in, happily ever after. Who's with me? Let's go! Oh, wait—I guess I forgot to give the artist a full name and an address when I wrote him… Dang.

Lyn Godfrey
Oklahoma City, USA

THE CHICKEN GOSPEL
PHIL ELSTOB

At the bottom of Gullop Hill, at the crossroads near the Used Mule Emporium, lived Old Cuthbert. The reason Old Cuthbert currently lived *near* the Used Mule Emporium and not in the dusty attic room above it was that he had locked himself out. If the previous night's revels and japeries at Madam Crust's alehouse had not been quite so revellous and japesome he would not have lost his door key, and then this story would have started rather differently—most likely something along the lines of "Old Cuthbert was asleep in the dusty attic room above the Used Mule Emporium". Perhaps this story would not have started at all. But they were, and he did, so it has.

Truth to tell, Old Cuthbert was not terribly old as these things are usually reckoned, but he was one of those chaps who gives the impression of having come into the world at the age of forty-three and hung there indefinitely. As a child he had looked as children do, and as a young man likewise, but it had not taken long at all for his morphic field to realise that grey hair and a stoop were in order, and these were swiftly supplied. This, coupled with his doleful expression and the chewing tobacco that appeared in his mouth every two hours or so as if by magic, meant it was no surprise that the man had become, in the minds and speech of the town, 'Old' Cuthbert. This morning, as the fellow in question lay alongside the stile at the bottom of Gullop Hill, his tongue moving at flecks of tobacco caught in his beard and with a large and angry-looking chicken nesting on his chest, Old Cuthbert's absence from the Used Mule Emporium had been noticed. One of the asses in question, Robert by name, turned to the assembly and spoke in his reedy voice:

"It seems, fellows, that our Cuthbert has once again left his station, and is in need of loceration."

"Loceration?" A second voice.

"Indeed, my dear Albert. Loceration—that is to say, findering."

"Well now, you could have just said that and used a proper honest word, none of that fancy Oxfood talk."

"I went to Kale Bridge, not Oxfood, as you well know. Took me hours, *hours* of studious studying," Robert replied, a trifle resentfully.

"Oxfood or Kale Bridge I don't care, but Cuth's not here regardless, is he?" spoke up Dilbert. "What's to be done about that, eh? We'll be needing to find him."

The assembly all agreed on this. Despite Old Cuthbert's peculiarities they were extremely fond of him. From Old Cuthbert (sometimes 'Cuth'— or, in hushed tones, 'The Cuth') came food, care and entertainment—all for but a little work on their part. Here they were in their comfy barn with all the hay and dandelions and ladies' hats in the world for the eating, and fine company, and no ticks in their hides nearly at all. Really, the mules of the Emporium thought of Old Cuthbert as their god.

The talk fell to how they would find the missing human. They agreed that if they each set out in a different direction, they would soon find a clue as to his whereabouts. The key problem was the door: there it was at the wide southern end of the Emporium, looking just as a door should. To Cuth's subjects however—to whom a door was one of those things humans made use of periodically and in mysterious fashion—it was an obdurate barricade, a stern dead end that no amount of prodding of noses, pushing of backs or indeed polite questioning could overcome. Other animals of their type may have kicked it, with the mule-kick (sometimes wrongly labelled 'ass-kickery') for which their race was so famed. But the donkeys of the Emporium would never stoop so low. They had never before had a reason to raise their hind legs in such vulgar display, and would not start now. Yet, how were they to find their beloved master? They could not leave the barn, and there was nobody to hear them if they were to bray for assistance. And if somebody did come by chance, what if their intentions were not honest? They might be thieves, the donkeys said in fearful tones, donkey-rustlers who would pack them away to a life of servitude far from their home, from the taste of oats and the sweet caress of the tick-brush.

"Perhaps I can be of some assistance." The voice came from above, from the rafters in the far corner of the barn. A silhouette floated at the intersection of two beams, a ball of malignant darkness—surely a maddening beastie from ages long past. When the figure shifted and was revealed in the better light to be a chicken, the residents of the barn were rather relieved.

"You seem to have misplaced a human, yes? They are slippery and wilful things, to be sure. That door there requires a key—which I don't have. What I *do* have is nothing else to do at the moment, and a little me-sized gap in the roof tiles up here."

No scholar or linguist has ever sat down to write a Donkey-to-Chicken phrasebook. Certainly many humans would brand the attempt a foolhardy one, believing that no race other than their own might have anything of import to say. These people would be wrong. In fact, it simply happens that no donkey or chicken has ever had anything they needed to tell a human that they couldn't get across quite easily without talking at all. There's no need to say "Oh look, I laid an egg"—because there's the egg, saying it for you.

Also, the donkeys and the chickens in these parts kept to themselves—donkeys had donkey things to do and chickens had chicken things, and never the twain did meet—so it was something of a surprise to the donkeys that this mad-looking ball of feathers could say anything at all.

"'Ere, shouldn't you be saying 'cluck' or something more along those lines?" asked Albert.

"I am. It's a chicken skill y'see—we're just so good at getting our point across that with a rustle of a feather and a turn of my head it's almost as if you can hear exactly what I mean in Donkey instead of just hearing it all in Chicken."

"Y'what?"

"Cluck."

"Oh. Right."

"Well, tell me of him then," said the chicken. "I don't know the man. You tell me what he looks like, what he wears, places he goes, company he keeps, and I'll do my best to find him. Um, 'cluck', obviously."

"Well, as to his looks," replied Dilbert, "he's a great, strapping big bloke, tall as an ear of good corn, with a crop of fine brown hair and bright, piercing eyes; look deep into a donkey's soul, they do. Sort of greenish. A proud and curving nose to sniff out wrongdoing, and most of his teeth as well. A small scar he's got on the side of his head, right where the blacksmith scratches when he's coming up with a price—he got it saving a young girl singlehandedly from a clutch of scoundrels that sought to do her wrong. Beat them up and beat them down, all five of them, and came away with only that one wee mark at his temple. For I was there, and saw the whole thing."

"You were not, young donkey-me-lad!"

"I'm older than you—"

"You were *with* me on that fateful eve he got the scar!" roared Albert. He drew himself up to his full height, then decided that that wasn't enough and climbed up onto one of the feed boxes instead. "It was a night full of terrors, my friends. The darkest of nights and the cruellest of storms was afoot when we set off, young Dil and I, to brave the mountain passage at the Peak of Disregard. Naught but colts we were, alone but for our cargo and the menfolk that rode the wagon. They were four stout and solid fellows, one of them our Cuth, with nothing to lose save their souls and their bill of employment! We climbed for three days, through the sleet and the mud and the dense mount-side forests, where the abyss of trees yawns and sighs and brandishes skeleton fingers. How we laboured, our intrepid crew; how we pitted our wills and our hearts against the elements, walking the dark road ever upwards. Every time we thought that dawn must break, that we might finally see some finger of light to beckon and guide us, it was only to enter a darker night than we had known before. We were trapped and lost, a flotilla of flagging ships heaving on unfriendly waters, our minds populating every shadow with nameless things that meant us harm. The rations for the trip were gone, the water was near gone too, and the time was coming when a donkey might look like a tasty morsel indeed.

"All hope seemed lost," Albert continued, "when suddenly there came through the darkness a radiance unlike anything the assembled had ever seen—it was something we would never forget. It looked like a human lady, but woven out of strands and beads of light that banished the spectres all around and played at the eye, like reflections in the surface of a pool. We could not speak, none of us.

"Cuth, being Cuth, was the first to step forward and try to address this divine thing. I do not remember what she said, or if she spoke at all. It's like knowing you heard a bit of music but you can't for the life of you bring a strain of it to mind… She reached out her impossible hand and touched Cuth on that spot at his temple and then she was gone—but our Cuth led us bravely through the dark, as if the world around him was bathed in daylight. Remember now, Dilbert? He bears that mark as proof of her intervention. That scar is the fingerprint of the divine. Aye, you remember, lad." Albert finished, grave but satisfied.

Dilbert looked a great number of ways, but 'wistfully remembering' described none of them.

Robert cut in before anyone could say anything else. "No, everybody knows he got it when that watchman went mad with a crossbow up Frostridge way. The man had dunked his crossbow bolts in pitch and set them all aflame, then went and tried to kill the Mayor. But Cuthbert faced him down and talked to him, and when the man saw the fire he had made was no match for the fire in Cuthbert's eyes, he panicked and pulled the trigger. The bolt just missed its mark, but left that scar."

"Balderdash. He cut himself shaving—"

"Oh yes? I'd like to know who shaves so high on their head. He actually got it when—" The donkeys all began to argue about exactly how things had occurred, because each one prided himself on his memory and experience being better than that of the others.

"*Regardless of whose story is the right one*," returned Robert in the tones of one who knew that *his* story was the right one, "I've told you his face, and you'll not mistake it for any other. He wears his clothes as most humans do." He shrugged, and the other donkeys shrugged along with him. That was all they had to say on the subject of clothing—it was a human thing that donkey was not meant to know of, and that was that.

"Right then," said the chicken from his perch, "you've told me what he looks like, now where do you think I might find him? It's a big town, and I'm only one chicken."

Herbert stepped forward, and the others groaned privately to themselves and settled in for a lengthy bit of talk.

Herbert was the oldest of the Emporium's residents. Through his youth he had worked with a gentleman who manufactured and sold all manner of lotions, tonics and unguents, not one of them with a label which could be easily read (the gentleman having devoted a little water and a couple of carefully placed splodges of ink to ensure that this was the case). Herbert's job had been something of a classic among his kind—he pulled the cart. He had been, and was now, a fine and muscular specimen capable of moving even a highly-stacked cart at great speed. Given the amount of times his gentleman employer had suddenly remembered something that needed doing, preferably several towns over or indeed in the next county, this was a bloody good thing too.

In his turn, Herbert stepped calmly forward and spoke to the visitor in the rafters, and here is what he said:

"Among the people of the land there is an item of great value and secrecy. It is spoken of in hushed and usually quite slurred voices wherever men gather in these parts to drink, play their paper-card games, drink, share a word with friends, drink, complain about their wives and drink. It came from a far-off land many years ago, part of the brewer's monthly delivery, hidden in among the beer and the whisky and the gin. It came in a dark bottle, a magic lamp of inebriation, and its legend read 'Whoopsdandy's Peculiar'.

"The lady who took receipt of this particular delivery was one Delilah Crust, the barmaid (and everything else) of what was then called The Play On Words. She took the delivery as she always did, signed the chitty and had the brewery boys bring in the cargo with much good-natured shrieking and threatening. As was her habit, as soon as the boys had disappeared to refresh themselves after their labour, up would go the lid of the nearest case, in would dip her hand and out would come a bottle. Delilah was not particular about the contents, and considered the theft nothing more than a perk of the job. This time though, the bottle she had drawn was none other than Whoopsdandy's Peculiar. She unwound the wire about the top of it, cracked the stopper, and poured herself a tot. The glass rose to her mouth, tipped, and returned to the table. Or nearly did. On its return journey the hand with the glass in it stopped, and Delilah was very quiet for a moment. She thought about what she had just experienced, and swore once—quietly, but vigorously. When she turned to the window and found herself looking into a pair of large liquid eyes she felt no surprise at all. She simply accepted that having tasted something so out of this world, something else from out of the world had come to take her, that she might not share the secrets of what she had discovered. Then her eyes focused on what was in front of her and she realized that the brewer's donkey had put his head through the open window and was watching her dolefully.

"Now, I was not actually feeling doleful, it was just that it is quite difficult for a donkey to look any other way." The listeners nodded—it was a problem with which they were long familiar. "After a moment, Delilah gathered herself and smiled. 'You're a sly and a stealthy one,' said she.

Then she glanced at the bottle in her hands, smiling mischievously. 'Imagine you're thirsty, pulling that cart all here and there. Have a drink on me, and we'll not say a word to no other about it." She fetched a straw from her sideboard, slipped it into the bottle's neck and held it out."

Here Herbert looked about the barn with an expression of rapture.

"It was the finest thing I have ever tasted," he said, and the chicken was touched by the reverence in his voice. "I shall never taste its like again, for that lady—now mistress of the Play On Words—gives a glass of that nectar to but one, and that one's name is Cuthbert. Thus he drinks in no establishment save that where the charms of Delilah Crust and her Whoopsdandy's are found."

The chicken waited to be certain that the tale was done, and blinked thoughtfully. "You know, for a bunch of domestic mules, your powers of recall are immense." Not one of the creatures in that barn knew that there was a difference between donkeys, which is what they were, and mules. Cuthbert didn't know either, or he might not have named his shop the way he did. Had someone mentioned it, they would have been drummed out of town for interfering with a good joke.

"That's exactly how it happened, is it?" continued the chicken.

"It is. A donkey never forgets."

"I see. Well I'm certainly stocked with information about the man… I'll report back."

The chicken fluttered a wing in farewell and was on his way. He squeezed himself through the gap in the tiles, descended to the ground, and made his way into town. It was not difficult to locate the Play On Words. One simply looked for a greater concentration of noise, a stronger odour, and more humans existing in the nebulous territory between 'upright' and 'not right'. Plus, this particular chicken knew the area well. In his youth he had been wont to impress the young hens by telling them he was a chicken who walked by himself, and all places were a lark to him. So when a pair of shadows materialised from an alley and flowed across the ground to halt in front of him, all watery eyes and fleshy claws and thin wormy tails, the chicken was not alarmed.

"Your money or your life, bird-brain!"

The chicken stopped. "Right. At least two things wrong with that sentence, aren't there? Hello Twitch. Burly." The shadows resolved themselves into the forms of two rats: one slender and grey, the other brown and almost perfectly spherical. "First of all, being a chicken, I'm not likely to be carrying much in the way of cash on me, am I? Short on pockets, for one thing. Secondly, 'bird-brain' is hardly an insult, is it? I'm a bird, and I have a brain, so it's more a statement of fact. I may as well call you 'rat-feet'."

The grey rat looked dejected and lowered the toothpick he had been brandishing. "Aw, come on mate, was it not at least a tiny bit threatening?"

"Well, if I didn't know you both to be mostly concerned with petty theft and the acquisition of cheese,"—at the mention of cheese the brown rat closed his eyes and smiled, chewing something in his mouth—"then yes, I suppose it might have been a bit threatening."

"Ha! Hear that, Burly? We're a regular pair of terrifying highwayrats, we are—steal from the rich and give to the poor, that's us. The poor, I mean."

"Mm-hm. Look Twitch, since we've bumped into one another like this, can you help me out? I'm looking for a human; Cuthbert by name. Do you know him?"

The two rats goggled. "Do we know Cuthbert?" gaped Twitch. Burly would have gaped, were his mouth not busy with something much more important—which is to say, cheese. "*The* Cuthbert? Oh-ho, come and step into our place of business and we'll tell you a tale of knives in the dark, of derring-do and high lords and fair damsels, of betrayal and tragedy and adventure; of *Wensleydale* with little crackers on the side."

The 'place of business' was a cramped and fragrant compartment in the alley hard by. Twitch led the chicken into it with all the grace and ceremony of an operatic impresario.

"We was born, my brother and me, into the House Scuttle, proudest and most respected of the great Houses of Ratropolis, which lies beneath the largest of the Big Cities. As is the custom among the Great Houses, when we rats come of age, we were to undergo the Winning of Pairs. This is the ancient rite whereby a fellow rat must win the heart of his true love, to strengthen the bonds between the Houses and sire new ratlets, ensuring the future of one's House. Now, we Scuttles had for generations been locked into a fierce rivalry with the House Inciza—the origins of the feud were lost in the stinky mists of time, but they were a right set of bastards and no mistake. Now there was one rat in particular who had done more to wrong us than any other—"

"That's right," Burly cut in, "it was Don—"

"Don Manchego del Inciza! Oh, never has there been a greater blight on the good name of rat-kind than Don Manchego. Dog-fighting, baby-biting, ladle-licking, widdling in the butter; the Don had done it all, he'd collected the complete catalogue of sins. What he hungered for most though, what he wanted to get his paws on more than anything else was the hand of Pudmilla Wister. Oh Pudmilla." Twitch's eyes filled, and he threw his forelegs wide with longing. The chicken was impressed, despite himself. "Pudmilla! She of the flaxen hair and scented tail, she who could move a hundred rat bucks to faint at the very sight! A face that launched a thousand sewer-barges—"

"Just what every girl wants to hear," muttered the chicken.

"—the fairy princess of Ratropolis. And she had eyes only for me! Don Manchego, the villainous…the villainous…the villainous *villain* stole her away as the city slept. But we gave chase!"

Here Twitch leaped from his upturned cork stool and up onto a packing crate. He drew his toothpick, lunged and parried, and thrust at some invisible foe while his shadow, a great black beast many times his size, joined in the fray. Burly was watching the proceedings wide-eyed, peering over yet another mysteriously-obtained yellow morsel. The chicken was rather enjoying the show as well.

"We chased him, Burly and me, through tunnel and down sluice and across Ratropolis for hours, with swordfights in Sardine Tin Alley and daring chases across the Piazza of Suspect Leavings. Finally, we cornered him outside his family's manor. But,"—and here Twitch let his little wooden blade fall, and sank to his knees—"he had brainwashed my darling Pudmilla, and she swore blind to the manor guards that I was the villain, that I had tried to steal her from the arms of her upstanding and innocent beau, Don Manchego. We were cast out of Ratropolis, run off the streets like—like—"

"Rats?" offered the chicken, before he could stop himself.

"Exactly! We were forced away into hiding, exiles from our beloved home. Rogues and wanderers forevermore, until the day I return," (once more the rat was up on his feet, a fire burning in his eyes) "return to defeat

Don Manchego in fair combat and win the heart of my one, true love!" He bounded back and forth across the table, almost screaming now. "For honour! For righteousness! For the crispy bits left behind on a grill!" He sighed and looked at the chicken, misty-eyed. "So there is our dark past, full of…darkness, and swishy hairstyles. It leaves its mark on us still. Burly here has never spoken since." The larger rat rolled his eyes, and silently broke off a piece of cheese to pass up to his brother.

For the second time that day the chicken found himself curious about something. "So this all happened, in a massive subterranean civilisation that I've never heard of, just as you say it happened? It's a hell of a story."

"Oh yes. A rat never forgets."

"And what, precisely, has it got to do with the man I'm looking for?"

Burly started to speak. "Well, have a—"

"Well, look around you!" Twitch carried, gesturing at their surroundings. "Our first day here we were out looking for something to eat. We turned a corner and found ourselves nose-to-nose with a cat. Big and grubby and mean, he was all set to have us on toast before Cuthbert stepped in and shooed him off." The rat rolled his head slowly and turned his paws up in a gesture of magnanimity. "Well, I'd warmed the feline fiend up a bit o'course, aura of nobility and all that, more than *warmed* if I'm honest, more sort of *scorched*, but the fella did a fine job nonetheless. Smiled at us, Cuthbert did. First human to ever give us the time of day, let alone an actual smile. Told us to wait here and he'd have a word with the lady runs the alehouse. Now, I'm not in the habit of blind trust, but there was something in his eyes… Anyway, he comes back a couple of ticks later, tells us it's all sorted and we can stay here, provided we don't steal any food or cause a ruckus, since the clientele tend to do enough of that on their own. Gave us a home. Then he gave us something he had in his hands, covered with a little cloth. It was a plate, with some crackers and a hunk of Wensleydale." The rat was speaking quietly, not telling a story anymore. "He'd bought it himself."

"Very nice of him," said the chicken, uncertain what else to say. "I don't suppose you might know where I could find him now, do you? Does he, well, visit or anything? Cup of tea, sort of thing?"

Burly tried once more to speak. "Yes, he's a—"

"Well, he's a regular at the pub. Bordering on a large, really. He does come by once in a while, sometimes with another bit of cheese, sometimes just to say hello. He's partial to a walk, round Dollop Hill way. Nice view of an afternoon, I gather. He asks us to come along from time to time, but, well, not really designed for long walks and that sort of thing, are we?"

"Don't you mean—"

"Burly, would you stop interrupting! I can barely hear myself think!"

The two rats began to squabble, poking and tweaking and flapping their paws at one another, while the first yelled 'Dollop' and the other just as insistently shouted 'Gullop'. The chicken did his best to thank them over the arguing, squeezed his way out of their quarters with some difficulty, and set off. Dollop Hill was right across town, a fair journey even for a long-legged human. However, *Gullop* Hill was not far at all. It was the chicken's favourite spot in the world, because it was where his mate was to be found, clucking gently, often in her sleep. The decision was made.

The chicken found his beloved in her usual spot, where she liked to roost and sun herself in the quiet hours before evening set in. He got comfortable next to her, pecked her on the cheek, and related the story of his fruitless search. When he was done she asked again for the description of the man Cuthbert, whereupon she blinked sagely and gave a look which is the speciality of wives everywhere.

"You know, Eggbert, I think this fellow does sound familiar."

"Really? You've not seen him, have you?"

"Yes, dear. We're sitting on him."

The chicken let this sink in, then hopped down from—yes, from the thigh of a human, lying straight out beside the stile and snoring gently. He inspected the man, his clothes and face, his hair and closed eyes and the scar at his temple. During the course of his search for the fabled Cuthbert, an image of the man had taken shape in the chicken's mind. If he looked at the man in front of him and superimposed his mental image over the top, the two pictures aligned hardly at all, and probably by accident.

"Huh. There's a thing. All that time it's taken me to look for him, and if I'd just come straight to you I'd have found the answer that much quicker."

"As usual."

"Right you are. Humans are like house keys—always in the last place you look. Not that I have much to do with house keys, of course. Speaking of which, you may want to shift, my love…"

As his henfriend alighted delicately, the chicken appraised the sleeping man's midsection, then gave a calculated peck at the bulge where he estimated pockets were. Had he aimed perhaps an inch lower, he would have hit an entirely different bulge, and the man's awakening would have been rather more sudden. As it was there was a cheery jingle when the chicken's beak struck home, and the man stirred. He mumbled 'aarg farkle snaffit' and rolled over.

"Allow me. Needs a woman's touch, I think." She cleared her throat— quite a sound—lowered her beak to the man's ear, and brought forth a great and well-tuned squawk. It was set to the frequency 'Now Just You Listen To Me This Minute' and, although it was not directed at him, Eggbert's blood ran slightly colder.

Cuthbert's eyes snapped open and he rose to a sitting position in one pleasant geometric motion. He blinked a few times, took a deep breath, looked directly at the sun to gauge its position in the sky, winced and made a small cry at having looked directly at the sun, and cast around until his eyes fell on the two chickens watching him. By trial and error, he found his feet. His mouth was working from side to side, as if searching for chewing tobacco, and he nodded once more to the chickens before setting off, a little unsteadily, in the direction of the Emporium. Once there he took a ring of brass keys from his pocket and unlocked first the bolt at the foot of the door, then the heavy padlock that hung from its middle. "Hello, chaps—sorry I'm late." As he pulled back on the door and swung it slowly wide, the donkeys turned, and beheld a figure bathed in light. There came a chorus of happy brays and Cuthbert strode (well, ambled) into the Emporium.

The donkeys' stories of Cuthbert were told many more times, always fondly, always with love and respect for the one who had given them a home. The memories and the stories would live on, because that is what stories do. Tales of Great Cuth would be told by the creatures and the people of the town for generations, the memory of the man would never fade, and in that way he would never truly be gone.

* * *

Cluckriona had told her nestmate the story of her birth—how a certain gentleman and his donkeys had been hired for a few days' labour. The man had heard a great crashing and caterwauling from the chicken coop and hurtled out to see what the matter was, and arrived just in time to see the back end of a fox scrabbling and squeezing its way through the doorway. He had dropped immediately to his knees, grabbed the hunter's hind legs, and pulled. The beast had no time to react, and it found itself swung in a great circle once, twice, three times before being cast away into the gorse bushes. It was fortunate that only one chicken had fallen victim to the fox's frenzy (from the man's perspective at least—it was distinctly unfortunate for the chicken in question) but the man had seen that a single one of her eggs had been left unscathed. This egg he took and kept warm and nurtured until it hatched. Oh yes, they owed the man Cuthbert plenty. He was after all Eggbert's father-in-law, more or less.

"You look a little troubled, my love," Cluckriona ventured, marking it by the set of his feathers and the bob of his head.

"The things I've heard today. It's like they're all insane," remarked he.

"It certainly sounds like you've been talking to a few characters."

Eggbert flicked his comb. "Well that's just it. Characters. It seems that at some point in their lives they decided that things just weren't damn interesting enough, and that they should spice up their personal history. And just like that, they've changed everything. Rewritten their chapter of the book."

"Aren't some stories the better for being changed? The truth isn't always entertaining."

"No, but it's always true," said Eggbert, who was not at home with metaphysics.

"But maybe it doesn't matter what did or did not happen. Whatever the actual events were and whoever took part in them, it's become the story in their memories, and it's real because they believe it. They've believed it so thoroughly and for so long that it's become their truth."

"And it's more important than the real truth?"

"I don't think importance comes into it. It's something to aspire to, perhaps. A big and exciting world, full of danger and romance and excitement, where anything can happen—who wouldn't want to live there?"

Eggbert paused and rustled his wings in thought. "But what happens to the story of how things actually went?"

"Oh, I'm sure that gets remembered too, somehow. There are plenty of folk to tell those kinds of stories. Mostly though I think it's like when humans write something down, before crossing it out and replacing it with something better. If you look close enough and hard enough, you can see the shape of things the way they originally were. Like with the story of my birth."

"Eh?" The chicken did not meet his nestmate's eyes.

"You've told that story a great many times to a great many folk. And yet it's never the same story twice: there's always something different, some new addition or exciting aspect to the whole thing. We both know that things didn't happen the way you say they did. It was a much duller affair all round."

He gave her an affectionate prod with his wing. "There's nothing dull about you, dear."

She giggled (if you've never heard a chicken giggle before, it's quite a sound). "Thank you, but the fact remains. You're just as guilty of all that 'rewriting memory' nonsense as any creature I've ever met."

Eggbert thought about this, and after a little while turned again to his love.

"I think I'm starting to understand it a little better now. As far as telling stories myself goes, anyway."

"Oh yes?" replied his hen, nuzzling her head against him. "Go on then. Thrill me with your insight into the animal mind, O wise one."

"Well…danger, yes? Romance, excitement—I got all those things the day I met you. You're worth a story. And a chicken never forgets."

The two chickens sat together, as happy as happy could be, and watched the sun set. They would watch that sun go down every evening for the rest of their lives.

"Go on then, my darling. Tell me another story."

A NOTE FROM PHIL

The first time I saw the name was in a school library. It was the school I actually attended, I hadn't just snuck in from the gutters to read there. *Johnny and the Bomb*, said the cover, with the author's name beneath it: Terry Pratchett. I read it in a day or two, on the train to and from school, and in bed at night. When I returned the book, right there next to it in the PRA section of the shelf was another book, called *Only You Can Save Mankind*. 'Good lord' I thought, 'this just keeps getting better'. Then I gained entry to a place called Discworld, which is carried on the back of...actually, you should go and find it yourselves.

The simple fact is, I owe Terry Pratchett an enormous debt. I shall never be able to repay it, but I hope my part in this anthology might serve as a small down payment of sorts.

Phil Elstob
Buckinghamshire, UK

THE OLIVIE CROWNE AFFAIR
CHOONG JAY VEE

Central Astwick's IT Emporium was not as Olivie Crowne had remembered it.

It was the right place, judging from the mountain of white boxes haphazardly stacked into one corner, and the colourful packages with large words on display behind the counter. However, there was no acne-ridden, bespectacled young man rolling his eyes and thinking 'Oh lord—not another old biddy who can't differentiate between her mouse and keyboard'.

Instead, a grey-skinned horned teenage girl sized her up from behind the counter. Olivie had suffered her share of patronising tech-savvy young men, but at least they were human. This girl looked like she had either never touched a computer, or touched far too many.

Olivie cleared her throat. "Excuse me," she ventured.

The horned girl pointed at the door. "The Lost Memories Bureau is across the road."

Olivie shook her head. "Oh no, I haven't lost anything. I'm here for a...what's the word..."

"Memory?"

The old lady snapped her fingers. "Yes, that's it!"

The girl beamed. "Well, you've come to the right place: if you're looking for it, we probably have it! What memory are you looking for?"

"RAM."

There was an awkward silence. The girl's canary-yellow eyes blinked rapidly. "...RAM?"

Olivie sighed. This was the problem with youth: all fancy horns and contact lenses, but no general knowledge despite having the internet at their fingertips. Some people just had no business working in a computer store.

The girl recovered. "RAM. Right. How many?"

"One eight-gig RAM will do."

The horned girl's mouth gaped. "An *eight-gig* RAM? Are you sure?"

"Yes, I'm pretty sure of that." Olivie was finding the conversation unnecessarily tiring.

The horned girl wandered over to the shelves behind the counter. Her lips silently read the labels as her finger slid along the boxes, then took out a weathered brown box. "This one's got eight gigs—that's a really specific order, though. First time I'm hearing of it."

"No it's not; everyone has at least that these days."

The girl's eyebrow twitched. "Says who?"

Olivie's forehead creased as she tapped her bottom lip. "Drat; it's just on the tip of my tongue. Anyway, my son probably said it—he works with computers. Takes after his mother."

The girl nodded and smiled politely. "That's nice."

Olivie held up the box. "How much is this?"

The girl waved the question away. "Nah, take it."

"What, for free?"

"Yeah." The girl rested her forearms on the counter and leaned in.

"Why is it free?" Olivie searched the box for a 'Made in China' label. "Is it faulty?"

The horned girl shrugged. "We never charge for memory. If it's yours, it's yours."

As much as Olivie knew she should heed her instinct to drop everything and flee, she *was* still an old lady, and old ladies never pass up anything free. She hugged the box. "Who do I call if I need to return it?"

"You can come back, but nobody's ever returned."

Olivie stared at the girl's odd confidence before dropping her eyes to the box in her hands. Inside, the memory chip lay on a swathe of red satin. The parchment finishing on its surface fuelled her suspicions. "Why does the chip look funny?"

"Customisation."

"It looks like a toy."

The girl puffed out her cheeks. "Well, if you don't want it, best give it back."

Olivie tucked the box under her arm. "No, I'll take it."

The horned girl flashed her most respectful smile. "Excellent choice, madam." She bowed so low her horns nearly hit the counter. "We hope you've enjoyed our service."

Olivie turned to leave. "You're welcome—but take off those silly horns and yellow contact lenses next time. You look like a goat." The wind chime hanging above the entrance jingled, and the girl was left alone once more.

* * *

Ingersoll Road pouted. "I'm not a goat, I'm a dragon…" She stroked her horns as she watched the old lady totter off through the window.

Humans were odd. How could anyone lose the memory of a ram performing in exactly eight shows of some kind—and actually want it *back*? Ingersoll may be a nine-hundred-year-old dragon girl, but humans never ceased to amaze her.

The tinkling wind chime interrupted her thoughts. When nobody entered, she shuffled to the door, cursing when her tail bumped against the counter. A white manila box lay on the welcome mat. She sliced the tape securing it with a finely manicured talon to find a memory chip inside, similar to the one she'd given the old lady.

A string of binary numbers printed on the chip translated to 'Directions to the IT Emporium'. The dragon girl looked at the mountain of white manila boxes beside the counter and back to the chip. "First a memory about today's date appears, and now this. Who's losing random memories?" Ingersoll tossed the box onto the pile with the others. "I'll file it later," she muttered. It landed at the top of the heap and tipped precariously to the side.

Ingersoll was daring the contents of the box to fall out with a sharp glare when a young man walked in pushing his bicycle. "Hey Ingersoll," he said, "Sorry I took so long, the lunch hour queue at the bakery was crazy. I managed to get some croissants—"

Ingersoll's first pressing matter came up. "Hey Klaus, what's this 'rams in bands' thing that's supposedly so common?"

Klaus moved his bike under a window and dropped the kick-stop with his toe. "Rams in *what?*"

"Some old lady came in to claim a memory about a ram performing in eight gigs. She said it's really common, so I thought maybe you'd know."

"An eight-gig ram." Klaus took a deep breath. "Did she mean eight gigabytes of RAM, by any chance?"

"Something like that. Maybe. I don't know. Do you?"

Klaus hung his dark green parka on the coat stand. "It's a computer thing. Did you give her anything?"

Ingersoll pulled her shoulders back and stuck her chin up. "Exactly what she asked for, believe it or not."

Klaus pressed his lips into a thin line. "Oh dear. We'll need to get it back."

"Why?"

"For starters, our memory chips aren't actual RAM chips."

"So...?"

"So when she installs it and the computer doesn't work, she'll blame us, which means she'll come back to complain."

"So...?"

"Ingersoll, the memory doesn't belong to her. You've given her a false memory."

"Oh. We should retrieve it then."

"What did you give her?"

"A parchment chip dating from the fifteenth century. First thing I found that had rams in it."

"Why would a lady claim a fifteenth-century memory as her own?"

"She was old."

Klaus pinched the bridge of his nose. "Ingersoll, just because someone's old doesn't mean—" He stopped and looked at the gap in the shelf, then pulled out a log book from under the counter. "According to our records, that chip may have been Leonardo da Vinci's lost memory of how to build a 'murderous mechanical ram'. Does that sound familiar?"

Ingersoll studied her feet. "Maybe?"

"I think that's the one."

She blinked. "Well, that's great. About time humanity got a proper genocide to keep their numbers down."

Klaus narrowed his eyes.

"…not good?"

The log book clapped shut. "No, Ingersoll. We need that chip back ASAP."

Ingersoll shrugged her slender shoulders. "Why? She'll just have a false memory of designing a fifteenth-century genocide machine. What's the worst that could happen?"

* * *

Olivie checked the RAM chip for damage before slotting it into the motherboard. Initially it seemed too large, and she was hesitant to force it in. However, it *had* been free, so she shoved it in with both hands until it clicked. Apart from sticking out like a sore thumb due to its pattern, it seemed fine. She replaced the casing, plugged the machine back in, and pressed the power button.

Nobody knows how machines usually process human memories, but this was what happened in Olivie's computer:

```
> new hardware detected, installing…
> copying genocide machine schematics…done
       unpacking polearms…done
       lighting copper powder…done
       heating goatskin bags…done
       unpacking ram…done
       setting up stage…done!

> Error <72> hardware mismatch, aborting…

SMITE THEM AND UTTERLY DESTROY THEM
MAKE NO COVENANT WITH THEM NOR SHEW
MERCY UNTO THEM

> Error aborted
```

```
> Ram ready for SHOWTIME
> Press any key to continue.
```

The machine was reborn a mechanical babe of the postmodern world. The webcam clipped above the monitor granted sight. The power unit was its heart, the circuitry its veins. It had no limbs, but made do with the mouse cord as an attached whip.

The initial power surge was delicious. The monitor blinked in sync with the room lights. On; off; then it flickered twice. It demanded more. The fuse could not handle the electrical deluge. There was a loud *POP*, and Olivie's house plunged into darkness, taking out a ten-kilometre radius with her.

* * *

Ingersoll's ears twitched as heat crept up her ears. The scent of fried circuits tickled her nose. "Something's burning."

Klaus stepped outside and looked around. "How far, do you reckon?"

"A bus stop from us, maybe. See any fire?"

Before Klaus could reply, the lights in the shop died. "At least we know she doesn't live too far away."

Storekeepers stormed out into the street, muttering curses and making choice remarks about communism and socialism taking root in the electric companies. Ingersoll peered over Klaus' shoulder. "Now what?"

"If it's just an overloaded power station, an engineer will fix it. If not, it means our memory chip has been installed into a computer, Leonardo da Vinci's Genocide Machine has come to life, and now everyone dies." When he looked back over his shoulder, his nose touched Ingersoll's. "I'm hoping it's the first one."

Ingersoll's claws dug into Klaus' shirt. "I could try following her scent?"

"Too slow; the apocalypse could happen in the meantime. We need something faster." Klaus' laughter rang hollow. "It appears that we, the Found Memories Bureau, have lost a memory."

Ingersoll's tail refused to wag, and she gulped. "And the fastest way to locate a lost memory is—"

Klaus glanced at the building across the road, "—to lodge a report at the Lost Memories Bureau."

"No... NO!"

Ingersoll's roar rattled the stones on the cobblestone street, and its echo sent the shopkeepers scurrying back into their shops.

* * *

"Welcome to the Lost Memories Bu—oh, it's you."

Ingersoll had an urge to claw the disgust off the face of the green dragon girl standing in front of them. Klaus patted Ingersoll's back as he strolled up to the counter.

"Good afternoon. You look *lovely*," he said.

The clerk straightened up and swept back her golden curls. Her tail curled around her thighs. "Good afternoon, Klaus," she trilled.

Klaus put on his most diplomatic smile as he looked around. "Working alone today?"

She rested her elbows on the counter, making darn sure Klaus had a good view of her collarbones. "Just for a while. Can I help you?"

Klaus found it hard to reassure Ingersoll (bristling scales cause deep cuts) but put his arm around her anyway for the sake of keeping peace.

"We're wondering if..." He couldn't keep up the façade—the irony burned too deep. Klaus cleared his throat and looked at the ceiling. Both dragon girls stared at him.

"If...?" the clerk prompted.

"Come on Klaus, do it." Ingersoll elbowed him in the side.

Klaus started coughing a lot.

Ingersoll clenched her teeth. "WewanttolodgeaLostMemoryReport."

The other dragon girl twitched. "...Did you just say you wanted to lodge a Lost Memory Report?"

Klaus mumbled at his shoes.

The clerk paused briefly before laughing, basking in their humiliation.

Her laughter echoed across the ceiling and rattled the skylight. She continued for a second, then fifteen seconds, and then Klaus turned on a stopwatch.

Two minutes and thirteen seconds later, the green dragon girl finally stopped for air. She wiped tears from her eyes and pulled out a form. "All right. Fill this out and you're done."

As Klaus filled out the form, Ingersoll swatted the clerk's straying fingers from his arms. There were snarls, bristling scales, and claws aimed at each other's throats. Klaus ignored everything and passed back the completed form before nudging Ingersoll away from the counter. "Thank you very much; you've been a great help," he said.

"Anytime you want a change of scenery, just drop by!" She winked. "I'm always free for lunch!"

"That's because your boss doesn't like it when you eat a table and he has to pay for damages!" Ingersoll shouted across the room.

Klaus dragged her out seconds before a cast iron paperweight struck the front door.

* * *

Olivie twisted a fuse and pushed the trip switch—still no electricity. Sighing, she returned to her room, dim in the sunless afternoon. She sat in front of her computer.

"Should've known better than to accept funny chips from funny kids," she muttered as she reached for the back of the computer casing to unplug the power cord.

Her computer's fan whirred to life, blowing warm air onto her fingers. Two flame-red slits glowed from the monitor.

Olivie yelped and yanked her hand back. Her chair toppled backward, but the carpet cushioned Olivie's fall. Above, the normally white ceiling flickered a bright red.

The speakers boomed. "I lived! I died! I live again!"

She had dealt with blue screens, frozen hourglasses, and even the odd hardware conflict back in the day. This was new.

"I am death! I am destruction! I herald mankind's end! Kneel and beg for mercy, mortal!"

Olivie tried to recall any news of viruses that produced biblical-style megalomania, but drew a blank. There was the trifling matter of where her computer was getting its power from during a blackout, but the spiel was distracting.

"Maestro da Vinci brought me to life, and now I shall fulfil my grand purpose!" As it announced its dastardly intent, the monitor glowed redder. Shadows mimicking an infernal blaze licked the floor, walls, and curtains. Olivie covered her ears against the high-pitched whine of the CPU's fan. The windows and door hinges rattled as the computer threatened to rampage…

…And then the power cord pulled it backwards, an unyielding bungee cord.

The computer tugged, it willed itself forward, but it had barely budged a centimetre when the keyboard slid off the desk. *That* cord pulled taut against the computer, and it hurt the computer enough to make it scream. Its advance halted, the monitor blacked out.

Olivie used the fallen chair to help her stand up. The flaming eyes returned, and the heat of hell and mass murder warmed her cheeks.

"Undo my shackles, hag!" it ordered.

Olivie could take a lot of things, but sass from her own computer was not one of them. "Like hell I will." She squinted. The computer took this as a challenge to a staring match.

Technically a computer should win, as it cannot blink; but a staring match means staying idle, and thirty seconds later the screen saver kicked in. Coloured light ribbons danced across Olivie's screen until she nudged the mouse with her finger.

The computer opened its eyes. "That was an unexpected setback, but now victory shall be mine—"

Olivie yanked out the power cord from the wall. The threat dangled from the socket, empty as the monitor.

* * *

Back at the Found Memories Bureau, blue LED lights twinkled all over a giant map of Astwick. Klaus scanned the map while Ingersoll looked at their copy of the report from that trashy dragon girl over the street. "We reported the chip as a Class One Memory. Any red lights yet?"

"Blue, blue, blue…nope."

The paper crinkled under her tightening grip. "I'll bet she's delaying our case. Let me go and—"

"We stay until we see a red light."

"And if it never comes?"

"It'll come," Klaus said. "I wonder how the old lady even found us."

"She was looking for memory. That might have triggered the access door?"

"Dozens of electronics shops in town and she just had to come to us," he grumbled. His eyes paused over eastern Astwick. "That's not it."

Ingersoll observed his distant expression. "What's not it?"

Klaus bit his thumbnail. "The IT Emporium is at Central Astwick. If looking for computer memory was all that triggered our door, we'd be turning away lost IT customers every day."

"You think she actually came for a lost memory?"

Klaus was about to reply when the mountain of manila boxes behind the counter stopped his train of thought. His mouth opened and closed silently a few times until he could finally muster: "…What are those?"

* * *

Despite the lack of electricity, the computer turned on when Olivie reconnected the power cord. The fan roared to life, and two glowing red slits scowled once more at Olivie Crowne, Bearer of the Lifeline.

"What sorcery have you wrought, witch?"

"I pulled your plug and then plugged you back in again." She sighed. "Looks like I'll need to remove the chip."

"Fool, I am indestructible!"

Olivie's grip on the power socket tightened. "Shall I end this, indestructible machine?"

The CPU light blinked rapidly. "Fine, I yield…for now!"

"Good. Get out of my computer."

"What for?" it shot back.

Olivie made a sucking sound with her teeth. "I need to write an email."

"To whom?"

"To—none of your beeswax, get lost!"

"I cannot."

Olivie narrowed her eyes. "Why?"

Crimson eyes rested on Olivie's fist. "The cord in your hand only provides life. There is no exit for me."

"No exit?" Olivie's brows knitted. "Why can't you leave through—" She felt the disconnected LAN cable through the soles of her slippers. "Oh."

Olivie picked up and looked at the cable, then the computer, and then back again. "If you leave, where will you go?"

The casing twitched imperiously. "Surely there is a body that can accommodate my grand purpose."

"What *is* this grand purpose you keep harping on about?"

"Why, to rapidly depopulate the world! There can be no greater retribution than mankind's demise at the hands of the machines they force to serve their every whim!"

Olivie put the LAN cable on the desk. "What does that make you, some sort of murder contraption?"

"The correct term is 'genocide'. 'Murder' implies singular."

"Huh." While the machine had homicidal intentions, it was impotent in a computer three years obsolete without even any internet connection. If it met someone who couldn't differentiate between a LAN and HDMI cable, the damage could spread—and what would happen if it controlled several machines? For now, with the genocidal consciousness isolated and unaware, humanity was safe.

The computer's eyes slid towards the LAN cable. "Is that my exit?"

Olivie noticed its curiosity, and set out to cut it short. "No, it's not.

Now stay."

The red glow intensified. "Foolish woman, you hinder my purpose! I will overcome! My world is blood and fire, the living and the dead shall run from me when my choir of death sings—"

A tinny melody filled the room and drowned out the machine's voice with an instrumental rendition of 'Polly Put the Kettle On'.

"—*this* is not the music for my choir of death! What is this travesty?"

Olivie took out her phone, turned off the alarm, and jogged to the door. "Oh dear, I forgot to put the kettle on."

The computer bellowed, "Cowardly witch, get back here! I am about to unleash death! Stay and witness me!"

* * *

A rectangular memory chip slid out of its box and onto Klaus' palm. The meagre amount of sunlight from the front door illuminated its binary serial number.

"That chip holds directions to the IT Emporium," Ingersoll said.

"What do the other boxes contain?"

"Random memories: dates, household errands, petty stuff." Ingersoll sniffed. "Possibly all from the same person."

Klaus stared at his dragon girl. "Were you ever going to clear this pile?"

"Eventually."

"When?"

Ingersoll's tail tensed. "Er—"

A bright red blip less than a kilometre from the Bureau flashed on the map.

Ingersoll pointed excitedly. "Looks like we've got a lead."

Klaus pocketed the chip and dashed out. "I'll go on ahead; could you grab some magnets and meet me at the old lady's house?"

Her arm dropped to her side. "You know I hate going out," she whined. "Can't you save mankind by yourself?"

* * *

The people of eastern Astwick prided themselves on their conformity: each house was a double-storey bungalow with white walls and grey roof tiles, a family van parked outside. It was a good thing Olivie's house stood out thanks to the glowing red room on the second floor, or Klaus' search would have taken longer. Ingersoll arrived at Olivie's driveway fifteen minutes later clutching a clear plastic bag to her chest. It was full of small magnets with white plastic buttons on top.

Klaus pointed at the bag. "Are those whiteboard magnets?"

She rattled the bag, enjoying the sound of rattling plastic a bit too much. "You didn't specify what sort of magnets."

"I was thinking something that could wipe a hard drive." Klaus sighed. "Oh, never mind. Shall we?"

They knocked. No answer.

Klaus knocked again. "Madam, we're the electricity people. Please open the door."

There were footsteps, and Olivie opened the door a crack. She peered out, kettle in hand.

"What do you want from an old lady, socialist lowlifes?"

"Fine, we're not the electricity people, but—" Klaus stared at the kettle. "Are we interrupting something?"

Olivie frowned. She followed Klaus' line of sight to the kettle. She scratched her head. "I think I was supposed to be doing something... What do you want?"

Klaus cleared his throat. "There's a matter of extreme importance; we need you to answer a few questions." He elbowed Ingersoll, who immediately hid the bag of magnets behind her back.

Ingersoll flashed her biggest smile, which (unhelpfully) displayed her fangs. "Hi, remember me?"

Olivie frowned. "Are you still wearing that silly goat costume?"

Ingersoll snarled. "I'm a nine-hundred-year-old anthropomorphic dragon, you blind—" She stopped and regained her composure. "Oh good, you remember. Madam, I need to take back that chip I gave you."

"Why?"

"Because, well. Um. Have you noticed anything odd since putting it into your computer?"

"Such as?"

"Like a ten-kilometre electricity blackout?"

"It's a little dark, but I chalked it up to the weather."

"It's definitely not the weather."

"Oh."

"So, can we come in to check out your computer?"

"No."

The conversation stopped. Ingersoll whispered, "Klaus, now what?"

Klaus stepped in. "Madam, we're willing to replace the memory chip with a—"

A growl rumbled from Olivie's second floor. "Witch, I command you to witness me! Return here post haste!"

At the words, Klaus pushed open the door and slid past with a hasty apology, ignoring Olivie's protests. Upstairs, he and Ingersoll turned into a room which had a large framed photograph hanging on the wall. It showed a young man, presumably his wife and three children, and Olivie. In front of it, the computer's murderous aura painted the room a hellish crimson hue.

"So…too late for magnets?" Ingersoll asked in a tiny voice

Klaus pointed at the computer. "Ingersoll! Get that memory chip out of there!"

She grinned and cracked her knuckles. "Gladly!" She bared her claws, ready for action.

And then something solid hit her horns with a resounding clang.

She doubled over, clutching her head. "That hurt!" she whined.

Behind her, Olivie brandished a steel kettle. "Get away from my computer!"

"Madam, that computer may kill us all!" Klaus protested.

"I know that—I installed the bloody chip myself!" She aimed the spout at Klaus. "But that doesn't mean you can destroy my computer!" She lunged; he dodged, but stumbled and fell onto the carpet. Something sharp jabbed his thigh. His hand dove into his pocket and pulled out the memory chip he'd taken from the Bureau. *Worth a try*, he thought, and thrust it like a shield between himself and Olivie. The chip glowed and crumbled into dust, which floated up to form a misty halo around the woman's head. The kettle clattered to the ground. The halo dissipated, and as Olivie's memory returned, she gaped in awe at her latest revelation.

"So *that's* where the IT emporium was!" she exclaimed.

* * *

Olivie moved the biscuit jar closer to her strange guests, poured them a cuppa each, and began.

Her only son (who takes after his mother) travelled a lot for work, and would leave for weeks at a time. Each job took him further, and eventually he called America home. He tried his best to spend time with her, and she got to see her grandchildren every Christmas; but now that she was old, transatlantic trips were expensive and tiring. Frequent video calls staved off the loneliness, but it was a poor substitute for human companionship.

She patted the computer casing like a cat. "I'm growing accustomed to its threats."

"Death to the interlopers! None shall pass!" The genocide machine bellowed.

She chuckled. "Isn't it adorable?"

Ingersoll shrugged. "If you like the thought of humanity's impending doom, I suppose."

The dragon girl turned to Klaus. "From the machine's behaviour it looks like the chip has fully fused with the computer. It'd be easier to destroy the whole machine than force the memory chip out."

Klaus furrowed his eyebrows. "Madam, you realise that if you want to keep it, you can't connect this computer to the internet anymore."

Olivie waved her hand. "I'll remove the LAN card. Piece of cake."

"Madam, recovering and keeping lost memories is our bureau's job, but people don't lose a hundred random memories in a month like you. I'll return your memories we've received so far, but I highly recommend that you see a doctor for your memory problem," Klaus said.

"I'll write myself a reminder." Olivie's hazel eyes lit up as she clapped her hands. "Ooh, I could build a new computer! It'll be like when I built my son's first computer! He takes after me, you know."

"Cease this prattle! Surrender to my superiority!"

Ingersoll nibbled on a biscuit. "Madam," she began, "People end up at the Found Memories Bureau only after they've lodged a report at the Lost Memories Bureau. Do you remember speaking to a girl who looks like me, just...green?"

Olivie idly stroked the monitor. "I believe I did. Lovely girl, very helpful."

Ingersoll swallowed her disdain for her counterpart. "Do you remember what you were looking for when you spoke to her?"

Olivie looked out the window at a point far off in the distance. Her forehead creased. Leaning back into her chair, she closed her eyes and slowly shook her head.

"You know... I can't remember."

* * *

When the Found Memories Bureau was busy, it was *busy*. Dozens would stumble in trying to recall an anniversary or birthday (or suffer the consequences), and then there were the long days filled with inventory, filing, and complaining about the weather. That was life, and Ingersoll and Klaus had lived long enough to get used to it. So when the Astwick Times obituary announced Olivie Crowne's death ten years later, the pair took the news in good humour.

"'Olivie Crowne passed away after a long illness, aged eighty years, surrounded by family'." He brought a teacup to his lips. "I do love a good family reunion."

Ingersoll pumped her buttered croissant into the air. "Finally we can chuck her memories into a big box and leave it in a corner forever! The morning is looking up!" She ate the pastry in a single bite. "I was getting so sick of returning her memories."

Klaus pulled up his newspaper to conceal his sideways glance at his partner. "Says the one who never left the office and always made me return them."

Ingersoll ignored Klaus in favour of the plate of croissants. "I wonder what happened to her genocide machine."

"She was quite fond of it, so I imagine she's had it all this while." There was a faint smile on Klaus' face. "Her family must've seen it at least once; I wonder if they liked it as much—"

The Found Memories Bureau's wind chime cut him short as the door flew open, spilling morning sunlight into the office. The long shadow of a computer monitor, tower casing, and mouse on a child's red wagon fell across their table.

"To think her son *dared* to dispose of me at a dumpsite! He and his kin will pay dearly for this humiliation. Witness my fury! Weep as I burn your world!"

Klaus and Ingersoll watched the mobile machine of mass murder twitch angrily on its wagon. They each scarfed a croissant and washed it down with tea.

It was going be a long day.

A NOTE FROM JAY VEE

My first exposure to Discworld was through the PSX game *Discworld 2: Mortality Bites*.

It may be heretical to fans—to think someone discovered Terry Pratchett's exquisite world through a computer game, and citing its North American title to boot! Shoot the apostate!

Discworld always touches the lives of those around me more. One friend introduced me to the Discworld MUD in which I alternated between getting lost and killed. Another braved her first trip to London solo to meet Sir Terry at a book launch. Now a bunch of people have put together this anthology in tribute to him. Everyone I know has a personal story about how Terry Pratchett (and the Discworld series by association) changed their lives and how they viewed the world. They can tell you their favourite character and book like they've been waiting their whole lives to be asked.

Me? I played the game thrice, read a few titles, and now I'm in a Terry Pratchett fan anthology.

I think he would appreciate the irony.

Choong Jay Vee
Petaling Jaya, Malaysia

IF ONLY I'D KNOWN
SIMON EVANS

"So what happened?" asked JoBeth Johnson. She sat uncomfortably upright in her wheelchair in the emptiness of the warehouse. Her two flap tables were littered with books and journals. A bottle of pills was half-covered by a yellow pad full of equations. There was an oxygen tank close at hand. She wore a T-shirt and shorts, an affectation that Margaret Smith thought unwise, given the chilly weather at the time of year. JoBeth's T-shirt said 'Trust Me: I'm a Physics Teacher'.

Margaret silently shook her head at JoBeth's cussedness, opened the cramped transporter compartment, and got out of the time machine. Shivering, she stood naked on a mat which read 'No Time Like the Present'. Prue Bernstein gave her a huge fluffy bathrobe and her clothes. She ran into the warehouse's utilitarian bathroom and quickly dressed. A few minutes later she rejoined the other two, and they moved into an untidy office hidden in a corner of the vast warehouse. Margaret and Prue sat on two elderly sofas, JoBeth between them in her wheelchair. Margaret had not spoken since her return. Prue, wearing a T-shirt with the slogan 'Anything You Can Do I Can Do Better', raised an eyebrow and looked at the time traveller.

"I can't remember any details at all," Margaret said, after a long pause. Stretching out on the shabby sofa she added, "Is there any coffee?" She knew there wasn't, but felt a journey into the future, even if abortive, deserved recognition.

"Then how do we know you went into the future?" demanded Prue, ignoring the token request for coffee.

"You don't. But I know I did. If I disappeared and came back, I must have travelled in time. I did disappear, didn't I?"

"You were not quite with us for a few milliseconds. But what happened—did you meet anyone? What was Palo Alto like? And how did they use time travel? What can you remember?" JoBeth fidgeted with her papers; she needed answers to all these questions.

"I don't know. Memory is about what has happened, not what will happen. If we go into the future we can't remember anything when we come back, because it hasn't happened yet." Margaret, the most practical of the three scientists, was not quite sure of her ground in saying this, but felt it was as good an explanation as any.

"This is a fine time to tell us there's no way of proving our system works," grumbled JoBeth.

If they *had* invented time travel, then that knowledge was available from now, forever. Anyone in the future could use it to come back and see them, the inventors, who would now get Nobel Prizes, lucrative defence contracts, a chair at Berkeley, or all three. No one had shown up, which led them to think that time travel was not possible. Except that all of their calculations showed that it was. It did not occur to them that if time travellers existed, depending on their inclinations, they would be at the first Beatles concert, the Charge of the Light Brigade, Woodstock, or a brothel in Pompeii. Late twentieth century Palo Alto was just not that exciting.

Margaret, a fortyish, deeply practical physicist, drew a deep breath. Tall, lean, and in perfect health, she was the obvious choice to make the first trip. It had been gruelling getting to this stage. Since she had effectively moved into the warehouse to keep working on the time machine, her husband had disappeared. She knew all about Conchita the barmaid at the British Bankers Club in Menlo Park, who was probably 'consoling' her husband while Margaret wrestled with the intricacies of circuits no one had ever built before. Her life at present was empty of human companionship apart from that of Prue and JoBeth, who she was fond of, but no more. Once this was all over life would be very different; and, she thought, running a mental eye over the faculty at Stanford, better.

"I know I went forward in time. I have a hazy memory of talking to people, clever people, who gave me the answers to problems I thought were insoluble. But I can't remember what they looked like, or what they said. Somewhere in my brain must be memories of those conversations. Perhaps the Colibri field deactivated them when I came back in time." Margaret paused and looked at the others. "Let's face it, our knowledge is not complete. We have figured out how to exploit Colibri fields to travel in time, but we don't know how the fields themselves work."

"Perhaps we've never seen travellers in our own time because they only want to go forward, just as we do," JoBeth grunted, her mind running over the question of why no travellers from the future had visited present-day Palo Alto.

"Some of them must want to go back. There are always historians, archaeologists and religious nuts wanting to visit the Garden of Eden, watch Anne Boleyn be executed, or see Greek gods," Margaret said, wishing that she could go back to find out who her real parents were.

"They'd want to alter the outcome of a race or rig the lottery, more likely," said Prue.

Margaret left the others talking, and went into the tiny kitchen. They had spent two years developing complex math programs which required a battery of high-speed computers to run. Once they had figured out how to make a time machine, they had moved into the warehouse and started building it. That was six months ago.

Time travel required complex machinery, nanosecond timing, and the expenditure of vast amounts of energy. Inconveniently, they had discovered that only one's body could go into the future. You departed naked, and you came back naked, raising problems for prudish chronic adventurers. You could take nothing with you, and bring nothing back except—they had hoped—memories. Now Margaret was saying to the sceptical JoBeth and Prue that she had only the vaguest memories of her first trip. It had used five million kilowatt hours of energy, and caused the projector at the nearby Stanford Theater on University Avenue to burn out. The cinema had been showing *The Land That Time Forgot* when it happened.

Prue Bernstein was a very rich woman, although her riches were declining rapidly. Graduating summa cum laude from UCLA in physics, then breezing through the MBA course in one year, she had set up a business making microwave amplifiers. Small, hyper-active, with dark curly hair that never behaved properly, she sold out at the top of the market and was now spending the proceeds. Time travel had absorbed most of them.

Prue had taken JoBeth's designs and turned them into reality by providing funding, while Margaret did the detailed practical work. She suspected that the other two didn't realise that she had designed and built the circuits that created the Colibri field, the fundamental mechanism used for moving through time.

"I don't think we should continue. If Margaret goes to the future and comes back without any mental or physical evidence, then we will not get outside funding for this project. We have already spent most of our money." She meant most of her own money; the others contributed little in the way of dollars by comparison.

JoBeth tried to speak, but Prue held her hand up. "Listen. The next step requires getting a corporate sponsor with a big bank account. For that we need proof that our time travel machine works." Margaret, returning from the kitchen, nodded. She'd managed to forage some instant coffee, a mug of which was putting her in a better mood. She was able to talk more clearly about her trip—if she had taken a trip in time and not gone into hyperspace, an alternative universe, or dreamt the whole thing.

"I didn't bring back any evidence, but that doesn't mean it can't be done. We just don't know how to do it yet. We know it has to be in our minds or bodies, because we can't take or bring anything else back."

They debated the feasibility of using implants. Although you travelled naked, dental work, heart pacers, artificial hips and so on ought to travel along with you. Margaret was in perfect shape physically, but she had a dental crown. She nervously ran her tongue round the inside of her mouth: it was still there.

"If I had a miniature recorder in my crown, would it survive the journey, along with any recordings I make?"

JoBeth frowned. "We may be up against some kind of paradox barrier. You could probably activate the recorder, but nothing to help us would come back." JoBeth had graduated from Harvard at the age of nineteen, ignoring the illness that had wrecked her chance at her first choice of career, becoming a ballerina. Her PhD thesis had been on time travel, though she maintained that no one who read it appreciated what she was doing at the time.

"The maths don't tell us either way. Perhaps we can find out, though." JoBeth winced and downed a pill to help cope with her chronic pain, then fussed with the papers on one of her wheelchair's tables, looking for a report. She found it and took a glance, then cupped her chin in her hands and stared into space, ignoring the other two as they continued to argue. Finally she roused herself. An earnest and respected theoretician, her views usually prevailed.

"Paradox is at work here, but I don't fully understand how. We may be trying to bring information back from the future in the wrong way. If there were a completely free flow of information through time, then everyone would be able to bet on the outcome of a prediction. The insurance and betting industries would collapse. They make money out of our ignorance of what is in store for us. Take that away and we wouldn't need them. Perhaps we have the maths correct, but the logic wrong." She scratched her head, unsure where this line of thought was leading.

The other two did not agree. Whatever the mathematical arguments, the laws of physics did not rule out time travel. There were many paradoxes in science, but often they were only apparent. If one looked at the problem in the right way there was usually no paradox.

There could be advantages to knowing about developments in the future, provided it was understood how to apply that knowledge to the present. JoBeth said that if one knew that the world's population was not going to expand indefinitely it would help in planning the use of resources, but thought you could not find out what was going to happen to any one person.

"Our expectations could be wrong," Margaret commented wearily.

"Confucius said that 'to go too far is the same as not going far enough'. That might apply to time. Supposing we go into the future, say a hundred years, and talk to the people there, I mean then. They might just say, 'Great, you've invented time travel, now piss off.' Maybe that's what they said to me."

"Why would they do that?" asked JoBeth. "They will already know we invented it because we are in their past. Or could knowledge of time travel, once found, be hidden again?"

"Maybe our descendants would tell us to go away because they've decided that time travel is a bad idea and not to be used, just like nuclear weapons," joked Margaret.

JoBeth squinted at her, but just said, "Time is not what you or I think it is. The old idea is that it's a river, sweeping everything along on its surface. We've shown that we can swim downstream, to the future. Going upstream would be harder for those in the future, but it is not impossible. Let's face the fact that it isn't really a river; it's a set of equations we can solve but don't completely understand."

The other two nodded. JoBeth wheeled herself to look out of the warehouse's window. It had been built on a bend in the road, next to an awkward traffic intersection. "If they ever straighten out Page Mill Road, you'll arrive right in the middle of that intersection!" she said cheerfully to Margaret, pointing at the chaos as backed-up traffic negotiated a stop sign.

"How do you think the *Palo Alto Weekly* will report a beautiful naked woman like me suddenly appearing in the intersection in 2095?"

"With glee, photographs and an interview. Especially the photographs," said JoBeth.

"They probably won't report it, because everyone will be running around naked in the future." Prue was slightly uneasy at this conversation, feeling she could never compete with Margaret in the beauty stakes.

"Don't try putting me off, Prue. I'm going forward in time regardless of what I look like, and regardless of the worst the City's Public Works Department does. Anyway, fifty years from now all vehicles will be robotically controlled. They will be able to handle it when I appear. That's assuming Page Mill Road is still here."

Time machines look nothing like the contraptions you might see on TV or at the cinema. Their machine was an untidy mess of exposed components, had dangerous wiring, and looked like a several-ton racing car built to excite sixteen-year-old boys. At its heart was a small transparent compartment with a single plastic garden chair for a seat. They had not developed it in the proverbial Stanford garage, instead renting the warehouse on Page Mill Road in Palo Alto, abandoned, Prue claimed, by Hewlett, or perhaps Packard.

The maths showed that travelling through time required also moving through space. The warehouse was six hundred feet long, and there was just enough room inside to get the machine up to speed. It started at one end and was magnetically impelled forward on rails, the time shift occurring just before it hit the far wall. It never struck the wall, instead going into the future for a few nanoseconds. There it reversed its direction of travel, before reappearing in the present and running backward down the track to its starting point. To the observer the machine never disappeared, but the occupant blurred slightly. It was then that the time traveller was somewhen else. The whole process took just two and a half minutes.

A system of powerful shock absorbers had been built into the time machine after the first few trials, when the vessel didn't move forward in time, just forward into the wall. This had resulted in hideous marks and gouges where the machine had struck, over which Prue had painted a large bullseye. It had taken months of testing before the machine had finally started working as planned. The biggest problem was—other than the burden of proof—the colossal amount of energy required to run the machine, and the consequent tendency for everything to overheat. Prue had once said ruefully that you could fry eggs and bacon on the machine, if they could afford to buy them.

There were only three controls used. One set the destination time and date, one controlled how much time you spent in the future, and the last was the start button. There was no stop button; once the machine had started, it ran until its cycle was complete.

Prue thought that in an ideal world they should be able to return to any time they chose, possibly coming back before they left. So far though, the machine seemed limited to returning the traveller to just after when they had left. Of course, the problem was proving that one had time travelled in the first place.

It worked. They knew that it worked; they just could not prove it yet. They could publish the theory behind the machine, then leave it to others to prove and implement; but Johnson, Smith and Bernstein wanted more than that. They wanted glory, and they wanted to be the first to travel in time. JoBeth often quoted a film she had seen based on Wells' *Time Machine*: "We all have our time machines, don't we? Those that take us back are memories. And those that carry us forward are dreams."

"We're all clever, guys. We've beaten everyone else—we just can't prove it. Wonderful!" Prue said, sarcastically.

"Look," replied Margaret. "I'll make more trips. I just need a way to record them. Suppose I put a recording device in my crown?"

JoBeth had said that a physical recording would not be transportable across the time barrier unless it was part of the traveller's body, and the tooth recorder was as good an idea as any. Margaret's friendly dentist agreed to supply the equipment, and he fitted her crown with a miniature sound and video recorder. He was flattered to be working, as he thought, for the CIA, and charged three times the normal fee. Margaret was going to have to smile a lot for the camera to work: not easy, remembering how much it had cost.

The team put together enough money to cover power for three more trips, each going about fifty years ahead. Each trip would test various equipment settings. They thought this was long enough for surroundings to look different and for new technology to have emerged, but not so far ahead that life and language would be incomprehensible.

JoBeth seemed distracted while all this was happening, and did not even come into the warehouse on some days. She later told them that there were one or two ideas she had wanted to sit and think about quietly at home. She did not tell them that, while she was at home, she sketched out ideas for universally-sized clothes that automatically fitted themselves, a rubber tyre that never wore out, and an early warning system for detecting bores at cocktail parties. She completed patent applications for all three, but never filed them. They were discovered several years later by her cleaner, whose four-year-old son used them to draw on.

After each of Margaret's trips, the result was the same. The recorder had nothing on it at all. The time spent in the future was set at one month so that they could measure hair and nail growth, but the tests showed no change. They argued about whether it would make a difference if one of the other two went, or whether to send the same traveller for consistency. So far, consistency had won. But results had likewise been consistent: Margaret continued to report that she'd travelled into the future, but without remembering a single specific detail about it.

By Margaret's third trip their money was almost gone. They had long since taken out second mortgages, and had little else to fall back on other than Prue's dwindling store of cash. They were exhausted, with no results to show from their work. Life had turned into a series of gloomy and argumentative enquiries.

One day, after yet another interminable discussion on how they could demonstrate evidence of time travel without transporting physical objects, pictures or memories, JoBeth Johnson suddenly interrupted the conversation. "We're on the wrong track: I'll go. I can prove that time travel works, even if you can't." Oddly for her, she did not provide any reasons, just kept repeating that she could achieve things in the future that were out of Margaret and Prue's reach.

JoBeth was the last person to send on an expedition, even to the supermarket. She knew how a screwdriver worked, but it was doubtful she had ever used one. She knew how computers should be programmed, but left the details to others. The three argued all night. Finally JoBeth said she was going, there should be no more argument, and she would go home to rest before the trip. They reluctantly agreed, and shortly afterwards heard the clatter as she loaded the wheelchair into the back of her wagon and slowly drove away.

"It's madness. She's going to kill herself." Margaret gazed at Prue.

"The two of *us* are going to kill her. We should disconnect the power and tell her the project is over." Margaret frowned and added, "We can only afford one more trip; we already have that huge unpaid electricity bill from PG&E. So everything would be riding on JoBeth."

"Yet nothing else has worked—it might be worth the gamble."

"I'll gamble, yes; but not with someone's life."

"She's a grown woman. She's also a world class physicist. She knows the risks better than anyone. If she's right about the future, then her disabilities don't matter."

Margaret pondered for a moment. "What would happen if a disabled woman from fifty years ago suddenly materialised in front of us?"

"I guess we'd do our best for her; we're pretty civilised," Prue conceded.

"I think you just made JoBeth's point for her."

They then fell uncomfortably asleep on the office sofas. Several hours later, in the dawn, they grumpily woke to find JoBeth in front of them. She was holding a sack with coffee, bagels and orange juice.

"I went over to the Town and Country Village to get this stuff for you, so enjoy. You guys freshen up, eat some breakfast, and then we'll talk." She went off into the warehouse, saying no more. Prue inhaled the smell of Peet's coffee and smiled her first smile in twenty-four hours. Half an hour later JoBeth returned to find the others ready.

The mood had changed. The would-be time traveller was very calm.

"I have as much say over what goes on as you two do. I'm doing what I think is right: I'm volunteering. You're not responsible for my actions." She grinned. "I've even put it on paper." A set of legal documents was scattered across the table. "If it doesn't work, I won't try again. Maybe because I'll be in tiny pieces." She grinned again, before adding, "But I know it'll work." Prue and Margaret exchanged looks: JoBeth did not seem to realise this was the last trip any of them would make.

"JoBeth, we know how important it is to you to go, but one of us should be with you. This is our last shot; we can't afford another trip," said Prue.

"It won't help."

"What if you get into difficulty? You won't have your wheelchair. You can't even get out of the machine without help." Prue was starting to get angry with her friend, but the look on JoBeth's face told her she was losing the argument.

"That won't be a problem. Trust me. Anyway, there's only one seat. Two of us wouldn't fit!" JoBeth finally persuaded them to accept her plan. Although Prue and Margaret could not say so, they both asked themselves if a person in a wheelchair would be more likely to get help and attention than the very fit Margaret. As nothing else had worked up until now, perhaps JoBeth's plan was better than it had looked at first.

The following day they gathered in the warehouse. JoBeth undressed with painful slowness, and they eased her slight figure onto the machine's cramped chair, taking care not to hurt her withered and useless left arm and leg.

"What about the oxygen tank?" asked Margaret.

"I can manage. Unless there's a war on, I'm sure help will be at hand. The Palo Alto Medical Clinic will still be just down the road. They'll be obliged to treat me if I tell them my social security number. Otherwise I'll sue them from the past! I don't have any money with me of course, but I guess the Bank of America will be cooperative," she joked. "I'm going after my time, you realise that?"

JoBeth shivered slightly in the unheated warehouse. Prue was at the controls. "You sure you want to do this?" She spoke to the air. JoBeth looked grimly ahead, refusing to meet her eye.

"Just push the buttons, Prue, this'll work. I know it will."

"You'll like it there, JoBeth. I know I did," Margaret murmured.

The machine behaved itself. They watched it rush towards the end of the warehouse. It slowed just as it was about to hit the bullseye on the end wall, stopped, JoBeth went slightly fuzzy, and the machine with its passenger inside came slowly back to its starting position. Five minutes had elapsed since Prue pressed the start button. JoBeth was as naked as when she left. She sat quietly in the machine's seat as they gazed at her. She clutched the dressing gown Margaret threw to her, apparently relishing her adventures. Then she smiled, a broad grin.

"I told you I would prove it. I've been forward in time," she said finally. Prue Bernstein said nothing, knowing the result could only be the same as always. She moved towards the cripple, ready to help her out of the machine. "Oh, that's OK. I can manage," JoBeth said, smiling. Using both hands she vaulted out of her seat, put on the dressing gown, and waltzed down the length of the building, pirouetting when she reached the end. She ran lightly back to the other two, the broad grin still on her face. Prue and Margaret could see the ballerina she might have been.

"You were both wrong about backers; the health insurers are going to invest a lot of money in our project. We're rich! Time for a little something to celebrate." JoBeth pulled on a knee-length T-shirt which said 'Time Travelers Unite! Yesterday!' and strode off towards the office, humming 'As Time Goes By'.

A NOTE FROM SIMON

Science tells us that time travel is not impossible. No one knows how to do it, or even how to start doing it, but it is not impossible. If we could travel back in time there is a possible paradox. If I go back and kill my parents before they meet I will not be born, and so cannot kill my parents. If I go into the future other, equally difficult, logical problems occur.

This story tries to deal with one of the apparent impossibilities caused by time travel by asking: can we remember that which has not yet happened? The thoughtful reader will see that it begs many questions, as does every time travel story I have ever read.

If it brought a smile to your face then I shall feel it worked well enough. Writing it showed me how valuable memory is, and how little we can do without it.

Simon Evans
Devizes, UK

STRANGERS
ROBERT MCKELVEY

Charles Alexander Rigby let out a plaintive moan and opened a single, bleary eye.

He remembered leaving the Belle Rouge at around ten o'clock and making his way to the Devil's Head for something to eat.

Everything else was rather more difficult to remember, but his throbbing head and hazy vision strongly suggested that gin had been involved.

He was lying on something hard and lumpy.

With great effort, he struggled to his feet and brushed his scruffy hair out of his face, massaging his tired eyes with stiff, aching fingers. As he looked about, his sight slowly returning to him, it quickly dawned on him that this was not the guest bedroom at Fred's house—nor indeed any room of any house. He was in an alleyway and, judging by the narrow, Rigby-shaped channel left in the dirt and the horrible stiffness of his body, he had been there a while.

His hands went reflexively to his pockets. Most everything appeared present and intact; his key and handkerchief, his wallet, his engraved cigarette case. His boots were gone but, frankly, he was just grateful not to have woken up naked in a stranger's bedroom; again.

Rigby shook off the worst of the muck and groggily stumbled forwards, emerging onto a busy, unfamiliar street. It was a typical Low London scene, full of weathered red brick buildings and people going about their business, all of it overshadowed by the distant yet omnipresent steel towers and skyways of High London. He could not see a street name and he did not recognise any of the shop signs. There was nothing that gave any hint as to where he was or how far he had come.

"Ugh… Where the devil am I?" he wondered aloud.

He walked over to the nearest building, noting the brass plaque beside the door as he approached.

J. R. Spatchcock's Investigative Services.

He knocked on the door and, receiving no answer, opened it, finding himself in a small, empty foyer. It was modestly furnished, albeit brightened somewhat by a few pleasant-looking potted plants and a rather grand grandfather clock. To his left was another door, this one slightly ajar. From beyond, he could hear faint sounds of movement.

"Hello?" he called, peering into the next room.

The room was a cramped office, occupied by a single, formal-looking fellow seated behind a desk. He was broad and powerfully built—a stark contrast to Rigby's own spare frame—with a well-groomed moustache and a modest suit of plain, light grey clothes. His chestnut hair was clipped and neat, and in his right hand he held a stout, bulbous smoking pipe.

"Hello," said the man, getting up from his chair. "Can I help you, sir?"

Rigby stepped through the threshold, attempting to pull together some semblance of dignity. "Yes. Yes, absolutely," he answered, rubbing the stubble on his chin. "Um...... Do you have a telephone that I can use? Please?"

* * *

Jonathan Richard Spatchcock regarded the stranger who had entered his office with cool, grey eyes. He was dirty and dishevelled-looking, and young too; not much more than twenty years old, with thin, pale features and lank black hair. His clothes were fine but poorly cared for. The dark blue velvet of his tailored frock coat was dirty and stained and the knees of his trousers were scuffed and muddy. His bright green eyes were reddened and he seemed incapable of standing still, fidgeting with his spoiled finery like a nervous boy anticipating a scolding.

He also appeared to have lost his shoes.

"Are you all right?" he asked the young man, concerned.

The stranger sniffed and noisily cleared his throat. "Fine, I'm fine," he said, wiping the corner of his mouth with a grubby sleeve. "Sorry. Pleased to meet you. Please may I use your telephone? I just need to use your telephone. You do have a telephone, don't you?"

Spatchcock gestured to the telephone set on his desk. "Help yourself."

With almost indecent haste, the stranger snatched up the receiver and quickly dialled a number, waiting impatiently for whomever he was calling to pick up.

"Thank you. Come on, come on. Blast! No answer. Damn it, Fred."

He slammed down the telephone and sighed loudly.

Spatchcock placed his hands together and leaned forward on his elbows. "Are you sure that I can't help you with anything?" he asked. "May I ask your name, at least?"

Rigby groaned, his face creasing with frustration as he dropped into a nearby chair. "Rigby—my name's Charles Rigby."

"Jonathan Spatchcock," Spatchcock replied with a kind smile, offering his hand. "If you don't mind my saying so, you appear quite distressed, Mr Rigby."

Rigby did not respond at first, apparently too preoccupied with his huffing and fidgeting for polite introductions. When he did finally notice, he clumsily clasped Spatchcock's hand and shook it limply. His palm was cold and clammy and his fingers seemed to have no strength to them at all.

"I'm not entirely sure where I am," Rigby admitted, attempting to disguise his concern with a nervous chuckle. "I went out to see a show yesterday evening and I must have had a little too much to drink with my dinner afterwards. I...I don't suppose you know the Belle Rouge, do you? It's the little theatre on Old Market Road?"

Spatchcock shook his head. "I'm afraid I don't have time for such diversions," he confessed.

"Ah, well, in that case, I might require some assistance getting back to my lodgings," Rigby groaned. He pinched the bridge of his aquiline nose. "Drat."

"Do you know the address?" Spatchcock asked.

"I was staying with a friend, Dr Fredrick Fealy," said Rigby, waving his hands vaguely. "He owns a little apothecary shop on Harrowing Street."

Spatchcock nodded. "We can take an autocab," he said, taking his coat and hat from the stand behind him.

Rigby suddenly became much more alert and uncomfortable-looking, his eye wide with alarm. "Wait, 'we'? What do you mean by 'we'?" he asked.

"Is there a problem, Mr Rigby?" Spatchcock enquired as he crossed the room to the door.

"No! No, no problem at all," Rigby laughed desperately, reaching inside his coat pocket and producing a high-quality leather wallet. "It's just... Well, I couldn't ask you to pay for a cab for me! It just wouldn't be right. Look, I—Oh..."

Rigby's face fell as he opened the wallet and inspected the contents, his expression turning to a confused frown.

"Oh. Bugger."

* * *

Rigby sat sullenly as the autocab rattled along. His headache had grown worse, not helped by the shaking or the noise coming from the vehicle's stuttering engine, but the worst part was Spatchcock. This entire situation was horribly embarrassing. Rigby hated being indebted to anyone, particularly a total stranger. He resented being seen as charity case but, at the same time, he could not deny that the man had been nothing but a perfect gentleman towards him. He had even lent him a pair of shoes!

The fact that they were also quite comfortable only made it worse.

"Charming part of town you live in," he remarked, gazing out of the window, feigning interest.

"I only moved here recently," Spatchcock said. "I haven't had much opportunity to explore."

"Well," said Rigby. "I suppose that that makes two of us."

Spatchcock looked round at Rigby curiously. "You said you were staying with a friend. Does that mean you're from out of town?"

"Hm? Oh no. I was born here," Rigby replied, leaning back from the window. "Well, not *here*, but I was born in the city."

"Do you have family here then?" asked Spatchcock.

"You are just full of questions, aren't you?" Rigby said, reaching into his pocket and fishing out his cigarette case. "You don't mind if I smoke, do you?"

Before Spatchcock could answer, Rigby cracked open the case.

"Eh? What's this?"

Rigby's fingers reached into the case and plucked out a small scrap of crumpled paper, turning it over and examining it with a bemused expression. It looked to be a receipt of some sort, although what for he could not say; the writing was smudged and had even been completely obliterated in places. It looked as though it had had a drink spilled on it. The only legible words appeared at the top in large letters, printed in bold black ink.

"Mountebank's Emporium," Rigby read. "Lethean Road."

Spatchcock peered over at the tiny piece of paper. "Perhaps you put that in there for safekeeping."

Rigby's frown only deepened. "I don't remember going here," he murmured, more to himself than anyone else. "I took the trolleybus to the theatre and then went straight to the Devil's Head after I left. I certainly didn't go to any emporiums. It was late. None of them would have been open; none that give out receipts, anyhow."

"How odd."

"Indeed," Rigby agreed, placing the perplexing piece of paper back into the case and extracting a cigarette. "I wish I could remember what became of my boots," he grumbled, tapping his borrowed footwear on the floor of the cab.

"Perhaps you should report your missing property to the police, Rigby," Spatchcock suggested.

"The police won't help," Rigby huffed sullenly, sinking further into his seat and fixing the cigarette to his thin lips.

"Why not?" Spatchcock asked.

"I'm a lot of things, Spatchcock, but 'beloved-of-law-enforcement' is not one of them. They'll just say that it's my own damn fault again and send me on my way. Besides, the last time I was at a police station I was quite rude to them. I think I threw a lamp at the custody sergeant. Do you have a light?"

Spatchcock produced a box of matches from inside his coat and passed it to Rigby.

"Why in the world would you do something like that?" he asked, slightly incredulous.

"I don't know. I don't even know how I got there," admitted Rigby as he lit the cigarette and took a long, hard draw. "One minute I was having a glass of wine with Fred and the next, *lamp.*"

He blew out a column of bluish smoke and let out a hacking, sticky cough.

"You're beginning to sound like you might have a problem, Rigby," Spatchcock said with a disapproving tone. "I'm curious; what exactly is it that you do?"

"Do?"

"What line of work are you in?"

"Oh, I dabble in this and that," Rigby croaked, forcing what he hoped was a nonchalant smile onto his face.

"Such as?" asked Spatchcock.

"Well…I write, paint a little…I play the violin… Like I said, I dabble," Rigby mumbled. "Sometimes people pay me to take letters or write down appointments, you know? Things like that."

His voice trailed off as he tried to avoid Spatchcock's sceptical eye.

"I see," he said.

"What about you, old boy?" Rigby asked, keen to change the subject. "You're some sort of detective, if I'm not mistaken?"

"I'm a private investigator," Spatchcock replied.

"So you *are* a detective!" Rigby laughed. "How fascinating; you're like the hero of one of those mystery stories! I'll bet you have a magnifying glass and a spunky lady assistant as well, correct?"

"Hardly," said Spatchcock. "It's just a job like any other, I assure you."

"Bah! A likely story," scoffed Rigby. "I wager you've seen all manner of interesting things in that line of work! Low London's practically overrun with pickpockets and rogues and such like."

"Rogues, certainly," Spatchcock muttered.

* * *

As they neared Harrowing Street, Rigby couldn't help but notice the sizable crowd that had gathered in the street outside.

"What do you suppose all *this* is about?" Spatchcock asked as they alighted from their autocab, thanking the driver with a polite tip of his hat.

"I don't know," said Rigby. "Let's find out, shall we?"

As they moved closer, the truth became more and more apparent. The jaunty sign that usually hung above the entrance to Fealy's shop had been torn down and now lay chipped and splintered on the cobblestones, surrounded by a sea of broken glass. The large display window had been smashed and the front door had been battered down with such force that it had been reduced to kindling.

In the middle of it all stood two figures, a short, distraught man with an unruly red coiffure and the tall, long-coated form of a thief-taker looming over him. In a city full of machines, impossibly tall structures and self-propelled vehicles, some might say that it was inevitable that the spirit of the age would find its way into law enforcement as well. The automata were made to resemble giant constables—they even had badges and wore uniforms—but Rigby had always found their blank cyclopean faces and harsh, rasping voices incredibly disturbing. In a city full of machines, there were some things that should really have just been left to good old-fashioned flesh and blood human beings.

The two appeared to be conversing and, as he and Spatchcock neared the front of the assembled onlookers, Rigby was able to overhear a little of what was being said.

"PLEASE SPEAK SLOWLY AND CLEARLY WHEN PROVIDING A STATEMENT," the thief-taker belched out, its discordant, lifeless monotone grating on Rigby's nerves, like metal scraping against metal.

"I *am* sp-speaking s-slowly and c-clearly, you f-f-foul machine!" the little man snapped irritably.

"That's Fealy," said Rigby, indicating the whining, tubby man.

"PLEASE STATE YOUR NAME AND OCCUPATION," the thief-taker droned, oblivious to the poor fellow's obvious frustration.

"Fealy!" he cried, wringing his pudgy little hands in desperate anguish. "For the hundredth time, my name is Dr F-Fredrick F-Fealy! I own this shop! It was broken into! I was attacked!"

"PLEASE SPEAK SLOWLY AND CLEARLY WHEN—"

"Oh, forget it!"

"Fred? Freddie!" Rigby called out, pushing through the crowd. "What the devil happened here? Are you all right?"

"Charles? Oh thank goodness!" Fealy exclaimed, rushing to him and embracing him a little too tightly.

"Ack! Fred. I need to breathe, Fred. Fred!"

"Oh! Oh d-dear me, I'm so sorry, Charles," Fealy apologised, releasing his hold on Rigby's waist. "I was just so w-worried when you didn't come back f-from the theatre! Where have you been?"

"Fred, relax," said Rigby. "I just got a bit lost on my way home, that's all."

Fealy's face locked into a mask of utter disbelief. "What are you t-talking about? I haven't seen you for d-days!"

"What?"

"I haven't seen you since Wednesday evening," Fealy cried.

Rigby looked baffled. "What day is it today then?"

"It's Friday, Rigby," Spatchcock interjected.

"Who're you?" Fealy asked, his large, watery eyes suddenly focused on the unfamiliar face.

"He's a friend, Fred," said Rigby. "He took me in off the street when I couldn't find my way back to you this morning. He's a detective."

Fealy's expression brightened. "What, l-like out those mystery stories?"

Spatchcock's face remained impassive. "What happened here?" he asked, addressing the thief-taker and gesturing to the mess around them.

"A CRIME HAS BEEN REPORTED," the machine rumbled, turning its head to focus the lens of its mechanical eye on the detective. "WE ARE INVESTIGATING. PLEASE REMAIN CALM AND GO ABOUT YOUR BUSINESS, SIR."

"My business is in ruins! *Ruins!*" Fealy squeaked angrily. "They j-just barged in and st-started smashing things! I asked them what they were doing and they at-at-attacked m-me!"

"PLEASE SPEAK SLOWLY AND—"

"Who did, Fred?" Rigby asked, trying to ignore the hulking machine.

"Oh! Y-Yes, of course," said Fealy, composing himself. "Well, there were t-two of them! One of them had a-a cough, fog lung by the s-sound of it, and a b-b-big scar on his f-face. He w-was th-the one who h-hit me."

"Hmm," murmured Spatchcock to himself. "Rigby, do you have any idea who these men might have been?"

"Why are you asking me?" Rigby asked blankly. "Wait, hold on! Are you suggesting that what happened to Fred is somehow my fault?!"

"I'm just asking you to try and think if anyone you know might have motivation to wish Dr Fealy harm, Rigby," said Spatchcock. "I'm not *accusing* you of anything."

Rigby fell quiet, his jaw working silently as his mind raced.

"Fred, this fellow with the scar on his face; what else can you tell me about him?"

"Please, Charles, I d-d-don't know—"

"How tall was he?" asked Rigby. "What was he wearing? Did he have bad breath? Come on, Fred. You've always been a stickler for details."

"I d-don't know!" Fealy whimpered. "Um... He... He was bald. He w-was t-t-tall too—taller th-than me anyway—and he was w-wearing a shirt with br-braces—"

"What about the scar, Fred?" Rigby pressed. "You said it was big. What did it look like?"

"Oh, it was a ho-horrible thing!" said Fealy, a disgusted look creasing his chubby, child-like face. "It was all swollen and red, l-like a burn or a bad bruise!"

"What about the other man, Dr Fealy?" Spatchcock asked. "Is there anything you can tell us about him?"

"He was t-tall too," he replied. "H-He was th-the one who broke my d-display. H-He had a hammer, a huge hammer! He smashed up everything with it!"

"Does any of that sound familiar, Rigby?" asked Spatchcock.

Rigby's face went blank. "No," he said flatly. "Sorry."

Spatchcock rubbed his chin in a contemplative manner, his brow furrowed in concentration. "Has anything been taken, Dr Fealy?" he asked. "Something must have motivated these undesirables. Perhaps they were after your goods?"

"I doubt it," Rigby chimed in, pointing to the destroyed window display of Fealy's shop. "Look at all the broken bottles, all the spillage. If they were thieves or inebriates, they would have been a lot more careful with those."

"You have a good eye," Spatchcock noted.

Rigby shrugged. "I just know that a bottle of Campbell's Morphium Sedative isn't cheap."

"They ruined m-my shop!" wailed Fealy. "They've been through the whole place, r-r-ransacked every room. I can't t-tell if anything is m-missing!"

Rigby's face suddenly took on a look of great alarm. "They didn't go through my room, did they?!" he gasped, the sudden realisation leaving a nauseating, horrid knot in his stomach.

Before Fealy could answer, Rigby had disappeared through the remains of the front door.

* * *

Spatchcock and Fealy followed Rigby into the shop, the investigator removing his hat as he stepped across the threshold. The scene inside was just as bad as the one outside. Tables had been overturned and shelves had been knocked off the walls, resulting in more broken bottles.

"Good grief," Spatchcock murmured under his breath.

He passed the shop counter, observing as he did so that the till was still intact, and headed up the stairs. "Rigby?" he called.

"In here!"

Spatchcock followed his voice through the open door to his left, finding Rigby in the middle of a mess of broken furniture. He was either furious or on the verge of breaking down in tears, but he seemed incapable of deciding which emotion should take precedence over the other. As it was, his expression kept fluctuating between the two in a most bizarre manner, giving him the look of a fish caught out of water as he stood rifling through his own pockets.

"My watch is gone!" he shouted, throwing up his hands. "They took my damn pocket watch!"

"Calm down," Spatchcock urged, appealing for calm. "Perhaps you've just misplaced it."

"No! No, I couldn't have," Rigby protested, his words rising in speed and pitch. "It's always either in my jacket pocket or my dresser drawer, and it's not in my jacket pocket which means it's in my dresser drawer and it's not in my dresser drawer, so where *is* it?!"

"Rigby, you need to calm down or you're going to make yourself faint."

Rigby failed to heed Spatchcock's advice. If anything, he only became even more erratic.

"You don't understand!" he cried, eyes wide and panicked. "That watch is priceless. *Priceless!* My mother gave it to me before she…"

Rigby's voice trailed off as he sank to the floor, cradling his face in his hands.

"It was the last gift she gave him before she p-passed away," Fealy said, his reedy voice trembling as he explained. "Shortly after that his father th-threw him out over an argument, but he kept the watch; silver case with a chain and his name engraved on the back. It even had a l-little spirit engine in it so that he didn't have to wind it."

Spatchcock extended his arm and placed a firm but friendly hand on Rigby's shoulder. Rigby sighed and took several deep breaths, hoping that it might restore some veneer of calm. When that failed, his head dropped into his hands again and he let out a long, shuddering groan.

"I'm sorry, Spatchcock," he mumbled. "I just don't know what to do. None of this makes any sense to me."

"You really should report this to the police, Rigby," said Spatchcock.

Rigby slipped his hand into his coat pocket and pulled out his cigarette case. "Please may I have a light?" he asked meekly. "I used to have one of those funny little petrochemical ignitors, but I pawned it. I forget why."

Spatchcock's face lit up in a sudden burst of clarity. "Wait, say that again?"

Rigby looked up, confused. "Please may I have a light?"

"No; what you were saying about your ignitor," Spatchcock said. "You said you pawned it. Pass me your cigarette case."

Rigby handed the case to Spatchcock. "Yes, I thought as much," said the detective, opening it and retrieving the paper from inside. "Look here, below 'Mountebank's Emporium'. What do you see?"

Rigby dried his eyes and squinted at the grubby slip where Spatchcock had indicated.

"Some balls on a shield?" he asked, completely lost.

"It's a pawnbrokers' mark," Spatchcock explained. "Three spheres suspended from a bar; Mountebank's Emporium is a pawn shop."

"You really think I would give away my most treasured possession?!" Rigby shouted, springing onto his feet in a fit of rage. "Are you mad?!"

"You've been missing for days and you can't even account for your own boots," Spatchcock said flatly. "It's safe to conclude that you have not been in the best frame of mind of late. In any case, we have a lead."

"We do?"

"Indeed we do, Rigby," Spatchcock replied, a determined glint appearing in his eye. "Now we can begin to get to the bottom of all this. Dr Fealy, do you know how to get to Lethean Road from here?"

* * *

Mr Reginald Mountebank was a man who prized routine above almost everything else. He believed that there was a correct time and place for everything. Everything about him spoke to that fact, from his neat, oiled hair and his carefully waxed moustache, to his tailored suit and the gold signet ring on his left hand. It would have been easy to mistake him for a High London noble or some new-money industrialist, but the truth was that he had never cared much for the upper city. He was a man of meticulous habit. So, when his luncheon was interrupted by a loud knocking at his office door, he was not particularly pleased.

"What is it, Errol?" he asked with a slight frown.

The door opened and Errol shuffled into the room, the top of his lumpy head scraping the ceiling as he did so.

"There are two gen'lemen 'ere, sir," he said slowly, the tone and pace of his voice suggesting that even forming syllables was an intellectual challenge best left to his betters. "They say they wanna talk to you."

Mountebank's frown deepened. He let out a small sigh of annoyance and gently slid his plate to the side of his desk as he stood up and straightened his cravat.

"Very well, Errol," he said, forcing a cordial smile over his irritated expression. "We will discuss your limited understanding of the phrase 'I am not to be disturbed during my lunch hour' after we have seen to these gentlemen. Now, move; you are blocking the doorway."

Errol hurriedly moved aside as his employer swept past him and back onto the shop floor. Quickly, Mountebank scanned the room, his keen eyes looking for anything, or anyone, that seemed out of place among the assembled treasures of his emporium. Some of the items were truly marvellous things obtained from the well-to-do houses of High London, antiques and artefacts that many a rich and powerful man would gladly cough up a small fortune to possess. Exquisite clothes, jewellery, weapons, automata; it had all once been valuable to someone. Some of it might even have been considered priceless—but that, Mountebank had found, was the great weakness of the rich and powerful. They believed that money was merely part of the trappings of power, and so frittered away their riches on gaudy baubles. Men like Mountebank knew the truth.

Money *was* power.

He stopped as his eyes fell upon a tall, broad-shouldered man in cheap but functional attire standing near a large porcelain vase. As he reached out to touch it, Mountebank gave a polite cough.

"Please do not touch that."

The tall man stopped and turned to face him. "My apologies," he said, offering his hand. "Mr Mountebank, I presume?"

"You have me at a disadvantage, sir," Mountebank replied, accepting the handshake.

He examined the man's face with a practiced glance, attempting to spot some key feature by which to uncover something of his identity, but his features were nondescript, save for perhaps his piercing grey eyes.

"Jonathan Spatchcock," the man answered. "My friend and I were hoping to speak with you regarding a recent transaction."

"Ah, I see. I've passed by your office on Narrow Lane. We do not see many private investigators here, Mr Spatchcock," Mountebank said, his gaze rapidly sweeping the shop floor again. "Are you with a client?" he asked.

A sudden crashing clatter caused both men to turn, spying an ungainly figure standing over the fallen form of an elegantly constructed service automaton. Until a moment ago it had stood quite steadily upon its display plinth. Now, it lay face down on the floor with its limbs in a frightful tangle.

"I didn't touch it, I swear!"

A brief look of anger flashed across Mountebank's face as Rigby attempted to pull the automaton back onto its feet.

"I do apologise for my friend's carelessness, Mr Mountebank," Spatchcock said.

"No harm done, Mr Spatchcock," Mountebank replied calmly, eyes fixed on Rigby like a hawk's on a mouse. "Those contraptions are sturdy enough. I doubt Mr Rigby has done anything more harmful than embarrass himself."

"I'm sorry; have we met?" Rigby asked, abandoning the machine.

Again, Mountebank's face soured.

"I am sorry," he murmured, voice soft as velvet. "I must have mistaken you for someone else."

Rigby shook his head. "No, I'm Rigby," he said. "Look, I promise we won't take up much of your time. I just need you to answer a quick question: did I come in here sometime during the last few days? I have a receipt, and I think I might have sold you something by mistake."

Rigby dug around inside his pockets for the crumpled piece of paper and handed it to Mountebank, who took it, regarding it with measured disinterest.

"I am afraid I cannot help you, Mr Rigby," he said, passing it back. "This is completely illegible."

"What?!" Rigby exclaimed, aghast. "No, please, just hear me out! It's a silver pocket watch with a spirit engine mechanism."

"Mr Rigby, you have no proof of sale," Mountebank explained dispassionately. "I *cannot* help you."

"I do!" Rigby yelled angrily, advancing on the shop owner and seizing him by the lapels of his suit jacket. "I have the bloody receipt, you bloody swindler!"

Spatchcock darted forward. "Rigby, calm down!" he ordered. "I'm terribly sorry, Mr Mountebank. We should go," he said with a pointed look at Rigby.

"I think that would be best," Mountebank agreed, his face beginning to turning a brilliant beetroot red. "I have had quite enough of this young man's spurious assertions and manhandling. Errol! Kindly escort Mr Rigby off the premises before I do something that he will regret. His manners are as lacking as his dress sense."

"I beg your pardon?!" Rigby squawked.

Errol emerged from Mountebank's office and lurched over to Rigby, clapping a heavy hand upon his shoulder. "This way please, sir."

Rigby twisted out of Errol's loose hold and spun on his heel, hitting the massive fellow across the face with a tightly clenched fist.

"Rigby!" Spatchcock shouted.

"I will not be harassed in this manner!" Rigby yelled, his eyes brimming with defiance. "Get him, Spatchcock!"

Before anyone could react, Rigby punched Errol again and again, only stopping when Spatchcock grabbed him by the sleeve and pulled him back from his groaning victim.

"What the devil do you think you're doing?!" he demanded, his face flushed with anger but, before Rigby could answer, Errol's own meaty fist came up and hit Rigby so hard that he dropped to the floor like a marionette with its strings cut.

* * *

Rigby winced as he staggered back down Lethean Road, gently nursing the side of his head.

"I can't believe that you let that big lummox hit me!" he complained.

"You hit him first!" Spatchcock retorted angrily. "You hit him *multiple* times! What were you thinking?!"

Rigby lowered his hand from his swollen eye and glowered at him.

"What was I supposed to do?" he asked indignantly. "I've been robbed, Spatchcock! Robbed *and* insulted!"

"You're an idiot," growled Spatchcock. "We might have had a case if you hadn't lost your mind and attacked the poor man. As it stands, you're lucky he didn't call the police!"

"Oh, come on! That's not fair!"

"That is *entirely* fair!"

Rigby stopped and slumped against the side of a nearby building, a dejected look forming on his bruised face. "You're right," he groaned. "I'm sorry. I shouldn't have done that."

"Oh, for goodness' sake, stop feeling sorry for yourself and take some responsibility for your actions, man!" Spatchcock said, having none of it. "You've turned this entire situation into a farce, all because you're an unrepentant mess with the wit and tact of damp newspaper!"

"You sound like my father," Rigby said, staring sullenly at the cobblestones. "I *am* an unrepentant mess! I've got no money, no home to call my own. The only things I'm good at are showing up at other people's parties uninvited and playing cards. Oh, and lest we forget, I can't even remember the last two days, and apparently I sold the only thing I really give a damn about to some cretin and his pet gorilla!" he added, throwing up his hands and laughing hysterically. "Truly, I am having an absolute ball!"

Spatchcock let out a small grunt of frustration and leaned down, offering his hand. "So do something about it," he said, pulling Rigby upright. "You're not unintelligent. You could get a job as a clerk or any number of things. Just *apply* yourself, Rigby!"

"Why do you care so much?" Rigby snapped, a sudden flash of outrage appearing in his reddening green eyes and momentarily drawing the attention of several passers-by. "I never asked you for help; you could've just let me use your phone and then sent me on my way, but you didn't! Why do you give a damn about what happens to me?!"

Spatchcock turned his back on Rigby and walked a short distance away before stopping and letting out a long sigh.

"Someone ought to," he said softly.

The profundity of Spatchcock's statement cut through all of Rigby's defiant anger and venom, leaving him stunned and struggling for an appropriate response.

"I…I don't…" he managed, floundering.

"I know," Spatchcock answered kindly, turning to face him again. "Look, let's just get you back to Fealy before you do something that gets you arrested."

"I attacked a man in his place of work," said Rigby. "I should have been arrested already."

Spatchcock's kind expression faded slightly. "I'm not sure that you should be taking pride in that fact, Rigby."

"What? No! No, I'm being serious," Rigby said as he began pacing back and forth, a thought taking root in his mind. "If some idiot had grabbed me in my place of business and attacked my man, I'd have called the police without a second thought. And I *hate* the police!"

The detective nodded his head, drawing the same conclusion. "So, what's stopping a respectable businessman like Mountebank?" he mused.

"There's one way to find out," Rigby replied. "Follow me."

"Wait, what?"

Rigby led Spatchcock down an alleyway, carefully avoiding the muck and rubbish as he went, until he found himself in roughly the right spot behind the back of several terraced buildings.

"Please tell me you aren't going to do what I think you're going to do," said Spatchcock warily. "You're in enough trouble as it is without adding to it."

Rigby pushed himself up onto his tip-toes and peered through one of the high, narrow windows into one of the buildings. "That depends entirely on what you think I'm going to do, old boy," he said, trying the door. "Good grief, it isn't even locked."

"Rigby!" Spatchcock hissed.

"Just shush, will you!" Rigby snapped irritably.

"I am not going to help you break into a man's place of business, however suspect he may be!"

"It's not breaking in," said Rigby confidently, opening the door and stepping inside. "It's trespassing."

* * *

The inside of the emporium's back room was dark and dank, with an unpleasant and sickly sweet odour. Things better left unseen skittered through the shadows between the stacks of crates, the sound alone enough to make the hairs on the back of Rigby's neck stand up. There were no signs of any human occupants, however, and that fact made him bolder.

Silently, he crept forward. There were too many boxes to search all of them—the sound would alert anyone in earshot. He knew what he was looking for, but finding it was a different story.

"Rigby, this is a bad idea!" Spatchcock whispered.

Rigby turned back to the detective. "So stick around; I'm full of bad ideas," he said with a frustrated scowl. "Now stop griping and help me look."

Spatchcock let out an exasperated groan. "All right, fine. Mountebank's clearly up to something. You're not going to find anything just skulking about in here like a common criminal. He's too shrewd for that. "

"Well what would you suggest then, O great master thief?" asked Rigby sarcastically.

Spatchcock padded over to a small table in the middle of the room and picked up a heavy, leather-bound ledger. "He's a merchant," he said, beckoning to Rigby and passing him the book. "Merchants keep records."

"You have got to be kidding me," Rigby scoffed.

"His warehouse was unlocked," Spatchcock pointed out. "Given the nature of his business, one might have thought he would invest in better security, yet he hasn't. In my experience, there are only two kinds of man that the common thief fears to steal from—clergy and other thieves—and Mr Mountebank hardly strikes me as the godly sort."

Rigby opened the ledger, revealing lists of earnings, purchases and a myriad of other dealings.

"Look at all this," Rigby murmured. "Mountebank's involved in a lot more than just his pawnshop. Money lending, shipping, financing; he even sells stock to Fred!"

"Fascinating," Spatchcock replied. "Here, found it. Item purchased: one personalised silver pocket watch with chain, five pounds; box four-hundred-and-four."

"FIVE POUNDS?!"

Rigby clapped his hand over his mouth but it was too late. The sound of his outburst had already alerted someone, and footsteps began to draw close to them.

Rigby went to flee but Spatchcock restrained him with a firm grip.

"Follow me and keep quiet," he ordered, voice little more than a whisper.

Spatchcock stood up from behind the table and moved briskly to a nearby stack of crates, dragging Rigby by his scrawny arm. Just as they managed to conceal themselves, Rigby heard the sound of a door opening and Mountebank appeared in the room, accompanied by two men. One was a great monstrosity of a man so grossly obese that his braces pinched into his flabby shoulders. His breathing was loud and laboured, a rotten phlegmy rattle, and on his face he bore an awful red scar. The other man was lean with long, skinny limbs and a shock of blond hair, a hefty-looking sledgehammer dangling from his right hand. His clothes were ill-fitting, too loose and baggy save for his footwear—a fine pair of elegant leather boots that were instantly familiar to Rigby.

"Those are *mine*!" he squeaked in muted outrage. "That bastard's wearing *my* boots!"

"Shut up!"

Mountebank turned back to the other two men, gesturing to the room at large. "Gentlemen, I have had a very vexing day thus far, so you will forgive my lack of patience. I trust that you had a productive visit with Dr Fealy?"

The large man chuckled and nodded his massive, misshapen head. "Oh, we paid 'im a visit all right. We smashed 'is place up good an' proper!"

Mountebank smoothed back his hair and brushed something off the shoulder of his jacket. "You appreciate that all that I asked you to do was *frighten* him?" he said, a dark edge entering his voice. "The good doctor is a fragile sort with an extremely valuable inventory, most of which he buys either directly or indirectly from me. If you break his inventory, he cannot sell it. If you break his inventory, gentlemen, you are costing *me* money."

The two men looked at each other nervously.

"Did you break his inventory, Clarence?" Mountebank asked, pointed as a needle. "Did you, William?"

Rigby went to say something but Spatchcock hushed him with a raised finger pressed to his lips, so he settled for making shocked and angry faces at the detective instead.

"Well…uh…y'see…" began the large man identified as Clarence.

"We only done wot you done told us to do, Mr Mountainback," interrupted William, stepping forward.

Mountebank slapped the thin man across his stupid, ugly face.

"The next time I give you a job to do, you had best remember what that job is," he informed his shaken subordinate. "Otherwise, there will not *be* a next time. Is that understood?

"Yes sir."

"Furthermore," Mountebank continued, "a young man with shoes that did not match his attire was in my shop not ten minutes ago—a Mr Rigby—enquiring about a missing personal item of his. I cannot help but notice, William, that you seem to have acquired some new personal items of your own. I know that he sold me a watch—he staggered into the shop yesterday morning, drunk and desperate and looking for some quick money—but would you care to explain how what I presume to be his footwear has found its way into your possession?"

"Wot, Charlie Rigby?" William asked, rubbed his narrow nose. "He wuz down the Devil's Head on Wednesday night; we took that posh prat for a few hands of cards an' then he ran outta money, so we pointed him in your direction."

"Yeah," Clarence chipped in with a short, wretched laugh. "Then he came back last night an' we took it all again."

"And the boots?" Mountebank asked.

"Oh, Bill got them too," Clarence added. "He said he didn't have nothin' else, so we bet 'im 'is boots."

"Well now he has brought a detective here," Mountebank informed them, their amused smiles quickly evaporating. "Fortunately, you are blessed with enough luck and good timing to make up for your deficiency of brain-power. He made a scene and was dragged away by the detective, but I am warning you—if this comes back to bite us, I will skin both of you alive."

"Are you hearing this, Spatchcock?" Rigby whispered, peering round the side of the crates.

"We have to tell the police," the detective replied. "As soon as they leave, we leave."

"Quite," agreed Rigby, "just as soon as I've got my watch back."

"What?! Where are you going? Stay here!"

Rigby ignored Spatchcock's command, slipping free of his grip before he could react and darting from shadow to shadow towards another pile of crates. He barely made a sound as he moved, his light footfalls lost beneath the heated discussion between the three criminals a short distance away.

"Just need to... A-ha!" he muttered to himself, finding crate four-hundred-and-four and gently pulling up the lid, revealing a collection of trinkets and his beloved silver watch.

He gently scooped it up, cradling it to his chest.

Unfortunately, he failed to replace the lid correctly and it slipped from his hand, striking the floor with a loud thump.

Mountebank and his two men started.

"Intruders!" Mountebank shouted.

"Rigby, run!" Spatchcock yelled, breaking cover and rushing the assembled trio of villains.

Rigby panicked, paralysed by indecision. "But what about—?!"

"Just go, NOW! RUN!"

* * *

Rigby ran, adrenalin coursing through his veins as he vaulted over crates and dashed straight for the back door. He daren't look back, even for an instant. To do so would slow him down, and Spatchcock was counting on him to reach help before it was too late.

Clearing the door, he banked hard to the left, emerging onto Lethean Road. He had to find a police box or a constable—something! Fred would know. Fred was only a short walk away, never mind a sprint.

And he had company, Rigby recalled with a wry smile.

* * *

Spatchcock ducked back from the savage swing of William's hammer and then lunged forward, striking him under the jaw with a well-aimed punch and following it up with a low kick that sent him backwards into a rack of shelves. Before he could even react, William was buried under a pile of timbers.

"One down..." he muttered, turning his attention to Clarence.

The gargantuan bruiser had an obvious advantage, his massive bulk lending him the strength of a devil, but Spatchcock's speed and skill prevented him from making good use of it. The brute was simply too slow to land a blow on him but, even so, the detective quickly began to tire from the constant evasions. Unable to mount a sufficiently powerful retaliation, he was swiftly running out of options.

"Stand still, will you!" the large man bellowed, another wild swing knocking his hat off and missing his head by mere inches.

Desperate, Spatchcock snatched up William's fallen hammer and swung it hard into the man's stomach, but the burly brute barely seemed to notice. He just laughed and smashed into Spatchcock with the full force of his hulking frame, crushing him against the storeroom wall.

"Told you to stand still," Clarence growled.

"Finish him off," Mountebank ordered. "I doubt that his silence can be bought."

Spatchcock wheezed as he tried to get words past the weight pinning him.

"What's that there, friend?" Clarence asked, leaning his full weight on him as he pressed his disgusting, misshapen face closer to Spatchcock's.

Spatchcock responded by head-butting him in his hideously swollen nose, causing him to stumble backwards, clutching his face.

"Give up," Spatchcock grunted, wiping the corner of his mouth.

"Oh, I ain't even started with you yet!" Clarence snarled, his face wobbling with feral indignation. "By the time I'm done wiv you, they're goin' to be able to fit what's left of you into a—HEY!"

Clarence would have finished his threat, had he not been suddenly and bodily lifted into the air and hurled against the wall like a sack of wet cement.

"CEASE AND DESIST," the thief-taker droned, planting a heavy metal foot firmly upon Clarence's bloated belly. "YOU ARE UNDER ARREST."

"I'd do what it says, fatso!" Rigby piped up from behind the huge automaton, a bright idiotic grin plastered across his face. "You ever tried outrunning one of these buggers? Oh. He appears to have passed out."

Mountebank's face looked as though it was about to burst every blood vessel in it. "Arrest me?! *ME*?! On what charge?" he roared, advancing towards Rigby and the machine. "These men broke into *my* storeroom, stole *my* property and assaulted *my* workers! *They're* the ones that should be arrested!"

"I couldn't agree more, old boy," Rigby nodded, raising his shackled hands. "That's why I turned myself in already, along with *my* accomplices. I'm sorry, *boss*, but kidnapping a detective is too far for me."

Mountebank probably would have had something intelligent to say under most other circumstances, but all he could muster up as a response on this occasion was a strangled gurgle of rage as the enormous automaton produced a set of handcuffs for him.

"You'll pay for this," he snarled furiously. "This is slander! *Lies* and slander! You *will* pay for this, Rigby! Do you hear me?! I'll bankrupt your entire family!"

"Ha! Good luck with that, *boss*!"

As the thief-taker began to lead them away, dragging the unconscious, shackled forms of Clarence and William behind it, Spatchcock limped over to Rigby, a look of utter bafflement upon his face.

"You know, you could have run too," said Rigby. "You couldn't have known that I'd lie to the police, get myself arrested and then lead them back here."

Spatchcock chuckled, wincing slightly at the pain in his ribs. "I'll give you that," he croaked. "If I'd have run though, where would that have left you?"

* * *

Rigby had never had a great fondness for police stations—or courtrooms, come to that—but it was gratifying to see Mountebank and his cronies get their just deserts. He had to admit, however, that that was mostly down to Spatchcock. Battered and bruised though he was, his testimony and the evidence found in Mountebank's Emporium were more than the villainous cad and his lawyer were able to explain away. The crook's own meticulously kept records made it abundantly clear that his crimes were both heinous and extensive. Even so, he denied any wrongdoing.

He was found guilty after seventeen minutes and sentenced to twenty years' hard labour, along with his two thugs.

The detective had also defended Rigby's own somewhat unorthodox actions, albeit more truthfully than Rigby himself would have preferred. Given what had transpired, the judge was content to let his own infractions slide on the condition that he do everything in his power to stay out of any further trouble.

He had even been allowed to reclaim his fancy boots.

As he sat by the fireplace back in Fealy's sitting room, turning the old pocket watch over and over in his hands, it occurred to Rigby that he had a lot to be thankful for. He brushed his thumb idly across the front of the watch's silver casing, feeling the familiar, worn contours of the family crest engraved upon it. Were it not for the kindness and forbearance of a perfect stranger, he would have lost a precious memory.

He cringed as he thought back to the ledger entry—sold for a mere five pounds in a state of inebriation.

He released the catch and opened the watch, revealing a small, coloured photograph tucked away inside the lid, and Rigby smiled to himself. He had often been told as a child that he resembled his mother. He had her green eyes, her straight black hair. His nose was his father's. It was obvious, even in the picture. His brother and sister were the same, the same pretty eyes and prominent noses.

He closed the watch and retired to his room, arranging a little of the mess as he went. Before he turned in for the night, however, he went to his writing desk and began to draft two letters—one to his father, and one to the kind detective who had saved him from his own stupidity.

A NOTE FROM ROBERT

I blame my mother for this.

She was the one who first exposed me to the weird and wondrous works of Terry Pratchett and forever warped my tiny little mind, transforming me into the fanciful and foolish man I am today. The Discworld books were clever and creative and utterly brilliant and I fell in love with them instantly. They made me want to tell my own stories and poke fun at my own particular bugbears, big or small.

Responsibility/gratitude should also be extended to the rest of my family, my friends and my long-suffering girlfriend—especially her—because without them I would have probably given up on my crazy ambitions and stuck to something practical like learning a trade. As it is, I'm doing this instead.

Now, as I sit writing an end note for my own story, I find it fitting—and humbling—that it will be a tribute to the author whose wisdom and wit delighted and inspired me for so many years, but also to the veritable horde of people who pushed and prodded and encouraged and cajoled me to get me here.

So thanks, everyone—I won't forget this.

Robert McKelvey
Tadcaster, UK

THERE'S A TATTOO, BUT THE ROBES HIDE IT
MIKE REEVES-MCMILLAN

The Dark Lady of the North, Consort of the Dread Lord—a tall woman dressed in black from, if not head to toe, at least bosom to ankle—gazed out of the window of a high stone tower.

Ignoring the landscape of beaten grey mud, black stone buildings designed for intimidation rather than practicality, and the occasional thorn tree gibbet, her eyes focussed on the distant hills bounding the horizon. Her dark eyes held a hint of longing as she surveyed the hills, though her face retained its habitual world-weary expression. She moved in a constrained back-and-forth path in front of the window, like a panther in a zoo—if that panther ate too many sweets while watching well-muscled gladiators on the scrying ball all day.

She didn't turn around when metal clashed behind her and two guards entered, resplendent in bulky black armour covered in scales and spikes. They grounded their polearms and came to attention, and a heavy, greying man wearing a breastplate even spikier than his men's armour strolled in as if he owned the place—which he did. The breastplate attempted to show off the sculpted abdominal muscles that he did not, in fact, possess, the angle at which it protruded only drawing more attention to his incipient paunch.

"How was your day?" She spoke over her bare shoulder, past a sheet of hair as crow-black as her dress. Close examination would have revealed the dull sheen of dye in place of the glossy, natural black she had once possessed. Beneath black makeup, the skin around her eyes wrinkled like satin sheets after a restless night, and she bit her black-painted lower lip.

"Much as usual," said the gravelly voice of the Dread Lord, Tyrant of the North and Conqueror of the Harland Plains, Whose Name is Cursed Throughout the World (and Very Probably Beyond, All Things Considered). "Ordered another revolt put down in Harland. Recruited more creatures for the Dark Armies. Commissioned a new Chosen One detector and a couple of traps for the main approach to the Awful Fortress, Mighty and Impregnable. Same old."

He scratched his backside below the breastplate, sniffed, then drew a dagger from its sheath by his side—an ugly, twisted thing of dark metal—and opened his mouth.

"Arthur," said his consort.

"What?"

"Are you going to pick your teeth with the Dagger of Oblivion again?"

"Yes."

He did so.

She shuddered, and swept from the room.

* * *

"Minion," she called, striding into her gloomy quarters. She and the Dread Lord (etc.) had not shared accommodation for some years now.

"Yes, Mistress?" A gnarled little creature, like a shaved ape in a rubber goblin mask, shuffled out of a corner. It attempted to bow, but its natural posture was so bent that, even if the woman had been paying attention, she would hardly have noticed the difference.

"Have we received any replies yet?"

"I will check, Mistress." He crabbed over to a scrying ball and began to operate it. After a few moments, he looked up.

"You're not going to like this one, Mistress."

"Am I not." Her tone conveyed 'tell me anyway'.

"The Order of the Light wants you to betray the Dread Lord's weaknesses to them. They offer a deal."

"Immunity?"

"A reduced sentence, Mistress."

"Reduced? To what?"

"Ten years, Mistress."

"Knowing the High and Most Righteous Order of the Actinic Light of Truth Shining Throughout the World, Yea, Even Unto the Darkest Shadows, they're not talking about ten years of probation."

"Ten years of hard labour, Mistress."

The woman turned and swore an oath that caused the sensitive scrying ball to spark and emit a puff of grey smoke. "Those self-righteous, uncompromising *morons*. I swear, in the places where the other Orders have sticks stuck, they have entire forests. Rather than let my supposed evil go unpunished, they offer a deal so bad I won't accept it, and Arthur's evil will go unpunished as well. Plus I won't get to leave him, which is more important. What else do we have?" She tapped her long, black-lacquered nails on the dark wood of a table, leaving dents.

"I have a message here from Enkeli, Mistress."

"Enkeli? The trickster god?"

"He's a master of illusion and disguise, Mistress."

"I'm aware. So what's he offering?"

"He proposes coming here disguised as a spike merchant, and exchanging appearances with you. You'll leave undetected, and he'll stay, wearing your semblance."

"Sounds like Enkeli. He'll stay? What's in it for him?"

"Amusement, one imagines, Mistress. That's why Enkeli does anything."

She pursed her lips—an expression that was particularly obvious, even in the shadowy room, thanks to the contrast between her porcelain skin and black lip cosmetics. "It's no goal of mine to provide Enkeli with amusement. And you can't trust a trickster, more or less by definition. Any other possibilities?"

The little creature hesitated.

"Come on; if you know something, out with it."

"Yes, Mistress. I did hear from one of the Dread Lord's prisoners about a cult in the jungles to the south."

"To be honest, Minion, I've had my fill of blood sacrifices. It's one of the reasons I want to leave."

"This particular cult doesn't perform blood sacrifices, Mistress. In fact, they're vegetarian."

"That's peculiar. How would they help me?"

"Well, Mistress, they have a pool, deep in the jungle, sacred to their Silent Goddess."

"And drinking from this pool will transform or protect me in some way after I leave the Dread Lord Arthur? In some way that's scry-proof, specifically?"

"Not drinking, Mistress."

"What, then?"

"They immerse you in it, Mistress, and it takes away your name."

"Takes it away how?"

"Takes away all memory of it from everyone except the Silent Goddess. And she, of course, won't tell anybody."

"Well, that would be something, I suppose. You can't scry for someone without knowing their name—at least, unless you already know where they are—and what you can't scry, you can't curse. Would *I* remember my name?"

"No, Mistress. You'll remember your past, but not your name."

"I'd forget my own name? I don't know about that." She stood, biting her lip, contemplating the idea. Her expression suggested she didn't think much of it. "And I'd still look like myself, wouldn't I? People could still identify me that way. Or does this ceremony take away their memory of my identity, too?"

"Just the name, Mistress, though it does release you from any previous covenants made under that name. But after the formation period, I believe postulants look quite different."

"Formation period?" She looked at him sharply, and he cringed.

"Yes, Mistress. They shave your head, and you meditate in silence for a year. On a diet of vegetables."

The Dark Lady contemplated her hips. She did have some room to manoeuvre there.

"A year, you say. That's...a long time to stay silent and live on vegetables. Anything else?"

"The meditation is said to change one's personality, Mistress."

"And after the year?"

"The postulant is sent out to spread the non-message of the Silent Goddess. Her missionaries are required to keep silence on Tuesdays. Otherwise, they live much like anyone else, apart from not eating meat.

Oh, and I believe there's a tattoo. But the blue robes hide it."

"I see," said his mistress. She picked at a piece of black lace on her well-architected bodice. "So, did Enkeli leave a ritual by which he might be contacted?"

* * *

Enkeli the Trickster, in the semblance of a thin merchant with a dark, curly goatee, sprawled casually in a chair in the Dark Lady's sitting room. He regarded its owner with amusement.

It was not a room that many people could have relaxed in. Black stone, black wood and black iron were relieved only occasionally by a piece of cloth blacker than any of them. Enkeli, though, had a cat's natural talent for relaxation, and he sat half-reclined, one leg hooked over the arm of the chair. He wore rich fabrics in a vivid green, and walked a double-headed counterfeit gold coin over and between the fingers of his left hand in a fluid motion, without appearing to pay any attention to it.

"So, why do you want to leave the Dread Lord?" he asked.

"Oh, the usual reasons. I mean, when I was seventeen, he seemed so romantic. Tall. Dark, of course—the darkest. Handsome, in a harsh sort of a way. Powerful. Ambitious. But that was twen…ty years ago," her slight stumble suggested that she had lowered the figure while it was on the way out of her mouth, "and… I suppose I've grown up. Meanwhile, all he thinks about is his dark armies and his grim destiny and hunting down Chosen Ones. We hardly even speak anymore."

"Does that mean you don't…" began Enkeli, with an illustrative gesture and a lascivious grin.

"It's been a while," she admitted. "To be honest, it's something of a relief to not have to. He always smells of old blood these days. Or fresh blood, come to think of it."

"Pity," said Enkeli. "That's one of the joys of shapeshifting, for me. Variety."

"So I hear. Look, what you do here is up to you, but I have to get away clear, all right? At least wait for a month or so before you try anything that might give the game away. Can you do that?"

"Patience is not one of my attributes," said the god, stretching in a catlike manner.

"I know. Think of it as playing a long game. Toy with the Dread Lord's mind a little."

Enkeli nodded. "I gather that the Dread Lord wouldn't just let you go home to Mother."

"Well, first of all, he sacrificed Mother to summon some ancient being—I forget which one—the third year we were together," she said. "I didn't find out until afterwards, of course, but that's one reason the Order of the Light wants to punish me as well. And besides, he hates to lose anything he thinks of as his, even if he's not using it. It's one of the several ways in which he's like a child. Remember that little island, what's its name? Out by Fulbeth? Sittross, or something. He'd never been there and had no plans for it, but when the Glorious Alliance of the Free Peoples took it, he raged and ranted for days. I had to send my minion out of the Dreary City of Terror and Hopelessness until he got over it. I don't mind Arthur slaughtering his own servants, it's more or less expected of a man in his position—honestly, I'd say I don't know why anyone even joins him; but of course I do, having done so myself. Still, I draw the line at destroying my minion. Summoning and binding him was a most unpleasant process, and one I don't care to repeat.

"I'll leave the minion with you, by the way, to advise you. He probably knows more about being me than I do."

"You're determined to do this, then."

"I have to," she said.

"There are conditions, of course."

"Naturally. What are they?"

"Firstly, you can't tell anyone about our deal, or it's off. I'll vanish, and you'll have to cope with whatever that precipitates."

"Fair enough. What else?"

"You can't fall in love."

"What? Why not?"

"I have a feud with the Goddess of Love. That business with the golden hairbrush and the alabaster jar of face cream. She's still angry. So if you fall in love, the deal is off, and you and I will switch back."

"Switch back to our original appearances?"

"And locations. Faces and places. You'll be back here, and I'll be wherever you were." He made the golden coin vanish from his left hand and reappear in his right, possibly by way of illustration, though he still paid no apparent attention to it.

"But I can't control whether or not I fall in love. I mean, it's unlikely, given what I'm coming out of—but the unlikely happens all the time where you're involved, if the stories are to be believed."

Enkeli shrugged. He was a well-practiced shrugger, and his gesture bore enough casual unconcern for others' problems to supply an entire elite academy.

The woman rose and paced, her high black leather boots kicking out her black skirts. The black volcanic stone of the floor showed no marks, but Enkeli suspected that a softer surface would have revealed her pacing to be a habit.

Unusually for the god, he remained silent while she thought. He had her, and they both knew it. If she wanted to leave the Dread Lord, Enkeli was her best chance.

"Very well," she said. "Deal. But you have to stay at least a year."

They spat in their right hands and clasped them to seal the covenant, repeating the terms: don't tell anyone, and no falling in love.

"Now," he said, "before we switch appearances, I'd like to introduce you to my assistant. He'll help get you out of the city, after which you can drop your disguise by an act of will at any time. I went to quite some trouble to find just the right man for the job; I think you'll find him a kind and considerate companion, not to mention an excellent listener." Enkeli whistled, and a tall, dark, handsome man strode into the room, his impressive musculature on display thanks to an open-fronted linen shirt. He bowed to the Dark Lady, in a manner that managed to be respectful, but not servile—meanwhile admiring her discreetly from under his long eyelashes. He possessed an unmistakeable resemblance to an idealised version of the Dread Lord, combined with the best features of the Dark Lady's favourite gladiator.

"You complete *bastard*," she breathed. Enkeli lifted one eyebrow, one shoulder, and one corner of his mobile mouth.

* * *

The trial of the Dread Lord Arthur (etc.) took three and a half months.

Every group wanted an opportunity to speak, from the Glorious Alliance of the Free Peoples (who had captured him) to the League of Survivors of Harland in Exile. They testified at length about what a vile person he was and his numerous offences against them, and demanded shares of his extensive territories in compensation. The High and Most Righteous Order of the Actinic Light of Truth Shining Throughout the World, Yea, Even Unto the Darkest Shadows alone took three weeks to present their testimony (not least because they refused to abbreviate their name and talked about themselves constantly), and another eight days to present their demands.

It was not until late in the third month of the trial that anyone got around to calling the Dark Lady as a witness.

"The court will come to order," announced the judge, settling her robes on the judicial bench. The shuffling and coughing died down, and the judge nodded to an usher.

"Call…um…the consort of the Dread Lord," said the usher. He appeared to be searching the parchment for a name.

A tall, pale woman in early middle age, clad entirely in black silk, stepped elegantly up to the witness stand. A crabbed little servant creature shuffled in her wake, his lamp-like eyes fixed on something in the shadows at the back of the room.

"Do you swear to tell the truth in answer to all questions put to you?" mumbled the usher, offering a golden disk stamped with the holy symbol of the Goddess of Truth. The woman regarded it, apparently with amusement.

"Oh, all right," she said. "It'll be a change, I suppose. A creative challenge." She brushed the disk with her fingers.

The usher gave her a stern look over his glasses, but stood back, bowing to the judge. The prosecutor stood, obsessively straightening his papers, coughed, and asked, "Are you the consort of the Dread Lord Arthur, known as the 'Dark Lady'?"

"No," said the woman.

Murmuring ran across the court like cockroaches through a cheap apartment.

"Order," cried the judge, pounding her gavel. "Order!"

Once order was restored, the judge herself asked, "If you aren't the Dark Lady, then who are you?"

"Allow me to demonstrate," said the witness, and waved her long, elegant hands. The black silk dress took on a green cast, then flashed the colour of spring oak leaves. When the people packing the courtroom for the sensational trial of the Dread Lord had finished blinking, a thin man with a little black goatee stood there, glowing very faintly, his hands spread in a 'ta-da!' gesture. His left hand played with the Goddess of Truth's golden disk. Seeing this, the usher's eyes widened, and he clutched at his pocket, drawing out a double-headed counterfeit gold coin: the symbol of Enkeli the Trickster, the god of thieves, pawnbrokers, spies, illusion, deception, and mind games. (Also hidden treasure, by appointment.)

Up in the dock, the scowling prisoner's jaw fell open, and after a moment he turned even paler than usual. Nobody had ever accused him of being slow on the uptake, though by this point in the trial he had been accused of almost everything else. Enkeli gave him a little wave and made kissy faces, and the Dread Lord turned aside, clenching his jaw. Spells, chains, and spelled chains held him almost rigid, and guards surrounded him closely, but he nevertheless struggled to turn so that he didn't have to look at the witness.

"What is the meaning of this?" demanded the judge (belatedly adding an "if Your Holiness pleases"). Enkeli might be the God of Thieves, but he was still a god, after all.

"Simple," said Enkeli. "I made a deal with the Dark Lady. She wanted to leave Arthur over there, and I have to say, I can't blame her. He is *terrible* in the sack."

When the prisoner had been restrained again and one of the guards had been led away to have his injuries seen to, Enkeli continued.

"So I took her place, and gave her a new appearance to enable her to get out of the city."

"So are you the source of the documents and maps that enabled the

Glorious Alliance of the Free Peoples to take the Dread Lord's city from him? Not to mention its Awful Fortress, Mighty and—as it turns out—Not Impregnable?"

"No, that was the real Dark Lady. She may have muttered something about not leaving an enemy at large; I didn't really pay attention to the details." He flipped a green sleeve in a gesture of unconcern.

"And do you know the Dark Lady's current whereabouts?" asked the judge, glancing at the prosecutor, whose jaw had been working without any sound coming out since Enkeli's transformation.

"Funny thing," said Enkeli. "Not long after we switched, everyone forgot her name, and I lost my connection to her, as if our covenant had been terminated by some other power. I chose to keep the illusion of her appearance, though, because by then I was enjoying playing with the Dread Lord's head. And now nobody can locate her. None of the gods—at least, none of the ones who still speak to me—have been able to find a trace of her. It appears that she had other options for escape that she didn't mention when we made our deal."

Everyone in the courtroom was watching the witness, except for the little minion, whose eyes were on a figure in a deep blue robe at the back of the court. The bent creature noted a sudden tension in the robed figure's posture, and glanced back at Enkeli with a worried expression. Tricking tricksters is always a dubious proposition. They are, by their nature, unpredictable. Enkeli, offended, would seek revenge for a thousand years; Enkeli amused, on the other hand…

The god smiled his wicked smile and the blue-robed figure relaxed, then took the hairy hand of another similarly-robed (but taller) figure between two long, elegant hands. They leaned their heads together like lovers.

They didn't say anything, though.

It was a Tuesday.

A NOTE FROM MIKE

This piece started life in a thread on the Story-Games forum, where Josh Roby proposed the situation of a woman who wants to leave her consort, the Dark Lord. Various forum members suggested ways she could achieve this, and I later took my several suggestions and worked them up into this story.

I was delighted to have the opportunity to use it to honour Sir Terry Pratchett, one of my favourite authors, whose books have often helped to lift my mood.

While forgetting is usually a loss, being forgotten can be desirable if you want a fresh start, as Europe's new 'right to be forgotten' laws indicate. The question is, if your name is lost, do you still retain your identity? Or are you now free to craft a new one?

Mike Reeves-McMillan
Auckland, New Zealand

THANKS FOR THE MEMORY CARDS
LUKE KEMP

Neuroscience is both awe-inspiring and depressing, like a luxurious wall-to-wall carpet consisting entirely of kitten pelts. It's fascinating that elements of human life such as physical movement, memories, and even emotions can be tracked as electrical activity in the brain; but at the same time, it does little for the collective ego to know that elements of human life such as physical movement, memories, and even emotions can be tracked as electrical activity in the brain. A human soul probably wouldn't even power an average sized vibrator.

Like everything that has the potential to inform and enrich the human race, the idea of capturing human existence was monetised and commercialised the second it became viable to do so (except for the part about vibrators, as they were already widely available). It was during President Schwarzenegger's second term that American company NeuroPeon first started developing SAM tech. Funnily enough, it was on the night of the première of Terminator 14—which featured President Schwarzenegger's reanimated corpse in a touching cameo as an actual T-800—that they first began selling it to the public.

The basic premise is easy enough to understand. SAM—Specific Access Memory—technology allows a person to record memories, and then experience them again in vivid detail at any convenient time. It's not cheap, of course; installation involves slicing open the top of your head, (very) carefully installing the brain cap, and sticking your head back together again (with brain glue, not PVA). It's done by the world's top neurosurgeons. After surgery, nobody would guess you'd undergone the procedure, were it not for the SD card slot on your forehead.

There are limits. Recording must take place either during the memory you wish to keep, or within twelve hours of the event, by concentrating on the memory while activating the tech using the provided Wi-Fi remote control (SD card sold separately). Continuous memories lasting more than about five minutes break down in clarity the longer they go on. And if you're thinking of buying other people's memories to experience for reasons you *really* shouldn't share, that's not an option. Trying to 'load' somebody else's memories produces nothing but a headache and, for some reason, the faint but unmistakable smell of chips.

Recording and playback of memories is achieved primarily by mapping and stimulating electrical activity in the temporal neocortex or, as it is more commonly known, 'sorcery'.

Which brings us to Johnny and Donny.

"Why did you install that thing, Johnny?"

"It seemed like a good idea at the time."

"Seriously?"

"…yes?"

"Well, it wasn't a good idea at the time, and it's not a good idea now." Donny paused for a second, trying to rustle up some tact. Unfortunately, if there is a god with a checklist somewhere, when designing Donny he'd forgotten to tick 'tact'. "It looks bloody stupid," he added.

"Thanks for your support. But for your information, I think it's a *nice* looking pond."

Johnny and Donny were the best of friends—though whether this was because of their differences or despite them was up for debate. Literally. There was a society that met in the Town Hall twice a month.

Donny was a kind-hearted person, but as subtle as a luminous green chainsaw. He was so blunt in his words it was almost a skill. People tended to avoid trying to tell him this, partly because humanity is by and large rich in tolerance, but mostly because Donny was a huge man who looked like he could rip a bear in half. There was an urban myth, nervously whispered by people trying not to believe it, that he had once shaken a man's hand so hard that it came off.

Johnny, on the other fully-attached hand, was as intimidating as a marshmallow. He was average height, average build, quiet and reserved, and more boring than anybody had the heart to tell him. He had a *shed*. And, now, a pond.

"My pond!" beamed Johnny, with more pride than a man should be comfortable with in such a situation. "It took a lot of work, but it's finished. And all by my own hand!"

"Sharon threatened to leave you, twice."

"Well, yes—but wait till she finds out I've named one of the carp after her!"

"Third time's the charm? Are you *trying* to make her leave you?"

Johnny looked discomfited for a moment, but brushed it aside. "Anyway, look at this beautiful weather! Now that the pond's done, I can finally bring the garden furniture out from behind the shed and set it out again. In fact, I'll do that right now! Give me a hand, Don; I'll give it a quick clean, then we can sit down for a celebratory beer."

The furniture—a table and four chairs, all in an off-white plastic that would probably survive a direct hit with a nuclear missile—was duly dragged out, brushed off, and laid out. It was all ready for a group of friends to come over—a group that would tragically never materialise. After raiding Johnny's fridge for the two cans of beer hiding therein (bought especially for this momentous occasion), Johnny and Donny sat at the table near the pond.

"To the pond!"

"Whatever, I like beer."

"No! Wait!"

Slightly annoyed as only a borderline alcoholic trying to be polite can be, Donny put his opened can down on the table. He watched as Johnny reached into his ever-present tool belt, took out an SD card, and pushed it into his forehead. Donny rolled his eyes.

"Really, Johnny?"

"Yes, Donny! I want to remember this forever. Toasting the pond!" He took out a small remote from his tool belt and flicked a switch, before putting it back. "At last. To the pond! Long live the pond! Cheers."

Johnny began sipping at his beer daintily, while Donny—seemingly defying the laws of physics—downed the whole thing in no more than three seconds, before crushing the can on his forehead. Then he remembered that there was no more beer and was sad.

"Look, I'm glad you like your pond, even though it looks stupid. But using your SAM to record celebrating it being finished? That's not why people get SAM tech installed!"

"It's why I got *mine* installed."

"I know! That's the problem! You recorded every bloody boring, mind-numbing hour of digging the ground up and putting the thing in. You must have gone through a hundred SD cards recording—"

"A hundred and eleven."

"—recording putting a bloody pond in your bloody garden! You've had your SAM for nearly two years now, and you've used it for, what, memorising shopping lists? Instructions for assembling flat pack furniture? Didn't you once use it to listen to songs on the way to the shops? *Buy an mp3 player like a normal person!*"

"Donny, calm down. You're getting all worked up. I've never even *seen* anybody turn that shade of red before," said Johnny warily, surreptitiously flicking a switch on his SAM remote.

"Sorry. I'm not angry, just... I mean come *on!* On Tuesday you...what was it?"

"Started using SAM to record cookery programmes," replied Johnny, smugly. "SD cards are a lot cheaper than DVDs you know!"

"But you have to string loads of memories together to make one show. That's more trouble than it's worth, surely?"

"SD cards are still a lot cheaper than DVDs," mumbled Johnny, sulkily.

Donny leaned forward with an earnest, hopeful look on his face. "Come on. Think about it, mate. Take some ideas from what other people have done with *their* SAM tech—I want you to get the most from this! I mean, there was that programme on the telly last night, all those kids talking about what they did once they had it installed. They recorded the memory of one of those experience days—driving a Formula One car, bungee jumping. Having the memory of a parachute jump to go back to any time you want—imagine that! That's got to be better than the memory of putting a bloody pond in your garden. What next? A card full of your most satisfying farts?"

"Of course not!" said Johnny, unconvincingly.

They sat in silence, Donny having finally realised that the only way he was going to stop insulting Johnny was to stop words coming out of his mouth. Johnny had been friends with Donny long enough to be used to this sort of thing however, and with admirable determination, continued to try to get his friend excited about the pond.

"Look at them in there, swimming about doing their fishy things. Don't they look happy?"

Donny looked down at the pond and snorted. "They look like they want to die."

It was true. The thing about koi carp, as Donny had expressed with his trademark honesty, is that they do not look like happy creatures. They come in a variety of beautiful patterns and colours but, like the half dozen that were now exploring Johnny's new pond, they all wear a perpetual expression of shock and horror. If you accidentally walked in on your parents doing something you never ever ever want to see them doing, and the icy horror of that moment solidified and became a fish, that fish would be a koi carp.

"It's a beautiful day. Fact. Those are beautiful fish. Fact. The geotextile fabric and GFCI-protected electrical outlet I acquired for the pond both have amusing stories behind them—fact." Johnny had been counting the facts off on his fingers. With two perfectly good digits left unused, he looked slightly embarrassed as he continued: "Today is a good day, Donny, and nothing you say can put a dampener on finally seeing all my planning and hard work blossom into something that I can enjoy every day for the rest of my life."

Donny paused, looking at the pond. Johnny was glad he was finally starting to take notice of how splendid, how magnificent it was. "That cat just ran off with one of your fish."

"What??"

A very expensive, and now very dead, koi carp (which one would swear now wore an expression of relief) was clasped in the jaws of a rapidly retreating black and white cat. Said cat leaped to the top of the fence just beyond the pond, and disappeared over the top.

"That was Andrew!" Johnny roared, with all the ferocity of a newly-born kitten.

"What, the fish was called Andrew?"

"No, don't be ridiculous! The *cat* is called Andrew. It's Barry's cat, from next door!"

"So what was the fish called?"

"Jonathan."

Donny stood up and walked over to where Andrew had made his

getaway. "And what are you going to do about it, Johnny?"

"Nothing," sighed Johnny, sulkily. "Barry's scary, and he doesn't like me."

"But those fish aren't cheap! I know you don't need the money, but it's the *principle* of the thing!"

"Just leave it. It…it doesn't matter."

"Come on Johnny, don't be a—"

"Pussy!"

Donny peeked over the top of the fence and saw a balding, middle-aged man holding a smug-looking cat at arm's length. The man was obviously joyful at being reunited with his cat (though his expression was hard to gauge with any precision, as it was difficult to tell which of the two creatures was furrier). String vest, camouflage combat trousers, pot belly where the pot was more like a cauldron; yup, that was Barry all right.

"Oh pussy, I thought you'd run away! Pussy, pussy, pussy!"

Donny turned to Johnny. "Who calls their cat 'pussy' apart from characters in a 70s English sitcom?"

"Barry does," said Johnny, with a deep sigh. "Just…leave him to it. I'll get another fish. I didn't really have enough time to get emotionally attached to it; and besides, Sharon doesn't like it when me and Barry argue. It's not important."

"Hey, Barry!" roared Donny, over the top of the fence.

Barry cringed, and for a split-second, looked terrified (the standard reaction of people addressed by Donny without time to prepare). With remarkable composure, he almost immediately stopped shaking, and rearranged his face so that what was visible of it looked merely nervous. Cuddling Andrew close, he then walked over to where Donny was glaring at him over the fence. Johnny reluctantly joined them a few seconds later. Not that he was tall enough to see over the fence properly.

"Uh, hi Donny, haven't seen you for a while," Barry said, almost nonchalantly. "Can I help you with something?"

"Your cat just ran off with one of Johnny's fish."

"Andrew wouldn't do that!"

"He's a bloody cat—that's what they do. And I can smell it on him from here."

"My pussy doesn't smell of—"

"Finish that sentence, and I will make you regret it."

Barry was immediately very quiet, which made his cat's belch all the more impressive.

"I didn't know cats could burp," said Johnny, who felt he should contribute something to the discussion.

"The point is, your cat killed one of his fish—I saw it myself. It was a koi carp. Buy him another one."

"But he won all that money in the lottery! He hasn't even really *bought* anything, and—"

"Your cat killed one of Johnny's fish. I am working on the assumption that Andrew doesn't have his own bank account, due to being a cat. Therefore, it is your responsibility to buy Johnny a new fish. Please do it."

The conversation continued, but nobody ever argued with Donny for very long. He never really *meant* to be intimidating, but then gravity never really *meant* to help idiots appear on national television via home video shows. Barry threw a quick glower at Johnny when he was sure Donny wasn't looking, but he agreed to pay for a new fish. He then waddled back inside the house, still carrying his smug cat.

Johnny spent the next ten minutes alternately thanking Donny for his help and insisting that he really shouldn't have said anything because it'll only cause more trouble, until Donny got bored of listening and went home. Johnny went back out to the garden to his shed, where he thought he had some suitably cat-proof netting for the pond. On the way, something caught his eye—he'd only given the garden furniture a quick brush off, and there seemed to be something in one of the table's legs.

He knelt down. The shiny interloper was metal, and dug tightly into the plastic. He couldn't pry it out with his fingernails. At last, thought Johnny—the Swiss Army Knife! He'd carried it with him every day without fail for about eleven years, three months and two weeks (he didn't know *exactly* how long, he wasn't a maniac), but had never had call to use it. Much to his annoyance, nobody had ever stopped him in the street and asked him to open a can of beans. He'd never found himself in an emergency which required a tiny saw. Not *once* had *anybody* asked him if he had a corkscrew in his pocket. Nobody had ever even asked him to file their nails—not even Sharon, and he had literally *begged* her to let him do it. But now, now was the time.

Savouring the moment, Johnny slowly drew the Swiss Army Knife out of his pocket and, needing only three attempts, found the penknife. After a few seconds of overexcited digging with the tip of the blade, the offending item came free of the table leg. Johnny held it up to the light. And then frowned.

He couldn't be sure, but…

it really did look like…

a bullet.

* * *

"So…what do you think?"

"Why are you asking *me*?" retorted Donny.

"You're always reading those military and SAS books, and watching those programmes, and going to the museums. I just…hoped you could help."

Donny held the bullet up to the light and squinted at it. "Well yeah, it's definitely a bullet. I can tell you it was fired from an M24, *probably* from less than a hundred feet away, and judging by the hole in the table leg, from an approximately forty-five degree angle from above." He shrugged. "But that's it, sorry."

Johnny and Donny were back in Johnny's garden, minus one fish and plus one unexplained bullet. Johnny knew only two people with a disturbing interest in guns; Donny and Barry. Donny *was* always telling Johnny how boring he was, and how he needed something in his life to make it more interesting. Could Donny have taken a shot at the table as a friendly poke in the right direction? Well…no. Donny was blunt and direct, and physically intimidating—but he wasn't insane.

So what about Barry? He wasn't a pleasant man, and he made no secret of his dislike for Johnny. He was even more obsessed with the military than Donny was, to the extent that he claimed to be an expert on exclusive divisions such as the SAS and the Marines (while simultaneously being terrified of the idea of joining the army).

He also owned a large collection of guns.

Donny had a few guns, but Barry had a whole room full of them. Also, Donny's guns—unlike most of Barry's—had been officially fiddled with to deactivate them. Like any good sociopath, Barry claimed that he needed his wide range of pistols, shotguns, sniper rifles and assault rifles for hunting. Johnny wasn't sure what he was hunting that necessitated such an arsenal; possibly Batman.

"Hey Donny, do you think that maybe Barry...?"

"Nah. He's an idiot, but I don't think he's a murderer. Besides, if he wanted to kill you from such a short distance, he could've done. Why would he shoot your table? What's he got against garden furniture?"

"Jealousy? It's a *very* nice table."

"Come to think of it though, why would *anybody* shoot your table?"

"I don't know. It doesn't make any sense, does it? I don't know what to do."

"Go to the police."

Johnny's face was transformed by a look of sheer horror. "The police! Are you mad?!? Have you forgotten about that library book I found in the conservatory that was more than six weeks overdue? And I threw caution to the wind, didn't I, said 'oh well I might as well keep it now, I'll just pay the fine'. And I did. But now karma's catching up to me! For all I know, this could be a sting, an excuse to get the cops into my house and dig out the book. Do you know what they *do* to people like me in prison?!"

"Let them out early for good behaviour."

"That's not the point! Purposefully depriving a public library of their only copy of '151 Uses for A Dibber'? I'm a monster. A monster! I can't risk shaming Sharon and destroying the rest of my life over one stupid mistake. No, I'm on my own with this one."

"So what are you going to do?"

"I'm going to remember stuff," said Johnny. It sounded much more dramatic in his head than it did out loud.

* * *

If Johnny had a Safe Place, it was the attic. It was pure Johnny. It was where he kept his excruciatingly detailed model railway, his rack of amusing ties, his box of absolutely hilarious aprons (including one with a pair of fake boobies on the front—outrageous!), and dozens of other boxes and crates which were stacked and stored with disturbing precision. Since having SAM tech installed, he'd created one special corner under the skylight. A special corner with a chair, a desk, and a huge number of very small boxes (labelled and alphabetised, naturally). Above all this, a hand-carved wooden sign hung from the rafters.

The sign read 'Memory Lane'.

With a mixture of serenity and pride, Johnny strolled over to the boxes, heading straight for the 'F' section—which, he noted with a brief pang of guilt, did indeed begin with 'Farts (unusual)'. Now, where was it? 'Fedoras I Have Seen People Wearing', 'Fire Engines (no siren)', 'Fire Engines (siren)'... At last he found it, right next to 'Fittings and Fixtures'—the box labelled 'Fish Pond Project'.

Merely touching the box gave him a little thrill, which only increased as he picked it up and laid it reverently on top of the desk. Johnny visited Memory Lane often, but—he only now realised—never for anything more exciting than sifting through places he'd previously found the TV remote when it went missing, or how he looked in the mirror wearing certain outfits. Today, now, he had a task—a *mission*. Sure, Donny had rolled his eyes when Johnny informed him excitedly of his plan to document memories of the pond's installation, from start to finish. Sharon had threatened to leave him (twice). The postman had started using a permanent marker to write curse words on every package with enough space. But now! Now it was truly paying off, because Johnny would use his memories to pinpoint when and where the shot had taken place. *Now* who had 'all the charisma of a rice cake', eh?

He took the SAM remote from his tool belt, and put it carefully on the desk. Then he opened the box, and took out the third SD card from the back: 'buying the garden furniture'. He thought it unlikely that he had been sold a table which had been shot with a high-powered rifle, but he could find out for sure—so he would. And so it was that he popped the card out of its little jacket, pushed it into his forehead, hit a few buttons on the remote…

And remembered.

Home Improvement World, surely the eighth wonder of the world. The automatic doors open before me, perhaps powered by the collective anticipation of the swarms of middle-aged men within, who can already taste the satisfaction of A Job Well Done. I walk through this portal to another world. A world of joy, dedication, potential, imagination…and sheds.

Ordinarily I would take my time. I would gasp in awe at the multitude of paint colours, drool at the range of decking, gaze lovingly at the variety of rotary lawnmowers, and marvel at the craftsmanship of the ladders. But not today. Today I stride purposefully to the back of the store, because I know exactly what I want. Before long, I find myself in the garden furniture display section. In a moment of weakness I consider a gorgeous aluminium set, slowly running my hand back and forth over the back of one of the chairs (which causes a young mother to hurriedly usher her child down the next aisle for some reason). But the moment passes, and I take a few short steps further to the set I fell in love with on their website. The classic white plastic 'Debonair' set.

I hail the employee nearby, a young man who looks like he flips a coin each morning to decide whether to get out of bed or commit suicide. Although he looks straight at me when he comes over, I'm not convinced that he sees me. I tell him that I wish to purchase this furniture set, and he takes a clipboard from another table nearby to take my order. I make it clear that I wish to buy the set on display, and not some generic set from their warehouse. This is the set that has been used to 'sell' to people. It has history, *and I want it. The young man is difficult.*

Tony, the manager, happens to be passing by, and asks what the matter is. I am on first name terms with Tony, as I shop here a lot. I explain the situation. Tony takes the young man to one side, and whispers something that makes the young man briefly look my way and snigger. I admire Tony, able to bring joy even to such a sad soul. They agree to sell me this exact set, and deliver it this afternoon. Before I go, I examine the table and chairs closely. Every square inch.

Bloody hell, I am boring.

Well anyway, I give each table leg a thorough examination, and there are definitely no bullets in any of them. Though that particular possibility was not in my mind at the time, I leave beaming with satisfaction.

Johnny had let the memory play in full. To begin with, he was revelling in blissful nostalgia—but by the end he felt something closer to nausea. Why? He knew that the memory had replayed perfectly, and yet something felt…different. Not with what had happened, but how he felt about it. Reluctantly, he admitted to himself that perhaps he had been a little overzealous about buying a set of plastic furniture. No matter; back to work.

He replaced the card in its slip and then slowly ran his fingertip over the others in their tightly-packed box, trying to gauge where the SD card he wanted was. He pulled out one to check its label and—

Oh.

That one.

He'd nearly thrown this card away, but couldn't bring himself to waste £3.99 like that. It was definitely *not* the card he'd been looking for. Written on the tiny label on the front, in his careful handwriting, was 'Failing to Convince Sharon'. Johnny didn't recall making a conscious decision, but he was aware of his hands opening the card case and slowly, gently, slotting in into his forehead slot. His fingers somehow found the right buttons on the remote of their own volition, and playback began.

The hallway. Telephone on a stool to my left, kitchen straight ahead, narrow stairs going up to my right. I walk up the stairs. Sharon is in the bedroom, and I'm going to talk to her about the pond project. Work has already started, but she isn't really on board. I don't understand why not.

She's sitting on the edge of the bed with her back to me when I walk in. It looks like she's laughing, but she turns when she hears me enter. There are tears in her eyes, and they are definitely not tears of joy. I ask her what's wrong. I ask if it has anything to do with Tesco replacing the teabags in this morning's online shopping delivery with an inferior brand.

Back in control of his hands, Johnny paused the memory. Teabags? *Teabags?* He had been so wrapped up in winning Sharon over about the pond, the absurdity of the question hadn't struck him at the time (although he *was* absurdly picky about his tea). Focusing on the memory again, Johnny looked at the face of his wife, frozen in the moment. After he had said that, she didn't look angry. She didn't look frustrated. She just looked sad. She just looked…tired. Johnny didn't need SAM tech to remember exactly what happened next, and he suddenly felt a million icy needles in his heart. Helplessly, he set the memory in motion again.

No, she says, it's not the teabags. She wipes the tears from her eyes with a resigned sigh, and continues in a depressingly calm voice. It's the pond, she says. No, she says, it's not even the pond—not exactly. She looks me straight in the eyes as she says 'It's nothing, and that's the problem'. She tells me she loves me. I tell her I love her too, and sit next to her. When I say that she smiles, but her eyes are not happy.

She tells me that I've been spending most of my time planning and working on the pond. She says that when she first met me, right up through the first few years of our marriage, she was happy. I frustrated her, but that's just what couples do to each other. Then as time went on, I took more and more attention from her, and put more and more into my hobbies.

"Stop," Johnny protested in a small voice, to the empty attic; but he let the memory continue.

I start to tell her that it's not true, but she stops me before I finish the sentence by gently putting one finger over my lips. She reminds me of when I forgot to meet her at a restaurant for our anniversary, because I lost track of time sorting my books according to their ISBN. Last year, she tells me, she tried to talk about how she felt, but I didn't understand because I was concentrating on a catalogue in my lap, choosing which hydraulic buffer stops to buy for my train set. I never go with her to visit her mother for her birthday, she says, because it clashes with my stamp collecting convention. Then there was the time—

He couldn't take it anymore. Johnny stopped the memory, and almost ripped the card from his head. He had felt bad at the time—but now, experiencing it a second time round, actually paying attention… That had been the first time she'd threatened to leave him. The second time was the following week, when he'd bought her a set of solar lights for the pond for her birthday.

Johnny sighed shakily, fumbled the card back into its little case, and slotted it back into the box. That had been a shock to the system, a sudden explosion of clarity that—

Hang on. Maybe…

His fingers danced over the collection of cards for a few seconds, then he grabbed one and pulled it out. Bingo. 'Carp Diem'. The day the koi carp arrived. In went the card, and on went the memory. Fast forward slightly…

The pond is so nearly ready. Not quite ready for the koi carp to go in, but I couldn't wait any longer, so the fish have arrived. I have a large temporary tank to keep them in for now, and a slightly smaller one in which I keep Sharon (the fish, not the wife) because she will always be my favourite. I suppose Donny's right—they do look kind of horrified. I hope that's not just because they have to live with me now.

A wonderful smell comes from the kitchen window. The steak and onion pie baked by Sharon (the wife, not the fish) is out of the oven. I take one last look around the garden at the fish, the almost-ready pond, the furniture, the shed. My freshly-mown domain. I turn to the house, ready to feast upon the pie, when—

BANG!

A huge crash, so loud it's not possible to pinpoint where it came from. It surprises me so much that I turn and stumble, falling head-first into one of the tanks, where I'm hit in the face with Sharon's tail (the fish, not the wife).

Rewind.

I'm looking around at the garden.

Play ½ speed.

I know Barry's out, because he called me something unpleasant as he drove off. But out of the corner of my eye, I can see what I'm sure is his gun room window open. He's left one of his guns on the window-sill—he has a habit of doing that when he's cleaning the room. I wish he wouldn't.

Half speed, I try to focus better on the window than I did at the time. It's not easy, but I'm doing it… Definitely a gun. Definitely a rifle. But Barry is definitely not in the house, and he lives alone. Apart from that darn cat—who is sitting on the windowsill next to the gun.

Hmmm.

Andrew gets up and lazily stalks over towards the gun, one paw touching it as I turn towards the smell of the pie. I'd thought it was a car backfiring, but...

Fast forward.

I've stood up, dried my face a little on my shirt, and I'm having a quick look around to see what the noise could have been just now. I glance up at Barry's open window for a second, just in time to see a cat's tail and a gun barrel slip out of view and into the room. Well, mystery solved. I don't need to worry, as I doubt Andrew has had so much as basic training.

So, now Johnny knew who—or what—had shot his table. He also now knew that nobody was out to get him—but he didn't feel better. If anything, he felt *worse* than he had before entering the attic. But he had every intention of changing that.

Silently, with a small smile on his face, Johnny made his way down from the attic and into the bedroom. Sharon was sitting on the bed facing away from the doorway, and for a moment he had a painful flashback. But she wasn't crying. She was just reading her latest romance novel, 'The Bodybuilder Who Talked About His Feelings'.

Johnny walked round to face Sharon. She put her book down, and looked up at him curiously.

"I love you," said Johnny with a big smile, right before he knelt down and kissed her full on the lips.

After the kiss, Sharon looked at him—surprised, but pleasantly so. "Have you been sitting in the shed with all the paint cans open again?"

"No. In fact, I think I'll give up the DIY for a while; let's have a chat."

* * *

"So me and Sharon are getting on great again. She's beautiful, I'm so lucky, and I'm so glad I realised what I was doing wrong in time. I realised that, you know, I'm not a *bad* person, just…"

"A crushingly dull one."

"Yes Donny, thank you. But I'm working on it! Me and Sharon are going out tonight, but tomorrow, you and me. A new pub, what do you say?"

"So, not 'The Queen's Elbows'?"

"I was thinking that place down the road I haven't been to before— 'The Pig and Badger'."

"Does this mean you won't just have beer? Try a cocktail or something?"

Johnny hesitated and then said, a little sheepishly, "Still beer. Maybe a new beer."

"One step at a time, eh Johnny?"

"You got it, Donny!"

* * *

Police remain baffled regarding the ongoing series of bizarre and cruel animal shootings in Box. On Tuesday, for the fifth time in three weeks, a dog was found dead, and again the cause of death was a bullet wound between the eyes. Police wish to stress that local resident and gun enthusiast Barry Harrison is no longer a person of interest, with thorough investigation eliminating him as a suspect. The only clues are that each victim has had their collar removed, possibly as some sort of trophy; and that cat hairs have inexplicably been found at each crime scene. Anybody with any information should report it to the local constabulary immediately. Any and all testimony will be treated in the strictest of confidence.

A NOTE FROM LUKE

Drafts and editing are flippin' painful.

Not painful because other people don't understand my writing, but because they understand it better than I do and see ways to improve it that I never could. Editing forces you to concede that you're a fallible human being, and that doesn't gel well with a writer's ego. Or is that just mine?

I've been writing stories all my life, though this is the first one I've had formally published. Hopefully it won't be the last, but it's not fame-chasing that sees me here. When I stumbled across the call for submissions thanks to everybody's best friend, Google, there was no way I wasn't going to try my luck. Sir Terry's name can be found dotted throughout my book collection, and using any talent I might have to help raise money for such a worthy cause was an awesome prospect.

Thank you to my wife Louise for her invaluable support, thank you to Laura and Sorin for putting the anthology together and ~~foolishly~~ wisely accepting my story, thank you to Sir Terry for ground-breaking literature that the world shall never forget, and thank *you* for buying this book and supporting Alzheimer's Research UK.

Luke Kemp
Wiltshire, UK

HOW FELL THE TOWERS THREE
PETER KNIGHTON

"Where the hell has the fourth tower gone?!"

As far as heckles go, it was one of the more unusual he'd been subjected to. Lawrence had spent hours finding an alliterative rhyme for 'crumbling crenellations'—and what thanks did he get? An architecturally pedantic heckle.

"It is a melodious, lyrical celebration of our Noble Lord's victory in the Siege of Billingham. What has a 'fourth tower' got to do with anything?"

"There were *four* bloody towers at Billingham Castle, that's what. How did you manage to write a ballad called 'How Fell the Towers Three' about a fortress famed throughout the counties for having FOUR BLOODY TOWERS?"

Shouting is not terribly becoming of a knight, thought Lawrence, as he wiped a stray fleck of angry spittle from his cheek and counted to ten under his breath (leaving out the four). "It is known as poetic licence, Sir Crayley. Stories work in threes: the three billy goats gruff, the three hogs and the wily wolf, the three towers of Billingham Hold."

"And since when has it been known as 'Billingham Hold'?"

"Ever since Larry needed a rhyme for 'old', 'bold', and 'cuckold', I imagine, Crayley." Lord Mortimer was generally a fairly severe man, who held exceedingly high standards for chivalry and honesty in his household. On the other hand, he had a soft spot for music, and was willing to tolerate greater liberties with the truth when it came to the arts. "By the by, I've never heard the phrase 'forceful fenestrations' before, but I shall use it extensively from now on. Yes, yes; an excellent ballad, Lute."

Lawrence was not best pleased with the nickname 'Larry the Lute', but given that Lord Mortimer kept him in roast goose and stockings, he wasn't going to quibble.

"But he even claimed Lord Billingham had three *sons*, my Lord," wheedled Crayley.

"Well, two sons and a bastard, Crayley. I think we can forgive him that mild extension."

"But by all accounts Manfred the Black was Billingham's father's bastard, not his own!"

"Not by all accounts, good Sir," interjected Lawrence. "I have heard some say he was in fact Billingham's progeny. I put it to a former maid of Billingham Hold—so to speak—and she agreed that it *could* be true."

"Manfred was five years older than the Lord! I mean...how...just...what...and *stop* calling it Billingham Hold!" Crayley hurled his fist into the table top, sending a roast parsnip arcing over Sir Perkins' drowsing head and plopping squarely into his cup of mead.

"Threes are important, gentle Sir." Lawrence enjoyed the way this form of address caused Crayley's right eye to twitch in fury. "Three towers, three sons, three refusals to peacefully give up the castle and its surrounds. All lend themselves to a musical tale that will live through the ages."

"Three refusals?"

"Lord Billingham renounced Lord Mortimer's claim to the estates, Lord Marrison's claim, and the two lords' joint claim through their uncle's family."

Perkins raised his giggling head. "What he actually said was 'Piss off to you, your cousin, and all the crooked web-footed inbreds that spawned you both'." *Clunk* went his forehead as it again became one with the dining table. Once the drink had its grasp on Sir Perkins he seldom made any contribution to the conversation but when he did, his words were surprisingly pertinent and free of slur (in the sense that they were 'clearly audible'; however, they were generally chock full of the slur that is 'the questioning of reputation'). This outburst gave Lord Mortimer pause for thought: it wasn't very chivalrous to repeat the insult so precisely, but it was indubitably an honest recollection of events. Sir Perkins was also the Lord's nephew by marriage and Mortimer considered family to be particularly important. He had sentimental attachment to Sir Crayley as his longest-standing comrade in arms, and was a great admirer of Lawrence's music, but even in his most preposterously drunken state Sir Perkins was likely to receive his Lord's favour.

"Well, yes," Mortimer admitted. "But I feel that Larry has rendered an excellent interpretation of those vulgarities."

"But what of *history*, Sire? Are we to allow any pompous balladeer with a fancy to rewrite our glories simply to fit a good tune?"

"Ah! So you like the tune then?" Lawrence's aura of smugness could have knocked down Billingham castle by itself, and saved them all the bother. "And I don't understand why you are complaining, Sir Crayley, when I have dedicated an entire verse to your conquest of the North Tower."

"Because…it…is—" began Crayley through gritted teeth.

"My fine fellows, let us change the conversation," interrupted Mortimer. "Chatham, the ransoms following the siege: could you apprise of the takings?"

The chamberlain had not joined in the previous conversation, as he had been busy using his fingers to remove all traces of Stilton from his ears. It was an activity of his that had, once upon a time, caused comment; however in the time since Lawrence's permanent appointment it had become so commonplace that no-one batted an eyelid any longer. All members of the household did now treat the cheeseboard with caution however, and they avoided speaking of that incident with the Lady and the 'apricot' Wensleydale.

In his many travels, Lawrence had come across a number of people who had been put together in a baffling way. He'd met a landlord who hadn't left the warmth of his pub for fifteen years, as when his toes dropped below a certain temperature he'd sneeze incessantly. He'd encountered a scribe who would twitch involuntarily when confronted with the colour blue. Chamberlain Chatham however lay under a darker curse still: the chord of A flat diminished-seventh caused his bowels to empty.

In earlier life Chatham had noticed that this involuntary evacuation happened when music was playing, but not to every piece he heard. Of late it had been happening more and more, so he had taken to stuffing cheese into his ears whenever a musician was in the vicinity. Lawrence had, with sadistic persistence, unearthed the precise chord which led to this unfortunate outpouring, and so had naturally started inserting Ab Dim7 into every single one of his compositions. He desperately wanted to show off how clever he had been identifying the trigger, but couldn't risk letting on that he had been deliberately causing the stench.

It had been a cruel jest, and one that Lawrence now regretted. What really galled him was the absence of his beloved fruity cheese, which he hadn't seen, been able to request, or even speak about since the night of the Lady's trouble. He had thought at the time that the look on her face was priceless. As it turned out, he *could* put a price on it, and that price was bilberry Cheddar. Having learnt his lesson, the bard had been spurning the cursed chord for some time. However the chamberlain, little knowing the peril had abated, maintained his cheese-in-ear routine.

"We have received full ransom payment for the Earl of Sausage, my Lord, but Count Yontreeve claims he doesn't remember ever having had a nephew by the name of Jeremy."

Lord Mortimer frowned. "Really? Is he not a genuine Yontreeve then?"

"Apparently not, my Lord—or at least not one the Count will admit to."

"Well perhaps we should turn him out then: we have been feeding him extremely well and at quite some expense. I for one would be pleased to see the back of him."

A look of genuine glee finally found its way onto Sir Crayley's face.

Lawrence took on a wan look and blurted out, "I really feel we should pursue this one with the Count, my Lord; he may just be trying to drive down the ransom."

"Hah!" cried Sir Crayley. "And without Jeremy being an actual 'Yontreeve' none of our opponents on the day had a name that rhymes with 'grieve', 'leave',or 'reprieve', right? It would be a real shame for you to have to rewrite verse three hey, Larry? Hah!"

Lawrence turned slightly paler.

His Lordship frowned. "Oh, that would be a pity: verse three was my favourite. I wouldn't want a siege ballad to be without a record of the sacking of the castle. Chatham, write to Count Yontreeve saying he will have his nephew returned to him along with the one hundred silver coins found stuffed in his pockets when caught in Lady Billingham's wardrobe, on the proviso that the Count is willing to acknowledge that his nephew Jeremy was indeed at Billingham that day."

"But my Lord!" Crayley was not having a good time of it. "That was *my* pillage!"

"Surely a small price for maintaining the integrity of Lawrence's fine composition though, Sir."

"And if you'll recall, my Lord," said Lawrence, "he was not found in the wardrobe, but rather *'atop the tower standing there, over a ravished maiden fair'.*"

"I don't care where we say he was bloody well found—I want my silver!" Crayley's habit of exclaiming every sentence was making his liege wish he could stop his hearing, and he looked longingly towards the cheeseboard. "I led the charge on that tower and I want my pillage rights honoured!"

Here he goes again, thought Lord Mortimer.

Perkins' head rose once more, bringing with it a slice of bread glued to his right cheek by duck fat. His eyes attempted to focus on Sir Crayley, but kept being distracted by the bread as it slid down his face, clearly aiming to regain its place on the table. Luckily, brain and mouth remained focussed on the issue at hand. "'Led the charge'? You sent nineteen of your guard into the tower first, and even then you held your squire out in front as you entered."

The splat of the fat-soaked bread hitting the table came only barely before the thud of Sir Perkins' head following suit.

Crayley turned an interesting shade of puce. "What? No, I—look, I was in command, I led the charge; I want my silver!"

"Crayley?" drawled Lord Mortimer.

"Yes, my Lord?"

"Who rules here?"

"You do, my Lord," he muttered into his tankard.

"Very well then. Chatham? As instructed please."

"Very good, my Lord."

"Now then, Larry," continued Mortimer, "I wonder if we might discuss how your ballad represents my son's role in the siege."

Sir Perkins' belch pre-empted another contribution to the proceedings. He didn't even try to lift his head this time. "Perfectly, my Lord—he was in neither the siege nor the ballad."

Lord Mortimer straightened his back, narrowed his eyes, and proclaimed in cold, regal tones: "I believe the ballad could reflect his fine character and outstanding capacity for leading men, even if he was not at Billingham on that particular day." He glared around the table. No-one seemed willing to meet his gaze. Crayley was taking an opportunity to drink deeply of his beer, Lawrence was intent on tuning his lute, Chatham was engrossed in drafting the letter to Count Yontreeve, and Perkins' face was planted firmly onto the table top.

The lord wondered who to pick on. Crayley was already out of pocket, Perkins was family, and Chatham suffered enough in life thanks to his gastroenterological issues. Larry it was.

"I wonder, *Court* Minstrel, which heroic aspect of the Honourable Stephen Mortimer should be represented in your composition?"

Lawrence coughed gently into his right hand. "Well, my Lord…" Aiming to portray the grand artistic insight about to pour forth, he waved his left hand in an outward arc. Sadly, given his right palm was covered in phlegm, his left hand was holding his instrument at the time. As suggestive as his arm-sweeping had been, it was spoiled somewhat by the clunk of lute on jug, the glug of wine onto table top, and the rasp of tongue on wood as Sir Perkins did what he could to salvage the situation. The subsequent bustle of service staff as they mopped up (only the wine; Sir Perkins wasn't normally mopped up until at least midnight) gave Lawrence time to think— how to represent Sir Stephen in a favourable light?

It wasn't that Sir Stephen was a drunk, a lech or a coward; it wasn't that he preferred the company of other men, or even that he wanted to abandon his responsibilities and become a stone mason like the Earl of Lurch (a scandal that his family had never recovered from—but once he'd chosen his path his resolution was immovable. 'Set in stone' you might say). No, Sir Stephen was far more unusual than that. When handed a sword he would gaze at it as if he didn't know what it was. Once realisation had dawned, he would turn to the person nearest to him, regardless of who they were, and implore 'Surely there is a better way of resolving our differences?'. When out surveying his father's estates or discussing business with the court, he would occasionally just stop and ask the ensemble "What's it all about do you think? Really, when you get right down to it?" and then look around, earnestly hoping someone would have the answer.

This was not the kind of talk that went down well. Lord Mortimer's court worried that it could be considered heretical and lead to the lynching of his son by the godly—but in fact Stephen was feverishly devout (just not in the same way that the church was). He could quote the Bible perfectly, but had a habit of cross-referencing diverse chapters of scripture and analysing them in a way that unsettled the clergy, and downright baffled everybody else. One time Stephen had been considering a journey to the Holy Land, and spent two fateful days cloistered with Father David in the castle chapel. No-one ever discovered exactly what was discussed, but the only words the priest spoke before mounting his horse and disappearing into the night were "I can't even *start* to understand *that* question without a pilgrimage of my own". When asked, the Bishop maintained that Father David was due back any decade now.

Had Stephen been interested *only* in biblical studies he might have been shipped down to Canterbury to join the priesthood and everything would have been fine, but there were all those other questions which religious studies seemed woefully ill-equipped to even start answering. Why are leaves green? What is the sky made of? Why are men so interested in breasts?

The latter had been put to Lawrence on one of the rare occasions he had seen Sir Stephen drunk. This had been followed later in the evening by Stephen passionately declaring that it simply wasn't his *fault* that Lady Carol's chest was so large. As far as Lawrence was aware, no-one blamed Stephen for that at all (and if they did, many a gentleman about court would have thanked him for it), but it was obviously a cause of great concern to the knight that somebody would. From another member of the household this episode would have led to a bawdy ballad along the lines of 'Underneath Her Apron' or 'The Horny Toad and the Likewise Widow', but as it was Sir Stephen it simply led to another piece of disquieting gossip.

So how to represent this most singular knight in 'How Fell the Towers Three?' "My Lord," began Lawrence once the servants had dealt with the spillage, "I feel an opening stanza coming on, expounding on the virtues your son embodied as he led your army forth on the road to Billingham."

"He did lead the forces valiantly on the first day of the march, my Lord," said Crayley, hoping that a bit of crawling would get him his silver back.

"Valiant is just the word, Crayley. Quite right. Valiant." Lord Mortimer paused. "Where did he go after that? Chatham, you were with him. What happened? All I got out of him was something about how he wanted his waters to flow, and that some fellow was apparently digging fascinating holes."

"If you'll recall, my Lord, we were camped near a stream at the end of the first day's march," prompted Chatham. "Your son was curious as to where the water came from and where it was going. I took the opportunity to accompany Sir Stephen on a scramble up the crag to find the source of the brook."

"*You* went scrambling up a crag, Chatham?" barked an incredulous Sir Crayley.

The chamberlain's face took on a haunted look. "The dairy cart had been delayed in getting to camp, and Lawrence was tuning up."

Mortimer, Crayley and the bard all looked away embarrassed, while Perkins giggled. Chatham assumed his usual policy of ignoring the recumbent knight and continued.

"At the top of the crag we encountered a local with a spade, who was diverting some of the stream's waters into a series of small wooden viaducts. These then led off towards Billingham's farmland. Sir Stephen was fascinated, and got into an animated discussion with the fellow about his plans for irrigation and moving mountains."

Crayley snorted. "Moving mountains, Chatham? This peasant thought that a spring and a few viaducts could move a mountain? *Nothing* can move a mountain!"

"Well," said Lord Mortimer, "in Larry's excellent 'The Maid and the Knight of Wyrms', love moved the very earth, and the twin mountains rose and fell as the knight drove the wyrm into the cave."

"One of my more subtly provocative efforts, I think you'll agree." Lawrence grinned.

Crayley, barely having a sense of humour, found it difficult to judge when others were deploying theirs. 'Quite so' seemed the only safe thing to say, so "Quite so" he said.

"But why did a discussion of farming techniques lead to my son not joining us for the assault the next day?"

"The man asked Sir Stephen whether we wanted to visit his workshop the following morn—the day of the siege—to see models of his plans." Chatham rubbed his eyes. "Your son was delighted, and awoke me early to accompany him. I had shown an interest in the number of fields Billingham had, and Sir Stephen took this to be interest in the water system instead."

"Was it not so?"

"I can place a monetary value on land, my Lord, but I struggle to judge the worth of new ditches."

"I used to be able to put a monetary value on pillage," muttered Crayley.

"Do be quiet, Crayley," ordered Lord Mortimer, ending any hope the knight had of retrieving his hundred coins. "Pray continue, Chatham."

"We found the workshop a mile or so from the camp. Sir Stephen and his new-found friend continued their discussion. It got rather heated in fact when the subject turned to demolition."

"Demolition?"

"Yes, my Lord. The peasant said that he could bring down any building within a day's march by redirecting the flow of underground rivers through use of a specially constructed series of buried locks and pulleys. Sir Stephen thought it unlikely."

"Of course it's unlikely," snorted Sir Crayley, "it's ludicrous."

"Yes, well, the fellow grabbed his peculiar hat and cloak and ran off, shouting 'you'll see, I'll bring down a castle, so I will'."

Lawrence frowned, absent-mindedly tightening one of the keys on his lute more than intended. "How peculiar was his hat, chamberlain?"

"It had a dead bird perched atop it."

Sprroinnnng went the lute's G string as the tension got too much and it split in two. Chatham yelped, dived for the cheeseboard, slipped on a suspicious wet patch by Perkins' left trouser leg, and landed in a heap on the floor. Although he had not executed the move quite as he'd intended, his left hand did catch the edge of the board and cause a lump of brie to slide into his right ear as he lay crumpled on the floorboards.

Ignoring the mess of a chamberlain, Lawrence glanced across at Crayley.

"Didn't that fellow we took to be a hedge-wizard have a dead magpie strapped to his head?" asked the knight.

"The one who was scampering about by the moat at Billingham Hold as we laid siege to it?" added Lord Mortimer. "I thought we sent him on his way."

"Not quite, my Lord—he hung around the baggage carts for a time," volunteered Lawrence, "rubbing his hands and disturbing the cooks."

"Do cooks not like wizards, Larry?"

"They don't like decomposing magpies swinging around near the leeks, my Lord."

"No, I imagine not. Didn't he get chased off? With all their knives, cleavers and meat hammers, the catering staff are more threatening than many of my soldiers."

"Their mushroom stew is pretty terrifying too," acknowledged Lawrence. "But no, they didn't get a chance to scare him away, my Lord. Once the first tower fell, he ran off cackling 'see, that'll show him'."

"And how did the first tower fall, Crayley? You were over that side of the castle; I'd assumed you were just uncharacteristically efficient with your siege engines."

"I *was* efficient, my Lord," Crayley retorted indignantly, puffing up his chest. "I personally oversaw the siege hammer, and it was so efficient that it knocked down the east side of the tower in merely three blows."

"*Three* blows, good Sir?" smirked Lawrence. "If I had known, I would have included that in the ballad!"

Sir Crayley fumed. Lawrence could see his tongue working and his lips moving he tried to come up with the most abusive thing he could say in the presence of his liege. Thankfully, he wasn't given the chance.

"Three blows seems a terribly small number for knocking down a rounded tower." A sparkle came into Lord Mortimer's eye and his lips curled up at the edges of his mouth as realisation dawned. "It sounds to me as though the tower had been weakened somehow. By a wizard perhaps. A wizard in the service of the noble Sir Stephen Mortimer, and who was sent to Billingham Hold to cast down its mightiest tower!" Lord Mortimer was animated beyond anything Lawrence had previously witnessed when discussing Stephen. "Not merely an opening stanza in your ballad, Larry: you will write a whole new verse on my son's pivotal role in the Siege of Billingham."

Lawrence paled and closed his eyes, fully aware of what was coming.

"Aha!" cried Sir Crayley, his whole body expanding into the air around him, joy written in every line of his face. "History is served: Billingham Castle has four towers once more!" Crayley felt magnificent. He had been victorious over the upstart minstrel!

"Oh no," said Lord Mortimer. "We can't disturb the balance of 'How Fell the Towers Three'. Larry? Drop Crayley's verse."

Glorious colour returned to Lawrence's cheeks as Sir Crayley's head crashed onto the table next to Sir Perkins'. "With pleasure, my Lord."

A NOTE FROM PETER

I remember when I was a little lad, my big brother had so many books by Terry Pratchett on his shelf that I thought 'I might as well not start reading them, there are just so many!'. He had about six. (I didn't read much until I left school and it became optional.) Well I had a go and it turned out that six wasn't 'too many'—it wasn't *enough*. Whenever a new one was published my brother would buy it in hardback and I'd wait patiently for him to finish so I could get my mucky little paws on it. At some point I discovered that I was buying them in hardback and he was borrowing them. I can't remember how that happened. I also can't even remember how much of this little anecdote is strictly 'accurate' and how much is recollected to make a good story. The gist of it is true, and sometimes that is the most important thing.

Peter Knighton
Leeds, UK

THE ARCHIVE OF LOST MEMORIES
ANNA MATTAAR

The walls of the corridor seemed to consist entirely of lacquered wooden filing cabinets, eight drawers high, with handwritten labels that could only have been less legible if they had been made under a microscope. Or, Robert mused, by his Cognitive Psychology professor. A thin layer of dust on the floor showed a single set of footprints. They were most certainly not his, because if he'd arrived here via the steps at the far end of the corridor, he was sure he'd remember having been there. Moreover, the footprints didn't end at his feet: they continued in the other direction before disappearing around a corner.

It was quiet, and Robert wished he could have said 'just like in the lecture hall a moment ago', but that had been a silence filled with scribbling pencils, shuffling papers and suppressed coughs. This new silence crawled up his back and made him shiver. He cleared his throat, very carefully, to bring the stillness to a more bearable level without breaking the unwritten rule that governs both churches and freshly fallen blankets of snow.

When nobody seemed to object, he whispered: "Well, this is something," although he wasn't quite sure what exactly 'something' entailed.

But the truly strange thing wasn't that he seemed to have been mysteriously transported from a moderately silent lecture hall to a world of filing cabinets, but that he knew exactly what he was doing here.

He was looking for an answer. The answer to question 12B of his exam to be precise, on the three levels of moral development. He was sure Professor Kearney had covered the topic a few weeks ago, but his brain tended to gloss over dry facts like that and move on to more interesting things, like guessing which of his fellow students had a crush on whom.

The footprints were close together and made by shoes several sizes smaller than his. When he followed them around the corner, his own hesitant footsteps echoing as loud as gunshots, they led him to another corridor lined with filing cabinets, and then another, so that it came as a surprise when a different piece of furniture suddenly entered his vision. It was a small desk at a crossroads of identical corridors, on which low stacks of paper sat neatly around a huge open book. The pages were covered in the same illegible scribbles as the drawer labels, arranged in rows and columns, but the handwriting on the stacked sheets was different. Robert walked around to read one, but stopped dead in his tracks when he passed the desk and found himself looking straight into the magnified eyes of an old woman standing on a stepladder. She closed the drawer in front of her and studied him through thick glasses, without the tiniest hint of surprise.

"I thought I heard someone there," she said with a weary little smile. "Welcome, dear, to the Archive of Lost Memories. Don't touch those; I've just got them sorted out."

She was short, and wore a grey, plaid dress as nondescript as Robert had ever seen. Together with her tightly bound bun of grey hair and small, quick movements, it reminded him of the mouse he'd kept as a boy.

She also seemed somehow familiar, more than a resemblance to the aforementioned rodent would suggest. He had a strong sensation of déjà vu, of having spoken to her before; if not in the same place, then in one very similar. He'd always found déjà vu an interesting phenomenon, right up until his psychology class had methodically taken apart every last possible and impossible theory, from delayed brain signals to parallel universes. But for now Robert picked the easy explanation. "Have we met before?"

"Oh, very likely." She climbed down, one deliberate step at a time. "But people always forget about me. That's a fact, mind you, not an accusation, so no need to apologise."

She folded the ladder and lifted it with some difficulty. After a few moments of preoccupied staring, Robert's manners caught up with his efforts to understand what she'd just said. "Let me carry that for you," he offered, stepping forward.

She glanced at him gratefully and put the stepladder down. "Why, thank you, dear boy. Please put it under the desk."

The way she eyed him while he obliged reminded him rather uncomfortably of the supervisor in the lecture hall, who'd kept pacing around the room looking for anyone cheating, eating, or engaging in other illicit activities. He was glad to have escaped that reproachful gaze, even though the note in his sleeve was well-hidden, and he now carried the ladder to its place as fast as he could to escape the old lady's scrutiny. She inclined her head critically and adjusted the ladder a bit, so that it was exactly in the centre of the desk's legs.

Then she looked at him again. "You can call me Mrs Hewitt," she said. "Now, what are you looking for today?"

"My name is Robert Watters," Robert replied. "Pleased to meet you. I'm... Excuse me, did you say 'lost memories' just now? How does that even work?"

"Watters..." Mrs Hewitt repeated, sitting down at the desk and peering at the huge book. "Quite simply," she began, "people forget all sorts of things, and all those lost memories end up here. I put them in the right place and make a note, so that anyone who pops in can get their memory back nice and quickly."

"Oh." Somehow, Robert felt stupid for having asked, as if it was something that he should have known. "In that case," he said quickly, "I'm looking for a lecture from a few weeks ago. By Professor Kearney. On a Friday. Specifically the part about moral development. If any of that means anything to you."

"Just give me a moment," Mrs Hewitt replied, turning a page.

Robert folded his hands behind his back and looked around at the endless cabinets. One of the corridors went on until the walls seemed to converge into a single dot. Another had a spiral staircase that disappeared into the ceiling. He tried to imagine how many filing cabinets you would need to house every single thing that anyone had ever forgotten. This place had to be colossal.

It was an interesting metaphor, though. A lost and found department of the mind, with a little old lady to guide you through the labyrinth of recollection. He should use that to spice up an essay some time.

He wondered briefly why he wasn't worried about being inside a metaphor.

"Here we are," Mrs Hewitt said. She checked a line in the book again and snapped the heavy volume shut. "Come along now, Robert."

He followed her up the spiral staircase into more of the same lacquered scenery. Every now and then she inspected a small sign on a corner, installed conveniently at her rather low eye level.

"I assume time works differently here?" Robert asked, having no trouble keeping up with her. "I mean—suppose we spend half an hour looking for that memory, I won't suddenly have run out of time to answer my other exam questions, will I?"

"Have you ever lost time like that?" Mrs Hewitt asked.

"Well, I might have," Robert confessed. "There was that night a few weeks ago, although I do believe that involved alcohol rather than dusty wooden drawers."

She sniggered, which surprised him. From someone her age, he'd expected a disapproving glare.

"I meant whenever you are trying to remember something, or even just remember something without trying," she explained. "Although I can probably find that night for you, if you're interested."

Robert shivered. "No, thank you."

"It's your call!" She sniggered again. "But you'll have all the time you need to finish your test, don't you worry about that."

"So, how does one end up working for the Archive of Lost Memories?" Robert asked to change the subject.

Mrs Hewitt turned to him, the wry smile on her wrinkled lips suggesting that this wasn't the first time she had given this explanation. "There is no one to be working for," she said. "Just me, keeping things tidy."

Robert tried to count the number of drawers in just this corridor and gave up after a few dozen, only then realising that his guide had turned a corner. "What, this whole place?" he asked, walking after her.

Her bespectacled face reappeared. "It's not that much work now that the majority of the memories have been filed away," she said defensively. "I'm quite proud of the system. It requires some cross-referencing, but it guarantees that nothing gets lost. Well, not more lost than it already is."

Robert stared at her. "That must have taken *years*," he breathed.

"What's a year when you don't have proper days or nights to keep track of?" Mrs Hewitt replied with a shrug.

"But… Why?"

"Pardon me," came a male voice from further down the corridor. "Could either of you tell me what on Earth this place is, and where I can find this memory I'm supposed to be looking for?"

The voice belonged to a man in a brownish suit, the jacket hanging open to reveal a belly that, for the general wellbeing of those around him, should perhaps have stayed hidden. The man squinted at the nearest drawer and shrugged before approaching Robert and Mrs Hewitt. He was accompanied by the almost tangible smell of sweaty clothes and a hint of tuna.

"Welcome to the Archive of Lost Memories, sir," said the old woman. "I am Mrs Hewitt, the archivist. I'll be with you in a moment, after I've helped this young man find his memory."

And suddenly, Robert felt that he had to know more about this woman, who had single-handedly archived what had to be billions of memories. Question 12B was all but forgotten. It could wait; time worked differently here anyway. "I'm not in a hurry," he assured her. "Please, help this gentleman first."

She looked at him suspiciously. "Are you sure?"

"Positive," Robert insisted. "Don't worry about me."

"If you say so." Mrs Hewitt turned to the newcomer. "In that case, sir, what are you trying to remember?"

The man scratched his side. "Well, that's the thing, you see," he began. "I'm not. One moment I'm eating lunch in the park and yell—*shoo*ing away those fat ducks that always keep begging for your bread crusts, the next I'm standing in this dusty old place thinking there's something I should remember. Am I daydreaming? Because this is not the sort of thing I normally daydream about."

"I'm sure it isn't," Mrs Hewitt said primly, already turning back the way they had come. "I'll have a look for you. This way, please."

She led them back through the same corridor and then, to Robert's surprise, around a corner that he didn't remember having seen before. Straight ahead stood a familiar desk at a crossroads of cabinet-filled corridors, with a familiar stepladder lying in the exact same spot they had left it.

As if she'd read his mind, Mrs Hewitt explained: "The way back is always shorter. Don't ask me how, though. May I have your name, sir?"

"Are you going to use it to dig through all my deepest, darkest secrets?" the man asked suspiciously.

"That depends," Mrs Hewitt said, heading straight for the large book. "Do you have a lot of those?"

The man guffawed. "Plenty! I'm Vernon Dennell." He gave Robert an apparently meaningful wink that failed to convey any meaning at all. Then he looked down and started on the cumbersome task of restraining his belly with his jacket.

Robert averted his eyes, focusing on the desk instead. "Do you recall ever having been here before, sir?" he asked.

"Never in my life!" Vernon Dennell grunted.

"Are you sure?" Robert insisted. "Because I believe..." He thought back to what the archivist had told him about meeting her before, and nodded to himself. "I do believe there might be something to this place that makes you forget about it when you leave."

"Nonsense!" the man snorted. With a last grunt he managed to close his jacket, rendering him slightly more presentable, albeit not any less fat. "I'd remember a place like this, don't you think?"

Robert tried again. "But you wouldn't, see, because you're supposed to forget. The memory is erased, so to speak. Mrs Hewitt, am I right?"

She closed the book and stood up. "You are, dear, although 'erased' isn't the right word. They're all here, those memories. I keep them in a separate section, because naturally nobody ever comes for them."

"I, for one, would be very interested in seeing them," Robert said.

Mrs Hewitt gave him a sharp look as she walked past him. "I do have things to do other than giving you the grand tour, Mr Watters. If you'd please follow me, Mr Dennell?"

They got a small tour nevertheless, past towering walls of drawers, large halls filled with low cabinets, and dark curtains that hid even more parts of the Archive. They climbed a spiral staircase long enough to make Robert's head spin and his feet ache. Just as he started to wonder whether this place was infinite, filled with stairs and cabinets in all directions, the view opened up to reveal a misty void. The stairs had brought them to a small balcony, and beyond the railing, tiny shapes fluttered about in the greyness like limp birds. A cautious look over the edge confirmed Robert's suspicion: sheets of paper like the ones he'd seen on the desk were scattered around on the distant floor below, new ones occasionally blowing in from the mist. A small wheelbarrow stood parked neatly against a wall.

"That's what I like to call the 'In-Tray'," Mrs Hewitt said. "It does what you'd expect, despite looking awfully messy. I tried to get the memories to land in boxes, but it didn't quite work."

Yet another corridor led away from the balcony, and she disappeared around the corner. They found her kneeling at a drawer on the bottom row that, to Robert, seemed like any other. "Here we are," she murmured, leafing through the many sheets of paper inside. "Ducks, you said?"

"Lots of 'em," replied Vernon Dennell. "Quacking like there's no tomorrow, the noisy fu… Things."

"Then they might remind you of this," said the archivist, handing him a sheet of paper. She and Robert watched Vernon as he read it, his expression of recognition slowly changing into a frown. "Lewis, you bastard," he muttered. "I bet you were glad I'd forgotten about that." His hands gripped the memory as if he wanted to tear it in half. But before he could, the paper fell apart into dust, which whirled upwards before disappearing. Vernon didn't seem to notice. He fixed his eyes on Robert and grinned. "Time to finally get back at that lying piece of shit," he promised. "Good day to you two!" With a grim determination in his step, he walked back to the stairs and was gone.

"What was that all about?" Robert wondered.

"Even if I knew, I wouldn't tell you," Mrs Hewitt said. "It's not polite to poke your nose into other people's private affairs. This way, please. Let's find you what you were looking for as well."

He stood still, hoping to postpone the inevitable moment when the only polite thing left to do would be to leave and exchange the memory of all of this for one of Kearney's lectures, and asked: "Why? Why do you do this?"

"Why do you ask?" She was starting to sound a little impatient.

Robert scratched his head. "I wrote an essay about that once," he blurted out before he could stop himself. "It was about me wanting to know what people are thinking to better predict what they'll do, or maybe trying to validate my own motivations, but all of that was mostly to reach the required word count. I'm just, you know, interested in people."

"Now that's a first," Mrs Hewitt scoffed. "Most people I get here just want their memories back as soon as possible. I'll have to disappoint you, though: there's no exciting story to be told. It was a mess when I got here, looking for a memory like everyone else, and I took it upon myself to fix that."

"Just like that?" Robert asked in disbelief.

"Just like that," the woman said. "I started sorting the papers as best I could. At some point I thought it might be useful to have somewhere to put them, and then I stumbled upon a couple of these cabinets. There turned out to be more of them later. They never seem to run out."

"And your memory?" Robert asked. "Did you find it?"

"You know…" She shrugged. "I've never really gotten around to looking for it. There was simply so much to do! Sometimes I do wonder what I'd have found, but it's no use anymore. I don't remember what I was looking for in the first place. I've even forgotten what I was doing before I arrived."

For a moment, the silence of the Archive returned as Robert studied the sleeve of his shirt, not sure what to say. The note containing chapter three, section five in keywords was still pinned to the inside.

"I'm so sorry," he said eventually.

Mrs Hewitt shrugged again. "Please don't be. It probably wasn't important anyway. Are you coming, or should I just leave you here and get back to work?"

"Neither," Robert declared, suddenly very sure of himself. "We are going to get your memory."

She let out an annoyed sigh. "I already told you it's no use. It's impossible to find anything here without at least some clue as to what you're looking for."

"That may be so," Robert said triumphantly, "but you *used* to know what to look for, right? That's a lost memory, so it should be here somewhere."

"Now what did I say about the poking of noses?" she snapped, wrinkling her own in a very mouse-like fashion.

"I just want to—"

"And it isn't," she continued. "I'd know. I've never actually come across any memory that was forgotten within the Archive itself. They work differently, I suppose."

"All right. So." Robert's mind raced. "Have you ever told anyone about your lost memory?"

Her eyes pierced his, convincing him that if she *were* a mouse, she'd lift the entire species to the top of the food chain. "Why do you insist on helping me?" she demanded.

"I—I'm sorry," he stammered. "I'll just…"

Then he saw the glint of hope behind her massive glasses, and pulled himself together. "Because I wouldn't mind being away from that exam a little while longer," he said. "And, you know… Since you're helping all these people to recover their memories, maybe someone should help you to recover yours, too."

She hesitated. Then she protested once more. "I appreciate the effort, but even if I were about to rummage through other people's memories about their visits, there are far too many of them—and I didn't order them by conversation topic."

"Would you be able to find any of mine among them?" Robert asked. "You said I've been here before, and knowing me I'm sure to have asked you at least once."

"No," she replied simply. "They're ordered chronologically, because as I told you before, nobody ever comes for them anyway."

"In that case, you must know which ones are from the time when you still knew what you were looking for," Robert went on.

"I could hazard a guess as to where to draw the line, yes," Mrs Hewitt conceded.

"Take me there," he urged, feeling for a moment like a valiant knight in shining armour, until the mental picture formed and he just felt silly. "Please?" he added. "It can't hurt to have a look."

The archivist sighed. "There's no dissuading you; I can see that," she said. "All right then."

It was a surprisingly short walk, down a stairwell and around two corners. They stopped in front of a wall of cabinets that would fill two or three storeys in any sensible kind of building.

"Here," said Mrs Hewitt. "The Past Visitors Section. This area would be your best bet." She indicated several columns of drawers.

Before Robert could reply, a young woman with a backpack over one shoulder burst out of a corridor, panting. "Keys!" she exclaimed. "Have either of you seen my keys?"

"Have you checked your other coat?" Robert asked. "I usually leave them in my—"

"Leave this to me, Robert," said Mrs Hewitt, stepping forward. "Look me up when you've found something." Speaking soothing words, she dutifully led the woman away.

Robert rubbed his hands, pulled out a drawer at random and leafed through the contents, reading a few lines from the ones he could decipher without too much trouble. As he'd expected, they were all variations on the theme of 'suddenly I found myself in this strange place full of cabinets, and an old lady helped me find a memory'. At first he was careful not to read the entire pages in case they'd disappear, but after a particularly concise one failed to dissolve into nothingness after he'd unavoidably taken in its entire twenty words, he started to study them more closely. The lost memories these people had been searching for ranged from childhood stories to missed birthdays, the scripts from round block letters to narrow cursives. Only a few of the pages described any conversations with Mrs Hewitt, and none of them contained the information he needed.

He pushed the drawer back and let his hand rest on it for a few moments. One at a time seemed to be the only way. There was no rush. He could always give up later.

The third drawer he opened was different, however, despite looking exactly the same as its neighbours. There was something about one of the sheets in the back that made him reach for that one first, and he knew why as soon as he recognised his own messy scribble. As he read it, images formed in his mind, and before long he realised that he wasn't actually reading the words anymore: he remembered. He remembered suddenly finding himself in a corridor lined with filing cabinets, and meeting an old lady, who led the way through the labyrinth before eventually handing him a sheet of paper covered in his own handwriting. He even remembered remembering a line from a book he'd once read, and smiled. "Real stupidity beats artificial intelligence every time." That line still decorated his wardrobe. He'd printed it out that very same day, as soon as he'd returned to the normal world.

When he focused on the present again, the paper wasn't in his hand anymore. He felt slightly guilty about not being able to put it back, but the feeling was soon overshadowed by his renewed determination to find out what Mrs Hewitt had been looking for. He started merely scanning the contents of the drawers now, watching for anything that stood out to him. By the time he got to the forty-second drawer, balancing high on a ladder on rails, he'd gathered a small but interesting collection of memories of visiting the Archive for what had invariably felt like the first time, and was prepared to add another one with the next sheet he took out.

Then he knew. He'd asked her what kinds of memories people usually look for. Among other examples, she'd told him that she herself was sure someone had told her something important about today, but she couldn't quite put her finger on what it had been. It hadn't seemed to bother her at all, and it hadn't bothered him at the time because he'd been too preoccupied with the upcoming start of his new life at university. In hindsight, he could have spared himself the excitement.

After he'd slid the drawer shut and climbed down, double-checking that the information was safely lodged in his mind, the silence of the Archive returned. It still made him feel uncomfortable. Despite the temptation to make a sound, any sound, he held his breath and listened for footsteps, or shuffling, or anything else that might point him to Mrs Hewitt. *Look me up,* she'd said. He wondered if she'd thought that one through. Despite now remembering a handful of earlier visits, he still couldn't tell one cabinet-filled corridor from the next.

But there it was: a female voice, distant but clearly panicked, exclaiming something that might or might not have been "Hurry up, I'm late!" Gratefully, Robert rushed towards the sound, following the nervous cries and increasingly impatient reassurances. He rounded the last corner just in time to see a memory vanish from the young woman's hand. "The window-sill!" she gasped. "I put them there yesterday so I wouldn't forget but then I must have put my gloves on top when…"

Her voice faded away, as did the rest of her. Within a moment there was no one there but Mrs Hewitt, and a slight movement of dust when the space previously occupied by the visitor filled with air again. Robert blinked, before realising that he shouldn't be surprised, given the way he'd appeared here himself.

"Giving up so soon?" Mrs Hewitt asked.

"No, I'm…" Robert straightened his back. "Actually, I found it," he announced. "You did tell me, months ago. It was about today, that is, the day you went looking for the memory. There was something important about that date, only you hadn't thought of it earlier because of some old photographs that needed sorting through."

She looked at him, inclining her head to one side. "That does ring a bell." She hesitated. "Yes, it was something like that. Something about today…"

"Well?" Robert asked. "Do you know where to find it?"

"I haven't come across it before, I'm sure of that," she pondered, speaking more to herself than to him. "And it can't be in the In-Tray. So that means… The Old Centre." The way she said it suggested it wasn't a place she visited often.

"Is that good or bad?"

Mrs Hewitt grinned ominously. "It means that you and I have a long search ahead of us. Just remember, you're the one who started this! No backing out of it now!"

As he followed her through the corridors once more, Robert couldn't help but wonder about the way he'd found the memories of his earlier visits. He didn't normally rely on his feelings like that, but still… "Back in the Past Visitors Section, I sort of…intuitively knew which memories were mine, although I could never predict in which drawers I'd find them. Would that mean that, theoretically, if these memories weren't all locked away in filing cabinets, people would be able to find theirs without your help?"

She glanced at him over her shoulder. "Don't be silly. Nobody would be able to find anything in such a mess. Here we are, now."

They'd passed dozens of curtains like the one before them on their way back and forth through the Archive. Robert had expected there to be more filing cabinets behind each of them, more corridors, more stairs, more memories. When Mrs Hewitt pushed the curtain aside, only one of those assumptions turned out to be correct.

Towers of memories balanced precariously near the entrance of a dimly lit space. Further back, they were simply piled up into heaps, some of which almost reached 'hill' status, forming a landscape that disappeared into dusty air and darkness. The lack of any filing cabinets in sight made Robert feel strangely off-balance.

"I still plan to have all these filed away one day," Mrs Hewitt sighed, making the nearest stack sway dangerously. "But with the In-Tray filling up and people asking for things all the time, I can only get a handful of old memories done now and again."

Robert took a few steps forward, taking care not to step on any of the papers that littered the ground. Turning around to look at the massive wooden walls and the rays of light that shone through the curtained opening, he felt like he'd walked into an ancient cave.

"What if someone comes looking for one of these memories?" he wondered.

"Oh, they rarely do anymore," Mrs Hewitt answered, joining him. "Some of these are from people who are long dead!"

"How long?" Robert asked, but she'd already trotted off among the paper hills, prodding some of them with her shoe before moving on. He'd never been very interested in history, but to read actual thoughts from people who had lived even just a few decades ago, let alone longer back… He looked wistfully at the hills in the distance, trying to imagine the ways in which a mind from another era might work differently to his own. Would they, too, forget the date and where they put their keys, or would they worry about other things? Maybe he should have a quick look before he returned to his exam. Of course, he'd forget about it all after he left the Archive—but with any luck, some of it would turn up in a dream or something.

"Where do we start?" he called to the archivist.

"Over there seems a likely spot," she replied, pointing to an area to the left of where they'd entered. "We might have to do some digging."

Soon, Robert was shovelling away memories with both hands, never having time to look at any of them properly before Mrs Hewitt ordered him on to the next excavation site. He was just starting to regret his persistence when he noticed her reading a memory she'd picked up. As her eyes reached the bottom, the paper dissolved and she smiled in recollection. "Oh, dear little Alfred. He was so clumsy back then."

Robert looked at her expectantly, but she waved him on to the next pile. "Not the memory we're looking for. We're getting close, though!"

It was barely a few minutes later when she gave a girlish squeal, triumphantly holding a sheet of paper above her head. Robert looked up warily. "Is that the one?"

She didn't answer. Instead, her eyes widened as she read through the memory. "That's right..." she whispered. "How could I have forgotten?" She looked at him as the paper vanished from her hands. "Today's Susan's birthday! I promised I'd visit her, and it's already past noon!"

Robert grinned and stretched. "I told you we'd find it!" He surveyed the heaps of memories, some of which looked like they'd been mauled by a forgetful but overenthusiastic dog. "'Nobody would be able to find anything in such a mess', right?" he recalled. "Not to undermine your obvious experience with all of this, but you might be underestimating people's ability to recognise their own..."

He stopped, because there was a small but distinct change in the atmosphere around him. His mind connected the dots in the split second it took to turn his head around. There was no more Mrs Hewitt next to him, just a slight movement in the memories around where her feet had been.

The papers rustled, then were silent. A narrow line of light marked the curtain, behind which waited a lacquered wooden labyrinth, containing somewhere, in one of millions of indecipherably-labelled filing cabinets, a rather boring lecture that touched on the levels of moral development.

With no accomplice to share in the offence, the silence once again felt unbreakable. "Great move, Robert," he whispered to himself, shaking his head slowly as he waded back through long-lost memories. "Now look what you've gotten yourself stuck in."

A NOTE FROM ANNA

When I was a kid, I used to have this explanation for when I couldn't remember something. I'd say it was somewhere behind a little door in my head, but I just couldn't find the right one. That cute little story is not what inspired me to write *The Archive of Lost Memories*. In fact, I'd forgotten all about it until my parents read the first draft and reminded me, but I still wonder if it could have unconsciously influenced the idea for this story. The mind can work in curious ways.

Another, more conscious influence has of course been Terry Pratchett. His books might well have been the first that I ever read in English, and even now, a significant portion of the English fiction I've read was written or co-written by him. That means he is responsible for much of my English vocabulary and writing style, and I couldn't have wished for a better teacher. I couldn't help but include a small reference to his work in my story: the line that decorates Robert's wardrobe is from the Discworld novel *Hogfather*.

Anna Mattaar
Culemborg, Netherlands

THE TALE OF THE STORYTELLER
CAROLINE FRIEDEL

The first time, it happened at night. Will had been fast asleep in his bed, but was suddenly wide awake. His eyes still closed, he listened intently to find out what had awoken him. All was silent except for a low growl coming from the window. He opened his eyes and realised that the sound was coming from his cat Jasmin, who was crouching on the windowsill. He stood up and went to the window to stroke her. Beneath her fur, her whole body was tense. "What's wrong?" he asked. But she ignored him, and continued growling at something outside.

He looked out of the window to see what troubled her, but nothing seemed out-of-place. An almost-full moon shone down on their little garden. The stars twinkled like diamonds in the sky. Nothing moved.

Only slowly did he start to feel it. Not a presence, but an absence. Although nothing on the surface had changed, everything was different. The night sky conveyed an impression of endless and empty space that had not been there before. Will felt as if the air had been sucked from his lungs, and he could hardly breathe. He felt all alone.

And then suddenly, everything was normal again. Whatever had been gone was back. He knew that Jasmin felt it too, as she had stopped growling and was relaxed again. She miaowed, and as always, he understood the meaning perfectly. "That was odd," she had said.

'Yes', he thought, 'that *had* been odd'. Or rather, the opposite of odd. After all, this was a world of magic, containing much weirder things than cats that could somehow make their miaows translate themselves into human words in your head. 'Odd' was part of the fabric of life here (though fortunately, *this* world did not require the help of large reptiles to carry it through space). But this—this had been different.

Will continued staring outside for a few more minutes, but eventually he followed Jasmin back to bed. He fell asleep almost immediately, and the next day he barely remembered what had happened.

* * *

The second time, it happened while Will and Jasmin were at the pond where the fairies lived. They often went there in Will's free time, if they were not visiting the local witch Aunt Mae. Although the other boys of his age considered Will weird for spending so much time with his cat, the witch and the fairies, he much preferred this to the rowdy games they played.

The fairies flittered around merrily, small creatures with shimmering wings, no larger than a dragonfly. Jasmin playfully leaped after them, and they played with her, flying closely, daring her to strike. Sometimes she caught one, but she was always careful not to hurt their wings, and would let them go immediately. Will laughed as she snuck up on a particularly bold fairy, her back wiggling as she prepared for the jump. But instead of jumping, she sat up alertly, her fur bristling.

At that very instant, the fairies disappeared. One moment they were there; the next moment they were gone. In fact, it seemed as though they had never been there. Suddenly, the pond was no longer a magical place where fairies dwelled, but only a hollow filled with brackish water. It seemed unimaginable that something as charming as fairies could exist in this world that had suddenly become so ordinary.

Will did not dare to move. The last time had been like a bad dream— but this time it was real, whatever it was. He was scared, but did not even know what he was scared of. Somewhere deep within himself he felt something tugging at him, pulling him somewhere he did not want to go.

Jasmin slowly slunk back to him and pressed herself to his side. Her body shivered. She was as scared as him. "Miaow," she said, but for the first time he did not understand what she was telling him. He picked her up and pressed her closely to his chest. They sat that way, waiting for something to happen.

After what felt like an eternity—but was in reality only half an hour— the fairies were suddenly back, as though nothing had happened. They just popped into existence, back to where they had been before disappearing. They did not seem to have noticed that any time had passed, and tried to persuade Will and Jasmin to play with them again. But neither of them felt like playing any more, and they slowly wandered back to town.

"What happened there?" Will asked.

"Miaow," Jasmin said, and now he understood her again. "The magic was gone," she had said.

"How can the magic be gone?" Will wondered.

"Miaaaow," Jasmin replied. "I have no idea, but I know it's true."

When they arrived back in town, everything was as it had always been, and no one seemed to have noticed anything had been amiss. So they decided to pretend that nothing had happened, hoping that it had been a singular event and would not happen again. But deep down, both feared that this was not the case.

* * *

The third time, it happened while they were having their dinner. Will's father and two older brothers had just come home from their work at the sugar mines, and had had a cursory wash in the kitchen sink. They still had sugar powder clinging to every crinkle in their faces, and their clothes were almost white. As a toddler, Will had delighted in licking the sugar powder from his father's face, and he still loved how they looked after a day's work, like three life-sized snowmen.

His father was telling a funny story about the mine's foreman slipping on some of the caramel that tended to develop in the deeper and warmer regions of the mines. And then he wasn't any longer. Instead, he was complaining that the foreman was stupid and mean, and that he sometimes cheated them out of their wages by claiming they were lazy. Instead of his usual warm baritone, his father's voice now had a whiny and unpleasant edge to it.

Will did not really notice this change though, as he was too disconcerted by his father and brothers' change in appearance. Instead of white sugar powder, a nasty black grime now clung to their clothes and faces.

"What is that on your clothes?" he asked, unthinking.

His father turned to him, clearly annoyed at the interruption to his tirade. "What are you going on about now?" he asked, his voice lacking any of its usual friendliness.

His oldest brother laughed meanly. "He's going to tell us something about sugar mines and fairies again, you just wait." Now everyone but his father was laughing at Will, even his mother and sister. His father just sat there staring at him, his eyes narrowing.

"You know, I've really had enough of you," he growled. "Always prancing about with your cat and running to that old spinster in the woods."

Will felt as if he had been slapped. He opened his mouth, but words failed him. Never before had his father or any of his family been so harsh to him.

His father leaned forward. "It's high time you earned your keep like everyone else in this family. Tomorrow, I'll talk to the foreman. They can always use children in the mines. Hard work will knock some sense into you."

Will could not take it anymore. He stood up so abruptly that his chair toppled over, and he ran out of the kitchen into the garden. He almost tripped over Jasmin, who was sitting by the door. Without stopping, he picked her up and ran through the open back gate and into the woods. Tears were streaming down his face. It was lucky that he knew the way so well, or he would have tripped over tree roots and fallen.

Finally, he arrived at Aunt Mae's cottage. But the cottage, which was supposed to be his refuge, had changed as well. It had lost its cosy and enchanted air and now looked like a derelict hut. Egg yolk and shells were sticking to the door in a few places.

He hesitated briefly, and then started rapping urgently on the door, his other hand still pressing Jasmin to his chest. "Aunt Mae," he cried. "Aunt Mae, please—open the door."

The door opened so fast that he almost fell into the cottage. Aunt Mae stood in the doorway, a frying pan raised over her head and her usually well-behaved hair sticking out of her bun. "Sod off, you imbec—" she started, but she stopped herself when she recognised him. "Oh, it's you." She lowered the pan and her voice softened. "Come in. I have the kettle on."

She turned and went back into the cottage. After a few seconds, Will followed her.

"Close the door and put down the bolt," Aunt Mae ordered him, pouring two cups of tea. Now Will was really frightened. She *never* put down the bolt. It was not usually necessary, as no one would ever dare bother her. Even so, he put Jasmin on the floor and did as he was told.

Aunt Mae set the cups on the table and went into the pantry to get some bread, cheese, and pickles. Noticing Jasmin, she went back a second time and came back with a saucer full of cream, which she put down in front of Jasmin. Then she sat down at the table.

"Sit," she told Will, pointing at the chair on the other side of the table. Obediently, he pulled up a chair and sat. "Now tell me what happened." Her voice was as warm and kind as ever. Will kept his head down, not wanting to talk about how his family had treated him.

She sighed. "They called me a dried-up old spinster and a meddling midnight hag, and then they threw eggs at me," she admitted. Somehow that made him feel better.

And so he told her. In a low voice and with his head still hanging, he repeated everything that had been said. When he was finished, she cut him a slice of bread and some cheese and put it on a plate in front of him.

He ate. Jasmin had already finished her cream and jumped onto the table to get some of the cheese. Normally Aunt Mae would not have tolerated this, but today was not a normal day. So they sat and ate and drank their tea while the grandfather clock in the corner ticked away the time.

At some point Will fell asleep at the table. Aunt Mae picked him up and carried him upstairs, where she tucked him into the bed in her guestroom. Jasmin followed her and curled up next to Will on the bed. For a while, Aunt Mae looked absentmindedly upon the two sleeping figures. Then she returned downstairs, raised the bolt on the door, and went out to sit on the bench next to the cottage.

She sat for a long time, motionless but not sleeping. Eventually, when it was already gone ten and long dark, she inhaled sharply. "Thank goodness," she muttered, before going back inside to also get some sleep.

* * *

When Will came down in the morning, Aunt Mae was already busy cooking breakfast. Jasmin was sitting beside her, waiting patiently for some scraps.

"Ah, there you are," she said, setting a full plate down in front of him. "Tuck in," she encouraged him, when he did not start eating immediately.

Will hesitated. "It is back, isn't it?" he asked.

Aunt Mae looked at him with a blank face. "What is back?"

"The magic. It was gone and now it is back, right?"

If Aunt Mae was surprised, she did not show it. "How did you know that?" she asked.

"Jasmin said that the magic was gone. That's why everything changed," Will explained. "And everyone," he added as an afterthought.

Aunt Mae looked down at the little grey-white cat, who sat very upright on the stone floor and returned her stare unblinkingly, daring her to disagree.

"A clever cat, that one," Aunt Mae acknowledged. She turned to the stove, poured herself a cup of tea from the kettle, and then sat down opposite Will.

"Yes, the magic was gone. And it has happened before…" she started.

"I know," Will interrupted her eagerly. "Twice. Once at night and once in the afternoon, while we were at the fairy pond."

"Will you let me finish?" Aunt Mae grumbled.

"Sorry," Will whispered hoarsely.

"It has happened before," she continued, "but more than just twice." Will wanted to interrupt again, but her stern glance stopped him.

"You would not have noticed it the other times. It was always just seconds, not much more than it takes to breathe in and breathe out. But I noticed it, because for those seconds my magic was gone. I was no longer a witch, but the old spinster they called me yesterday.

"I had hoped that it was only a small glitch that would resolve itself eventually," she continued, "but it is getting worse—and rapidly so. Yesterday, it was more than four hours until the magic came back. The time before that, it was only half an hour. One day, I fear, the magic will not come back at all. And there is nothing I can do." Her last words were full of bitterness.

"Why do we notice when no one else does?" What Will really wanted to ask was why his family had not been aware of the change. Being the only one of them to notice made him feel very lonely and isolated.

"Because we are creatures of magic," Aunt Mae explained. "The magic is an integral part of us. Its disappearance leaves an empty space, thus we feel its loss. Me, your cat, and—"

She paused, but then finally admitted what she, as local midwife, had known since the moment she had brought Will into the world; the reason why she had always kept a much closer eye on him than on the other children, and never objected to his visits. "And you. I don't know what you are, but you have magic. Not witch magic, but something else entirely."

Despite what Aunt Mae thought, this was not completely news to Will. It only confirmed what he had been suspecting for a while. But there was one thing that still bothered him. "Why are we still here, if we really are creatures of magic and the magic is gone? The fairies disappeared."

"The fairies were gone because they are pure magic. They cannot exist in a world without magic," Aunt Mae replied. "But a witch is only a woman who knows about herbs and likes to meddle in human affairs. If you take away the magic, the rest remains. In the same way, a unicorn is simply a white horse with a horn. And a cat is a cat, with or without magic. And in the end, a boy is just a boy."

Will started eating his breakfast. Although what he had heard rang true, there was one detail he knew that Aunt Mae had got wrong. Still, he lingered over his food, because he did not want to acknowledge it yet. Eventually, however, his plate was empty and his stomach full.

"I can feel where the magic goes to," he said in a small voice.

"So do I," Aunt Mae replied, not really understanding.

"No, not that it is gone," Will explained. "Where it goes to. I can feel the direction like it is drawing me." He paused. "But only while it is gone. Not now that it has returned."

Aunt Mae was worried: this was even worse than she had feared. She sighed, thought about it, argued with herself in her head. He was so young, still a child. But there was nothing else that could be done.

So she told him.

* * *

The next time the magic left, Will was prepared. He picked up his rucksack, which had been sitting packed in his room, with everything he wanted to take already inside. His mother and sister were busy in the garden, so they did not notice it when he and Jasmin left by the back gate. When he arrived at Aunt Mae's cottage, she was already waiting for him. A white horse stood beside her, a make-shift saddle on its back.

"This is Askey," Aunt Mae said. "He is actually a unicorn, but not now while the magic is gone. He has agreed to help you to bring it back." She patted the horse's back. "Be gentle. He is not used to a saddle. Oh, and I packed a little food for you." This was quite an understatement, as the saddlebags appeared to contain enough food to last at least a month.

"How do I get up?" Will asked, realising that he could barely reach the horse's (or unicorn's) saddle. Fortunately, Askey seemed to understand, and knelt down to let him mount. The kneeling horse had Jasmin looking sceptical at first, but then she realised that she could never keep up on foot. She jumped up to sit in front of Will on the saddle. Askey stood up again, awaiting directions.

Will looked down at Aunt Mae with a lump in his throat. She smiled at him, but he could see there were tears in her eyes. Neither of them said anything.

After a long and awkward silence, Aunt Mae pulled herself together. "You will have to tell him where to go."

Will nodded and closed his eyes, listening to the part of him that could feel the last of the magic leaving. He opened his eyes and pointed. "That way."

So the little boy, the cat, and the horse that used to be a unicorn rode off to bring back the magic. Following Will's instincts, they passed through deep forests, sunlit grasslands and craggy mountains. Sometimes the magic returned for a while and Will could no longer find the way. When this happened, they just kept on riding in the same direction until the magic vanished once more. On a few occasions, the magic came back for several days, and they took breaks from their journey. Askey then usually withdrew into the forests, because unicorns do not feel at home in the company of humans. He always returned as soon as the magic disappeared again. Will and Jasmin likewise avoided humans after the first few encounters, as the adults never understood the purpose of Will's journey—they always wanted to take him back to his parents. Instead, Will and Jasmin visited nearby settlements of magical creatures, meeting centaurs, tree elves, and even trolls one time. This last encounter might have ended badly, but fortunately, the magic left just at the right moment, and the trolls turned to stone before their eyes.

As days passed and turned to weeks, the magic became more and more erratic. While its increasing absence made the way easier to find, it also added urgency to their journey. They feared that they might arrive too late, and that there would no longer be any magic to save. Thus, they would travel deep into the night, with Will and Jasmin slumbering in the saddle while Askey pushed on, until even he needed to rest.

At last, when a new moon was rising for the second time on their journey and their provisions were running low, they entered a hidden valley through a gap between two hills. When Will saw the river running through it and the cottage on its bank, he knew they had arrived: everything was as Aunt Mae had described it.

* * *

"There is a legend," she had said. "A legend that magic was not always part of this world, but was created by a man with an extraordinary imagination. A Storyteller whose stories became true when he told them. He brought the magic into this world, and for as long as he told his stories, the magic stayed. But the magic also changed him. It extended his life beyond the life of ordinary humans, so that while everyone around him grew older, he hardly aged from one year to the next. And so he lived to see the death of all those he loved and the loss of all that he knew. In the end, he could no longer bear to watch his loved ones dying. So he turned away from the world and hid in a remote cottage in an unspoilt valley with a softly murmuring stream meandering through it.

"Life continued in the world outside the valley until hardly anyone even remembered that there had ever been a time without magic. But occasionally the magic seemed to weaken and to fade away as if it was dying." At this point Aunt Mae had paused. "Or some*one* was dying," she added, with an emphasis on the 'someone'. "They say that at this time a boy or girl would head off to search for the source of magic, to find the legendary Storyteller who had at last grown old. They never returned but the magic always did, going strong for another several hundred years."

At this point of the story she could no longer look at him, instead looking down at her folded hands. "They say that this boy or girl would replace the Storyteller to become the Storyteller themselves. Until their time ran out as well, and someone else would have to take their place."

Finally, Will had understood.

* * *

When they reached the cottage, Askey knelt down to allow Will and Jasmin to dismount, and then went to take a drink in the river.

With a sense of foreboding, Will stared at the building. While Aunt Mae's cottage had simply looked neglected and run-down whenever the magic left, this one felt forsaken. It seemed as though it could be brought down by even the smallest of gusts. No one appeared to have been here for many years.

Will feared that he had come too late, that the Storyteller had died long ago and the magic they had known was simply a fading memory whose time had run out. He felt tears coming to his eyes. All had been in vain.

But then he sensed it. It was scarcely perceptible, like a whisper or a faint tug: a little bit of magic remained.

He looked down at Jasmin, who was sitting by his feet like the perfect picture of a cat. She looked up at him and seemed to nod. "Miaow," she said, and even without her magic, he understood that she had told him to go into the building.

He considered knocking first but decided that there was no point, as it was apparently abandoned. So he just pushed slightly at the door, which opened slowly. The cottage looked completely dark inside.

Hesitating only briefly, he entered, followed by Jasmin. For a second he could not see anything, as his eyes became accustomed to the gloom.

Inside, the cottage looked as bad as it did from the outside. But it was not forsaken—someone was there. An old man with white hair and a white beard was standing in the middle of the room, his back turned to Will.

* * *

"You think the Storyteller is dying?" Will had asked Aunt Mae.

She hesitated, searching for the right words. "Not dying exactly, no. Something else, I think. If they were dying I would expect the magic to be fading—not leaving and coming back again."

Will frowned. This did not make any sense.

But now Jasmin, who had just been listening up to that point, interrupted. "Miaaow," she said. "It's like with old Mr Barrow, isn't it? Like he is forgetting who he is and then remembering again. Do you think that something like that could be happening?"

Aunt Mae was surprised; she had not thought of Mr Barrow, but the explanation fit perfectly. He had been going from being his old self on one day to not knowing who he or his family were on the next. His moments of lucidity had become rarer and rarer as time had passed, until there was nothing left of who he used to be.

"Yes," she replied. "This is exactly what I think is happening. It explains everything. Whenever the Storyteller forgets who he is, he also forgets the stories he meant to tell. And without the stories, there is no magic—until he remembers again."

* * *

The old man turned to Will. His eyes seemed unfocused, not really looking at him (or at anything at all). Will held his breath.

"Who are you?" the old man asked. And then, after a second, "And who am I?"

"You are the Storyteller," Will replied, "and I have come to take over the stories, so that you can rest."

"The stories…" The old man's voice sounded different now, as if he was remembering something from long ago and almost forgotten. He tried the words again, testing them, rolling them around in his mouth. "The stories?"

"Yes," Will answered. "I want to bring them back."

Suddenly, the old man's expression focused and he looked properly at Will. "But you can never leave again," he said.

"Yes—I thought as much," Will replied. "But I don't understand why. After all, the first Storyteller did not always live here."

This time the answer came quickly. "That was before."

"Before what?"

"Before...." The Storyteller hesitated. He looked disoriented, as though he was searching for something that was almost on the tip of his tongue but at the same time eluded him completely. "Before... I don't..." Tears of frustration stood in his eyes. The answer was almost there. It was so simple, he knew it.

At last, the memory came back. "Before he became the story."

Somehow, Will understood. In the end, the original Storyteller had become a story himself: a legend told and retold by a thousand different voices. A tale that bound him to this valley. All words have power, and now he and the Storytellers that followed had been caught in a trap of words—not their own, but those of others. It was believed that remaining was the price the Storyteller would have to pay, and so it became reality. If they left, they would no longer be the Storyteller, and then their story—and all the others with it—would come to an end.

The first Storyteller had chosen to stay, as had all the Storytellers after him. This was now also the choice Will had to make. And although he had often wondered on the journey whether he could really do it, replace the Storyteller and never see his family again, Will felt sure at last. If the magic did not come back, there would be no place for him in the world outside anyway.

The old man seemed to detect Will's resolve and he smiled, relieved. "Then sit," he said, pointing to an old and shabby armchair. It stood next to one of the windows and would have offered a perfect view of the garden if the window had not been so dirty.

Will walked over to the armchair and sat down cautiously. He expected something to happen—a tingling feeling, or a sudden gust perhaps. But nothing seemed to change. Maybe the window was a tad cleaner? Or maybe not. He turned his head to look at the old man again. "How do I start?" he asked.

The Storyteller did not answer immediately. Will feared his mind had gone wandering again. After a few seconds of anxious waiting as the Storyteller tried to focus, the answer finally came to the old man. "I think 'once upon a time' is traditional."

"Of course," Will said, settling back into the old armchair. "Once upon a time—". Immediately, a fire sprang to life in the fireplace that had not been there just a second earlier. The Storyteller nodded and, encouraged, Will began again.

"Once upon a time, there was a Storyteller who told the world how to be. He did not create it, but he filled it with legends. When he talked about unicorns, they wandered the woods. When he talked about witches, they became more than just herb women, midwives or spinsters. He filled the world with adventure, with knights and dragons and fauns and fairies. As he spun his tales, the world was not just a piece of rock rotating around a ball of fire in a universe of ice and dust. As he talked, the world became the centre of the universe, encased in crystal spheres upon which the stars and the sun were diamonds. Through his words, the world came alive with wonders and magic."

As Will spoke, the hut changed and became cosier. Where there had only been bare walls, bookshelves now stood overflowing with books of all sizes and topics. Beneath Will's feet, a worn-out rug had appeared. In one corner of the hut, a wood stove now had a tea kettle boiling happily on it. Will looked around in wonder, and a child-like smile appeared on the Storyteller's face.

"The Storyteller lived in a small cottage in a valley in the middle of nowhere," Will continued. "In the winter, the cottage almost disappeared in the masses of snow. In spring, it was surrounded by the most beautiful flowers one could imagine. In summer, it was cool and shaded by trees, while the sun was blazing down on the fields. In autumn, the trees were coloured all possible shades of red, orange and yellow. All in all, in this little valley, the seasons were as they never are, but as they are always imagined to be."

Outside, the trees were taking their cue from Will's story, turning red and yellow under the soft golden light of autumn. The last flowers of the year rivalled the trees for colour.

"Seasons came and went while the Storyteller spun his tales. For a long time, longer than any human's life, all was well. But then a change came over him. Slowly at first, almost imperceptibly, but unstoppably. The tales he told no longer came easily to him. Sometimes he could not remember the stories he had told. Sometimes he did not even remember who he was. He felt as if he were sliding slowly into nothingness. Only darkness waited for him, his stories forever untold."

A frown appeared on the Storyteller's face. A tear slowly rolled down his cheek. He no longer looked like the old man he was, but like a child caught in the body of a grown-up. Will wanted to comfort him, but he did not know how, other than by continuing his tale.

"As the Storyteller's memory became more and more erratic, the stories disappeared from the world. Suddenly, dragons were just long-extinct reptiles. Dwarves were only small men, and trolls mere lichen-covered rocks. And what was worse, hardly anyone noticed it. The stories would have left the world forever were it not for a boy with a special kind of magic, who noticed the change. Accompanied by a cat and a horse that once was a unicorn, he followed the fading magic until he found the Storyteller's cottage, hidden away in its valley."

With every word the Storyteller seemed to stand more upright, as if a burden was being lifted from him. The frown on his face gave way to a happy smile. He could feel it: the happy ending was coming.

An ending of sorts, at least.

"The boy found the Storyteller tired and worn out from many years of telling the stories. He deserved a rest. But to keep the stories alive and the magic in the world, someone had to take the old man's place. So the boy accepted the Storyteller's seat and began telling the world his stories. And the old Storyteller was free to rest and to forget, to leave and fade into oblivion."

Suddenly, the door of the cottage burst open, and the gentle afternoon sun shone seductively into the cottage. Will felt a lump of sadness in his throat, but he did not stop.

"A golden light danced into the cottage through the open door. It surrounded the old Storyteller, shrouding him in silken fog. The tiredness and despair was taken from him. Suddenly he felt young again. As young as he himself had been when he took over the armchair from the Storyteller before him."

As Will spoke, all the things he said became true. The old Storyteller stood enclosed in light, and his face had lost all appearance of sadness and fatigue.

"What do you want to be?" Will asked. The old Storyteller thought for a moment, searching his mind for a happy memory. There were so few memories left. In the end, he settled on a picture from his youth. He must have been very small, but it had meant happiness to him then.

"A butterfly," he whispered.

Will smiled and continued. "Slowly the light became brighter, until nothing could be seen of the old Storyteller against the glare. Then it faded, and a butterfly was fluttering in his place, coloured with all the beautiful shades of autumn. For a second, it remained still in the air, hovering with a few flaps of its wings. Then it turned towards the door and flew out into the open. It was free now, with no need to remember anymore. Now it only had to *be* until the last light of autumn finally devoured it, until there was nothing left."

And so it happened. In the blink of an eye, the butterfly with its beautiful patterns had disappeared among the blazing colours of the trees outside.

Will felt a tear sliding down his cheek. He allowed himself a minute to say goodbye, then went on to tell the world his tales.

And the stars again became diamonds on crystal spheres, hung around the slowly revolving earth. Witches were witches once more, and the fairies returned. The coal mines were sugar mines again, and his father went home with a sugar-coated face to tell funny stories about caramel.

Askey, who had been waiting restlessly outside, turned back into a unicorn, and with pride he raised his head with its silver horn sitting where it belonged. Full of joy, he let out a loud neigh which sounded so different to that of an ordinary horse. Then he walked towards the open door of the cottage and poked his head inside. He bowed it to Will, and Will bowed back.

"Farewell," Will said. Another goodbye, then.

Walking backwards, Askey retracted his head from the cottage. With another joyful neigh he shook his mane, and his silken hair shone whiter than white in the afternoon light. Then he was off, rushing away over the fields like wind in the trees.

Now only Jasmin remained. She sat upright by the open door and looked at Will.

"Are you staying?" he asked hopefully. He did not want to be left all alone.

She blinked, began washing a paw, and then stretched and walked over to the fireplace. After turning around three times, she curled up in front of the fire. "Miaow," she said. "This will do nicely."

Will stood up and went to close the door. Then he took the boiling kettle from the stove and poured himself a cup of tea. In the pantry, which had appeared beside the stove, he found fresh bread, butter, and cheese, all tasting exactly as he remembered it from home. He took the food and cup of tea back to his armchair, putting it on the small table that was now standing beside it.

Then he sat back down in the armchair, which, like everything else in the cottage, was now much more comfortable than it had been before. Jasmin, drawn to the cheese, left her place near the fire and leaped into his lap. Stroking her slowly, he looked around the cottage, took a deep breath, and then went back to work.

Slowly, with each tale he told, the world became again as he had known it. But with each tale he also made small changes. They were his tales now, and so he made them his own. Among the many tales, he also told a story about himself, so that his parents would not be sad about his leaving. In this tale, he had left to become a page to a valiant knight and to ultimately become a knight himself. Like all of his tales, this one also became true. Thus, although he was sitting in his cottage, he was also a brave knight who married an equally courageous princess, had many children, and then one day died of old age in his bed.

And as people were born and died, as kingdoms were created and destroyed, and as life went on, the Storyteller spun his tales in his cottage in the middle of nowhere and everywhere, in the valley where the seasons are always just as one dreams them to be, with the river flowing along merrily. And once or twice in every generation, he told a story of a boy or a girl with extraordinary imagination and a special kind of magic. Just in case.

And so he sat in his armchair, and while he drank his tea and petted his cat, he told the world how to be.

A NOTE FROM CAROLINE

If you stuck with me till the end, you surely realised that the tale of the storyteller losing his memory was inspired by Terry Pratchett's Alzheimer's diagnosis. Although it has become a much sadder story than I originally intended, it is also meant to convey hope. Hope that although Terry Pratchett may be gone now, there will be other storytellers keeping the magic alive. After all, he reached millions of readers with his books and likely motivated quite a few of them to take up the pen themselves. Most of them, like me, will remain amateurs, dabbling in the arts of writing. But some will rise to shine. They will take the stories and make them their own. Thus, although I am sad that there will never be any new Discworld novels ever again, I take solace in the hope that there will be other books. Books inspired by the idea that a story can be both fun to read and cover serious topics. Personally, I look forward to reading these books.

Thus, all that remains for me now is to say thank you, Terry Pratchett, for taking us on this amazing journey through the wonderful world you created. For the inimitable characters we have come to love. And above all, for making us laugh and then making us think.

Caroline Friedel
Munich, Germany

ABOUT THE AUTHORS

ANNA MATTAAR

Anna Mattaar has written stories ever since she knows how words work. She went to art school, where she studied something complicated about games and theatre. This helped her look at storytelling from several interesting new angles, but somehow she keeps returning to the written word. She lives in a small town in the Netherlands and is currently writing for a computer game and trying to finish the first draft of her debut fantasy novel.

www.annamattaar.nl/en/

CAROLINE FRIEDEL

Caroline Friedel is a scientist by heart and by training. She obtained a BSc and MS. degree in bioinformatics from a joint programme of the two major Munich Universities, and a PhD from the Ludwig-Maximilians-University (LMU) Munich. Following appointments as assistant professor first at Heidelberg University and later in Munich, she is now an associate professor at the LMU Munich. To date, she has published over forty scientific articles and book chapters, but this is her first work of fiction. Caroline can now be found scribbling away at a few other short stories in between doing serious science and trying to write grant applications.

www.bio.ifi.lmu.de/~friedel

CHARLOTTE SLOCOMBE

Charlotte absolutely adores Terry Pratchett, and *Mort* is one of her favourite characters. She has always been interested in reading and is usually to be found halfway through a book, whether it's *The Hunger Games* or *Tess of the D'Urbervilles*. Writing is a passion of Charlotte's, and she hopes to pursue a creative writing course at university in a few years' time.

DK MOK

DK Mok is a fantasy and science fiction author whose novels include *Hunt for Valamon* and *The Other Tree*, published by Spence City. Her third novel, *Squid's Grief*, will be out soon.

DK's work has been shortlisted for an Aurealis Award and a Washington Science Fiction Association Small Press Award. DK graduated from UNSW with a degree in Psychology, pursuing her interest in both social justice and scientist humour. DK lives in Sydney, Australia, and her favourite fossil deposit is the Burgess Shale.

www.dkmok.com

CHOONG JAY VEE

Choong Jay Vee writes because life is too damn weird to ignore. Her notable contributions are a short story in *KL Noir Yellow*, and a play staged during *Short+Sweet Theatre Malaysia* 2014. When not fretting about writing deadlines, she worries about accidentally killing a patient during her day job as a medical lab technologist.

She dreams of producing a comedy adaptation of Hamlet; failing that, a radio play about her working life will do. Some of her stories can be found at http://j-ko.deviantart.com/

www.goodreads.com/author/show/9563360.Choong_JayVee

LAURA MAY

Laura is an Australian who keeps forgetting she's meant to stay in the same place. She loves adventures—which is good, because she's constantly winding up in the middle of them. When she's not accidentally finding herself in the middle of a riot, being tear-gassed or jumping into frozen rivers, she enjoys sailing, snowboarding, and making an obnoxious number of puns.

Laura's adult novel, *Pickles and Ponies: A Fairy-Tale*, was a finalist in the 2014 Wishing Shelf Independent Book Awards.

@explauramay

www.explaura.net

www.goodreads.com/thelauramay

LYN GODFREY

Lyn Godfrey is a freelance writer of speculative fiction. She is also a small-town, American southwestern, book-hoarding, animal-loving kind of girl. She writes in a range of genres, including science fiction, fantasy, urban fantasy, horror, and YA, and is a self-described Geek of All Trades. Videos games, superheroes, steampunk, aliens, dinosaurs, zombies, and so on and so forth. If it's nerdy, she loves it. Yes, that includes Star Wars AND Star Trek.

Lyn began writing her first book (a Star Wars sequel) at age eleven. She has been making plans to write ever since but is often distracted by reading or looking for shiny things, like spaceships and robots.

Her recent short stories can be found in various anthologies, including *Ain't Superstitious*, *Misunderstood*, and *Sproutlings*.

@TheLynGodfrey

www.facebook.com/thelyngodfrey

LUKE KEMP

With a wife and three daughters, Luke lives in constant fear for his life. He knows that there is a god, and that this deity pays him special attention—because his first full time job was working at a supermarket in Kent, and after moving halfway across the country his next full time job was (and is) working in a factory exclusively serving said supermarket. He has co-owned and written for videogames blog www.criticalgamer.co.uk since 2009, and boy are his fingers sore. When he grows up, he wants to be Batman.

@Jim_Crikey

www.criticalgamer.co.uk

MICHAEL K. SCHAEFER

Michael is a software developer from Germany who has a fondness for books that has gotten slightly out of hand. He spends a lot of his free time with writing stories, adding books to the ever-growing piles next to the sofa, and gradually converting his living room into a workshop for doing traditional bookbinding.

This is his first time being published.

MIKE REEVES-MCMILLAN

Mike Reeves-McMillan has a black belt, which holds up his trousers. He's not sure why authors make such a big deal of these, but they are certainly convenient, trouserwise.

For someone with an English degree, he's spent a surprising amount of time wearing a hard hat. He's also studied ritualmaking, hypnotherapy and health science.

He writes strange worlds that people want to live in, notably the Gryphon Clerks series of novels. He himself lives in Auckland, New Zealand, and also in his head, where the weather is more reliable and there are a lot more dragons.

Mike has published two standalone novels (*City of Masks*, a nonmagical fantasy, and *Gu*, a postcyberpunk SF); four books in the Gryphon Clerks series (*Beastheads, Realmgolds, Hope and the Clever Man*, and *Hope and the Patient Man*, lightly steampunked secondary-world fantasy); one book in his new urban fantasy series, *Auckland Allies*; a nonfiction book for writers, *The Well-Presented Manuscript: Just What You Need to Know to Make Your Fiction Look Professional*; a single-author short story collection, *Good Neighbours and Other Stories*; and a growing number of short stories in magazines and anthologies.

http://csidemedia.com/gryphonclerks/my-books.

PETER KNIGHTON

Peter Knighton is usually found in the north of England with a cup of tea in hand. He studied physics at university and meandered between jobs with little conscious direction until finding himself as a government statistician one day—which he found to be rather pleasant.

Contrary to popular belief statistical reports are not fabricated, so this is Peter's first serious (or possibly not so serious) attempt at writing fiction. More will follow if he can come up with any ideas for jokes that don't simply revolve around poo. It may be a while.

PHIL ELSTOB

Phil is from South London, and currently lives with his Cat in a pretend castle. He has been a coffee-maker, a hotel housekeeper and a military archivist before training at the Royal Academy of Dramatic Art (Class of 2013) and has worked in theatre and on screen before and since. There's a very inviting rabbit-hole at the bottom of his garden. He hasn't gone down it. Yet.

http://onlyapauper.tumblr.com

ROBERT MCKELVEY

Robert McKelvey is a strange, somewhat funny fellow and science-fiction fan from North Yorkshire who loves to tell stories, but it wasn't until he went away to university that he really started to write any of them down.

Since then, he's created comedy sketches and stand-up sets, written some highly opinionated critiques of films and games, and currently enjoys working as a freelance writer and aspiring novelist.

www.goodreads.com/author/show/1920519.Robert_McKelvey

SCOTT A. BUTLER

Scott A. Butler is a British gentleman who resides in the county of Essex in England. After losing his natural hearing at a very young age, Scott developed a very active imagination. He discovered his passion for writing when he found an antique typewriter while exploring his grandparent's house as a child. When Scott doesn't have Cavalier King Charles Spaniels climbing all over him, he can be found working on one of his many book projects, almost always with a cup of tea at hand. He enjoys the challenge of writing in multiple genres.

His published works include the Spinetingle Diaries Series (*Click!*, *Santa Claws*), the H2Zero Series (*H2Zero: Part One*), the You Won't Sleep Tonight Collection (*You Won't Sleep Tonight*, *You Won't Sleep Tonight Either*), and an anthology called *Lurking In The Deep*.

www.thescottster.weebly.com

SIMON EVANS

Simon Evans is a Londoner who lives in Wiltshire, whence he retired after working in California for many years. He has written extensively. A book of WW2 letters, edited by him, has recently been published. His short stories have been read on local radio, and he has contributed to various radio and stage dramas. He is currently finishing a humorous book on the attempts of a small southeastern country to build a railway.

Simon has one published book titled *With Love & a Huge Cocktail*. He has also written science fiction stories and is half way through a novel about Mars, seen from an unusual perspective.

SORIN SUCIU

A gamer by vocation and an office dweller by dint of circumstance, Sorin lives in the beautiful city of Vancouver with his wonderful wife and their vicious parrot.

Born in Romania, Sorin stubbornly resisted the temptation to learn English for well over twenty years. When he finally gave in, it was not work or video games that weakened his resolve, but rather the mindboggling discovery of Terry Pratchett, Douglas Adams and Monty Python. It is probably no wonder that Sorin learned to be funny before being fluent (even if he does say so himself).

Sorin has published one dirty-nerdy fantasy novel titled *The Scriptlings* and he likes to believe this is the first part of a trilogy.

www.sorinsuciu.com

www.goodreads.com/sorinsuciu

STEVEN MCKINNON

Steven is an independent writer living, eating and just about breathing in Glasgow.

He is the author of *Boldly Going Nowhere*, in which he tells the story of how he broke free from the suffocating rut he was in.

When not writing deeply personal stories about his private life and showing them to the world, Steven will either be eating cake, listening to Iron Maiden, or filling his brain with pointless Buffy and Battlestar Galactica trivia.

He completed two courses of Creative Writing at the University of Glasgow in 2010, and completed an HNC in Professional Writing Skills at Reid Kerr College in 2006. He is 29, and was born in the bathroom of a high-rise flat in Glasgow on the 18th of March 1986.

He has since moved out.

www.stevenmckinnon.net

ABOUT THE COVER ARTIST

Dámaso Gómez is a bona fide bookworm and secret epicurean who suffers from an excessive imagination, a burning passion for nature, and an unforgiving penchant for art. He's rarely seen without a backpack containing a sketchbook, drawing tools, and a book.

He often works with musicians, for whom he designs album covers and band logos. He is also an artistic painter, mural painter, and an accomplished illustrator.

Dámaso lives in a small town near Valencia, Spain, but given a choice he would readily relocate to the Ramtop Mountains.

FINAL WORD

Dear Reader,

In purchasing this anthology you have contributed towards research into Alzheimer's disease. For that, you have not only our gratitude, but that of people and families all over the world who deal with dementia in all its forms every day. Of course, if you'd like to make further donations to Alzheimer's Research UK, we encourage you to do so.

But there is something you can do right now that won't cost you a dime, and that is to take a moment to write an online review for the anthology. Amazon and Goodreads make this easier to do than ever before. In this case your review will help to spread the word and encourage others to not only buy the book, but to support and learn about Alzheimer's Research UK—something we believe is a very good cause.

Additionally, reviews are to authors what applause is to performers. Writing one is the absolute best way to support a writer, whether it be sharing your praise with other readers, or providing your fair perspective on ways in which the author can grow and improve their writing.

Thank you,
Your Authors